dark horse

kate sherwood

Dreamspinner Press

Published by
Dreamspinner Press
4760 Preston Road
Suite 244-149
Frisco, TX 75034
http://www.dreamspinnerpress.com/

Dark Horse

Cover Art: Justin James http://www.wix.com/qpm2010/justinjames
Cover Design by Mara McKennen

ISBN: 978-1-61581-465-7

Printed in the United States of America
First Edition
June, 2010

eBook edition available
eBook ISBN: 978-1-61581-466-4

To the Eventers: without your encouragement I wouldn't have tried, and without your support, I wouldn't have succeeded.

part 1

chapter 1

DAN likes the routine of the job, the rhythm of it all. He likes knowing that the horses expect to be fed at six, two, and eight o'clock, and will try to kick their stalls down if their expectations aren't met. He likes it that every piece of equipment in the barn has a home, and every piece of tack has its own hook or rack to rest on. And he likes the riding, the "warm up, work, take a break, work, cool down" pattern. It lets him turn his brain off a little, lets him stop thinking and just work on doing. On being.

So he's not exactly welcoming when something happens to break the rhythm. Molly and Karl both know this and generally try to shield him from intrusions. Not because he's a prima donna, just because they're caring people—caring people who don't like it when their head trainer yells at prospective buyers.

They try, but they don't always try hard enough, Dan realizes as he sees Molly waving at him from outside the ring. He sighs and brings Chaucer to a walk. They were just getting somewhere, too, with the big gelding finally seeming to realize that his nose doesn't need to go up to the sky every time he's asked to change paces. As a final reminder, Dan asks Chaucer to trot on the way over to Molly, and then go back down to the walk. Both times Chaucer's nose stays where it should be, so Dan gives him a congratulatory slap on the neck and lets him have his head.

Molly is strong and athletic but middle-aged, and Dan isn't used to seeing her jitter around like a teenager. "The California people are early. Robyn's getting Monty in from the paddock, but he's filthy, of course. We need you to help her get him polished up."

Dan doesn't like the sound of that. "If they can't see through a little mud, they don't deserve Monty."

Molly's excitement turns to frustration pretty quickly. "When you're in charge of the bills around here, you can tell me who *deserves* what horse. Until then, we need to make a sale, and it's the horse that's being looked at, not the buyers." She turns and heads toward the barn but then stops and comes back a few steps. "You behave yourself. These people have more money than God—they could buy and sell this whole place with their pocket change." She looks like she might have more to say, but a group of people is coming out of the barn, so she puts her happy face back on and walks over to meet them.

Dan takes Chaucer out of the ring on the far side and avoids the crowd. The gelding is hot from the exercise, and Dan doesn't want to make him stand still in the cool spring breeze. When they reach the door of the barn, he jumps out of the saddle and quickly untacks the horse, then throws a cooler on him. The light blanket will be enough to keep the animal from catching a chill, but Dan still wants to find a way to cool him down properly. The barn's hot-walker broke down several weeks earlier and has still not been repaired. Dan spares a moment to wonder just how important this sale is. Molly's right; Dan has nothing to do with the finances of the place, so he doesn't really know the state of things. There never seems to be enough money, but that's always been the case. Have things gotten worse than usual? Dan forces his mind away from thinking about the likely cause of any financial woes. He's at work—not the place to get maudlin.

Monty is already in the crossties, with Robyn working away at him furiously with the curry comb. The Hanoverian hasn't lost all of his winter coat yet, so despite being clipped short, he's shedding hair as well as mud. Dan has to admit it to himself: the horse *is* a mess, and Robyn could use some help. He runs a hand down Chaucer's chest, feels the heat and sweat still pouring off him.

"I can walk him, if you need." The offer comes from behind them, and when Dan turns to look, he sees only a dark shape silhouetted against the bright sunshine outside. The shape moves forward and becomes a man, maybe forty or so, a decade older than Dan, his dark brown hair just starting to gray in the stubble around his mouth. "Jeff Stevens," the man says, sticking his hand out for shaking. "We've met, but only briefly."

Dan searches his memory. He really doesn't think he'd have forgotten meeting this guy. He's got a great face: lines creased in all the right places, warm, intelligent eyes, and from what Dan can see of the body, the guy might be a bit older but he definitely takes care of himself. And he's dressed for riding, so Dan expects the muscles are from working, not from the gym.

Jeff seems to realize that Dan can't remember him, and prompts, "Rolex, two years ago. You were a little… preoccupied." His smile is gentle. "I know you must've heard it a million times, but... I'm really sorry. About last year, I mean."

Dan nods automatically. The guy's right. He has heard it a million times, but it doesn't seem to have lost much potency in repetition.

Jeff obviously realizes that a subject change would be appreciated. "I'm the trainer for the Kaminskis—the folks in from California. We're a bit early, I know. Didn't mean to catch you all unprepared. So, like I said, if you have something you need to be doing, I can walk this one."

Dan mutely passes Chaucer's lead rope to the other man, and then turns toward Monty. He wouldn't usually trust a stranger with his horse, but somehow this feels okay. "Thanks," he mutters belatedly, and Jeff smiles easily as he turns Chaucer and leads him back outside. Dan grabs a curry comb and gets to work on Monty's off side.

It's a good thing there are two of them working, because it's only a few minutes before he hears Karl and Molly coming into the barn, their tag-team sales technique in full force.

"Oh, there he is!" Molly coos, as though she'd had no idea that Monty was being groomed. Dan grabs a clean rag and passes it to Robyn, who quickly mists it with show sheen and runs it over Monty's lean body. He dances a little at the sound of the spray, but isn't really spooked. He's used to being fussed over and takes it as his due.

Molly is walking next to a girl who is clearly going through her awkward phase, all angles and braces and shyness. Maybe fifteen, Dan guesses. Prime horse-crazy age, but she doesn't look strong enough for a mount like Monty. The guy with her, on the other hand.... Dan lets himself take an appreciative look before bringing his mind back to business. The guy would be a great match for Monty. They're both tall and well-muscled. Dan wonders if the guy bucks when he gets excited, and then has to call his mind back to work again.

The little group draws closer. "I'm sorry he's not looking better," Molly apologizes to the girl. "He was outside this morning, and, well, you know how boys are in the mud!"

Robyn looks a little offended. She'd practically performed a miracle on the horse, given the time she'd had, and it must sting to hear Molly dismiss her efforts. Dan catches her eye and shakes his head minutely. It's just a sales ploy, making it seem as though Monty is usually even better looking.

Molly is encouraging the girl to get closer to Monty, supplying a chunk of carrot to feed him. Dan swallows a sigh. Apparently the girl is the prospective rider after all. He hopes they have sense enough to find another horse.

Karl nods his head at Dan, indicating that he should join Karl and the tall guy farther up the barn aisle. Dan looks at Robyn and says, "Their trainer is walking Chaucer for me. Do you think you could go take over, send the trainer back in?" She nods and heads toward the barn door as Dan walks over to Karl.

"Mr. Kaminski, this is Daniel Wheeler. He's been riding Monty lately." Now it's Dan's turn to feel a bit slighted. He's been Monty's trainer for almost five years, since the gelding was first introduced to the saddle. Everything the horse knows, Dan taught him, and Monty knows a lot. So why is Karl making it sound like Dan is some stable rat begging for rides? He guesses it's another sales technique, but can't really figure out what the point of it is—other than to remind Dan of his place.

Kaminski smiles warmly and holds out a hand to shake, and Dan catches himself before he takes it, and holds up his own hands to show how they're covered in mud and horse hair. The guy is dressed casually, but he looks put together. Dan doesn't want to get blamed for mussing him up.

"Oh, that's fine, man; I don't mind getting my hands dirty!" Kaminski leans in a little. "And my name's Evan." He grabs Dan's right hand and gives it a few vigorous shakes, then looks over Dan's shoulder. "What do you think, Tat?" he asks. She beams back at him, and he laughs happily. When they're smiling, it's easy to see that they're related, both of them grinning so wide that their hazel eyes are almost invisible. "Looks like she likes him. Where's Jeff? We should get his opinion."

Dan turns to look in the direction Jeff should be coming from, and he appears as if by magic. He walks easily and confidently, taking a few steps to the side in order to look at Monty from directly behind, then continuing closer. He glances over for permission to approach the horse, and Dan feels a small satisfaction that he's the one Jeff looks at, not Karl. Karl takes over, though, apparently deciding that Evan is just along to sign the check, and that Jeff is the one who needs to be persuaded.

Karl moves toward the horse, waving his hand at Jeff. "Please, be my guest! Look him over, and then we'll tack him up, and we can show you what the big guy is capable of."

Karl continues with a stream of positive statements about the horse, and Dan finds himself agreeing with most of them. Monty really is exceptional, and Dan will be sorry to see him go. But he'll be more than sorry if he goes to a girl who won't be able to handle him, and who could get hurt by the huge animal.

Dan wonders whether he should say something to Evan, and glances over to see the other man watching him closely.

"He's a beautiful horse," Evan starts. "My sister, Tat… well, Tatiana, but 'Tatiana' doesn't rhyme with 'brat', so it doesn't seem so appropriate." Evan smiles to make it clear that he's joking, and Dan sees a couple dimples appear in the otherwise lean face. "Anyway, Tat's been wanting an eventer, and we saw the video of this guy, and it's like she fell in love!"

Dan nods warily, and then Molly is gesturing to him. "Dan, let's get him tacked up. They need to see him at work."

Dan isn't used to the almost manic energy Molly's projecting today. Monty is a valuable horse, Dan knows, and selling him would certainly be a help for the barn's finances, but usually Karl and Molly are a bit more laid back about things. They try to sell the horses, of course, but they aren't generally so *frantic* about it.

Dan gets Monty's dressage saddle and bridle. Might as well start slow—if the kid gets scared working on the flat, there's no point in wasting time with jumping.

Dan puts the tack on under Jeff's scrutiny, and finds himself appreciating the other man's attitude. Lots of people forget about a horse's ground manners, think it's only what happens under saddle that matters. As the one who worked so hard to train Monty to behave in crossties, Dan is gratified to see that someone appreciates his efforts. He has a slightly unsettling moment when he turns away from the horse to see Jeff looking not at Monty but at Dan himself, with an assessing expression similar to the one Evan had worn earlier. But Monty is ready, so Dan takes the reins over his head and looks to Karl.

Molly starts instead. "Okay, let's go out to the ring, and we can see how beautifully he moves!" She herds the visitors in front of her, and Dan falls in behind, leading Monty. Jeff watches over his shoulder for a few steps, apparently making sure that Monty's good manners continue once he's being led, and then he turns and focuses on where he's going.

Once in the ring, Dan gives the tack a final check and mounts up. He goes through the basic warm ups, getting Monty relaxed and ready to work, and then takes him through more advanced moves, essentially duplicating a standard dressage test. Monty is a bit shaky on his counter-canter, but he gets it eventually. Dan makes a note to work on that in their next training ride, and then wonders if there will be one, or if Monty will be leaving the barn before they get a chance.

Dan brings Monty to a halt next to the spectators. "Did you want to see anything in particular?" He addresses the question to the whole group, but he's really talking to Jeff. When Jeff shakes his head, Dan swings down off the horse and holds the reins out, about halfway between Jeff and Tatiana. They're both dressed for riding, and realistically, they both need to be able to get along with Monty.

Jeff nods at Tatiana and puts a hand on her shoulder. "Come on, let's give him a spin." They duck through the fence and walk out into the ring, heading for the mounting block. Dan leads Monty over to meet them. There's a moment to adjust stirrup lengths and re-check the girth, and then Dan stands at Monty's head while the girl climbs on. She's light and graceful, and settles into the saddle naturally, so Dan hopes the ride won't be a complete disaster.

The horse and rider head out to the rail, and Jeff moves toward the center of the ring. Dan moves toward the fence, but Jeff calls to him. "Dan, can you stick around? Let me know if there's any tricks we should be using?"

Dan obediently follows Jeff. The older man is watching the horse and rider carefully, and calls out a few suggestions to Tat. He has her work through a dressage test similar to the one Dan had done earlier, leaving out a few of the more advanced skills. Finally, he calls to her, "Okay, your turn, try out anything you want to have another look at." Then he half turns to Dan, saying, "Okay, now—what do you think, really?"

Dan is torn, so he tries to be neutral. "She's a good rider. They're a good match for dressage. For jumping—we'll need to wait and see, I guess."

"Is he going to be too much for her?"

Dan can't bring himself to lie. "I don't know. Probably. He's got a lot of heart, you know? And he loves to jump. He needs a pretty firm rider to keep him under control." Dan rubs his neck. "It's what makes him such a great eventer; he's totally fearless, full of enthusiasm." Dan doesn't think he needs to explain how that attitude could pose a bit of problem for someone as slight and inexperienced as Tatiana.

Karl has come out in time to hear the last of that. "Fearless and enthusiastic, that's our boy!"

Jeff smiles politely, but he obviously has doubts of his own. Karl sends Dan into the barn for Monty's jumping tack. When Dan returns, Jeff has Monty's saddle off, and they trade burdens so Jeff can have a chance to try saddling Monty. The horse is as good as Dan would expect, and they quickly trade bridles as well. Dan sometimes jumps Monty in just a snaffle, but he thinks Tatiana will need all the help she can get.

They take Monty to the grass ring for jumping, and as soon as they're out from behind the dressage ring fence, Monty starts dancing. Dan is leading him, and has no trouble maintaining control, but he's not sorry to see the horse act up a little. It's only fair for the buyers to know what they're getting. Monty's a sweetheart, but he's also a handful.

When they get to the grass ring, Karl gives Dan a leg up, and Dan takes Monty through his paces. They work up in size, and Dan is pleased with how cleanly Monty is jumping, and how little effort he seems to be putting in. But he can't deny that the horse is getting a bit worked up, and he only feels a little guilty when he doesn't do much to calm him. If Tatiana gets a healthy scare over these jumps, there's less chance of her really getting hurt by trying to ride Monty cross-country, a setting where even Dan has to work hard to control the gelding.

Monty settles well enough for a rider swap, though, and again Jeff asks Dan to accompany him to the middle of the ring while Tatiana rides. This time, Karl comes with them.

Tatiana and Monty take a couple low jumps without much trouble, but Dan can see the horse starting to get a little frustrated. "She needs to loosen up a bit," he tells Jeff. "I usually ride him pretty soft when we're jumping—he knows what to do, she needs to guide him, not order him." Jeff nods and passes the suggestion along, but there's not much evidence of a response.

"She's nervous," Jeff says.

Dan nods. "Monty's sensitive enough to pick up on that. He needs a confident rider."

Karl jumps in at that. "Well, obviously she'll be a lot more confident once she gets used to him! And at her own barn, without an audience...."

Jeff nods politely again, his eyes fixed on the horse and rider. "Circle him, Tat! He's getting too flat, you need to bring him back a little." Tat complies, and Jeff calls, "Again! Circle him until he comes back under you, until he listens!"

Dan murmurs, "Have her use her seat a bit more, her hands a bit less," and Jeff passes these instructions along as well. Eventually, Monty settles enough that Tatiana is able to take him over a couple more jumps, although he charges the second one so fast that only his athleticism allows him to get them over cleanly.

Tatiana pulls him to a dancing, prancing halt in front of a group that is not quite as enthusiastic as they were after the dressage riding. Evan laughs and slaps the horse's sweaty chest. "He gave you a bit of a wild time, didn't he?"

Tat grins, and Dan isn't sure whether to be disappointed or impressed that her enthusiasm seems undampened. "He's fantastic, though! It was like riding Pegasus, or something—so powerful!"

Dan can't help liking the girl, but he sees Jeff's serious expression and hopes that the trainer has some influence over the young Kaminskis. "That's enough for today, I think," Jeff says. "Let's get out of everyone's hair and let them get back to their day, and we can come back tomorrow if we need to."

Karl and Molly hear the pending rejection in that suggestion, and start trying to persuade Jeff to try Monty on the cross-country course. Dan is surprised to realize that he already trusts Jeff to stay firm, and he leads Monty a few steps away and adjusts the stirrups back to his length. He doesn't want the last thought in Monty's head for the day to be that it's fun to ignore his rider, so Dan needs to take him over a couple jumps.

Jeff is fielding the comments from Karl and Molly, and Evan wanders over to Monty and Dan. "He's a really beautiful animal," Evan says, and Dan is happy to hear a slight wistfulness in the other man's tone. Maybe Evan isn't totally clueless about the situation.

"He is. He's a supercharged sports car of a horse."

Evan bends a little, his hazel eyes catching Dan's and holding them. "And a supercharged sports car isn't a good car for a fifteen-year-old, is that what you're saying?"

Dan shrugs. "I'm saying you should listen to your trainer. I don't think he'll steer you wrong." He pulls the stirrup leather back into place. "And, Evan...." He pauses. "We have a lot of great horses here. You should have a look at Sunshine—she's almost as scopey as Monty, but a little less…."

"Supercharged?"

Dan grins. "Yeah, that."

Evan smiles back, and reaches out to shake Dan's hand again. "Thanks for the advice, Dan. I appreciate it." Then somehow the atmosphere changes a little. Evan is still smiling, but there's a bit of a strange edge to it as he continues. "It was really nice to meet you." Evan is still holding his hand, but not shaking it anymore. He releases it as soon as Dan starts to pull it away, and steps back as Dan nods and pulls himself up onto Monty.

As Dan takes the horse over a couple easy jumps, he tries to keep his mind on his job, not on whatever just passed between him and the handsome Californian. By the time he's over the third jump, the visitors are out of sight on their way back the barn, and Dan is able to focus on what he should be doing.

After he gets Monty listening to him, Dan cools the horse off and heads into the barn. He'd been about to have lunch when the Kaminskis arrived, so he's starving. But Karl and Molly are waiting for him by Monty's stall, and he has a feeling it could be a while before he gets any food.

He turns the horse in and takes his halter off, then slides the door shut and turns to look at his employers. Karl speaks first, his anger clear. "What did you say to them, exactly?"

Dan doesn't really appreciate being put on the defensive. "When? I didn't spend any time with them that you weren't right there."

Molly takes over. "When you talked to Jeff, or when Evan got you alone. Did you tell them not to buy Monty?"

Dan just shakes his head. "Come on, guys, do you really think they need to be told that? Jeff's obviously got a good eye. He could tell that Monty was taking over! And that was just going over a few arena jumps, not even a cross-country course." He turns and hangs Monty's halter on the stall door. "If they decided not to buy him, it's because they could tell he's too much horse for the kid, not because I told them not to."

Molly doesn't look convinced. "Oh, and you don't think they could tell what you thought? You don't think that your bad attitude came through clearly?" She glances at Karl before continuing. "Really, Dan, you should know why we need extra money! I just can't understand why you would sabotage us like this… *you*, of all people!"

Dan doesn't appreciate the attempted guilt trip. "Me of all people? You mean because I've only been getting every third paycheck for the last year? Or because I've been working overtime without claiming for it, trying to get these horses into the best condition they can be in for your buyers? Is that why I should be aware of how much you need money?" He looks at the couple before him, whom he'd been encouraged to think of as parents. "You know what *I* can't understand? I can't understand why the two of you wouldn't see a problem with letting a kid risk her life on a horse she can't control." He backs away from them, and his voice twists in bitter mimicry. "You, of all people!" Then he turns and strides angrily out of the barn. He's worked every single day for almost three weeks; he's going to take the afternoon off.

chapter 2

DAN lives in an apartment above the barn, so his storming out isn't all that satisfying. He really just wants to sit on the couch, have a few drinks, and sulk a little, but he isn't feeling quite churlish enough to be able to do that if he knows that Karl and Molly are right downstairs working away without him. So instead of going home, he climbs into his battered pickup and heads over to Chris's place. Chris will be at work, but Dan knows where the Hide-A-Key is, and he knows he's got a change of clothes over there. This isn't the first time Dan has wanted to hide out from Karl and Molly, although it is the first time he's been so angry about it.

By the time Dan gets to Chris's, it's already mid-afternoon. He rummages around in the fridge and takes a slice of pizza and a beer into the shower with him. Well, he leaves the pizza on the bathroom counter, but the beer goes right in. One of the best things about Chris's house is the window in the tub enclosure, with its wide sill, just right for holding a drink.

Getting clean calms Dan down a little, and once he's out of the shower he calls Chris at work. Chris is an up-and-coming young lawyer at the biggest firm in Louisville. Dan's understanding of these things is that Chris should be slaving away day and night, but somehow the man always seems more than ready to take off work early. This day is no exception, and he agrees to meet Dan at JP's in half an hour. Dan wishes he could afford to go someplace else, but he works a couple shifts a week bartending at JP's, and he can usually get a substantial discount when he goes in on off hours. Chris could probably afford to go to any restaurant in the city, but he knows enough about Dan's financial situation not to suggest a change—and enough about Dan's pride not to suggest that Chris pay for both of them.

So, JP's it is. Dan pulls jeans and a black T-shirt out of the duffel bag in Chris's closet, and reflects that it's just as well they're going somewhere casual. Kentucky may not be the Deep South, but it's far enough down that people believe in dressing for the occasion. And Dan is going to be dressed for a neighborhood bar, not a fancy restaurant. A quick look in the bathroom mirror confirms that, as usual, he could use a shave. He has fair skin and green eyes, and his hair is dark brown, so when he's got stubble, it makes his eyes stand out—glow, practically. He used to think that growing a beard would help make him look older, less vulnerable, but he's come to realize that for him, the opposite is true. Still, he can't be bothered to shave. He's just seeing Chris, after all.

He throws his riding clothes in Chris's washing machine, hoping he remembers to pull them out to go in the dryer when he gets back. It's a foregone conclusion that he'll be sleeping in Chris's spare room. He definitely intends to drink enough to make driving a bad idea, and a cab ride out to the barn would cost a week's salary. Not that he sees his salary most weeks, he reminds himself. But the anger's gone, and he's left mostly with a sense of confusion. He knows things are tight for Molly and Karl, but are things really so bad that they're willing to risk their reputations or even a kid's life?

He decides to walk to the bar. It's not that far, and it's a nice afternoon. Besides, things will be easier the next day if his truck is already at Chris's place. He arrives just as Chris pulls into the parking lot, and he waits at the door for his friend. Chris is driving his brand new truck, and Dan suppresses a little twist of jealousy. Just one more thing Dan's career choices don't pay for.

Chris nods as he gets out of the truck. "Hi, Danielle."

"Christine, you're here."

Chris grins. "I've been calling you Danielle for five years, and this is the first time it occurred to you that I have a girl's name too?"

Dan shrugs nonchalantly. "I was saving it for when the time was right. And somehow, just now… it felt right."

Chris just nods. "Well, in honor of the auspicious occasion—you can buy the first round."

They go inside, and Dan waves to the bartender and waitress. Chris is here often enough that he knows most of the staff almost as well as Dan does. They find a table near the back, and the waitress brings their drinks without waiting for them to order. "Are you guys gonna be eating too?"

"Yeah, probably. But not for a while."

The waitress nods and heads off to another table, and Chris and Dan sit back with their drinks. They've each got a beer and a glass of Wild Turkey. Dan looks at his glass thoughtfully, while Chris watches.

"Trying to decide what kind of night it's going to be?" Chris asks. "Shoot it or sip it?"

"Yeah." Dan regretfully picks the glass up and takes a sip. "I got stuff to deal with tomorrow. Better take it easy."

Chris looks a little interested, although he's also paying a good bit of attention to a blonde in a halter top over by the bar. "Dealing with stuff, huh? Anything I should know about?"

Dan shakes his head. There's no point in dragging Chris into things. Chris grew up across the road from Karl and Molly, so he might have some insight, but he might also have divided loyalties. Besides, Dan wanted to get away from the barn to clear his head, not to dwell on things. He asks about Chris's family, instead, and gets updated on all the goings-on of the Foster clan. The conversation flows easily, more drinks come, and food is eventually ordered and eaten.

There's a bit of a pause in conversation during the meal, but as Dan is mopping up the last of the gravy with a French fry, Chris breaks the silence with, "So, Danny—what are your feelings on threesomes?"

Dan takes a moment to carefully swallow his fry, and washes it down with some beer. "Just to be clear, are you one of the three?"

Chris grins and shakes his head. "You wish, sweetheart." He nods somewhat discreetly over Dan's shoulder. "There's a couple over there, about your four o'clock, both guys, and they've been eying you up since they got here."

Dan shakes his head. They've been through this a few times before. Chris seems to think that he can give Dan permission to start dating again, or at least to start having sex. Dan has tried to convince him that Chris doesn't really have that authority, but he hasn't shown any interest in Dan's opinion on the matter.

"I'm just saying, man. If I were that way inclined, I would be inclining all over these two. One of them's kinda grizzled looking, in what I imagine might be a sexy sort of way, and the other is fucking built. Tall, like I know you like 'em…." Chris stops, apparently realizing that the last comment might be a bit over the line.

Dan is too preoccupied by Chris's description to be upset by the reference. He frowns, and turns to look over his shoulder, then turns back to his friend.

"Chris, you idiot, they're not checking me out. They know me. They were looking at a horse today." Dan cocks his head. "And what makes you think they're a couple?"

"What, if they know you, they can't check you out? The two aren't mutually exclusive, you know." Chris shakes his head in mock dismay at his friend's lack of self-esteem. "And, trust me—they're a couple. You know my gaydar's better than yours, so don't even try to argue."

Dan has to admit that Chris is right about their gaydar. Dan's is terrible, and Chris's is shockingly good for an alleged heterosexual. "Don't feel bad, baby," Chris continues. "It's just because you're so pretty—you don't have to seek out the boys, they all flock to you like bees to a flower." Chris smiles beatifically, and then his grin turns wicked. "And they're checking you out *again*. I swear, the younger one just licked his chops!"

"Jesus, Chris, keep it down! I might have to deal with them again sometime, you know!"

Chris leans back triumphantly in his chair. "You might have to deal with them right now. They're coming over."

Dan groans. If Chris hadn't started all this, it would be a perfectly natural, casual meeting between acquaintances. With Chris's wild speculation playing through his head, though, Dan knows he's going to feel awkward. And then he's going to try to act natural, and that will make him feel more awkward, and the whole thing will just turn into a nightmare for Dan, and an endless source of amusement for Chris.

Chris's eyes shift from Dan to the new arrivals, and Dan turns to acknowledge them.

"Dan, hey. We thought it was you," Evan starts almost shyly.

Dan doesn't really understand that comment. They were twenty feet away—are they both so shortsighted they can't recognize someone from twenty feet? Or was it meant to be an insult, based on him not being memorable? But that doesn't make sense—they'd both been totally pleasant that afternoon, and even if they didn't like him they didn't seem like the kind of assholes who'd walk across the room to make their disdain clear.

Apparently Dan's rumination has gone on a little too long, because Jeff and Evan are looking at him somewhat strangely as Chris leans across the table with his hand outstretched. "I'm Chris. Sorry about Dan, he's… drunk? Or just socially awkward. Possibly a little of both."

Dan rolls his eyes. "Sorry, yeah. I'm not all here." He pulls himself together. "You're out without your sister?" he asks Evan.

"Yeah, well… I'm not her favorite person right now." Evan makes a face.

"You told her no on Monty, then?" Dan looks from Evan to Jeff, who nods.

"Yeah. And I wanted to thank you for that." Evan smiles. "I can be a bit bullheaded, and I didn't want to just take Jeff's word for it. So it was helpful to have a second opinion to back him up." Evan looks tentatively at Dan. "He reminded me… well, he made it clear how dangerous eventing can be."

Dan really doesn't want the conversation to go in that direction. "Well, I hope you give some of the other horses some thought. Like I said, Sunshine would be great, I think. She's a Hanoverian, too, so she's a similar type, but she's a bit less headstrong. She's not quite as athletic as Monty, but I don't think that should matter, at Tatiana's level."

Jeff nods. "Yeah, we called out this evening and arranged to see her tomorrow. If Tat's done sulking by then."

Evan grimaces. "It's too bad Karl and Molly built Monty up so much. I mean, they've got Tatiana thinking that she and that horse are soul mates or something." Evan shakes his head. "It's frustrating, really. I mean, I've met so many great people around horses, and then something like that comes up, where they clearly know it's not suitable and push it anyway…."

Dan breaks in. "Well, it was a judgment call. We can disagree with them without thinking they're evil or something." He might not be too happy with his employers, but he can't just sit around and listen to someone run them down.

Evan looks abashed. "No, of course. You're right." He grins apologetically. "See, like I said, I can be bullheaded."

Jeff puts a gentle hand on Evan's neck and shakes him ever so slightly. Even Dan doesn't miss the way Evan leans into the touch, and Chris looks like he wants to do a victory dance. Dan doesn't look forward to the gaydar-bragging that is sure to follow.

"Well, anyway, we'll let you get back to your evening. I just wanted to thank you again for helping us out today." Evan smiles sincerely before continuing. "Tatiana may not thank you, but—"

"She'll be grateful when she's calmed down a little," Jeff breaks in, "and when she's riding a horse that she can control properly."

Dan nods. "Well, I hope it works out. And I guess I'll see you tomorrow, if you're going out to the barn again."

The two say goodbye to Chris and head for the door. After they leave, there's a pause, and Dan braces himself.

"Well, they seem nice," Chris starts. It's innocuous enough, but Dan knows there's more coming. "Yeah, a really nice *couple*. Really, one of the nicest *gay* couples I've met in a while." Dan starts laughing. "And you know what, Dan? If I was right about them being gay, which, for the record, I was...." Chris nods proudly before continuing. "If I was right about that, then you should admit that I was also right about the other part... they were totally checking you out!"

Dan just laughs and shakes his head at Chris. Reality has never been much of a factor in Chris's decision making process, Dan knows, and sometimes there's just no point in arguing with him. "Yeah, okay, 'me, Jeff, and Evan, sitting in a tree....'"

Chris claps his hands triumphantly. "That's right, baby!" Then a more serious expression comes across his face. "But, in a tree? Really? I mean, I'm not an expert on the gay sex thing, but I think the first time at least you should be on the ground...." And the evening continues on as expected.

chapter 3

AS HE'D planned, Dan spends the night in Chris's guest room. Robyn is responsible for the feeding and day-to-day chores at the farm, so technically he can sleep in a little if he wants, but he finds himself waking with the sun out of habit. He has a quick shower and some leftover Chinese for breakfast—it tastes even better reheated than it had the night before when they'd ordered it. Dan pulls his work clothes out of the dryer and gets dressed, then heads out the door. Chris is still sleeping.

Dan isn't really looking forward to running into Karl and Molly, so he's relieved that they are nowhere to be found when he gets to the barn. It's peaceful there in the early morning, just the sound of horses happily munching their hay. Calm eyes follow him as he walks down the aisle, and when he stops at Monty's stall, the big gelding puts his head over the door in greeting, although he doesn't stop chewing while he does it. He's gotten a piece of hay stuck in his forelock, and Dan pulls it out and playfully tries to insert it in Monty's mouth.

Robyn comes down the aisle with an armful of lead ropes, her red curls already pulling out of the ponytail she's trying to control them with. "Admit it, Dan, you love that horse. You sabotaged the sale because you want him for yourself."

He knows Robyn is only joking, but it stings a little anyway. "What is all this 'sabotage' stuff? If they want to sell Monty to an inexperienced kid, they should find someone with a blind trainer." Dan runs his hand along Monty's muscular neck. "Jeff wasn't going to let the sale happen no matter what I said."

Robyn raises an eyebrow. "'Jeff', is it? You guys pretty close? And what makes you think the buyers would listen to him anyway? We've seen how well our bosses listen to you!"

"Well, I've got a feeling Jeff might have a few ways to convince Evan to pay attention." The words aren't much, but Dan puts a suggestive note in his voice, and Robyn picks up on it.

"*Really?* Does that mean what I think it means? And is it confirmed, or are you just guessing?"

Dan knows he shouldn't be gossiping, but he's worked with Robyn long enough to know that she has no malicious intent—it's just a way to make her boring job a little more interesting. "Let's call it an educated guess," he hints, and takes a couple lead ropes from her. "You taking the big boys out first?" He checks to see which horses are done eating—they always hang their heads over their stall doors as soon as they're finished with their meals, waiting to go outside.

Robyn looks like she would be shrieking if she didn't know better than to make a fuss around the horses. "Wait, wait... *how* educated are we talking, here?" Dan just grins at her, and puts the halter on Monty. Robyn stares at him. "You left early yesterday... your truck wasn't here this morning, so you didn't spend last night at home...." She grabs his arm. "Dan, please... just how educated is your guess?"

He laughs and shakes his head. He's taken this far enough. "No, not very educated. We just saw them in the bar last night, and they looked pretty close."

Robyn looks temporarily disappointed but then brightens. "Wait, 'we' were in the bar? Who were you with? Is there any gossip there?"

Dan slides the stall door open and runs the chain of the lead over Monty's nose. The gelding is usually well-behaved, but if he decides to act up, Dan knows he'll appreciate a little extra leverage. "Sorry, just Chris. I've given you all I've got on the gossip front." He stands aside and lets Monty leave the stall, then starts toward the barn door.

Robyn isn't put off for long. As Dan leads Monty outside, she follows with another horse, and calls up to Dan. "But that's pretty good already, Dan! It'll give me something to look for when they're here!"

He opens the gate to the field and takes Monty inside. "Just don't be obvious about it. Karl and Molly are already pissed at me. I don't need to get blamed for 'outing' customers."

"I'll be good, I promise."

Robyn brings her horse into the field and waits for Dan to shut the gate before releasing him. Dan takes the halter off Monty and watches fondly as the big horse takes a few springy trotting steps and then erupts in a series of high-spirited bucks. Dan knows he did the right thing the day before, so he doesn't feel guilty about being glad that Monty is still at the barn.

He helps Robyn take the rest of the horses out, except for Sunshine and a couple others that might be of interest to the Kaminskis. Karl and Molly haven't left him a note as they normally would, letting him know about the buyers, but it's a lot easier to leave a horse inside for an extra hour or two than it is to catch one that doesn't want to be caught. He also keeps Chaucer in, and sets to work grooming him and tacking him up. They'd done dressage the day before, so Dan puts his jumping saddle on today.

He keeps an eye out for the Kaminskis as he works with Chaucer but doesn't see them. He also doesn't see Karl or Molly, which is a bit unusual. They're both strong riders and do their fair share of work in the barn. He hopes something else hasn't gone wrong. Sunshine wouldn't bring nearly as much money as Monty would have, but at least it would be something. He gets an unpleasant churning in his belly when it occurs to him that they might be away because of a problem unrelated to the barn. He'd checked his cell that morning, but if they were still angry from the day before, maybe they wouldn't want to tell him….

When he's cooled Chaucer down and turned him out, Dan decides to take a walk over toward the main house. It's not that he's looking for Karl and Molly. Really, he'd be just as glad to avoid them for a while. But it's a little unnerving for them to not have left a note or anything.

He reaches the clump of trees that separates the house from the barn area, and peers around. He can see their car in the driveway, with another car and a truck parked behind it. He squints. The car looks like the rental the Kaminskis had been driving yesterday, and the truck really looks like Chris's. He knows Chris handles the barn's legal matters, but he wouldn't usually be involved in a simple horse purchase, and it doesn't make any sense for the Kaminskis to be buying without even trying Sunshine, especially not after the failure with Monty.

Dan leans a little farther, and then catches himself. What's he doing? Whatever's going on, he's established that everyone is fine, so he really has no excuse for further spying. He turns and heads back to the barn. He's frustrated about being kept out of the loop. If he hadn't run into Jeff and Evan the night before, he'd have no idea that buyers were expected that day. And without knowing the situation, he can't really make intelligent decisions about what to work on.

Robyn is still cleaning stalls when he gets back to the barn, and instead of figuring out which horse to ride next, he makes a snap decision. "I'm going to get changed and take a long lunch, okay, Robyn?"

"I thought you said the Kaminskis were coming?"

"Yeah, I thought so, but I don't really know. Maybe they changed their minds. Anyway, it's Sunshine—Karl or Molly can ride her if they need to."

"Yeah, okay." Robyn's brow creases. "You know it's, like, ten o'clock, right? That's a pretty early lunch."

"I'm taking a drive. It'll be almost lunch by the time I get there."

Robyn nods understandingly. "Oh, okay." Dan turns and heads up to his apartment, and Robyn calls after him, "Say 'hi' for me!" Dan waves to show that he heard but doesn't turn around.

He gets changed into jeans and a button down and heads down the stairs. There's still no sign of anyone but Robyn, so Dan scrawls a note on the chalkboard. *Back around 2—D.* It seems a little petty not to tell them where he's going, but he expects they can figure it out, or Robyn will fill them in.

He pulls out of the long farm lane and heads for the highway. He knows that he puts in plenty of hours at the barn, but he feels a bit guilty all the same. Leaving early yesterday, taking a long lunch today—it feels decadent. Then he thinks of where he's going, and his guilt subsides.

The drive takes about an hour, and then he's pulling into the beautifully landscaped grounds that give the place its name. "Willowbrook" may sound like a cliché, but there're a lot of willows and at least one brook, so it's hard to argue with. He finds a parking spot and heads into the main building. He signs in at the desk, as usual, and heads down the familiar hall. A couple of the nurses nod hello, and he smiles back. He can't imagine doing their jobs, dealing with all this every day.

When he reaches the door of the room, he pauses. He always needs a moment to prepare himself. After a deep breath, he puts a smile on his face and pushes the door open. He crosses the room to the bed and pulls up a chair. "Hey, Justin. Sorry I missed a couple days—your parents were having a bit of a fit, and I had to work some extra hours."

Dan pauses and realizes that he's waiting for a response. If Justin ever did say anything, Dan would be so freaked out he'd probably run screaming from the room, but it somehow just feels rude to assume that the man won't contribute to the conversation.

Dan reaches out and takes Justin's hand. "And Robyn says 'hi'. She's got a new boyfriend, I think, but she's being pretty quiet about it—I wonder if that means she's serious this time. And I went out with Chris last night. Just JP's, of course. I'm still working a couple shifts there. Chris seems good. He won that case, the one with the tire factory. And his sister's having another baby, he said—I think they're still trying for a girl." It feels strange to talk to Justin about new lives, so Dan changes the subject.

"We had some buyers in for Monty. Were your parents here yesterday? They might have already told you this." Another pause for the non-response, then Dan continues. "Anyway, Monty was really good. Well, you know—he was Monty, but he was good on the flat, at least."

Dan fills another ten minutes or so talking about horses, the successes and failures of life as a trainer. Then he pulls out the sandwich he'd picked up on the way. "None for you, man, sorry. This is from that place on Limestone, where we went that time with Kelly and Phil? They make good sandwiches, but, God, do you remember how nasty the soup was?"

He eats quietly and then tidily bundles up the wrappings and puts them in the trash. A nurse he hasn't met before comes through the door and stops when she sees him. "Oh, I'm sorry. I didn't know anyone was in here."

Dan resists the urge to point out that there's always someone in there, since Justin never really gets to leave. "I was just on my way out."

"Oh, don't let me rush you." Her smile is almost flirtatious. "I can come back later, if that's better for you."

"No, I really was just about to leave." Dan leans over and brushes Justin's bangs back, then kisses him on the forehead. "Bye, baby. I'll see you in a couple days, probably." Dan makes sure he doesn't inhale when his face is near Justin. There's no smell, but rather than making Justin seem clean, it just makes him seem… empty.

Dan nods to the nurse and heads outside. He's always so happy to get out of that room, and then even happier when he can leave the building entirely, breathing in the fresh outside air. He doesn't like to think about Justin being stuck in there permanently. He doesn't like to think about having to go back himself for his next visit. But he knows it's really not about what he wants. It's about doing the right thing. There have been times when Dan hasn't been sure what that was, but this isn't one of those situations. As long as Justin needs him, Dan will be there. He knows that as well as he knows anything.

chapter 4

WHEN Dan gets back to the barn, Robyn is at his truck before he's even turned the engine off. He actually has to wait for her to step back before he can open the door.

She stares as if waiting for him to say something. When he looks blankly back, she says, "You were with Justin? Is he okay?"

Dan doesn't really know how to answer that question. "I didn't actually talk to the doctors, but he seemed the same. Why?"

She backs up a few steps more. "Karl and Molly were down here looking for you, and it looked like they'd both been crying. They didn't say what was wrong, so I thought, you know…."

Dan feels a burst of panic, but fights to keep himself calm as he tries to work out the timing. "When were they here? I left Justin about an hour ago."

Robyn thinks for a moment, and then looks relieved. "No, it was longer than that ago. A couple hours, probably."

"It's still nothing good, though… they were *both* crying? I mean, Karl cries at TV shows, but Molly's pretty tough." Dan has only seen Molly cry once, when the doctors had first told them the extent of Justin's injury, and he really, really hopes to never see it again.

"Well, neither one was actually crying when they were here, but they both had red eyes. They both looked upset."

Dan doesn't know what to do with this new information. He hates not knowing what's going on. "Their car wasn't in the drive when I pulled up. Do you know where they went?"

"They said they were going into town… and, Dan… they said to tell you not to ride."

This makes no sense at all. "What? Not to ride anybody, or just not Monty or Sunshine or something?"

"No, they said not at all. Said you could help me, or take the afternoon off, but to not ride."

Dan pulls out his cell phone and hits a speed dial number. He hadn't wanted to involve Chris the night before, but things are getting ridiculous. When Chris's cell goes to voice mail, Dan tries his work number, but the receptionist says that Chris is in a meeting.

"Well. Great." He's at a loss. "Do you *need* any help?"

"Not really, to be honest. Without you guys around to mess things up, I'm actually ahead of schedule." Robyn shakes her head. "I'm starting to get a really weird feeling about all this, Dan. I mean... what's going on?"

Dan doesn't have an answer for her. Even though she'd said she didn't need it, he helps Robyn haul some hay in from the feed shed, and then he cleans tack until his fingers ache. There's still no sign of Karl or Molly by the time Dan has to go and get cleaned up for his shift at JP's. It's their turn to bring the horses in and do the evening feed, and he's a bit worried that they haven't appeared. He doesn't want to cause an inconvenience for his boss at the bar, but he also doesn't want the horses to be neglected if their owners don't come back from wherever they are. On a normal day, he'd be totally confident that Karl and Molly would look after their animals, but this has not been an ordinary day. Robyn solves the problem.

"I'm just going to watch TV anyway. Let me watch at your place for a couple hours, and if they aren't back in time, I can help out."

He makes sure she really means it, and then they go upstairs together, Robyn to the couch and Dan to the shower. As he heads out the door, he tells her to help herself to anything in his fridge, and she rolls her eyes. "I already checked. You've got beer and three different kinds of hot sauce. It's not exactly a balanced meal. But you've got a couple pasta dinners in the freezer—I can have one, yes?"

Dan grins sheepishly and nods, then reminds her to call him if she gets any news, to make sure Karl and Molly have his cell number if she sees them. He knows they do, but doesn't understand why they haven't used it.

He gets to JP's just in time for the dinner rush, and for the first couple hours he's too busy to think much. Things finally calm down a little, and he finds some time to tidy up and restock. In his peripheral vision, he sees a new customer come in and sit down, so he moves in that direction as he puts the final polish on a glass. When he looks up and sees the new customer, he's greeted with miles of tanned Kaminski. Well, there's not all that much tan showing, but Dan can imagine.

"Hi, Dan," Evan says. He smiles, and it makes him look like Tat. They both smile with their whole faces, their whole bodies, practically.

"Evan, hey, what's up?" This sounds a little vague to Dan, sounds like what he'd say to someone who *didn't* have some mysterious connection to Dan's employers and quasi-in-laws. He tries to clarify, make it clear that he actually wants to know. "You didn't make it to the barn today… did something happen?"

Evan goes from almost sheepish to totally awkward. "Uh, yeah, kinda… I know it sounds weird, but I'm actually not supposed to talk about it."

Dan's had about enough of being out of the loop. "Oh. What can I get you, then?"

"A Bud and a Jim Beam, please. And I didn't mean that I can't talk at all, I just can't talk about… that."

Dan moves to get the drinks but isn't really interested in playing games. "Okay, well, I don't really know what 'that' is, so it'll be a bit hard for me to avoid it." He smiles politely as he says it. Evan is now a customer in the bar *and* a potential customer at the barn, so Dan really can't be too rude to him.

Evan's return smile is much more genuine. "Yeah, I can see why that'd be a little tricky. I could just ask you questions…."

"Uh, well… I'm at work, Evan. It's not really the best place for chatting." Evan looks a little unimpressed, and Dan realizes something. "You've never had a job, have you?"

"No. I have. I do!" Evan's denials are a little too emphatic, and Dan closes in for the kill.

"Evan…." Dan walks to stand in front of Evan and looks him in the eye, trying to inspire honesty. "Evan, have you ever had a job at a business your family didn't *own*?" Evan casts his eyes down and Dan laughs. "Yeah, it's not quite the same, buddy." That's maybe a bit more casual than Dan should be, but Evan doesn't seem to mind.

"Well, still… I'm a customer… doesn't that mean I'm always right? If I say I deserve some attention, isn't it your job to give it to me?" The words would sound petulant if it weren't for the open, teasing grin on the man's face.

Dan doesn't really want to get involved in this, but he seems to be having some trouble resisting the eyes and the dimples. "Okay, fine. Is there something you actually want to know, or are you just being a brat?"

Evan's victory grin threatens to split his face. "There's *lots* of things I want to know! I'm just not sure where to start."

A customer down the bar catches Dan's eye, looking for a refill. Dan moves away from Evan, saying, "Well, you can have *one* question, so make it good. I'll be back in a minute." Dan pulls a beer for the other customer while wondering what exactly he's doing with Evan. It's not flirting, exactly… or is it? But Dan's not that guy. He doesn't flirt with other people's boyfriends, and he certainly doesn't fool around on his own lover. Chris is Justin's best friend, and as such has decided that it's his right to tell Dan that he can do what he wants, but Dan knows that it's not Chris's call. Chris and Justin may have grown up together, but Chris doesn't know Justin the same way Dan does. And apparently Chris doesn't know Dan too well, either, if he thinks Dan would ever want to cheat on somebody who's lying in a hospital bed.

Evan's just a typical rich kid, Dan decides, taking something that means a lot to somebody and turning it into a game for his own amusement. Well, Dan doesn't want to play. He has to be polite, since Evan's a bit too powerful to insult, but that's all.

Dan realizes that it's easier to make this sort of resolution when he's at the far end of the bar. When he's standing in front of Evan again, faced with the full warmth of the man's personality, Dan finds himself smiling a little more sincerely than he had intended. "You got one?"

"Like I said, man, I've got lots. I really don't think one is going to be enough. Is there anything I can do to earn a couple more?" Yes, Evan is definitely flirting. Dan knows he should shut it down, but he's a little curious to see just how far Evan will take it. And, if he's completely honest with himself, maybe he's enjoying the attention a little.

"I doubt it, but if your first one isn't too horrific, I'll think about it."

"Oh. Not horrific… I gotta be honest, that eliminates a lot of my ideas right off the top."

Another customer needs a drink, so Dan just raises an eyebrow at Evan and moves around the bar. When he returns, Evan is smiling happily.

"Okay, I've got one. It's easy, no horror whatsoever." Dan nods, so Evan continues. "How did you get started with riding?"

Dan knows that *should* be an easy question, so he can't blame Evan for asking it. Still, he doesn't really want to answer. "I was living with a family, and they had horses, and they taught me." It's a bit of a gloss, but it's not a lie.

"With a family? Like, not *your* family?"

"You got one question, man. Not two." Dan moves down the bar and picks up a glass to start polishing.

Evan shifts along to follow him, bringing his beer. "No, this is just a follow-up. A clarification, even. Your original answer was vague and incomplete!"

Evan doesn't seem like the type to take hints, and Dan is reminded again that the other man is a spoiled rich kid, used to getting what he wants. "Okay. No, they weren't my family."

"But you do have a family, right?"

"What do you think, Evan, I was hatched from an egg?"

Evan's face lights up. "Yeah, that's good! We'll exchange questions. That's a great idea!" Evan almost claps his hands. Dan is pretty sure the innocent enthusiasm thing is an act, but he's not quite positive.

Evan continues. "Okay, your question was, 'Evan, do you think I was hatched from an egg?' My answer to that is, 'No, Dan, I do not believe that at all, and I am sure you were born from a traditional union between a human male and a human female.'" Evan's smile is mock-condescending. "You'll notice, I think, that I answered the question fully, and even gave a little extra. Perhaps you could use that as a model for your answer to my next question." Dan refuses to smile, but Evan continues anyway. "Okay, my next question is… do you like your job?"

That one's a bit easier, so Dan decides to play along. He has a question he wants to ask Evan, after all. "Yes, Evan, I like my job. It's not perfect all the time, but in general, I enjoy it."

Evan nods, looking impressed. "Excellent, you're really picking the game up quickly. Okay, now it's your turn."

Dan puts down the glass. "All right, here goes… what were you doing at Molly and Karl's this morning?"

Evan's face falls. "Dan, damn. I'm sorry, but I really can't talk about it. Not now, at least. As soon as things are settled, you'll be the first to know."

That was about what Dan expected. "So, you refuse to answer? I guess that means the game's over." Dan moves around the bar, this time going to check on the coffee pot. Again, Evan follows him.

"Dan, seriously… I know this must be frustrating for you. But I was just hoping that… I don't know. I guess I was hoping that all that could be separate." Evan looks awkward, and Dan wonders if this is what's beneath the careless exterior, or if it's just another act. "I mean, you must have people coming on to you pretty much constantly, but, honestly, I'm not just—I'm not just after your looks, not looking for just—you know. I really like you, what I've seen so far, and I'd like the chance to get to know you better." Evan looks like he's surprised himself with his little speech.

Dan just stares at him, and then says, "Okay, how about I give you an alternate question, then?" Evan nods enthusiastically and waits for Dan to speak. "Here it is, then, question two… Evan, where's Jeff tonight?"

Dan can't read the expression on Evan's face, but his voice is agitated. "No, man, you've got it wrong. Jeff and me, we're not like that. I mean, we're like that, but we're not… I mean, believe me, Jeff has no problem with me being here tonight." Evan catches himself. "Well, no, that's not quite true. He didn't think I should come, but it's because he thought it was stupid, thought it was making things too complicated, not because he has a problem with it in theory. I mean—"

Dan is suddenly tired, and strangely sad, and he cuts Evan off. "Evan, you should go home. There's nothing for you here." He fixes Evan with a level stare to show that he means it. This time when he walks away, Evan doesn't follow.

chapter 5

EVAN leaves the bar shortly after Dan starts ignoring him. Dan feels mostly relieved, and tries to disregard the tiny little niggle of disappointment. Evan seems like a good enough guy, and Lord knows he's not hard to look at. Maybe in another life, Dan would have been interested, even if the Jeff situation is still a little confusing. But in this life, he knows that the whole thing is out of the question.

Dan helps close down the bar and then heads home to find a note pinned to his door. It's from Molly, asking him to come by the house the next morning at nine.

So, that's it, then. He'll find out what's going on in… he checks his watch. Six hours. He's really just fed up with the drama—he's been more than just an employee to Karl and Molly, and he doesn't understand what he's done to be shut out like this, and he doesn't really appreciate it.

He falls asleep quickly but wakes up, as usual, when he hears Robyn arrive to feed the horses. He tries to get back to sleep, but then the sun shines in his window, and he knows it's a lost cause.

He showers, dresses, and tries to think of a way to kill almost two hours. He settles on going down and helping Robyn take the horses out. Even if he's not allowed to ride, it's still calming to be around them. He and Robyn grill each other looking for extra information, but there's none to be had.

Finally, he heads over to the house. He's a little early, but he doesn't think Karl or Molly will mind. In better times he would have expected to mooch some sort of breakfast from them, but he doubts that's in the cards today.

He's only a little surprised to see Chris's truck in the driveway again. Chris hadn't returned Dan's calls the day before, which is totally unlike him, so Dan knows he must be involved in whatever the Big Secret is. There's no sign of the Kaminskis, though.

Dan wipes his feet carefully and then rings the doorbell. Usually, he'd follow that up with an opened door and a shouted "hello," but things just don't feel quite that casual anymore.

When Karl comes to answer the door, he seems reserved, almost nervous, and he doesn't seem to want to look Dan in the eye. He leads the way into the living room, where Molly and Chris are waiting.

Chris stands up, saying, "I'll just go tidy up some of the paperwork," as he leaves the room.

"Dan, come in." Molly says softly. "Please, sit down."

She's acting like he's made of china, and the change from her normal forthrightness is kind of creeping Dan out. "Yeah, okay," he says. Whatever it is, it can't be as bad as they're building it up to be.

There's an awkward pause, and then Molly begins. "We've… we've made several decisions. They're all connected, and they all involved you, and we just… we know you might not agree, necessarily, but we really want you to hear us out. Can you do that?"

Dan just shrugs. He's not going to start making promises when he has no idea what's going on.

Molly nods as though that's the response she expected, and Karl takes over. "You know we've gotten offers for the farm before, Dan, and we always refused them. We thought Justin would be taking over—that was always the plan." It's obvious that it still hurts Karl to talk about his son's injury, and Dan just sits still, making sure he doesn't do anything to make it worse. But Karl and Molly are looking at him as if they expect a response.

"You're selling to the Kaminskis?" he guesses. "But why would California billionaires want a Kentucky horse farm?"

"Not exactly… we're selling the land to Leincorp Developments. They're thinking of building a subdivision here, apparently."

"Oh." Dan takes a moment to digest this information. "So you're shutting the farm right down?"

Molly reaches forward and takes his hand. "But the Kaminskis are interested in buying all the horses! All of them! They've got a big barn out there, apparently, and they were going to just buy a horse for Tatiana, but now they're thinking of getting into the training business, and filling up the place."

Dan isn't shocked, really. In his time thinking about the possible reasons for the Kaminskis' involvement, he had come up with a variety of scenarios, and the Californians throwing their money around had come into several of them. He just isn't sure why it had to be such a secret. "Well, yeah, that's great. I mean, congratulations, I guess. Do you know what you guys are going to do instead?"

Molly and Karl exchange somewhat apprehensive looks. "We're just going to retire, we think." Molly says. "The last year—it's taken a lot out of both of us. We've used up most of our savings, but with the money from the land and the horses, we'll be okay."

Dan nods. "Okay. Well, yeah, congratulations. So you'll need me out of the apartment, I guess? What's the timeline on that?" Dan finds that he's not really upset about the idea of losing his job. Moneywise, he could do better with just working another couple shifts at the bar, considering how rarely he gets paid at the barn. And if he wants to work with horses, he knows he's got enough of a reputation to find a job in the field. Leaving the apartment is a bit tougher to think about—he and Justin had shared a life there, after all.

Karl says, "Well, the developers want in as soon as possible, but we told them we'd need some time to get things packed up, and obviously you will too. There's a bit of extra money available if we get out faster, so let us know how long you'll need, and we can split some of the bonus with you."

"And all of your back pay, of course," Molly hastens to add. "We've kept close track, and Chris has the numbers, and we'll pay you all of it, with interest." She moves closer to Dan and puts her hand on his arm. "We really don't know how we could have made it through this without you, Dan."

"No, it's fine. I wasn't going to leave you in the lurch. And I don't really have much stuff. I can get out as soon as I have a place to move into. So don't worry about that." Dan stands up. "So, when are the horses going? And no more riding before they go?"

"Well, the 'no riding' is just for while things are in flux. If we decided on a price, and then a horse got injured, it could confuse things. And we're still working out the details with the Kaminskis. But even if things don't work there, we can find buyers, don't worry. We might need to be a bit flexible about the prices, but they're good horses—we'll find homes." Molly sounds like she's trying to convince herself at the same time as she convinces Dan.

"So, the Kaminski thing isn't for sure?" Dan sits back down. "With the economy the way it is, people aren't buying a lot of horses. Have you thought about hanging on to the barn for a bit longer, until you're sure about where the horses are going?"

Karl looks at Molly and they both shake their heads. "No. The deal for the subdivision isn't open forever, and... we... we need this to be over." Karl looks down at his big hands. "You were right, about selling Monty to that little girl. That would have been a terrible thing. Could have been really dangerous. And you were right that we, of all people, should have known better—"

"It was a real wake-up call for us, Dan," Molly cuts in. "We realized that we've been pushing too hard for too long. We needed to stop, and think about things."

"Okay, yeah, I can see that." Dan can. He's been working for the Archer family for years, and has seen them before and after Justin's accident. Karl and Molly are really not the same people they were a year ago.

"But, really, it could be an opportunity for you, Dan." Molly says, and she seems to be trying to put some enthusiasm in her voice. "The Kaminskis are looking for a trainer. Apparently Jeff is mostly helping them out as a friend. He's got his own interests and his own business to worry about. Evan was really interested in getting you to come to California, to be the trainer. I'm sure it would be fun for you to work in a barn that actually has some money, for a change!"

Dan really doesn't want to think about just what Evan's trying to buy with all his money. "Well, obviously I'm going to be staying in Kentucky, even if I'm not working for you anymore. It's not like I can just leave Justin here." He stands up again, a little insulted that they think he'd abandon their son. "So, sure, I'll start looking for a place. Let me know how things go with the California thing, whether I should start working the horses again or not." He looks at them, waiting for them to stand and walk him to the door, or at least acknowledge that he's leaving. They don't.

Karl's voice is scratchy when he speaks again. "The farm... that's not all we've decided." Dan gets a sick feeling in his stomach. Maybe this next part will explain why they've been acting so strangely. He sits back down, and waits.

Molly starts. "We're going to have enough money to live

comfortably, and then some." Dan just nods. The farm is a good size and
not that far from town, and several of the horses are quite valuable. "We'll
have enough money to look after Justin and ourselves, if we're careful."
Dan nods again. Justin's in a private facility. Insurance covers the basic
care, but a lot of the extras have come right out of his parents' pockets. It's
why Dan has never resented his missing paychecks.

"We just wanted to be sure that our decision wasn't based on
money," Karl blurts out. He takes a breath to calm himself, and then says,
"We wanted to be sure we were doing what's best for Justin, not what's
best for our bank account." Dan's already queasy stomach flips when he
sees that Karl is crying openly, and Molly's eyes are brimming. He
realizes that the farm decision was just a warm-up for the main event.

Molly takes her husband's hand and looks at Dan imploringly. "He's
gone, Dan. The doctors have been telling us that for months. The seizures
are getting worse, and his heart has stopped three times now." Dan can't
look her in the eye as she continues. "Dan, it was wrong of us to let it go
on for so long. We wanted so much for him to be okay, and we let it blind
us to the truth." Her voice cracks and her tears are flowing freely now.
"Dan… Justin died almost a year ago. We've got to stop pretending he
didn't. We've—"

She breaks off, and Karl wraps his arm around her shoulder before
he continues for her. "We've signed a 'Do Not Resuscitate' order for
Justin. The next time his heart stops, or he has a violent seizure, or…." He
takes a moment to collect himself, and then speaks in a more level voice.
"The next time anything happens, they'll take steps to make sure there's
no pain, but they won't bring him back."

Dan is stunned. He remembers the conversations he'd had with
Molly and Karl when Justin had first been hurt. They'd all agreed that
Justin was a fighter, that he'd never give up. They'd agreed that they
would be as strong as he was, and wouldn't give up, either. What had
happened?

"Just because you made a bad call about a horse?" Dan almost
whispers. "You're going to let Justin die because… because why?" Dan
can't sit still, and stands to move around the room as his voice rises. "If
it's the money, you could put him in a simpler room, and I could
contribute more. You don't need to worry about giving me the back pay."
This makes sense, this is becoming a plan. "You could still sell the barn,
and the horses, if you want, and I could get a job somewhere else to help

pay. I could—"

Karl breaks into Dan's increasingly frantic monologue. "No, Dan! It's not about the money. That's what we were trying to tell you... we waited until we had lots of money, so we'd know that the money concerns weren't influencing us at all!"

"Well, what is it about, then? How can you give up on him?" Dan's shouting now, and he knows he should stop, but he doesn't seem to be able to. "He's your son. You're supposed to look after him, not stick him in an institution, and then abandon him!"

"Dan!" It's Chris, brought back into the room by the yelling. "Dan, you need to cool off." Chris doesn't look angry, exactly, but he doesn't look friendly, either. Dan is reminded again that Chris is only his friend through Justin, and that Chris has known the Archer family for his whole life.

"What, you're in on this too? You think this is a good idea?" Dan shakes his head in disgust. "First you tell me that I should be fucking around on him, and now you tell me I should let them kill him? What kind of friend are you?"

"Dan, you're way over the line!" Chris's voice isn't loud, but it's powerful. "You need to take a walk, calm down a little."

"Yeah? What else are you going to decide while I'm gone? Who else are you going to kill?"

Chris takes one look at Molly and Karl, curled up around each other on the sofa as if Dan's words hurt them physically, and then he grabs Dan by the shoulders and wrestles him toward the front door. "Out, Dan," he grunts.

Dan doesn't really try to resist. It feels as if all the fight has gone out of him. He'd always been jealous of Justin's relationship with his parents, how they could work together so well and still function as a family. Seeing them abandon him like this is bewildering. He lets Chris manhandle him onto the porch. Chris looks torn between going back and comforting Karl and Molly or staying out and keeping an eye on Dan.

When Dan collapses onto the porch steps, Chris sighs and sits down beside him. "They're not abandoning anybody, man. Justin's gone, and he's not coming back. If there was a shred of a chance, you know they'd fight for him. You know that." Dan just stares out at the front lawn. There's a big old maple tree out there. Justin had once shown him where he and Chris had carved their initials in the bark when they were kids. When Dan had looked wistful, wishing that he had that sort of history somewhere, Justin had gone and gotten a knife and carved DW right there beside the other two. Dan wonders if the subdivision developers will cut the tree down.

Chris is still talking. "They maybe made a mistake in not telling you everything they got from the doctors. I think they were trying to spare you, or something... I don't know. Maybe they just thought if nobody knew it wouldn't be true. But there's been no higher brain function since his first seizure, months ago. He's gone, Dan."

Dan can't answer, can't talk past the lump in his throat. There's a weird ringing in his ears, and his body is flashing hot and then cold. He's listening to Chris, but it's like they're far away from each other, or Chris is speaking a language Dan used to know but has forgotten. He pushes himself off the step and straightens up, then starts walking back to the barn.

"Where you going, Dan?" Chris calls after him, but Dan doesn't really hear him.

Dan has no plan, no real destination, but he knows he doesn't want to have anything to do with what's happening in that house. He's got no legal rights to anything, he knows that, knows there's nothing he can really do. He can't even say for sure what Justin would want. The three people back at the house have known Justin a lot longer than he has, and he knows that they do love Justin, despite Dan's accusations to the contrary. If they think Justin would want to give up, maybe they're right. Dan just can't understand how *they* can give up. Maybe Justin would want to quit, but that just means that it's their job to be strong for him, to lend him their will power until he's back to himself.

When Dan gets to the barn, he manages to make it upstairs without seeing Robyn, and he starts packing his few belongings into bags and some boxes he's able to find. He's not sure where he's going. Ordinarily he would have run straight to Chris's, but that doesn't work anymore. But it doesn't matter, really. The barn is going, and the horses are going, and Justin... Justin is going. So Dan is going as well. He just doesn't really know where.

chapter 6

DAN ends up arranging to stay with Robyn. He hadn't planned it, but she'd seen him packing his stuff into the truck, and hadn't even asked for an explanation. She'd just asked if he was going to Chris's, and when he'd said no, she'd asked where he *was* going. When he'd turned his face away instead of answering her, she'd taken out her keys and snapped one off the ring.

Dan pulls out of himself long enough to realize that Robyn is going to get some bad news pretty soon too. She'll be upset about her job but also about Justin. They'd all worked together at the farm for years. He decides to take the key but not make himself at home. If it seems like she wants some time alone, he can always leave.

He starts to drive into town, toward Robyn's apartment, and then makes a sharp turn and heads for the highway instead. The drive to Willowbrook passes too quickly, and Dan soon finds himself walking through the familiar hallways and pausing at the same old door. He wonders how many more times he'll be making this trip. Wonders if maybe Justin's parents will change their minds, if they have to watch Justin dying a slow death. How could any parent stand by and let that happen?

Dan braces himself as usual and then pushes the door open. He doesn't bother to even try to smile; it would be dishonest to pretend that he's not upset.

"Hey, baby, it's me." Dan pulls the chair from against the wall and sets it next to Justin's bed. He leans forward, resting his forearms on the bed, and takes one of Justin's hands in his. He speaks almost reluctantly. "Things aren't going so well, man. Your parents… I mean… you know they love you. They just—" Dan's voice cracks.

"Justin, I really need you to wake up now. You've got to show them they're wrong. I understand that you needed some time to heal, I get that, and maybe you got a bit lost in there or something." Dan moves a hand up to Justin's forehead and smooths his hair back. "Please, Justin. Baby…

we're running out of time, here."

Dan can feel the tears running down his face. "Justin, please." He leans forward and buries his face in Justin's chest. His voice is muffled in the sheets, but he talks anyways, willing the words to pass directly through Justin's skin to his heart. "Please don't leave me, Justin. Please don't leave me alone."

Dan isn't sure how long he stays there like that, but when he finally sits up, his face is dry, though stiff with salt. He takes a deep breath. There's been no change in Justin, but he hadn't really expected one. Intellectually, he knows that Justin's parents are right. Justin is gone. And he's not coming back.

Emotionally, it's a little harder to accept, to understand. What is Dan supposed to do with the Justin-shaped hole in his life? How can he say goodbye to all their plans, all their shared memories, when Justin is still right in front of him, looking not terribly different than he had before the accident? With a jolt, Dan realizes that maybe that's the reason for Karl and Molly's decision. Nobody can let go, not really, not while Justin's body is still here. But Dan doesn't think he's ready to let go. He still needs Justin, needs to let a tiny part of himself believe that things could go back to the way they were, back to being perfect.

Dan remembers meeting Jeff, remembers how Jeff said they'd met before, at Rolex. The Californian had seemed to be pretty understanding about the fact that Dan couldn't remember him. Dan knows he'd been in a daze that whole weekend. The Rolex Kentucky Three-Day Event is the top event in North America, and Justin had competed in it, on a horse that Dan had conditioned and helped to train. Add in the fact that they were from a local farm, with Justin Kentucky-born-and-bred, and they'd been treated like royalty all weekend long. And when Justin had won, an underdog coming from nowhere, he'd gone straight to Dan and pulled him into the messiest, goofiest, most enthusiastic kiss Dan had ever been a part of— and Justin had known that the TV cameras were rolling. Dan doesn't understand how to reconcile that vibrant, intense man with the body lying on the bed in front of him, but he also doesn't know how to let go of the only part of that man that's still alive.

It's ironic that Dan's best and worst days with Justin both came at the same event, but a year apart. Justin had been so driven, so determined to repeat his triumph. The previous year's victory had given a huge boost to the farm, with people clamoring for horses trained at the stable that had produced a Rolex winner. But Justin knew that the horse world was fickle, knew that he needed to keep winning in order for the farm's success to continue. He'd done well in the dressage competition, and he was confident that he could put in a good performance at the jumping, but the cross-country was his chance to really shine. Dan had known he was wound too tight, had tried to talk him down, but Justin had been almost manic in his intensity. The last words Justin had ever spoken to Dan had been, "Back off, Dan. Don't tell me how to ride!"

On a good day, Dan can comfort himself by knowing that he had at least tried to get Justin to ride safely. On a bad day, he wonders if Justin's recklessness had come as much from anger at Dan as from his need to win, if Dan's attitude had somehow disrupted the careful focus and concentration that was required to safely ride an elite cross-country course. He wonders what was going through Justin's mind during the approach to the twelfth jump, wonders whether Justin could tell it was going wrong, wonders if he was worried about himself or about Willow when the mare's front hooves hit the immovable barrier and sent them both tumbling forward in a tangle of horse and rider. He wonders if he'll ever be able to get the image out of his mind.

Dan hears the door open softly behind him. He turns to see Karl and Molly standing in the doorway. They look tentative, almost apologetic. "We can wait, if you'd like some more time alone, Dan." Molly's voice is soft.

Dan's stomach twists at her choice of words. He doesn't want time alone, he wants time with Justin. He stands stiffly. "No, that's fine. I've been here for a while." He moves toward the door, and the three do an awkward dance in the doorway.

Karl puts a gentle hand on his arm. "Dan…."

But Dan pulls away. He's not angry anymore, he understands what they're doing, but he just can't talk about it, not right now. "You've got my cell number, if you need to reach me about anything. Okay?" He tries to make it a little gentle, not as fierce as he was that morning. But he still can't look them in the eye.

Karl drops his hand and nods. "Okay." He sounds old.

Dan walks briskly down the hallway and out to the truck. He checks the time on his phone. It's later than he thought, and he's supposed to be working at the bar that night. He briefly considers calling in sick but then thinks about sitting around Robyn's apartment all night with nothing to distract him, and decides that work sounds like a much better idea.

If he hurries, he has time to drop his stuff of at Robyn's and see if she's still okay with him staying there. He wishes that he'd thought to ask Karl and Molly whether they'd spoken to her yet, but he guesses he'll know as soon as he sees her face.

And he does. When she opens the door to his knock, her eyes are red and puffy, and she doesn't say anything, just shuffles forward and burrows into his chest. He brings his arms up to enfold her, and they stand there in the doorway, rocking a little. It doesn't last long, and then Robyn is pulling back and brushing at her face, trying to put a smile on.

"Did you bring your stuff? The couch pulls out, and there's room over there for you to pile whatever you don't want to leave in the truck."

"Robyn, are you sure it's okay? I mean, this is maybe not the best time for a house guest."

"Don't be stupid. You're not a house guest; you're Danny." Her smile seems a little more genuine this time, and she says, "Come on, I'll help you bring stuff up. And then, are you working tonight? You could steal me a drink or two, help me feel better?"

"Absolutely." Dan nods and tries to fight back the lump in his throat. "I don't have much, but, yeah, if you don't get enough of carrying heavy things around all day…."

A few trips down and back, and then all of Dan's belongings are piled in the corner of Robyn's living room. He looks at the clock on the wall. He's a little bit late for work already. Robyn waves him off, tells him she's going to have a shower and then come to the bar for dinner, and Dan heads out the door.

He drives to the bar and gets to work. He likes being able to fall into the familiar routine. It's not as good of a distraction as barn work. There's too much thought required, and it doesn't use his muscles enough. Still, it's better than just sitting around.

Robyn comes in with her new boyfriend, and Dan chats with them a little, but both he and Robyn are pretty subdued, and the boyfriend seems to be really understanding about it all. They move over to a table to eat, and shortly after that Dan sees Chris in the doorway. Chris hasn't seen him yet, and he has a sudden, childish urge to run into the back and hide. He just doesn't want to deal with anything tonight.

But then Chris is making his way over, and Dan knows he's been caught. He pours a draft and sets it in front of Chris, and then reaches for the bottle of Wild Turkey, holding it up questioningly.

"Fuck, yes, man. Get pouring." Dan takes a minute to look at Chris, and sees that the man looks about as bad as Dan feels. But somehow, Dan is having a harder time forgiving Chris than he is forgiving Justin's parents. He's not angry, exactly; it just feels like he doesn't know Chris as well as he thought he did. Like Dan had thought they were better friends than they were. He pours and then puts the glass on the bar and goes to serve other customers. When there's a gap in the orders, he restocks the bar or polishes glasses, rather than going and talking to Chris like he normally would.

Chris drains his glass, and Dan has to go back to offer a refill. He isn't surprised when Chris tries to stop him from leaving again. "Dan, do you have a minute? We should talk."

Dan tries to maintain his calm. "Sorry, man, not really. I'm at work."

Chris snorts. "Dan, you're one of the top eventing trainers in the country. You shouldn't be worried about your job as a bartender!"

Dan turns back to him, this time a little more fiercely. "Well, as of this morning, this is the only job I've got, so if you don't mind, I'd like to keep it. If you have some sort of business you need me for, you can call me tomorrow—my schedule has just gotten really open."

"Well, if you're looking for work, you could consider the offer from Kaminski. He seems to be willing to throw a hell of a lot of money around."

Dan is done trying to walk away from this. "Okay, first, other than you and Karl and Molly rambling about something, I haven't actually gotten an offer from Kaminski—well, I have, but he wasn't interested in me riding a *horse*, exactly. Second, it's really none of your damn business what I do for a living—if you don't see fit to include me in decisions about my lover's *life*, then why the hell should I include you in my decisions about any damn thing? And, third, I'm not leaving Justin. So even if there is a job in California, I won't be taking it." Dan's voice has risen enough that people are starting to look over, and he takes a deep breath to calm himself. He continues a little more quietly. "So, this job is still pretty important. I'd appreciate it if you would try to not fuck that up for me."

Chris looks a little surprised by the depth of Dan's resentment, but he doesn't give up. "Okay, fine. No discussion, no conversation, but just let me give you one little fact."

Dan waits reluctantly, and Chris continues. "The offer from Kaminski for buying the horses—it's a really good offer, and Karl and Molly want it a lot. It's way better than they'll ever get for selling the horses individually, and it's quick and easy and stress-free, which would be great for them right now. But the deal's contingent on Kaminski being able to hire a suitable trainer for the horses." Chris pauses and takes a sip of his bourbon as Dan stands waiting. "Now, that's all it says in the contract, 'a suitable trainer'. But the contract says that it's Kaminski's place to determine who's 'suitable', and he's made it pretty clear that when he says 'suitable', he means *you*." Chris looks Dan in the eyes. "So, I'm not telling you what to do—I wouldn't know what to say even if you were interested in listening. But I wanted to be sure you had the information before you made any big decisions. It's absolutely your choice whether you want to take the job or not. But I just thought you should be aware that without you, the deal goes south."

Chris polishes off what's left in his glass and stands up. "So, if it's all right with you, I'll give Kaminski your number; have him give you a call." Dan nods distractedly, and Chris's expression softens. "Molly said you moved out of the apartment already. Have you got somewhere to stay?" Dan doesn't speak for a moment, so Chris continues. "You know you're always welcome at my place. Or if you'd rather not, if you need some money to stay at a hotel or something, I can get the firm to advance some money out of your back pay claim...."

Dan shakes his head. "No, thanks. I'm fine. I'm staying with a friend."

Chris winces a little but nods, and then his head swivels to look at the table where Robyn is sitting, trying not to eavesdrop on the conversation at the bar. "Yeah, okay. But, honestly, Dan...." Chris reaches over the bar, trying to grasp Dan's forearm, but Dan jerks back out of reach. Chris pulls his hand back, and continues softly. "If you need anything, Dan. Please, give me a call."

Dan doesn't really answer, just nods dismissively and moves away. There are several people waiting for drinks, and he busies himself with them as Chris heads for the door. Dan had felt overwhelmed before the conversation with Chris, and now it's like there's even more weight being piled onto his shoulders. He has an almost overwhelming urge to just leave, to get in his truck and drive until morning and start all over again somewhere else. He's done it before, after all.

A customer waves him over, and he goes. He resolves to lose himself in the job for tonight. Then he'll take a bottle home with him and drink himself to sleep on Robyn's couch. He knows that things won't be any better in the morning, but, hey, it's about time he got lucky—if he plays his cards right, maybe a giant asteroid will hit the Earth and he won't have to worry about any of this anymore. With that comforting thought, he moves around the bar and gets back to work.

chapter 7

DAN follows his plan to the letter, and wakes up feeling like his brain is too big for his skull. He almost welcomes the pain and fuzzy thinking; they're one more way to distract himself from reality.

Robyn has already left for work, he discovers when he gets up, and he feels totally aimless. He finds coffee made, and has one more reason to be grateful to his hostess. Then he has a shower, tidies up the blankets on the couch, and turns on the television. After fifteen minutes, he's climbing the walls.

He goes out and walks down the street to find a diner. He orders breakfast and reads the paper. He takes a half-hearted look at the want ads, but he knows that he's not going to find a job he wants in the classifieds. He's asked his boss at JP's to keep him in mind for extra shifts, so he's not exactly destitute, especially as long as Robyn will tolerate him sleeping on her couch. And he trusts Karl and Molly to get him his back pay and severance, although he's not really sure how long all that will take.

At ten thirty his phone rings, and he almost breaks a finger he's so eager to get it out of his pocket. It's not that he wants to talk to anybody specific; he just wants to *do* something. He hadn't realized how busy his job kept him until he didn't have it anymore.

He checks the call display and finds the caller identified as a local hotel. Probably Kaminski, then. Dan doesn't really want to talk to the guy, but….

"Hello."

"Hi, Dan, it's Jeff Stevens." This is a little easier to take, Dan decides. He may not be sure about the relationship between Jeff and Evan, but at least Dan can talk horses with Jeff.

"Hey, Jeff, how are you?"

"I'm good, thanks. Uh, Chris gave me your number." Jeff pauses. "Listen, Dan… this whole thing has gotten pretty jumbled up, but we're trying to get it back on track. Would you be free for lunch today? Evan has a business proposal for you. I know you've heard rumblings, but we'd like a chance to present the idea properly."

"Look, I don't want to waste your time… I can come by if you like, but I'm really not interested in leaving Kentucky."

Jeff's voice is level. "Yeah, we've got some ideas about that. Just give us a chance." Jeff takes Dan's silence as acquiescence. "It's your town—do you have a recommendation for where to eat?"

"Not really. You guys have probably eaten more restaurant lunches since you got to town than I have in the last five years. I'm usually at the barn."

"Well, we're at the Brown Hotel, right downtown. They've got a lunch restaurant called J. Grahams. Could you meet us there, maybe one o'clock?"

"Sure, that's fine."

There's a pause, and then Jeff's voice comes out a bit tentatively. "Look, Dan. I can't even pretend to understand how torn up you must be right now, and I know that it's not really any of my business. And, like I said, this whole deal has gotten way more jumbled up than it had to be, and Evan… Evan was an idiot for coming to see you in the bar the other night. The boy's got no sense at all. But he's got a good heart, and he *can* control himself if he has to." Jeff sighs. "I guess I'm just saying that I hope you can come into the meeting with an open mind. There's no pressure, no expectations, we're just putting an idea out there."

"No pressure?" Dan says. "If I don't sign on to be Evan's barn-boy, you don't buy the horses and Karl and Molly have to scramble around and try to find buyers in a totally messed up economy while they should be mourning their son? Is that what you mean by 'no pressure'?"

Jeff sighs again. "I wish Chris hadn't mentioned that to you. He's just trying to look out for everybody, I guess, but… it's really not that simple. We're not trying to be high handed about this, and we're totally open to negotiation. And the barn-boy thing… interesting imagery, by the way… Evan and I have talked about that pretty intensely, and… he's not going to make things uncomfortable for you. I promise." As far as Dan can tell from a cell phone conversation, Jeff is totally sincere. He pauses, and then goes on in a slightly less impassioned manner. "We're interested in hiring you because of your skills and your attitude—we were both really impressed with your honesty about Monty. The other part is totally separate, and if you don't bring it up, it is totally dead."

Dan doesn't really know what to say to that, but he can't really refuse to even *hear* their plan. "Yeah, fine, I'll... I'll try to have an open mind."

Jeff's smile transmits through the phone. "That's great, Dan. So we'll see you at one."

"Sure thing. Bye." Dan hangs up the phone with the beginnings of an idea in his head. He now wishes he wasn't hung over, because he's not sure it's a good idea, and a clear mind would really be helpful. Ordinarily he could call Chris, but that doesn't seem like a good option today. He thinks for a second and then pulls out his cell and dials it. He only hopes Robyn will be able to pick up.

A COUPLE hours later, he leaves the copy center and heads off to the restaurant, a thick manila envelope in his hand. He's not sure if he really needs the props, but getting them put together helped fill the time and calm his nerves.

When he gets to the restaurant Jeff and Evan are already there. They both stand and shake his hand when he walks to the table, and then they sit down and make small talk. Dan inquires about Tatiana, who has apparently gotten bored with all the business and flown home on her own. Evan raves about their housekeeper for a while, about how great it is to have someone in the house that he can trust with anything. Dan's not sure if it's meant to be a pointed comment. If it is, he's not sure what the point is meant to be. Possibly Evan is just rambling. The rest of the mealtime conversation is similarly benign, although Dan finds himself getting increasingly restless as time passes.

None of them order dessert, so once their plates are cleared and coffee is brought, Evan finally gets down to business. "So, Dan, I know this has been done kind of ass-backward, but I wanted to explain what we're looking to do with the eventing stuff, and how we'd like for you to be involved."

Dan nods. Evan hasn't even hinted at anything sexual all through lunch, and Dan isn't sure whether the other man has really given up on that or is just building up for a sneak attack. But Dan ate their meal, so he guesses he should hear their ideas.

"So, originally we were just planning on buying an eventer for Tat. Honestly, I think the last time you and I talked about this, that's where we were. But we wanted to keep the horse at our home. We've got a big barn and whatever already, but we were going to have to build a dressage ring and a jumping course and a cross-country course."

"Naturally," Dan agrees, and Jeff grins. Maybe Kaminski thinks that investing half a million dollars in top-of-the-line facilities is the only way for his sister to ride her horse, but Jeff and Dan have both apparently grown up in a slightly different world.

Evan continues unperturbed. "So, when Monty didn't seem like a good fit, we were going to get another horse. But then Tat said that she really loved Monty, and couldn't she have him, too, and we could buy an easier horse for her to ride until she gets good enough to ride him." The fact that Evan seems to have thought this was a reasonable suggestion tells Dan a little more about how different their worlds are.

"Anyway, I started thinking. It doesn't make sense to build all these rings and whatever and have just one horse using them." On that point, at least, Dan is in agreement. Evan continues. "We've already got the barn and there's loads of land, so why not fill the place up? When we heard that Karl and Molly were thinking of getting out of the business, it just seemed like the perfect opportunity." Evan pauses for a sip of coffee, and Dan waits patiently.

"So, obviously we can't have the horses just sitting there. We want to be an eventing stable. Tat can ride one or two of the horses, and Jeff can coach her, but he's too busy with his other stuff to work for us full-time. And besides, he says he prefers working with people to working just with horses." Dan wonders if Jeff also prefers to maintain some level of career that is outside the control of his mercurial young friend but doesn't inquire. "So, I need somebody to train the horses. Somebody who knows what he's doing, and who I know I can trust." Evan smiles. "Naturally, I thought of you."

Jeff takes over a little. "I know it sounds a little flaky, like he's just playing around, and he'll drop it all for the next shiny thing he sees." Evan shoots Jeff a look, and the man shrugs. "Sorry, kid, but that's how it sounds." He turns his attention back to Dan. "But it's really not like that." He pulls out a thick leather portfolio and passes it across the table to Dan. Dan looks inquisitively at Jeff, who just nods at the book. "Have a look."

Dan opens it up. It's full of press clippings, letters of reference, testimonials… all evidence of the business acumen and responsibility of Evan T. Kaminski. Evan looks embarrassed, but Jeff just grins. "Evan was born rich, no doubt about that. But he's been in charge of the family, and the family business, for the last six years. In that time, he's impressed a lot of people." Jeff reaches over and grips Evan by the back of the neck, shaking him gently. "But it's not always easy for a gorgeous twenty-six-year-old to get people to take him seriously." Jeff's grip on Evan's neck tightens a little. "Especially when he lets his dick lead him around about fifty percent of the time. So we put the portfolio together."

Evan looks sheepish, although he hasn't disagreed with anything, including the dick remark. "We did our homework on the eventing thing, Dan." He passes another bundle of papers across the table, and Dan looks down at spreadsheets, financial projections… a blur of information that makes his own envelope of homework seem paltry by comparison. Dan takes a moment to glance over the numbers. He's never had much interest in the business side of horses, but the papers look reasonable, and are projecting a modest profit by the fifth year. He notes that the salary allowed for the head trainer is significantly more than he'd made even back when Karl and Molly were paying him his full salary, and that there are generous allowances for other staff as well.

He looks up to see the two men watching him expectantly. "Okay, yeah. This looks good, I guess. But… look, Chris said the contract with the Kaminskis requires that you be able to find a suitable trainer. There's lots of people out there who would love to be part of an operation like this. Are you really going to let this deal fall apart just because you can't hire me? Or is that just a bluff?"

"We never actually said that we'd walk away without you, Dan." Evan explains. "But, yeah, it makes the deal a lot less attractive if you're not involved." Evan sees Dan's eyes narrow and speaks quickly. "I don't mean that in any sleazy way. And I'm sorry about the other night, for what it's worth. Jeff said it would complicate things, and I'm sorry if it did. But… we want you for the job because we want to be able to trust whoever we hire. I don't know enough about horses to really understand what you're doing, and Jeff's busy. And I want this to be a fun, relaxing little business… I mean, it's going to be set up at my home, not in some office somewhere. I don't want to be worrying all the time about whether my trainer's cheating me, or cheating someone else." Evan absentmindedly rubs his neck where Jeff's fingers had gripped. "So, if we can't find somebody we trust to do the job, we won't go forward. And right now, you're the only one we can think of who has the skills *and* has our trust."

Evan continues. "We understand that you've got commitments here, and we respect that. We can be flexible about the starting date, or we can figure out a way to get you enough time off that you can come back and visit, or… whatever you need. Seriously."

Jeff looks at Dan. "Ball's in your court, Dan."

Dan has to stop and think for a minute. He's been impressed despite himself. This job is a lot harder to turn down then he had expected it to be. But he had a plan, and he doesn't think anything's happened to make it a bad idea. So he takes a deep breath and pulls the envelope up onto the table. He opens it up and takes out a photograph.

"That's Monty. He's a seventeen-hand Hanoverian gelding, full brother to the mare that won Rolex two years ago, and he's had the same trainer. He's only nine years old, and he's already eventing—strongly—at the Intermediate level. He has great breeding, he's incredibly athletic, and he's brave and honest." Dan pauses for a moment. The two men are looking at him a little oddly, but he ignores them and pulls out another photograph.

"This is Sunshine. She's a Hanoverian, too, but a little smaller, only sixteen hands. She's got great bloodlines and could be a fantastic broodmare, but she's also capable of competing at a high level." Dan is on a roll now, and pulls out another photo. "This is Kip. He's a Thoroughbred stallion, came off the track, but he's totally sound. He's sixteen-one, eight years old. He's eventing at the Training level now, but he'll be ready to move up in a year at the most." Another picture comes out. "Chaucer. Hanoverian gelding, only six years old, so he's still learning. He's doing really well over jumps, and seems to have the courage and strength to be great at cross country. He's got the balance and movement for top-level dressage, as soon as he learns to stop fighting his rider."

Dan pauses, and Evan jumps in. "Dan, we know all this. I mean, I'm sure you know the horses better than we do, but we did check them out before we made the offer."

Dan nods, pulling out the other photographs as he speaks. "Okay, and that's what's confusing me." He fans the photographs out over the table. "Because these horses? These are *excellent* horses. And the way I look at it, if somebody has more money than God, and is genuinely interested in eventing, and that person sees these horses? That person will not be able to stop himself from buying them. They've been handpicked, carefully trained... this collection of horses is an eventer's wet dream." Dan pauses and shakes his head a little. "I'm only interested in working for somebody who has a genuine, strong interest in eventing. I'm only interested in working for somebody who would buy these horses even if he wasn't sure exactly who was going to be training them." Dan looks up from the photographs and sees Evan staring at him intently. Jeff is sitting back in his chair looking almost amused.

Dan decided he needs to wrap this up. "So, you can see why I'm confused. You say you're genuinely interested, but you're going to pass on horses like these just because you're not sure who your trainer is going to be? It doesn't seem right to me."

Evan leans forward and squints a little at Dan. "So, are you saying that if I buy these horses you'll definitely come and work for me?"

Dan shakes his head. "No, I'm saying if you don't buy these horses, I definitely won't. If you do buy them... I'll give it some serious thought." Dan decides to be a little more generous. "The job sounds a lot better than I thought it would," he admits, "and I do appreciate the flexibility in terms of my commitments here. I just...." He drops the businesslike facade and finds himself speaking to Jeff instead of Evan. "I just don't know which way's up right now. It's been an insane few days, and if I have to rush into a decision, I'm going for the option that keeps me as uncommitted as possible." Dan turns his attention to Evan. "So if you need an answer right now, the answer is no. If you're willing to wait a while, and if you're interested enough in the sport to invest in a damn fine string of horses...." Dan shrugs, and then stands up and holds out his hand. "Thanks for lunch and for the interest."

Evan and Jeff both stand and shake his hand, and Jeff smiles at him a little. "We're in town for another day. I'll give you a call to let you know how things are progressing." Dan nods, and Jeff continues in a softer tone of voice. "And, I don't mean to step over a line, but... you have our sympathies." Dan just nods again, and then he has to get out of there. All the horse talk had distracted him from thinking about Justin, but now it's threatening to take over again.

He heads out into the spring air and calls Robyn, as she had insisted he do. She had loved the plan and had been the one to e-mail the photographs to the copy place. She deserves to know that Dan hadn't been laughed out of the restaurant, at least.

When that's done, he finds himself at loose ends, again. He's not scheduled to work that night or the next, so he has literally nothing to do for the next fifty-two hours. He can't remember the last time he had that sort of freedom, and it scares him a little. When he gets to the truck he climbs in and points it toward Willowbrook. He finally has some maybe-good news to tell Justin.

chapter 8

DAN sits in his usual chair, in his usual pose, leaning forward with his arms braced against Justin's bed. He's just told Justin the whole story, the sale of the horses, the job offer, the counter offer… but there is one more thing he needs to explain.

He takes a deep breath before he continues. This is the hard part. For once, Dan is almost glad that Justin can't hear what he's saying.

"The thing is—I might have had a chance, Justin. I really thought about it. I thought I could use the California job as a way to convince your parents to keep you alive. You know? I could say that I would take the job, so they would get their money, as long as they agreed to not give up on you." He shrugs. "Even if they wouldn't agree, at least I'd have tried everything, right? I don't want to give up on you just because they did."

Dan pauses. This isn't something he wants to say out loud. It isn't something he even wants to think. "But I didn't do it, Justin. I don't know if that was the right thing or not. I just…." He's choking up again, and he wonders with some disgust if it's possible to dehydrate from crying so much. "I just wasn't sure that they were wrong."

He smoothes Justin's hair away from his face, runs his fingers over the neck and shoulders that used to be so strong. "I think maybe… I think maybe they're right. You're gone. It doesn't look like you are, but… the doctors have tests, they say there's nothing left. And, it's been so long, baby. More than a year now. I think… I think if you were going to make it back, you would have done it."

Dan's almost sobbing now, but he wants to get the words out, wants to say it at least once. "It doesn't mean I don't love you, Justin. You know that. You know I always will. I just… I just don't think you're here anymore, and I don't think you're coming back." He reaches for a Kleenex from the box by the bedside, blows his nose, and then takes a couple deep breaths to try to regain control of himself. "If there was a chance, any chance at all… you know I'd wait forever. You know that, right? You… you knew that." The verb tense seems wrong, but Dan thinks maybe it's something he just needs to get used to.

"Your parents love you too. I was mad at them… or hurt or whatever… that they didn't bother to talk to me before they… before they decided to let you go. They're big talkers on the family thing, I guess, but… maybe I was just being pathetic, thinking they'd care about me just because you do. Did." Yeah, *did.* Dan tries to wrap his mind around that.

"Anyway… they love you, and they're doing what they think is right. And… I don't know. Maybe I think it's right too." He leans over and kisses Justin's forehead. "It doesn't mean I'm going to stop coming to see you, and it doesn't mean I'm gonna stop hoping for a miracle. But… I've got to start figuring out how to say goodbye."

He stands and wishes there was an attached bathroom so he could wash his face without having to go out in the hall and see people. Then he laughs at himself a little. If he's going to start having wishes come true, he's got more important things to protect than his vanity.

"Okay, Justin, I'm heading out now. I'll be back in… I'm gonna try to start coming less often. I'll be back in a few days, okay? The nurses have my number. They'll call if anything goes wrong." Dan thinks of the calls he's received in the past, letting him know about Justin's health crises. With the DNR order in place, he probably won't be getting another call like those. The next time the hospice phones him, he thinks, they'll be telling him that Justin is gone.

He pops into the bathroom on his way to the truck. He splashes cold water on his overheated face and takes a moment to collect himself. Then he walks to the truck and is just opening the door when his phone rings. It's the hotel number, so he picks up. "Hello."

"Dan? It's Jeff."

"Hey, Jeff, how are you?" It's only been a few hours, so Dan expects Jeff is still just fine, but he has to open the conversation somehow.

"I'm tickled pink, Dan." Dan doesn't think he's ever heard a grown man use that idiom, but Jeff seems comfortable with it.

"Oh? About anything in particular?"

"As a matter of fact, yes. A good friend of mine has just gone off to finalize a deal to buy a string of really excellent horses, and I'm excited that I'm going to get a chance to work with them."

Dan hadn't realized how tense he'd been about the deal until he feels his body react to hearing the good news. He opens the door of his truck and sits sideways on the seat, his feet still out the door. "Are you serious?"

"I don't joke about horses, Dan." Jeff's voice is warm, as if he can read Dan's reaction and understand the reasons behind it. Dan may not be pleased with Karl and Molly right now, but he still cares about them and really wants them to be as happy as they can be. He especially doesn't want any decision he made to be the cause of their unhappiness.

"That's great, Jeff, really. Thanks for letting me know—it's really good news." Dan doesn't know where the next idea comes from, but he decides to go with it. "Look, Jeff, I'm about an hour out of town, but... would you be free in a bit, maybe to get a drink or something?" Dan panics suddenly. Did that sound like he was asking Jeff out, like he was trying to work his way into whatever Jeff and Evan have going on? "It's nothing big, I'd just... I'd appreciate a little advice, or... I don't know, exactly." He's just thinking of ways to back out of the invitation gracefully when Jeff speaks.

"Sure. That sounds good. Do you want to meet in the hotel bar, in about an hour?"

"Yeah, or, you know, if it's a nuisance, don't worry about it...."

"Dan, it's alcohol, and it's right downstairs. Couldn't be less of a nuisance." Jeff sounds amused. Dan is getting a little sick of amusing this guy, but he knows he has to blame himself for that, not Jeff.

"Yeah, right. Okay, the hotel bar, in about an hour. I'll see you there." Dan hangs up the phone and shakes his head. He doesn't think he's ever been less smooth in his life, and he's honestly not even sure what he's hoping to get from Jeff.

He's made the drive back to town so many times it's almost automatic now, although he does have to pay a little attention to keep the truck from driving itself to the barn. It's strange to think that he may never go back to the place where he spent so much time over the past five years.

When he gets to the hotel and goes inside, Jeff is there waiting for him. He's at the bar, but when Dan arrives he stands. "We can get a table, if you like."

"No, the bar's fine." Dan sits down and asks the bartender for a beer. He feels a little awkward, but Jeff seems to be taking things in stride. They sit on adjacent stools and swivel a little in, so they can look at each other if they want to, but not make it obvious if they want to look away. It reminds

Dan of standing at the edge of the paddock with Justin, leaning on the fence and speculating about the horses. He pulls himself out of that thought when Jeff speaks.

"So, I got another call from Evan. It sounds like things are going smoothly with the sale. He should have it all wrapped up in time for dinner."

Dan nods. "That's great. It's… I was a bit nervous."

Jeff smiles. "I would think you would be, playing with someone else's money like that. But you didn't let it stop you from making your case, so… unpleasant for you but not something that anyone else has to worry about." He takes a sip of his drink. "And you impressed Evan, even more than you had before. We went into this thinking you were talented and honest, and now we know you're smart too." Jeff smiles warmly at Dan. "It's made him even more determined to hire you."

Dan groans a little. "I guess that's what I wanted to talk to you about. I mean… I love the horses, and it'd be great to keep working with them. And it looks like you're going to be building a top-notch facility, so that'd be good too. And I appreciate that you're trying to find ways to make it work with… with Justin." He shrugs. "It just all seems a little… intense." He thinks about his words. "Evan seems a little intense."

Jeff nods, and seems to think for a moment before speaking. "Evan's parents died six years ago, and he had to grow up pretty fast. Had to take over the family business, and take care of his sister. He's done well by going after what he wants and not letting anything get in his way, but he hasn't learned a whole lot of subtlety yet. That's how he is with business, and that's how he usually is with his sex life." Jeff grins at Dan's wry eyebrow. "But he's a pussycat with his friends, and his sister has him wrapped around her little finger."

Jeff looks appraisingly at Dan. "When you first met him, in the barn the day we looked at Monty—did he seem too intense then?"

Dan thinks back. "No, actually, he just seemed like a guy. Like a pretty good guy."

"That's Evan in family mode—laidback, polite, friendly." Jeff smiles to himself. "I respect business-Evan, but it's family Evan that's the real draw."

This seems like the perfect opening to ask more about Jeff's relationship with Evan, but Dan holds back. He and Jeff are friendly, but they're not really friends. "So, which Evan would I be dealing with at the barn?"

Jeff smiles. "He's serious about finding a way to make the thing make money, but he's mostly setting it up as a hobby for his sister. As long as she's interested, it'll be family mode. And if she loses interest and it becomes solely a business venture, you'll rarely see him. The boy's running a multi-billion-dollar privately held corporation. A few horses are not going to be significant enough for him to devote much time to. He'll just assign you to some manager at the office, and you'll see Evan once a year at the Christmas party." Jeff grins. "And he'll have too much eggnog and make an inappropriate advance. You'll shoot him down as a drunk playboy, and you'll go back to your horses the next day, no harm no foul."

Dan shakes his head. "Does he not worry about sexual harassment lawsuits?"

Jeff grins. "Actually, he's usually really good at keeping it out of the office." Jeff's grin gets just a little wolfish as he adds, "Can't imagine what got into him with you."

Okay, Dan's going to take that as an excuse to pry a little. "It doesn't bother you? Him sleeping around?"

Jeff doesn't look surprised by the question, and just shakes his head. "We both like it this way. We're… we're committed, I guess, but… we both travel a lot, and neither of us is looking to be tied down to just one person." He shrugs. "It works. We get along well, with just enough of a daddy kink to keep it interesting. So no drama lurking there, either, if that's what you're worried about."

Strangely, Dan finds that he isn't curious about the relationship because he's trying to avoid drama, and he isn't curious because he's interested in Evan. It's Jeff that has him intrigued—Jeff, with his calmness and his compassion, with his warm smile and laughing eyes. Dan isn't sure what to do with this. He's had flashes of attraction since Justin's accident, but he's never, in the words he remembers from a Catholic family he'd once lived with, entertained the thoughts. Really, Dan's kept his thoughts more faithful *after* the accident than they ever were before Justin's injury. And given the events of the last few days, Dan is surprised that he's able to feel much of anything other than numbness.

Jeff's phone rings, and he glances at the call display. "It's Evan— mind if I get it?" Dan shakes his head, and Jeff flips the cell open. "Hey, kid, how'd it go?" There's a pause before Jeff says, "Congratulations.

They really are beautiful horses." Jeff smiles and nods at Dan, who smiles in return and then goes back to pretending not to hear the conversation. "Yeah, he's still here. I dunno, hang on." Jeff takes the phone away from his mouth. "Evan wants to know if he can join us for a drink. He's booked a flight back to California for tonight, so he'd like to check in with you before he goes."

Dan raises his hands. "Yeah, of course he can." It's nice that they bothered to ask, but Dan really wonders how often people say 'no' to Evan Kaminski.

"He says 'of course'," Jeff tells Evan. "And I've been telling him that you're not a total jackass, so make sure you mind your manners." Jeff's laugh is warm and intimate, and Dan has a quick flash of jealousy. He's shocking himself with this. Two hours ago he'd been crying at his lover's bedside, and now he's getting possessive about the affection of a virtual stranger? He'd told Justin he was going to find a way to say goodbye, but this really wasn't the method he'd had in mind.

Jeff hangs up and tells Dan, "He's on his way up from the lobby."

Dan nods and plays with the label of his beer bottle. He's feeling awkward again, anticipates feeling a little strange around Evan, now that Dan's realized that he's got a bit of a crush on the man's boyfriend.

Evan appears in the doorway, and Dan stands to greet him. They shake hands, and then Evan reaches out and gently grips Jeff's shoulder. Dan remembers having little coded greetings like that with Justin, and his emotion this time isn't quite jealousy, but he's not sure what else to call it.

"There's a booth free over there... do you guys want to grab it?" Evan is already moving toward the booth, and Dan feels a burst of resentment. He and Jeff were doing fine at the bar, and then Evan had to come along and ruin it. Dan squelches that idea fast—it's insane to start imagining a relationship between himself and Jeff, and if the new job has any chance of working out, Dan needs to go into it with a better frame of mind. And he knows that three people sitting in a row is not a good conversation layout, so it's not like he can find a fault in Evan's suggestion.

Dan stays behind long enough to settle the bar tab, over Jeff's polite objection, and then the two of them follow obediently in Evan's wake. Jeff slides in next to Evan, and that leaves Dan to sit on the other side, staring at both of them. He really misses sitting at the bar.

Evan seems pleased with the situation, though. He smiles expansively. "So, everything went really smoothly this afternoon, and I think you're going to like my new plan." He looks at Dan as if he expects the admiration to begin flowing immediately, but doesn't seem at all put out by Dan's blank look.

"Well, the facilities aren't totally ready for us in California—the barn's in good shape, but they're still working on the new rings and the cross-country course. Apparently getting the right footing is a big deal?" He looks at Dan for confirmation, and he just nods. Hopefully Evan already knows that, or he's not doing a very good job of supervising construction. "And Karl and Molly don't think they can be out of their house for at least a month. They've got to find somewhere else to live, pack up… whatever. So the new plan is for the horses to stay at the barn for another month or so. I can pay enough in rent to offset the loss from the developers, and you can keep working the horses just like you have been." Evan smiles. "I mean, I'm hoping you'll agree to take the job for at least that long. It can be a sort of tryout phase, you know? Tat'll probably want to fly out for a weekend or two and get some riding in, but otherwise it'll be just like it always was, but I'll be signing your pay checks."

Dan notices himself searching for a flaw in the plan, just so he can have the fun of pointing it out to Evan, but he has to admit he can't find anything, and he chides himself for being petty. Evan has gone out of his way to make this work for Dan, and he deserves at least a little appreciation. "Uh, yeah, that sounds good, I guess." He frowns a little. "Are Karl and Molly still going to be working there? If it's just Robyn and me, that's not really enough staff for twenty-three horses, not if we're going to be training them."

Evan nods. "I mentioned that to Karl and Molly, and they seemed willing to put in some time, but I told them I'd have to discuss it with you, that you'd have final say over hiring. Same with Robyn—she'll get her severance pay from Karl and Molly regardless, but if you want to hire her again that's up to you. It's short term work, of course, unless you want to try to bring them out to California with you…." Evan catches himself and smiles winningly. "Assuming you decide to come. We can talk about that more after we see how this goes."

Evan pulls a sheaf of papers out of his briefcase and passes them to Dan. "That's a contract for your own employment, totally open-ended for now—either side can end the contract for any reason at any time. Not that

I anticipate having to use that clause, but my lawyers' eyes were bleeding when I suggested that we put the terms in for you and not for us. And the next sheet has some names you should know. Payroll and purchasing will go through the central office, but I don't want you to get drowned in bureaucracy, so you can just call that number and speak to Becky, and she'll take care of what you need. And the other name is Linda Davis—she's my executive assistant, she knows everything that's going on everywhere at all times… it's a bit scary. So if you need something Becky can't help you with, call Linda, and she'll either help you herself or put you through to me."

Dan misses the tranquility of his conversation with Jeff. Evan isn't saying anything wrong, at all, but he's just saying a *lot*. Again, Jeff notices and tries to make things better.

He chuckles, and nods at Dan. "Another victim of Hurricane Evan." He points to Dan's beer. "Drink up. I think my liver curses the day I met the kid." Dan takes a long pull on the bottle, and Jeff continues. "I think the only decision you need to make right now is staffing, right?" He looks to Evan for confirmation, and Evan nods. The guy is trying so hard to subdue his energy that Dan worries that his head might explode. "Robyn is good, right?" Dan nods in confirmation, and Jeff continues. "And she'll probably be interested in continuing to work there?" Another nod. Jeff pauses for a drink, and to let Dan catch up a little. Even with Jeff's guidance, things are still happening pretty fast.

"So it's down to Karl and Molly." Jeff gives Dan an assessing but non-confrontational look. "Would it be uncomfortable for you to work with them? Either because they used to be your bosses or because of any personal issues?" Dan has to think about that one. He's been in charge of training the horses for quite a while, so he doesn't think there would be any change in the day-to-day dynamics of the barn. But he's less sure about the personal issues.

"How did they seem?" he asks Evan. "When you mentioned them working at the barn—did they seem like they wanted to do it, or were they just trying to do you a favor?"

Evan looks like he's thinking about what to say, for a change. "Honestly? I don't mean to intrude on personal stuff, and I'm sure there's tons I don't know and none of it's any of my business." Evan casts a look at Jeff, as if the older man has had to remind him of these points a few times. "But since you ask… from what I could see, they don't care one way or another about the jobs. They just seemed to be interested in doing whatever would make things easier for you." Evan shoots a look at Jeff as if he's afraid he's about to cross a line. "They seem like they really care about you, and they seem upset about some sort of rift between you." Evan seems like he might want to say more, but Jeff raises an eyebrow and Evan reconsiders. Dan notices the interplay—daddy kink indeed.

Then Dan is forced to consider the content of Evan's appraisal. Dan knows he needs to talk to Justin's parents. He's just not sure he knows what to say.

"The deal closes tomorrow at midnight—we made it super fast because the lawyers are worried that some horse could go lame or something and all the valuations will fall apart. So you've got tomorrow to figure out staffing." Evan is back into hurricane mode. "Contact Becky in the morning—I'll let her know to expect your call. You can set up wage expectations with her—I'll authorize a ten percent raise for Robyn… and we could maybe set the Archer pay at halfway between yours and Robyn's?" Dan nods. He guesses that makes sense. "Or, if you decide not to hire them, you can use the equivalent amount of money to hire whomever you need. If that's not going to work out for some reason, give Linda a call, and she'll sort it out." Evan's on a roll, and Jeff just sits back and watches him. "You're welcome to move back into the apartment if you like—I understand that it's good to have some employee on site in case there's trouble at night, so if you don't hire the Archers and you don't want to move back in, you should find someone else to live there, probably. And you can buy whatever supplies are needed for day-to-day operations; just send the invoices to Becky." Evan pauses. "What else? Am I micromanaging too much?"

Dan just raises an eyebrow. "No, I guess not. I think I know what I need to do. I just…." Again he finds himself looking to Jeff rather than Evan. "I just don't have any experience with this side of things. I mean, I know horses. That's about it. The hiring and supplies and invoices and executive damn assistants… I don't really know anything about that stuff." He takes a deep breath, because he finds that when it comes down to it, he really does want this job. He turns to Evan and says, "I think maybe you should be looking for someone else for the job, if you want them to look after all this stuff. I… I didn't even graduate high school. I'm not saying I can't learn it, but for what you're paying, you deserve to have somebody who already *knows* it."

Evan looks thoughtfully at Jeff, who just shrugs. Evan grins as he shakes his head. "That damned honesty, again, Dan! I love it! We can train you for whatever you need to know, but we can't train somebody else to be a stand-up guy."

Dan drains his beer. Evan is exhausting, but he makes it really hard to not like him. "Okay, then. If that's your call. Is there anything else we need to talk about tonight?"

"Becky will probably have a list of things for you—she'll want to set you up with a laptop and a fax and God knows what else. But I think the big stuff has been handled. You know what you're doing tomorrow?"

"Calling Becky and figuring out staffing," Dan recites obediently.

"Okay, then, I think we're good." Jeff stands up as Dan does, and Evan shuffles out of the booth to join the line for handshakes.

"It was really good to meet you, Dan." Evan says. "I'm really looking forward to luring you out to California!" Dan just laughs, and tries not to look awkward as he turns to Jeff.

Jeff has pulled a pen out of Evan's briefcase and reaches out for the sheaf of papers Dan has been given. He finds the page with the phone number, and writes another two on it. "Those are my numbers, home and cell. If you have any questions or need to talk, about horses or whatever, give me a call." Evan is looking at Jeff a little curiously, but Dan just nods and shakes Jeff's hand.

"Okay, well, it was good to meet you both." Dan represses the strange urge to wave to the two men and instead turns and makes his way out of the bar. It's odd to think that earlier that day he was thinking he might never see the barn again, and now he's going back to living and working in it. At least for a while longer. He decides to ask Robyn if he can stay another night with her, and then gives serious thought to trying to get her to go out to California with the horses.

It still doesn't feel right to think of going out there himself, not without Justin. But he knows that nowhere is going to feel right without Justin: not Kentucky, not California, not anywhere. He's not sure whether it would be easier to be alone in a familiar setting or in a new environment. The big change, he realizes, is going to be trying to live without Justin. Everything else is just a petty detail.

chapter 9

ROBYN readily agrees to keep working at the barn, even before Dan mentions the raise. And she's kind enough to not look overjoyed when Dan tells her that he'll be getting off her couch the next day. Then she's the one who raises the problem of other staff.

"I don't know...." Dan leans back on her couch and runs both hands through his hair in frustration. "Is it just going to be weird if Karl and Molly come back? Evan said they weren't too enthusiastic, and it's not like they need the money anymore. I don't want them there just to do a favor for me, you know?" Dan thinks for a moment. "You've gotten really good at riding—if I worked with you, you could take over a few horses a day, right?" Robyn looks a little hesitant. "I mean, if I found someone else to do the job you've been doing. It'd be easier to find a replacement for a stable hand than for a trainer."

Robyn's tentative. "It sounds great, Dan, and you know I've been looking to move more into that side of things. But... are you ever going to deal with Karl and Molly? You guys were all really close—are you just going to let that go?"

Dan tries not to show too much of his frustration. It isn't Robyn's fault, after all. "I don't know that we ever were all that close. I mean, I thought we were, too, but really it was just Justin. Without him... I'm just some guy who used to ride their horses." He pauses. "And that would be fine, as long as everyone admits that's all there is. But if anyone keeps pretending that there's more to it, it's just going to be awkward. You know?"

Robyn sighs. "I think you're taking things the wrong way, maybe. I mean, they always say that you're like part of the family."

"Yeah, I think they mean Chris. He's the one they talked to when it really mattered." Dan takes the bitterness out of his tone and smiles apologetically. "I've been 'like part of the family' before, Robyn... it never lasts. People say the dog is like part of the family, right before they get rid of it because one of the *real* kids gets allergies."

Robyn looks at him sadly. "So that's it? You just pack up and move on, and leave it all behind?"

"I'm not the one who packed up! I was sticking it out!" Dan shakes his head in frustration. "But if everyone else is packed and gone—sorry, I'm not going to hang around and wait for them to come back." The words remind him of Justin. "Nobody's coming back, Robyn."

He stands up suddenly and moves around the small living room. "But you're right; I should at least talk to them. Make sure they don't want the jobs for themselves. I mean, I can't see why they would, but since Evan mentioned it to them, I'd better follow up, I guess."

Robyn nods. "Tomorrow's my day off, so I guess they'll be at the barn most of the day… you could talk to them there." She stands, too, and walks over to Dan. "I was thinking of going out to see Justin. It's been a while, and I thought… I thought maybe I should…."

"Say goodbye?" Dan says softly, with a gentle smile.

Robyn tears up almost instantly and turns away. "God, Dan, I'm sorry. If I feel like this, how must you feel?"

"No, Robyn, don't be sorry!" He reaches out and gently turns her to face him. He tilts her face up and uses his thumbs to brush the tears away, but they're instantly replaced by new ones. "Everybody loves him, I know that. It's not easy for anybody." She buries her face in his shoulder, and he brings his arms around her, rocking her a little. "You'll be okay. We'll all be okay." He hopes that if he says it enough, he'll start to believe it too.

It's not long before Robyn pulls away, and Dan finds that he misses the warmth of contact after she's gone. "Sorry," she mutters. "I'm good now…. Hey, if this is your last night here, I'm gonna make dinner for us, okay? Anything in particular you'd like?"

Dan laughs. "Robyn, who do you think you're talking to? I know what you cook… I've got a choice between tofu stir fry, tofu spaghetti, or that tofu-chickpea-potato thing… which is really good, actually. Have you got the ingredients for that?"

Robyn's eyes are still red, but she raises her head jauntily. "As a matter of fact, I do." She takes his hand and pulls him toward the kitchen. "You can chop up the onion—I've cried enough for one day."

They cook and eat and go to bed early, and the next morning Dan wakes up and showers, makes coffee for Robyn, and then heads to the barn before he can change his mind.

He pulls up and opens the door of the truck, and takes a deep breath of the horse-y air. He wonders what it says that the smell of manure makes him feel at home. Most of the horses are already outside, and Dan walks over to the paddock where Monty and some of the other geldings are picking lazily at the short grass. Dan whistles and they all look up… and then go back to their grazing. Apparently they didn't miss him as much as he missed them. He ducks through the wood-slat fence and walks over to Monty.

Once he gets close, Monty raises his head and looks at Dan with a warm eye, and then takes a few steps forward to meet him. Monty snuffles at Dan's pockets and then hangs his head over his shoulder so that Dan can lift his hands to scratch both sides of Monty's neck at once. "Hey, buddy. How've you been?" Dan has always talked to horses. Justin said it wasn't strange to *talk* to horses, but it was a little strange to ask them questions. But then he'd kissed the back of Dan's neck and wrapped his arms around Dan's chest, so it really didn't seem like a criticism. "Do you want to go for a ride, buddy? Huh? We can't go today, but tomorrow, I'm back. We'll go up along the ridge, maybe. Does that sound good? And you can splash in the mud down by the pond too. It'll be an all-terrain day, my friend!"

Monty snorts a little and backs up enough to be able to rub his forehead gently against Dan's chest. Dan answers the request by bringing his hands up and rubbing Monty's face vigorously. The gelding's coat is clipped short, but he's still shedding a little, and his face is apparently itchy. Monty leans into it, and angles his head so that Dan hits all the right spots. Finally, Dan slaps Monty's neck to let him know the massage is over, and then turns back toward the barn.

At some point during Monty's scratch-fest, Karl and Molly have apparently become aware of Dan's arrival, and they're standing by the fence waiting for him. That's not bad, Dan decides. There are more distractions outside. Still, he's not exactly looking forward to the conversation.

He walks toward them, squinting into the morning sun. He aims for the fence a panel down from where they're standing and ducks through, then walks over to stand next to them, all three resting their arms on the top rail and watching the horses.

"Congratulations on the sale." Dan finally says. "I didn't hear a number, but Chris seemed to think it was a good price."

Karl nods and clears his throat. "It was an excellent price."

"Well, they're excellent horses." Dan replies. "Monty's gonna be totally bald if he keeps shedding like that, but, otherwise…."

Molly laughs a little. "Well, as long as it doesn't happen before midnight tonight, we're okay." She turns toward Dan a little, but he keeps staring out at the horses. "We wanted to thank you, Dan. For taking the job, making the deal happen…."

Karl interrupts gently. "We didn't want Chris to tell you. We didn't want you to feel at all obliged. But he said you needed to know all the information, that we'd gone wrong the last time by not telling you enough, not keeping you in the loop."

Now it's Dan's turn to interrupt. "No, wait, it didn't happen that way. Evan bought the horses because he wanted the horses. I told him I'd think about the job, but I didn't commit to anything. I didn't even say I'd do this month until after he'd already bought them." Dan glances over at the others. "Seriously. I didn't… they're just good horses, and he wanted them."

Karl and Molly exchange skeptical looks, and Dan sees them. "Don't you think they're good horses? I mean, he'd be crazy to *not* want them, right? And it's not like he's short on cash—and he's got a pretty good plan for making the business work, I think."

Molly raises an eyebrow, and Dan feels like an idiot. "I mean, obviously I don't really know much about the business stuff. It was all spreadsheets and whatever… but a guy like Evan, he'd know what he was talking about, right?"

"Dan, I'm sure you could judge his plan! I wasn't surprised by that, I was just… you seem to have spent a fair bit of time with him." Molly gives him an inquisitive look, and Dan feels defensive again. Can she really think that he'd cheat on Justin, with Evan or anybody else?

"Not that much time, really." Dan knows his voice sounds cold, and he really doesn't care. "But he did mention that he'd talked to you about working out here for the next month, just keeping things running as they were."

Molly seems to withdraw, so Karl steps up. "He mentioned it. We said we'd be happy to help out however you need."

Dan doesn't really like people thinking he needs charity. "Well, I'm sure we'll be fine either way. Robyn's staying, and she knows the system as well as anybody, so we can just hire some general laborers if we have to. I figured you might be busy packing up the house and finding a new place. But if you want to stay, of course the jobs are yours." He pauses for breath. "I told Robyn she could do more riding, so we'd have to shuffle around a bit to share out the barn chores, but… yeah, if you want another month, that'd be great." He hopes that was balanced enough. His spine is crawling at the thought of having conversations this awkward every day, but he knows that Karl and Molly would be really useful, and he knows that it would be rude to not give them the option.

"Well, we are going to be pretty busy getting the house packed up…." Dan starts to talk, to say it's no problem, but Karl raises a hand to stop him. "But we'd like to see it through here, as well. I mean, this place is our life's work. Those horses—I know you worked hard on them, Dan, but we did, too, and… well, it just doesn't seem right, somehow, to have them all still here, without us being involved somehow." Karl sounds a little choked up, and Dan is reminded that they had always planned to leave the farm to Justin. They're sad to see it go, but that's nothing compared how they must feel about the reason they've had to sell. "So, if it's okay with you, we'd like to keep working here until the horses go."

Molly steps around Karl and puts her hand on Dan's forearm. "We'd really like to have some more time with you too. We know… we *know* we didn't treat you fairly, deciding about Justin without talking to you. It honestly… we just had one terrible, horrible night of talking, and by morning we'd made up our minds. And once we'd decided, we couldn't go back, couldn't go through all that again." Molly is crying a little, and Dan only hopes he can keep himself under control.

He looks out at the horses for a minute and doesn't talk until he knows that his voice will be level. "I understand. And I don't really disagree with the decision. I'm sorry I yelled at you about it."

Karl is crying now too. "We're going to lose our son. We know that now. We just—" Karl makes a move as if to hug him, but Dan jerks back a little. He didn't plan to. He doesn't want to hurt them, but….

Karl's arms fall to his sides and he continues in a more subdued tone. "We just don't want to lose you too."

This isn't fair, Dan thinks. They can't say he's family, and then treat him like he's not, and then try to say he is again… he needs to maintain control over this, needs to remember that they're emotional and not thinking about what they're saying.

He takes a small step backward. "No, of course not. You're not losing me." He plasters a smile on his face. It doesn't matter what he says, it just matters what he feels, and he can keep himself from feeling anything for them if they'll just stop crowding him. "It'll be good to work together. No problem, everything's good."

Molly looks like he's said exactly the wrong thing, but he really doesn't know how to help her. He tries for a subject change. "I was thinking that Sunshine should probably get some more time on hills—work on her fitness, help her get her legs under her. Robyn could probably do that a few days a week, right?"

Karl and Molly look a little stunned by the new topic. Dan knows that the segue wasn't exactly smooth, but he really can't handle any more crying, so he charges on. "Is Casey still sore in front? We're going to have to get a good farrier for him. Next time Scott's here, maybe we could ask if he knows anybody out in California. In the meantime, though, is he sound to work?"

Karl takes a moment, but he manages to get back on track. "Uh… yeah, maybe, as long as we keep it light."

Dan continues making plans with Karl, and eventually Molly joins back into the conversation. They agree to keep the work schedules as they were, although all three of them will make a point of spending more time on barn duties in order to free up some of Robyn's time for riding. It seems a bit weird that Dan will be shoveling more shit *after* getting his new job than he did before, but he's not willing to go back on his offer to Robyn, and the Archers seem to understand.

Once everything is figured out, he leaves them and heads back to town. He knows that Karl and Molly weren't totally satisfied with the conversation, but he's really not sure what he could have done differently.

He calls Becky in California and is blown away by her efficiency. She has already arranged to have a variety of office equipment shipped to Louisville. He just needs to give her an address and the delivery will be there in a couple of hours. She collects information on names of the staff, and asks him to collect some basic inventory information on what's in the barn. Dan agrees to it all without too much thought.

He also calls his boss at JP's and asks to be taken off the schedule as soon as possible. Seeing the horses again that morning had made it clear to Dan that he was always going to want to work in the horse business, and with Kaminski paying him, he doesn't need to worry about making it from paycheck to paycheck, so the bartending job is no longer necessary. His boss isn't thrilled. It was only a couple days earlier that Dan had been asking for more shifts. But bartenders are not known for their long-term reliability, so the man doesn't seem too shocked and says that Dan doesn't need to come in at all anymore.

Then Dan drives to the University of Louisville and finds the bookstore. He's intimidated even walking into the place, but he finds a helpful sales clerk and asks for the textbooks for the first year business program. She asks a few questions and helps him find what he's looking for, and he walks out a few minutes later with three hundred dollars' worth of heavy, boring-looking books. He's not really looking forward to reading them, but he doesn't want to mess up with his new responsibilities.

He's tempted to go out to Willowbrook with them. If he's just reading, it doesn't really matter where he is. But he remembers his resolution to stop visiting so often, so he goes to Robyn's instead, picks up his stuff and heads out to the apartment over the barn. It doesn't take long to move back in, especially since he leaves most of his belongings packed up. Then he takes the least offensive-looking book and heads downstairs to find a seat at the picnic table. The book might be boring, and his life might still be a little unsettled, but he can see the horses from where he's sitting, and the sun's warm on his shoulders. Sometimes, you just take what peace you can find.

chapter 10

DAN is surprised by how smoothly things go over the next couple weeks. There are a few awkward moments with Karl and Molly, but it's not nearly as bad as he'd thought—as long as they have horses to think about, they're all able to work calmly together. Robyn does well with her new responsibilities, and Dan finds that *parts* of the business textbooks are actually fairly interesting.

He has a couple of phone conversations with Linda Davis, Evan's executive assistant, and finds her warm and charming, not at all the hyper-efficient robot Evan had suggested she was. Dan wonders if the poor woman has had to adopt a cold persona around her employer just to keep his enthusiasm under some sort of control. She keeps Dan up to date on the construction schedule in California, and then calls to see if they can arrange a time for him to come out to inspect the site and help them with hiring.

"I'm not even sure if I'm going to be coming out with the horses, though," Dan reminds her. "Right now, I still need to be here." It feels ghoulish to clarify the reasons behind his indecision, seems ugly to say that he will only move to California if Justin is dead. He doesn't even like to think about the implications of that himself. Now that he's admitted that he wants the job, does that mean that he has a reason to want Justin to die? Dan has a growing understanding of why the Archers wanted to make sure that money wasn't a factor before they made their decision to let Justin go.

"Well, I think Evan is hoping to take advantage of your expertise even if it's not a long-term arrangement," Linda says smoothly. "He'd like to get your opinion of what's been done at the barn, and what else needs to be done. And he's also planning to get your help in evaluating the skills and credentials of the candidates for the jobs." Dan can hear the smile come into her voice. "I think he's also hoping that once you see the place you'll want to come back. But that's really not the main reason for the trip."

"Well, sure, then, I can come out. Do you have dates in mind?"

"The ads have already been posted for the positions, and we've gotten a good response. Evan asked me to fax the applications to you for review, and then as soon as you get back to me with the names of the candidates you'd like to see, I can have someone set up the interviews." It occurs to Dan that Linda is probably working well below her pay grade, placing want ads and coordinating travel for a bunch of horse people. He wonders why this project merits special attention from Evan's own assistant, and the answers he comes up with make him uncomfortable but also a little flattered.

"Sure, yeah, that sounds good." Dan remembers something. "Oh, wait—I was talking to Robyn, the woman who looks after the horses here, and does some training… and she'd be interested in moving out, having one of the jobs." Robyn had just broken up with her boyfriend, and when Dan mentioned the possibility of her going to California with the horses, her eyes had actually glowed. "Uh, I think that'd be good whether I come or not—if I'm there, we work well together, and if I'm not, you'd have someone who knows the horses."

"All right, I can pass that along to Evan. I think he and Jeff Stevens were hoping to sit in on the interviews, along with Tatiana—Evan's trying to use this project as a way to get her more involved with the family businesses. But I expect they'd be interested in hiring someone you recommend, even if they don't have the chance to interview her themselves."

And only three days later, Dan finds himself being picked up in an airport limo (really just a car, he's relieved to see) and driven to the Cincinnati airport. He's never flown before. He's traveled lots, at least through North America, but at first he got around by hitchhiking, and later he drove with horse trailers. He and Justin had talked about taking Willow on the international circuit, but that was just one more thing that they hadn't gotten to do together.

The airport staff seem bored and vaguely hostile, but he manages to make it through security and boarding without too much trauma. He's a little nervous about taking off, but when it comes, the acceleration is nothing compared to what he's felt on a horse. Karl has lent him a couple books on horse farm management, and he's taken the smallest one with him. He doesn't want the California people to see it and realize how little he knows, but he also doesn't want to sit around wasting time when he could be learning something. This one is small enough that he can stuff it in his bag before he meets anyone.

Landing is a little scarier than taking off—again, the bumps and deceleration are nothing compared to what he's felt on a horse, but he's used to being more actively involved in the situation. It's against his nature to just sit there and trust that someone else will take care of things. They do, though, and he follows the instructions to get him off the plane and out to the arrivals area.

He had been told that someone would pick him up and to call Linda if there were any problems. He realizes when he gets outside the security gate that he has no idea how the person picking him up is supposed to recognize him. He's seen movies where drivers hold signs with their passengers' names on them, but he doesn't see any signs, or anyone else who's looking as lost as he is.

He really doesn't want to call Linda and bother her with this sort of detail, but he also doesn't want to be the idiot who stood around the airport for hours when a simple phone call could have straightened things out much earlier. He's playing with his phone, trying to decide, when he hears a voice boom out from behind him.

"Dan! Hey, sorry I'm late! Have you been waiting long?" Dan turns to see Evan, but not the Evan he's used to. In Kentucky, Evan had dressed to blend in, wearing jeans and button downs at his dressiest. Here, Evan is wearing a medium gray suit with a crisp white shirt and a purple tie. His hair is still a little long, but it looks carefully styled. For the first time, Dan finds the other man a little intimidating.

Then Evan grins and the effect is lost. "I told Linda I could drive you out, because I'd be at the airport anyway… but then my flight got delayed, of course!" Dan notices that Evan has a carry-on of his own slung over his shoulder, although Evan's is the folding suit kind and Dan's is a knapsack.

"No, it's fine, I wasn't waiting long," he finally manages.

"Oh, good. Hey, it's good to see you, man!" Evan looks like he might be working up to a hug, but Dan shoves his hand out for a shake and shoulder-slap instead. Evan doesn't seem to notice the shift. "So, did you check a bag or anything? No, me neither—I hate standing around waiting." Evan charges off through the crowd, and Dan just tries to keep up. Once they're out of the main building, Evan slows a little, and Dan moves up beside him, watching as Evan loosens his tie and unbuttons his collar. He sees Dan looking, and grins. "I really don't like the suits. But they do help people to take me a bit more seriously."

Dan nods, and then Evan's burrowing through his suit jacket to find his wallet, then the claim ticket for his car. "They have this valet service for parking here... I swear, I don't normally use it, I'm not a fat sixty-year-old, but I was totally running late for my departure flight, so I just wanted to dump the car and go...." Evan keeps up a running monologue as they head for the parking garage. He gives the claim ticket to the valet staff, and moments later they're climbing into a Jeep Cherokee that's not much newer than Dan's own truck.

Evan drives them out of the parking structure and into traffic. At the first stoplight he takes his tie all the way off and tosses it into the back seat. Then he rolls his shoulders a little, and Dan can see the way his muscles move even through the suit jacket. Evan is slowly nodding. "Damn, it's good to be home." Dan realizes that those are the first words Evan has spoken since they got into the car. He wonders if this is what Jeff was talking about, the transition between go-go-go business Evan and the more laidback home version.

They drive in silence for another few blocks, and then Evan asks, "Are you hungry, at all? I usually get a burger for the drive home."

"Sure, yeah, that's fine."

They go through the In-and-Out drive through. The chain hasn't reached Kentucky yet, so Dan actually has to pay attention to the menu. He finally just tells Evan to order two of whatever he's getting. Evan seems strangely pleased, as though he has finally earned Dan's trust in at least one tiny area.

After they get their food, Evan pulls into a parking spot. "I always drop food all over myself if I try to eat while I drive," he explains. "I'll eat the burger first, then I can drive with the fries."

Dan shakes his head. "No rush, man. I mean, as far as I know... are we supposed to be somewhere?"

Evan laughs, and then looks a little worried. "Probably. Linda schedules things pretty tight." He crouches down in his seat as if he thinks she might be watching.

Dan fights the urge to giggle. The mighty Evan Kaminski is afraid of his assistant. "Don't worry, man, I'll cover for you. Traffic?"

Evan grins ruefully. "I dunno... I use that one a lot."

"Uh... late flights?"

Evan almost whispers. "She checks the arrival times—they're on the internet."

Dan looks at Evan, and then slides down a little lower in his own seat.

They sit there, silently eating their burgers, Dan swallowing a giggle with every bite.

When Evan is done with the burger, he tidies up the wrapper and pulls the car out into traffic. Dan watches him drive. Evan is confident, but he's also polite, yielding to other cars and not getting frustrated by traffic. When a minivan cuts in front of him and then slams on its brakes, Evan's right arm shoots out to catch Dan as they brake hard to avoid a collision. Evan steers around the minivan and glances inside as he passes. He looks over at Dan and shrugs. "Damn, he's got a pack of kids in there—I bet they're driving him crazy!"

They head out of town. Evan shares occasional tidbits of information about the places they pass, but mostly they're quiet. Dan is surprised by how fast San Francisco's green lushness fades to dry scrub land, and he mentions it to Evan.

"Yeah, with the mountains and the ocean out here, we've got about seven different vegetation zones in a hundred mile radius." Dan looks at him oddly, and Evan laughs. "I used to want to be a climatologist."

"Gave it up for the life of a billionaire businessman?"

Evan looks a little rueful, maybe even a little sad. "Didn't have a whole lot of choice, you know?"

Dan is reminded of what Jeff had said: that Evan had taken over the family business after his parents had died. He wishes he'd looked into that more. The information must be public record, wouldn't have been hard to find. But he'd been too wrapped up in his own pain to worry about anyone else's. Or would it have been intrusive to read about something that Evan might prefer he didn't know?

"Sorry." Dan knows the word is inadequate.

Evan seems almost startled. "Oh, no, don't worry about it! I mean, I was going to end up doing the business stuff anyway, eventually. I just got into it a bit faster than I thought I would."

That isn't what Dan is sorry about, but he lets it go.

Evan finishes the last of his fries and looks for somewhere to throw out the container. Dan wordlessly takes it from him and puts in the bag with the other garbage. They drive for another few minutes, and then Evan starts pointing out landmarks with more regularity. They leave the highway and drive through a little town. Evan shows Dan a restaurant he and Tatiana love, and the hardware store that has everything he's ever thought to ask for, even though it's a quarter the size of a Home Depot, and the bar he and Jeff go to most Saturdays to hear live music.

Dan knows Evan is trying to sell him on the town, but it doesn't feel pushy like it did in Kentucky; it just feels sincere, like Evan loves it here and wants Dan to love it too.

As they pull out on the far side of town, Evan slaps Dan's shoulder and points to the bleachers at the high school. "First kiss—right there." He nods sagely.

"You went to a public high school?"

"Uh, no." Evan grins. "But she did."

Dan digests that little bit of information, adds it to his growing collection.

They leave town and turn onto an even smaller road, winding its way through foothills covered in rough scrub and pine trees. They reach a sort of plateau and Dan notices the fence stretching along the land on one side. It's vinyl, the kind that looks like wood but is stronger and wears longer, and Dan notices that the post holes are all freshly dug. He doesn't even want to think about how much it cost to install a fence like that this far away from any barn or buildings. Dan wonders if this is Evan's property or if the Kaminskis have neighbors just as rich as they are.

"Yeah, that's the start of our property," Evan says, as if he'd heard Dan's thoughts. "We've got about two hundred acres in this part, but then we bought another hundred just attached at the corners. We're building the cross-country course over there, but we figured we'd fence the whole place—if a horse gets loose, we'll have to catch it, but at least we won't have to worry about it getting on the road." Evan seems to be looking for Dan's approval.

"That's great, man." It's a fairly standard system for large horse farms, although Dan knows most of them don't use the most expensive type of fencing for their entire perimeters. "I'm looking forward to seeing the rest of the place."

"The guys have been working really hard. It won't be completely done by the end of the month, but it'll just be finishing touches left."

Dan nods as Evan pulls off the road and starts down a long driveway. There's horse fencing on both sides now, and a large barn comes into view on the left. There's a gate leading to it, and Evan stops the car in front of the drive. "We're putting you up in the guest house, if you don't mind. We can get you a hotel room if you prefer, but it'd be a lot easier if you were on site."

"Sure, that's fine."

"Linda's waiting for us at the house, but we can have quick look at the barn first, if you want...."

"Well, if Linda's waiting, shouldn't we go see her? The barn's not going to go away if we make it wait a couple hours."

Evan barks out a laugh. "Yeah, trust me... neither will Linda."

Dan really wants to meet this woman.

Evan reluctantly puts the car back into gear and steers it up the driveway. There's a branch off to the right, and Evan gestures to it. "Guest house is up there. We've got a couple extra cars around if you want to borrow one, but if you stay on the property everything is pretty much walking distance." Evan suddenly gets animated. "Or we have golf carts! I forgot about those, but they might be good—I think they're in the garage, maybe. Or there's ATVs, if we want to go out to the cross-country course. I don't... I don't actually know where those are, either, but I'm sure somebody can find them." Evan looks a little bashful. "That's not what's going to happen with the horses, though. It's like I said, the horses are a business as well as a hobby, and I'm much better at keeping track of business."

Dan nods. "That's good... horses don't do well if they get lost in the garage."

Evan just grins. "See, that's the kind of expert information we flew you out here for!"

There's a bend in the road, and then Evan is pulling up in front of the main house. The house isn't actually as imposing as Dan was prepared for. It looks big, but not huge.

Evan turns the car off and climbs out, snagging his bag from the back seat. Dan does the same and then looks up to see the front door of the house opened by a striking brunette. She's dressed for business, but looks so comfortable in her suit that she could just as well have dropped over for brunch. She comes down the steps toward them carrying a leather portfolio.

Evan grins at her. "Can't even wait for me to get inside, Linda?"

"Seems like I spend half my life waiting for you, Evan." She hands him a sheaf of papers from the portfolio. "You probably want to look at these as soon as possible." She turns to Dan and holds out her hand.

Evan remembers his manners. "Uh, Dan, this is Linda. Linda, Dan."

Dan shakes her hand. "It's really nice to meet you."

"And you. Welcome to California!" She smiles warmly. "Have you been out here before?"

"Uh, California, yes, but not this part. LA, mostly."

Linda wrinkles her nose delicately. "Well, this is like a whole different state, if not a different country." She smiles to take any sting out of her words, and then pulls another collection of papers out of her dossier. "Don't think I left you out... here's what we've got scheduled for you while you're here. And there are also copies of the resumes of the people we've arranged to have interviewed."

"Linda, seriously, can't you let us go inside first?"

She just shakes her head at Evan. "If I'd let you go inside, you would have offered him a drink, and then you'd have wanted to show him around, and you would have finished the tour by the pool and asked if he wanted a swim, and by the time that was over it would have been dinner time and you'd say it gives you indigestion to look at paperwork while you eat." She smiles again. "If I don't catch you now, the day is wasted."

Evan just shakes his head. Linda loops her arm through Dan's and leads him into the house. "Now, before Evan steals you away, I just need you to enter any four-digit PIN you want in this computer. It's our security system, you can enter the code on any keypad on the property and it'll open the door for you."

Evan grimaces. "And it tracks you, man! If she wants to know where you are, she can find out the last door you opened. It's Orwellian, and I paid for it!"

"It's an excellent security system, and if you would answer your phone I wouldn't have to track you down."

Evan leafs through his papers while Dan enters his code, and then makes an apologetic face. "I actually do have to deal with these… Linda, do you think you could show Dan around, get him settled in?"

She smiles. "I'd be happy to. And I can offer you a drink as well." She guides Dan down the hallway as Evan disappears through a door to the left.

It turns out the house is a lot bigger than it looks. Dan thinks there must have been a deliberate attempt to minimize its appearance from the outside, with parts set back from each other, hidden by shrubs, and built on different levels. There's an indoor pool *and* an indoor lap pool in the gym, and when they go outside there's a huge terrace with another pool, and Dan can see tennis courts around the corner. Linda sees him looking. "Tatiana used to play every day, but for the past year or two it's been all about horses."

"So you've worked with Evan for a while, then?"

"Oh, I've known him since he was a little boy. I used to be his father's assistant, got the job right out of university. It's why I can boss him around like I do. But don't be taken in—I know that he's in charge, and on anything serious I listen to him. He just needs a firm hand to help keep him organized."

Dan doesn't let his mind dwell on the "firm hand" comment.

Linda walks Dan up to the guest house and lets him try out the door code, and then shows him in. He'd been expecting some sort of tiny cabin, but it's a full-size house, with an open plan living and dining room, a full kitchen and three bedrooms. "It hardly gets any use, really. Evan's parents used to loan it out as a sort of artist's retreat, but Evan really isn't too interested in the arts, and I think he prefers to have a bit more privacy when he's at home."

They return to the main house and Dan is introduced to the housekeeper, Tia, who has also been with the family forever. She gets drinks for them and they go out and sit by the pool, waiting for Evan. Dan takes a quick glance at his schedule.

"So, this is it for today? Just getting settled in?"

"That's all I have scheduled for you. Evan really does need to get caught up on some of those issues, and I know he wanted to show you around the farm himself, with Tatiana and I think Jeff… so unless you're really restless, you can just relax and enjoy the view."

"Am I keeping you from anything? I mean, the company's great, but if you have somewhere you need to be, I'm fine by myself."

She checks her watch. "Well, if you don't mind, I should run in and see if Evan needs me to follow up on anything... can I get you something, though? A book, or...."

A deep voice comes from behind them. "It's okay, Linda. I can keep him company."

Dan turns and sees Jeff, and his stomach does a little flip. He'd thought he'd gotten over whatever he'd been feeling in Kentucky, but seeing Jeff again makes it clear that he was wrong. Jeff's beautiful in the late afternoon sun, and Dan can almost feel the warmth in the man's smile.

Jeff walks across the terrace and sits in a deck chair opposite Dan and Linda, who stands gracefully and heads into the house.

Jeff just looks at him for a moment and then smiles again. "Welcome to California, Dan."

chapter 11

DAN leans back in his chair and lets the sun hit his closed eyelids. He feels peaceful here, like he's wrapped in a safe cocoon, just the sun's warmth, the chill of the drink in his hand, the sound of the water hitting the edge of the pool… and Jeff. He opens his eyes again, because if Jeff's around, Dan wants to be able to see him.

Dan squints into the sun, and Jeff pulls his own sunglasses off and leans over to hand them to Dan. Jeff's back is to the sun, it only makes sense for Dan to have the glasses, but it still seems intimate somehow. He takes the sunglasses and puts them on.

Jeff smiles at him. "You just get in?"

"A little while ago. Evan picked me up at the airport, and then he had to do some work, so Linda showed me around."

Jeff nods. "He's in there now, working the phone. It's always a bit hectic when he gets back from being away."

"He seems to have a lot of responsibility. But, you were right, what you said in Kentucky… he does seem different out here. More relaxed."

"Yeah, he's a big homebody." Jeff's tone is affectionate, and again Dan is jealous. He decides to try to get the topic of conversation away from Evan.

"So, what about you? You have your own business, right?"

"Well, nothing on the scale of Evan's, that's for sure. I just try to teach rich people to ride, and then train their horses well enough that the riders think they've achieved something."

Dan raises an eyebrow. "Wow, cynical! Don't you have any good students?"

Jeff rubs the back of his neck and smiles apologetically at Dan. "Yeah, sorry, of course I do. It's just been a long day. A long few days."

A long few days because Evan had been out of town, Dan realizes. Their relationship still feels a little strange to him. They seem so casual about sex, but are clearly very attached emotionally. He tries to be mature about it. "I really am fine out here on my own… if you wanted to go in and check…."

Jeff shakes his head. "Nah, I poked my head in when I arrived. He knows I'm here. He'll come out when he can." He kicks his shoes off and rolls up the cuffs of his pants, then walks over and sits on the edge of the pool, dangling his feet in the water. He lies back, resting his head on the pool deck and looking backward at Dan. "Everything okay in Kentucky?"

Jeff's tone is gentle, and Dan appreciates the vagueness of the question. Dan can answer with any level of detail he wants. "The barn's good. I've got to tell Evan that one of his horses is lame, but we think he just pulled a muscle. And everybody's working well together." Dan pauses, and then pulls his own shoes and socks off, rolls up his cuffs and walks over to sit beside Jeff with his feet in the pool. He doesn't lie back, although he sort of wants to.

"Justin's the same." Dan keeps his tone neutral, is proud that he can say Justin's name without losing control.

"And you? You're okay?" This time the question isn't so vague, but the tone is still gentle.

"Me? I dunno… I'm fine, I guess." Dan doesn't really know how to answer. "I mean… I'm the same too."

Jeff nods as if that were a real answer. They both rest as they are for a few minutes, and then Jeff grips the side of the pool with both hands and pulls himself back up to a sitting position. One of his hands rests right next to Dan's on the pool edge, and Dan won't let himself look down, but he can feel the contact. His whole body knows that his little finger is stretched out alongside Jeff's. He feels like a school girl, but he won't move his finger, won't take it away or move it in closer. He stares out across the rolling foothills toward the ocean, thinks maybe he can see the water, and then realizes that he still has Jeff's sunglasses, even though they're both now looking into the sun.

He turns his head a little, enough to see the Jeff is looking at him. He raises his other hand to his face, starts to take the shades off. "Here, you should have these back."

Jeff shakes his head, and uses his other hand to guide them back to Dan. "Nah, you hang on to them." He smiles. "They look better on you anyway."

Dan knows that if Jeff made a move right now, Dan would be right with him. He'd feel terrible about it later, he's sure, for so many reasons. But his brain is not in control anymore, and his body knows what it wants, what it hasn't had for far too long. And there's something about Jeff, with his gentle awareness, his….

"Hey, Jeff!" It's a female voice, and as Dan and Jeff turn toward it they see two dogs barreling toward them, and Tatiana standing in the doorway to the house. The dogs head straight for Jeff, and he raises both of his hands, releasing Dan from the spell and letting him shift away from the furred onslaught.

"Hey, guys, settle down, settle down," Jeff chides the dogs and then looks over their heads to Dan. "They're totally friendly but not too well trained… sort of like their master." The dogs are done with Jeff and move on to Dan, a little more cautious but still very enthusiastic. Jeff points. "This one's Copa, this one's Trapper." He looks over at Tatiana. "You take them somewhere with you?"

"Callie got a new puppy, and they're trying to socialize her, so I took the big dogs for an introduction." She walks over a bit shyly, and Dan knows it must be because of him.

"Tatiana, you remember Dan?" Jeff prompts.

"Yeah, hi, Dan," she manages.

"Hey, Tatiana, it's nice to see you again." Dan knows that he's a better actor, but he's not sure that he's any more comfortable than the girl is. What if she had come out a few minutes later? But then Dan catches himself. Just because he had been overcome with temporary insanity doesn't mean that Jeff would have been or that Jeff is interested at all. Lined up pinky fingers are hardly a universal invitation to passion.

"Where's Lou?" Tat asks Jeff.

"Her stitches are still healing up. I didn't want to bring her over here to play and have her tear them out again."

Tatiana nods understandingly. Then she looks shyly at Dan. "How's Monty?"

Dan can't believe the girl still has that crush on the horse. He's not sure she'll *ever* be strong enough to ride him really effectively. "He's good. Still a bit headstrong, but… good." He decides to try a slightly different approach. "The one I'm really impressed with lately is Sunshine. Horses sometimes, it's like they hit plateaus in their training, you know?

They'll learn a bunch of stuff, and it'll be like they're improving every day, and then they'll just sort of go into a holding pattern and don't learn anything at all for a while. And then when they're ready, bam! They start learning again. And she's been learning like crazy the last week or so. Seems like every day I ride her she's gotten noticeably better." This much is true, and he doesn't bother to mention that some horses don't plateau. They backslide, seeming to forget everything they ever knew. That's one of the most frustrating parts of training, and he doesn't want to discourage Tatiana right now.

The girl smiles enthusiastically. "That must be so much fun!"

Dan nods. "It really is. She's the one I'm most excited about right now." He leans in a little, as though he's about to tell Tat a secret. They're still at least five feet from each other, but he thinks she gets the idea. "And she's a mare, which is great, because with the geldings... well, it can be hard to see them get old and lose their fitness and know that they're not good for anything but pasture ornaments anymore. 'Cause you still love them, but you can't really *do* anything with them anymore. You know?" Tat nods, and Dan goes in for the kill. "But with a mare, even if she's too old to compete she's still usually healthy enough to have at least a couple beautiful foals. And then you get the fun of loving them, and raising them up and training them, and it's like the horse you love continues, you know? Because you've still got her foals to remind you of her."

Tatiana is practically clapping her hands. "I wanted us to have foals, but Evan said he'd looked into it, and it didn't make sense to have a breeding operation, that it was more efficient to let someone else take all the risks of breeding the horses and then just go in and pick out the horses that are worth training."

Dan nods, and hopes he isn't making a mistake, setting up Tatiana for more disappointment. He glances over at Jeff who is standing behind Tat and watching the whole exchange. He grins, and makes a sort of 'go on' motion with his chin. Dan decides that he's so far in, he might as well keep going.

"Well, a large scale operation probably doesn't make sense. Or at least you'd need someone else to look after it for you, because I only know the basics about breeding. But I think if you're going to have a business that you care about, especially a business with animals... I think sometimes you have to just go with your heart." He shrugs. "Besides, Sunshine's got great bloodlines—I can show you her pedigree sometime, you should see all the famous horses that show up in it. She'd be a good bet for breeding."

Tatiana is enthralled and peppers Dan with questions about Sunshine and foals and training and how a friend of hers said that Thoroughbreds are better than Hanoverians, and how many Thoroughbreds are coming with the Kentucky horses, and are they really better, and….

After the first couple questions Jeff sketches a half-wave to Dan and heads into the house. Dan is temporarily distracted. Did he really just let himself be dragged into a conversation with a teenage girl so that Jeff could make an undisturbed booty call? But he reminds himself that Jeff and Evan are none of his business, and tries to get back on track with Tat.

He's distracted again when Linda comes out to say goodbye for the day. She reminds Dan of his schedule, and makes sure that he's got everything he needs in the guest house, and then chats a little with Tat about her day. The whole time Dan is thinking that now Jeff and Evan are alone, and they've been away from each other for a while, and does Jeff live here? Do they share a bedroom? Or are they in Evan's bedroom? Or Evan's office, afternoon light coming in through the venetian blinds, Evan sitting on the big wooden desk with Jeff standing between his legs, pressing in tight, Jeff leaning Evan back over the paperwork, working the buttons on Evan's shirt open while he sucks and bites at his neck….

Dan feels pressure against his fly and rips himself back to reality. What is he doing, about to let himself get hard ten feet away from a teenage girl? Is he really that desperate? That out of control? He swirls his feet in the pool a little more vigorously, hoping the cool water will help calm him down. Linda calls out her goodbye to him, and he waves in response, and then the door to the house opens and Evan and Jeff come out together, not looking at all as Dan had just been picturing them.

Evan grins at Dan's position by the pool. "Damn, did Jeff teach you that?" Evan looks over at Jeff's bare feet and damp lower pant legs. "The guy can't sit out here for two minutes without having his feet in the water."

Dan swirls his feet a little more. "I guess he knows how to live. You need to cut the legs off some of those chairs so you could sit like this and still have a backrest."

Jeff nods. "Now you're thinking."

The housekeeper comes out with a tray loaded with a variety of appetizers, and Jeff helps her set it up on the table. She comes back with a bottle of wine and four glasses, as well as a can of Diet Coke. Dan watches in amusement as Evan opens the bottle of wine while Jeff pours the Coke into a wine glass he hands to Tatiana. Then Tat drags him along to the far end of the terrace, wanting to show him where she thinks a squirrel has its nest. With one wine glass still empty, Evan looks at Dan. "We've got beer, if you'd prefer?"

Dan shakes his head. "No, wine's fine, thanks." Then he starts feeling a little intrusive. "But, maybe not a whole glass. I mean, you guys probably have some sort of family stuff to catch up on or something… and I've got things to do to get ready for tomorrow."

"What, read the resumes again? Come on, it's California… relax!" Evan fills the glass to the same level as the others and walks over to hand it to Dan. "Besides, you're here for dinner, right? There's no point in going away and then coming back again."

"Uh, I don't know. Am I here for dinner? I mean, I sort of expected a hotel, thought I'd be eating there." Evan looks a little startled by Dan's words. "I don't mean I *wanted* a hotel, I just… I mean, I'm your employee, right? Do you really want me eating all my meals with you?"

Evan is standing right next to Dan and looks at him for a little longer than is comfortable before softly saying, "Yeah, Dan, I do." He moves away a little and takes a sip of his wine. "Nice sunglasses, by the way."

Dan had forgotten he was wearing them. "Oh, yeah. Jeff loaned them to me. It was rainy at home, so I wasn't wearing any, and I don't think I remembered to pack any."

Evan nods. "They're from a trip we took to Costa Rica. Going down to the tropics, and we both forgot to bring sunglasses. And the shop only had one style that wasn't totally ugly, so we each bought the same pair, felt like one of those 'dress alike' couples for the whole rest of the trip." Evan takes another sip of wine. "I sat on mine on the plane ride back, totally crushed them."

Dan wonders if there's supposed to be some deeper meaning to the saga of the sunglasses, but can't really see it. Other than reminding Dan that this is an established relationship, that Evan and Jeff have history. Maybe that's all Evan is trying to say. "Well, I'll try not to sit on them."

Evan grins sunnily. "Whatever, they're just cheap plastic. It'd be good if his got broken, actually—then he could stop using them as evidence of his responsibility compared to my scatterbrainedness."

Dan is starting to be a little confused by this conversation in general, and is relieved when Jeff and Tatiana return from their nature excursion.

They sit by the pool and drink and eat snacks and chat, and any discomfort that Dan felt during his conversation with Evan is long gone. The housekeeper supplies a platter of steaks, and Evan mans the barbecue. Tat helps bring out table linens and place settings and then several side dishes.

The meal is delicious, the scenery is incredible, and everyone is pleasant and charming. Dan feels like he's stumbled into someone else's life. The world of eventing certainly has its share of wealthy participants, but there's usually a fairly clear divide between the patrons and the patronized, the owners and the workers. Dan really doesn't feel that here, and isn't sure what to make of it. He isn't sure he likes it, even... it's harder to keep things clear in his head this way, and he really thinks he needs to keep a clear head. He looks at Jeff, who's lazily smiling as Evan teases Tatiana, and wonders if he's a bit too late.

chapter 12

DAN wakes up the next morning and doesn't know where he is. California is three hours behind Louisville, so part of the problem is jet lag. When his body tells him it's time to get up, it's still pitch black outside his window. He dozes for a while, but each time he wakes it's with the same unpleasant sense of disorientation and displacement, and finally he gives up and gets out of bed. He finds his book and reads a chapter and then showers and gets dressed.

There's a coffeemaker in the kitchen, and he finds a bag of ground coffee in the freezer. He makes the coffee and finds a mug, then takes his book out onto the porch. It's still a bit chilly out, but the sun is coming up, and the porch faces east, toward the mountains. He doesn't really read, just sits there and enjoys his coffee, and wonders if this could be his life. If he actually lived here, of course, he'd be over at the barn by now, helping to feed the horses and turn them out, figuring out the training for the day. If this was his life, maybe he'd have someone in his bed upstairs, someone who would have dragged at him when he got up, tried to coax him back to bed.

He has to shut the fantasy down when his imagination puts Justin in the bed, when he starts remembering Justin hiding his eyes from the daylight and trying to wrap Dan up under their quilt. He has a brief flash of Jeff in the role, his gentle eyes watching Dan come out of the shower, his big hands resting on Dan's hips and pulling him back toward the bed, but then Dan shuts down that thought too. Nothing can happen with Jeff. It would be unfaithful to Justin and unfair to Evan, and if nothing's going to happen, then Dan should just stop torturing himself with thoughts of it. He thinks of Justin as he is now, lifeless and wasting in a sterile hospital bed, and that's as effective as a cold shower. No more fantasies for Dan this morning.

Evan had said that he'd be up by six and ready to get started by seven. It's not quite seven yet, but Dan figures that he can walk slowly, so he puts his book and mug inside the door and starts toward the house. He hasn't gone far when he sees the two dogs racing toward him. Evan's tall shape appears from a path in the trees and follows after the dogs, albeit more slowly.

Dan crouches to greet the animals, and is rewarded with kisses and cold noses against his neck. He straightens with a laugh and walks to join their master.

Evan turns to go toward the house with Dan, neither of them saying much. The dogs take off into the woods, and Evan grins. "We saw a deer this morning, and they had no idea what to do. But now every time a leaf moves, they're chasing after it like they've got something to prove."

"Not great hunters, then?"

"Well, they're… enthusiastic."

"Just as well. We had a dog when I was a kid, he'd bring back a dead something at least once a day. And if we buried it shallow, he'd dig it up and bring it home again, like he'd killed it twice, no matter how rotten and stinky it was. So we had to bury 'em deep."

Evan grins. "Sounds like a good job for a young whippersnapper like you."

Dan flexes his shoulders. "These are grave-digging muscles, boy."

They walk for a bit, and then Evan says, "Where was that? Kentucky?"

Dan shakes his head. "No, Texas."

"Oh yeah? Is that where you grew up?"

"Yeah, mostly." Dan doesn't think this needs to go any further. "So, Tatiana said she wanted to be there when I saw the stuff you've done at the barn. Did she mean it, or can we go by now?"

Evan makes a face. "Oh, no, she meant it. She talked me into letting her take today off school so she can 'be part of the new business'. She wants in on the interviews, the site inspections, everything."

"Linda said you *wanted* Tat to get interested in the business side of things."

"Yeah, if she's actually interested, that's great. I just wonder if she's pretending to be interested as a way to get out of school. And maybe…" Evan's lips twitch a little. "Maybe so she can spend a little more time with the dreamy new trainer."

Dan sputters a little. "Really? Does she not know that I'm gay?"

Evan laughs. "Well, she knows about Justin, she saw the video from when he won Rolex." Evan pauses to see if the mention has upset Dan and then continues. "It's kinda my fault—I'm pretty equal opportunity about things. I mean, I don't bring anyone home if we're not reasonably serious, but she's seen me with guys and girls. I don't know, I think she thinks everyone's the same way." Evan pauses.

"Oh. God." Dan isn't up to this.

"No, it's cool, she's really innocent. She might moon around after you for a while, but it's not like she's gonna make a move or something." Evan seems amused by Dan's alarm. "Jeff said you were really good with her yesterday. Said I might have to look at turning the place into a breeding operation, but otherwise… said you were good."

"Yeah." Dan doesn't want to get too far into this, but…. "I have a younger sister. I remember the age."

"Really? She's Tat's age?"

"No. She's only two years younger than me. But she was about Tat's age the last time I saw her."

Evan looks like he wants to ask a *lot* more questions, but he satisfies himself with one. "This was back in Texas?"

Dan nods, and they walk in silence until they reach the house.

They go in through a side door, and Evan grabs a towel to wipe the dogs' feet before they go into the main house. They follow the smells of food to the kitchen, where the housekeeper is laying the table.

Evan greets her with a kiss on the cheek. "Tia, something smells incredible." Evan reaches out to open the oven door and look inside, and Tia slaps his hand away.

"When Tatiana is ready, you can sit at the table and eat like a civilized person." Tia stirs something in a pot on the stove, and then turns to Dan. "Can I get you some coffee or juice, Mr. Wheeler?"

Dan grins at Evan's eyeroll. "Uh, coffee would be great, but I can get it myself if you're busy." He reluctantly adds, "And Dan is fine."

"No, you sit down. I'll get you some coffee."

Tia bustles off to take care of that, and Evan shakes his head ruefully. "The disadvantage of having longstanding employees. When a woman's changed your diaper, it's hard to get her to treat you with a whole lot of respect." Evan crosses to a box on the wall, and punches in a few numbers. There's a crackle, and then Evan speaks into the box. "Tat, let's go! Breakfast is served!"

The box speaks back in strident tones. "Leave me alone! I'll be down when I'm ready."

Evan winks at Dan and then says, "Okay, Tat, but Dan's here, and he's hungry, so let's not keep him waiting too long."

There's a pause, and then the box sounds almost meek. "I'm hurrying."

Evan walks behind Dan to get to his place at the table, and he affectionately ruffles Dan's hair as he passes. "This could be really useful. If having you around makes my little sister behave like a human instead of a troll... I'm sorry to say it, but you may have to give up on all this 'gay' nonsense."

Dan ducks away from Evan's hand, but he grins. "And marry into this? I dunno, man, it might be worth it."

"Well, better you than some of the guys she goes to school with, that's for sure."

Tia brings the coffee over and sends a dark look at Evan. "You be careful with that talk, Evan. If she thinks you're judging her friends, she'll stop bringing them home, and then what?"

Dan nods in smug support, and Tia rewards him with a pat to his cheek.

Dan helps himself to sugar from the bowl in the middle of the table, and then passes it over to Evan. He's curious about why there was only one call on the intercom. "Is Jeff not eating?"

Evan grimaces. "Maybe. He went home last night. His dog just had surgery, and she's all stitched up, so she can't really come over and deal with the beasts. But he wants to be here for the grand tour, and for sure for the interviews, so we'll see if he makes it for breakfast."

Tatiana arrives then, looking freshly scrubbed and sunny, and gracefully slides into a seat at the table. She's right across from Dan, and he thinks of Evan's earlier remarks and feels the heat rising up on his neck. Evan notices and grins.

"Morning, Tat. Is that a new hairband? It's really pretty." Evan smiles ingratiatingly at his sister, who looks back at him in bewilderment. Evan continues. "Isn't it a nice hairband, Dan?"

Dan smiles awkwardly, but decides to give it his best shot. "I don't really know about the hairband, but I like your hair pulled back like that. It brings out your eyes."

Tatiana blushes happily, and Dan smirks at Evan.

Tia is just serving up breakfast, some sort of waffle-esque pastry with homemade blueberry sauce, when the door opens and Jeff comes in. "Hey, I thought I smelled something good!" He kisses Tia's cheek and then goes around the table, bending to catch Tatiana's cheek and pulling Evan's head back a little to kiss his forehead. He grins at Dan, but doesn't approach.

Dan's eyebrows go up. "You're in a good mood. Or are you just this much of a morning person?"

"No, I'm in a *great* mood." Jeff turns to Evan, who looks confused and then excited.

"You got the show? Seriously?"

Jeff nods. "Two weeks in the Nachfelt Gallery, my paintings on the walls." He grins. "The message was on my machine when I got home last night."

Everyone's very excited, but Dan is reminded again that he's an outsider here. He hadn't even known that Jeff was an artist. And he doesn't know enough about the art world to understand the significance of getting a show, although he can tell that it's a big deal. When the commotion dies down, Jeff's eyes turn to Dan, who offers up a simple, "Congratulations."

"Thanks, man. Sorry for the fuss, it's just… I've been working for this for a while." Jeff smiles happily.

The meal resumes, with Tia bringing a plate for Jeff.

There's some talk about the show, about which of Jeff's paintings should be included, but eventually they get back to the day's business. Evan checks his watch before he mops up the last of the blueberry sauce with a piece of waffle. "So, the first interview is scheduled for an hour from now. If we go down to the barn and have a quick tour, we can interview until lunch, then interview some more, and then go up and check out the cross-country course before dinner?"

This is almost exactly the schedule that Linda had laid out on Dan's papers. He wonders if she'd passed the information along to Evan, or if she's just good enough to have read his mind in advance. He nods his acquiescence, and gulps the last of his coffee as he sees the others standing to go. Everyone leaves their dishes on the table, and Dan remembers that the same thing had been done last night. He wonders if the dinner remains are still out by the pool or if Tia started work early enough to tidy that up as well as prepare breakfast.

They walk down to the barn, and Evan and Tatiana show off all the features to Dan, while Jeff stands back and watches with amusement. There is potential mayhem when the siblings want to show off the shower stall, each trying to spray the other with one of the long hoses, but cooler minds prevail and no one gets worse than a soaked shoe. Most of the improvements have gone into the outdoor riding rings. Dan looks at the surface of the dressage ring and the round pen, and then they head over to the grass jumping ring. There's no sod laid yet, but the ground has been prepared with lots of sand and light loam, and there's good drainage in all the rings. It all looks great to Dan, and he tells the Kaminskis so.

The interviews are scheduled to take place at the barn, so once they're done with the tour they just poke around the tack room and the loft, while Jeff is a little more responsible and makes sure that there are some chairs and a table set up in the empty feed room. Evan lays out the game plan. He will start by asking the candidates basic background information. Dan will ask about their experience and try to get an idea of their general knowledge. Jeff will determine their familiarity with the local equestrian community. And Tatiana will ask if the candidates have any questions or would like to add anything. Dan mentions that Robyn is interested in moving out.

Evan beams. "Yeah, Linda told us about that! That'd be great. It'd be good to have someone you already know you can work with."

Dan doesn't really want to say it, but he wants to be sure he's being fair to these people. "It'll be good even if I don't come out. She's been working with the horses for years, so she'd be a really valuable resource for whoever your trainer might be."

Evan looks like he might want to argue a little, but Jeff quiets him with a nod, and then the first interviewee is there. Dan and Tatiana are both a little nervous, but they make it through the first one, and everything after that is easy. There's one great candidate, three that would probably be fine, and two that are disastrous. Dan feels a little bad for recommending them, but Evan points out that it's easy to look good on paper, and weeding people out is the whole point of interviews.

They troop back up to the house for a lunch of homemade soup and sandwiches, and then it's back to the barn for more interviews. The afternoon candidates are worse than the morning ones, with no one that's really great, two that might be okay, and three that are out of the question. One doesn't even show up.

At the end, Evan sums it all up. "Okay, so we've got the head trainer position hopefully filled, then there's two assistant trainers, we were thinking? So if one's Robyn, and one's Michelle from this morning? Then we want two barn staff... I say Devin and Sara from this morning."

"I'd like to see Michelle on a horse, if we're hiring her to ride, but otherwise that sounds good." Evan nods at Dan's comment.

Once they've decided on who they want to hire, Evan calls Linda and asks her to take care of contacting them, and then the four head up the hill to the cross-country course. Dan likes what he sees but wants to come back when he gets the opportunity, to double check some of the spacing and the landing surfaces. He has to admit, though, that everything looks really good. Evan has obviously spared no expense, but he's also hired someone who knows the demands of horses.

They're walking down from the cross-country course when Dan's cell rings. He's a little surprised they get service out so far, but then thinks the Kaminskis could probably have bought their own tower if they had to. He checks the caller display and his mouth goes dry. He reminds himself that there are lots of reasons for a call from the Archer house. There could be a problem with one of the horses, or a question about ordering supplies. But his mind goes immediately to the call he's been dreading for over a year.

He's stopped walking and the others have moved a little away to wait for him, but when he doesn't answer the phone, they look back curiously. Jeff starts back toward him, concern on his face, and Dan kicks into gear and flips the phone open.

"Hello."

"Dan? It's Chris." Chris sounds shaky, and there's no other reason for him to be calling Dan, especially not from the Archer house. Dan turns his face away from the others. He sees a boulder a few steps away, and moves over to lean against it.

"Yeah, Chris, I'm here." Dan is almost whispering.

"Danny…." Chris's voice breaks on the second syllable, and Dan can hear him taking a deep breath over the phone. When he starts again, his voice is stronger. "Justin had a heart attack this afternoon. They say he had an infection, it came on really fast, and it just put too much stress on his body." Dan knows what's coming, but he finds that he needs to hear the words. He waits, and finally Chris continues. "He's gone, Dan. It was really fast, there was no suffering." Dan nods, and then realizes that Chris can't see him. It doesn't seem to matter, as Chris continues anyway. "His parents are with him. They were gonna call you, but they're pretty wrecked. They said to say that they'll call later tonight." Dan nods again. "Dan, are you still there? Danny?"

Dan pulls himself together, at least a little. "Yeah, I'm here."

"Okay, so we need to get you home. Right? I mean, there's no rush, in terms of… you know, services or anything. But…."

"Yeah." Dan realizes that he's crying, but it's weird, his voice doesn't seem to be affected. His brain feels numb, feels like everything is happening far, far away. Dan went away for a day and a half, and Justin died alone.

"Dan, is anybody there with you? Maybe I could talk to someone about travel plans?" Dan doesn't really understand that. What does Chris have to do with travel plans? But he doesn't really want to talk to Chris anymore anyway, so he turns around and sees Jeff hovering a few feet away. Evan has his arm around Tatiana's shoulders, and they're both pretending to look down toward the house. Dan leans out toward Jeff, phone in hand, and Jeff steps forward and takes it. He holds the phone in one hand and reaches out with the other to grip Dan's shoulder.

"Hello, Jeff Stevens here. Yeah…. Yeah." Jeff moves closer to Dan. "Yeah, we'll take care of it…. Okay…. Yeah, we'll give you a call when it's sorted out…. Okay, bye."

Jeff folds the phone and puts it in his pocket, and then turns so he's standing in front of Dan. "I'm sorry," he says in his low voice, and Dan knows that he is, but he also knows that it doesn't really matter, doesn't change anything. The whole world could be sorry, and Justin would still be dead.

Dan isn't sure what he's supposed to say or feel. He looks up for a moment, sees the beautiful rolling hills, the distant mountains and the warm afternoon sun, and he hates all of it, hates to think that Justin will never see anything so beautiful, will never see anything again. He'd thought maybe he was used to the idea of Justin's death, thought that his plan to start saying goodbye would make things easier, but he can't imagine anything harder than this. He starts to slide forward, as if his legs no longer want to hold him up, but Jeff is there, his strong arms catching Dan's shoulders, and he leans forward and braces the top of his head against Jeff's chest. One of Jeff's hands comes up and runs through Dan's hair, and they just stay like that for what seems like a long while. At some point, Evan is there, and Jeff is talking to him in low tones, but then Evan is gone, and it's just Jeff again.

Eventually, Dan lifts his head up. He wipes his face with his sleeve. It's gross, but he doesn't have a Kleenex. He looks at Jeff. "I should go."

Jeff nods slowly, and his touch is gentle as he smoothes Dan's hair back from his face. "Evan's gone down to get Linda to change your flight. If you're ready, we should go down and get you packed up."

Dan doesn't know if he's ready, doesn't know if he'll ever be ready. But Jeff seems to think it's a good idea, so Dan straightens up. Jeff moves around beside him and slings an arm across his shoulder. The ground is really too rough for walking like that, but Dan doesn't think to object, and Jeff doesn't let go.

It's strange to walk down the same hill that they'd just walked up. When they'd been coming up it, Justin had still been alive. But that isn't true… Justin had been dead, and Dan hadn't known, had been walking around talking like the distance between two elements in a show jumping ring actually mattered. Dan wonders what he'd actually been doing when Justin died. Had he been interviewing some hopeless barn rat, or had he been choking on his soup as he laughed at Evan's impersonation of Tatiana? Or had it happened even earlier, when Dan had been sitting on the porch, looking at the mountains and imagining another man in his bed?

They take a shortcut to the guest house, and when they get there Jeff leaves Dan staring at the mountains as he calls the main house. He grunts a few times and then puts his phone away. "Okay, they've got you on a flight that leaves in two and a half hours. It's about forty five minutes to the airport, so we don't have a lot of time, but why don't you grab a quick shower, and I'll throw your stuff together." Dan hears him, but is again having trouble understanding why he should care. "Dan." Jeff's hand is on his shoulder, and he's being guided into the house. "Come on, kid, you're gonna be all right. Do you want to skip the shower? Let's change your shirt, at least." Jeff guides Dan up the stairs and into the master bedroom.

They go into the en suite bathroom, and Jeff turns the cold water on in the sink, lets it run for a second, and then puts the plug down.

"Okay, kid, shirt off, please." Dan doesn't see the point of this, doesn't see the point of anything. Everything is so far away. He feels Jeff's fingers undoing the buttons on his shirt and wonders vaguely what's going on, but he doesn't really seem to care. Jeff eases the shirt off Dan's shoulders and lets it fall to the floor. By the time the shirt is off, the sink is filled with water, and Jeff moves Dan over to stand in front of it. "Okay, I know it's weird, but I think you're gonna feel a lot better if you cool down. So let's go." Jeff holds Dan's waist and pushed gently on his shoulders, and Dan's face is lowered over the sink. "Okay, kid, I'm just gonna splash you a little." Jeff cups the cold water in his hands and brings it up to Dan's face, runs the coolness over Dan's forehead and down his cheek. Jeff dips some more water up and catches Dan's other cheek, then down his jaw.

The chill is welcome. Dan's whole face feels hot and swollen, and the next time Jeff's hand goes back to the sink Dan follows it with his face, pushing as much of his head as he can into the icy water. It's so cold it hurts, but it brings Dan back to himself, cools his brain and lets him think. He stays in as long as he can, and when he comes up for air he brings his own hands forward and uses them to splash water over the back of his neck and his upper shoulders. Jeff laughs gently. "See, I really think a shower would have been tidier, but, go to it." Jeff waits until he sees that Dan is functioning and then goes into the bedroom and starts rooting through Dan's backpack. Dan takes a washcloth off the rack and turns the cold water back on. He soaks the cloth and uses it to cool down his chest and his back.

When Jeff comes back in the room, Dan pulls himself up and looks in the mirror. His whole face is swollen, but it's not red anymore, and Dan feels like he might be able to function, as long as he doesn't let himself think. Jeff hands him a shirt, and as Dan is doing up the buttons, Jeff's hand goes to the back of Dan's neck and shakes him a little. "You're gonna be okay, kid. We'll make sure you're okay."

chapter 13

EVAN drives him to the airport, while Jeff sits with Dan in the backseat. Dan hasn't started crying again, but he's still not really functioning too well. Nobody's talking much, but when they do say things he has trouble making sense of them.

They get to the airport and Evan parks the car, and he carries Dan's backpack as Jeff walks beside Dan. Evan goes to the ticket counter, and then they get to the security gate and Jeff walks through with Dan, while Evan stays behind. Dan doesn't really understand that, but he doesn't worry about it much. He's trying to focus on the little details as he goes, trying to keep his mind off anything important, trying to keep his mind off Justin. He does math for a while, counting by threes and then by fours until he loses track and has to start again. He knows it makes him seem odd, unaware, but if he doesn't distract himself he'll break down again, and that was bad enough in an empty field with only Jeff. He really doesn't think it would be appreciated in a crowded airport.

The flight is called, and Jeff gets up with Dan. When they get to the Jetway opening, Jeff hands two tickets to the flight attendant. Dan is finally present enough to realize that something's going on.

"Wait. Are you flying with me?" Jeff just smiles, and Dan shakes his head. "No… man, I'm sorry, I'll be fine. I just… it caught me off guard or something. I can pull it together, don't worry."

Jeff's hand is on the back of Dan's neck, and he gives him a gentle shake. "I'm not worried, kid. I've got some business in Kentucky anyway. I might as well take care of it now."

"Business? When did you start having business in Kentucky?" Dan's mind still feels muddy, but he doesn't remember Jeff saying anything about this before.

Jeff smiles. "Is this really something you want to talk about right now?" They're walking down the Jetway, and then they get to the plane and are herded to the left, toward their seats. Jeff stands aside for Dan to go in first, and then takes the aisle seat. Dan feels like he's being protected.

Dan stares out the window for most of the flight, watching the clouds and counting in his head. Any other thoughts have a way of leading back to Justin. Thinking about horses is obviously impossible, but Dan also can't think about movies without remembering the ones he saw with Justin, music without thinking of Justin's favorite songs, or politics without remembering how passionate Justin was about his chosen issues. As far as Dan can recall, he and Justin never did math together. He's up to counting by seventeens when the announcement comes on to fasten seatbelts. The minutiae of landing and getting off the plane let Dan get into the airport, but when the security doors slide open in the Arrivals area, and he sees a grim-faced Chris waiting outside, he actually stops and turns around, starts walking in the opposite direction.

Jeff lets him take a few steps and then grabs his arm and guides him out of the way of the other travelers. Jeff looks at him in concern, and Dan manages to say, "I just need a minute, just a minute." The flight had been like a little break from reality. He'd never been on a plane with Justin, so as long as he kept his brain turned off, he could feel as if Justin was still on the ground, waiting for him. Dan knows that as soon as he steps past the door, as soon as he sees Chris's grief, the opportunity for denial will be over.

Jeff stands patiently, lets Dan take a few deep breaths, and then walks behind him with a hand lightly touching the small of his back. Dan feels a bit like he's being herded, but in a good way. This time he makes it through the door, and Chris sees them and watches as they approach.

"Hey, Danny." Chris's voice is low and scratchy. Dan nods at him, and Chris extends his hand for Jeff to shake. "Hey, Jeff. Thanks for making the trip."

Jeff nods, and then looks at Dan. "Are you okay with Chris, kid?" Dan just looks at him blankly. Okay to do what? Jeff tries again. "Chris is going to drive you back to the apartment, okay?"

Dan stares at him. The apartment where he and Justin lived together? They think Dan is going there? He starts walking, heading for the exit. He calls back over his shoulder, "I just need some air. I'll be right back," but of course they follow him, and when he gets outside, it's no better. He doesn't need air—he needs Justin.

Jeff moves closer again, brings his hand back to Dan's shoulder. "Do you want to go somewhere else? Do you want to stay at a hotel?" Jeff looks to Chris for permission as he says, "Or at Chris's place?"

Dan takes a deep breath and tells himself to stop being such a little girl. He manages a sort-of smile, although he suspects it looks about as real as it feels. "No, sorry, I'm being an idiot. Thanks for coming out, Jeff, and, Chris, thanks for coming to get me." He straightens up. "Yeah, if you could drop me off at the apartment, that'd be great."

Jeff is looking at Dan as if he's trying to figure out how much of that was an act. Chris doesn't seem too convinced either.

"You're totally welcome at my place, Dan—or at Karl and Molly's or Robyn's...."

Dan doesn't really want to break down in the airport, and that means he needs to get out of there soon. "No, thanks, I'm fine." He turns to Jeff but can't look him in the eye, knows that the kindness that he would see there would destroy the facade he's trying to build. "Thanks again, Jeff."

Jeff looks like he doesn't want to leave, but he's clearly being dismissed. He gives Dan a long look, but Dan still won't look straight back at him. He sighs. "Okay, kid, you've got my cell number, and I'll be in town. Give me a call if you need me, for anything." Dan nods, but he needs to get out of there. Jeff is honesty and comfort, and Dan can't let himself be honest right now, can't be comforted without collapsing. This is Kentucky, not California, and in Kentucky, Dan has responsibilities.

Jeff heads off, and Dan follows Chris to his truck. They ride quietly, and Dan is glad that it's dark out, glad that he can't really see much when he looks out the window, can't see the familiar landmarks, can't see the places he and Justin had been together.

They turn off the highway, and Chris starts to talk. "Remember the time we went up the Reds game?"

Dan isn't sure he can do this.

"It was Justin's turn to drive, and you and me were shitfaced before we even got to the park. Remember? Remember how pissed off he was? Just swearing at us the whole time." Chris might be crying a little, but he's keeping his eyes on the road. "And when we got to the game, we—" Chris breaks off, his voice unsteady.

"We snuck into the VIP section, and you met that girl, that redhead." Dan stops looking out the window, looks over at Chris instead. "Yeah, man, I remember."

"I thought I was in love, I swear. She went to the bathroom or something, and you were passed out over in the corner—"

"I was resting my eyes," Dan interjects, and his voice sounds almost normal.

"Yeah, okay. You were out of it, and I was going on and on to Justin about how I'd never felt this way, and it was like a lightning bolt, and all that crap." Chris's laughing a little, too, now, but they pass a street light, and Dan can see that Chris's eyes are still shining with tears. "And he'd been so pissed off all day, and I thought he was gonna shit all over me and my little dream, and then"—Chris glances over at Dan, and then jerks his eyes back to the road—"and then he looked over at you, and he said, 'yeah, sometimes you just know'."

Dan takes a minute. He's never heard this part of the story before. "He looked over at me all drunk and passed out, and he said that?"

Chris grins. "Dude, you were just resting your eyes."

Dan turns to the window again, sees a farm pass by, the lights in the house warm and welcoming. He turns to Chris again. "Give it to me straight, man… was I drooling?"

Chris's lips twitch. "Possibly there was a little drool." Then he looks at Dan, his face serious. "And he still loved you that much."

Dan takes a deep, shaky breath. "And now it's over."

They're at the farm, and Chris pulls in and parks in front of the barn. "If we're being honest, Danny… it's been over for a while." Dan doesn't want to hear this speech, opens his door to get out, but Chris grabs his arm. "Not like you shouldn't be hurting, just like… you're surviving, you're managing without him. You know? I know it hurts, but… you can get past it." He leans back in his seat and takes his hand off Dan's arm. "We can all get past it."

Dan has his feet on the ground, and he just sits there for a minute, breathing in the night. Then he stands, says, "Thanks for the ride, Chris," and shuts the truck door.

He knows it's late, knows he should go up the stairs to the apartment, but instead he opens the door to the barn and slips inside. The horses are asleep, and the barn is quiet. He walks down the aisle to Monty's stall, and looks over the door. Most horses sleep standing up, but Monty has a tendency to lie down, curled up like he's still a foal. He's lying like that now, and it makes him look peaceful and innocent.

Dan leans against the stall door, brings his head down to rest his chin on his hands, and looks at the horse. Dan believes that animals have emotions. He's seen too much anger and joy and frustration and confusion and fear from them to deny it. But he doesn't know if they feel love, and he doesn't know if they feel sorrow. Monty is a full brother to Willow, the horse that had fallen on Justin. And she'd been injured in the fall, too, broken a leg and lots of other things, been put down by the vets before she'd left the show grounds. But Monty hadn't even noticed that there was an empty stall. Dan envies that, sometimes. But then he wonders if it's worth the trade, if never feeling sorrow makes it worth never feeling love.

He hears a shuffling sound and looks down the barn aisle, sees Chris standing there bashfully. Chris comes a little closer, and Dan's eyes go to the bottle of Wild Turkey in his hand. Chris holds it up questioningly.

Dan takes a long look, and then nods his head. "Fuck, yeah. Let's go upstairs."

They mostly drink silently. Every now and then one of them will come up with a memory, check to see if the other remembers it the same way. After a while, Chris is falling asleep in his chair, and Dan pulls himself to his feet and slaps Chris's shoulder. "I think the blankets for the couch are still packed, man. Come help me find them, or you're gonna freeze your ass off." Chris staggers up and joins Dan by the pile of belongings that he'd never bothered to put away after he'd moved back. They rustle around a bit and find the blankets, and then Dan goes into the bedroom and pulls one of the pillows off his bed, lobs it at Chris.

Chris bundles himself in the blankets and collapses on the couch, pillow wrapped in his arm. Dan stumbles to his bed and climbs in, and he falls asleep before he even has time to think about how Justin will never sleep in the bed again.

It's like his head barely had time to hit the pillow before he hears the sounds of the horses being fed down in the barn. He wants to go back to sleep, wants to dream about a life where Justin timed the jump just a fraction of a second differently, where he took the turn a little wider and came at the obstacle a little straighter. But he can hear the horses making their "bring me food" rumbles downstairs, and he knows he's never going to get back to sleep. He stumbles to the kitchen and puts on the coffee, then heads for the shower.

He adjusts the water temperature and strips down, then climbs into the tub. He runs the bar of soap over his body, down to his groin. The shower used to be his standard masturbation location. It's ironic, in a way, that back when he was having lots of sex he used to jerk off all the time, and then when he stopped having sex, he pretty much stopped jerking off too. He hadn't given it up altogether, but it had changed from being a natural, instinctive way to enjoy his body into an emotional minefield. He couldn't manage to come without picturing something, someone, and before Justin's accident it could have been anyone, someone from a movie or a guy he'd seen on the street or, often, Justin in a particularly hot moment. But after the accident, Dan felt like it had to be Justin, but then he worried that he was living in the past and worried when the memories began to fade and became less vivid. It started to feel dirty, like he was taking advantage somehow. It felt wrong to want someone who was in no condition to want him back. It became easier to just turn the water a little colder and put the whole thing out of his mind.

On this morning, he's too hung over for it to be much of an issue, and he turns the water on cold to help shrink his headache rather than his erection.

When he gets out of the shower, Chris is awake, already drinking coffee. Dan grunts at him and stumbles toward the coffee pot. Chris grunts back and heads for the shower.

By the time Chris is out of the bathroom, Dan is dressed and has eaten a breakfast of cold cereal. He's thinking about going downstairs, but he's a bit afraid to see anyone. He can handle Robyn, he's pretty sure, but dealing with Karl or Molly would be torture. Chris pulls on his clothes from the day before, then gets a bowl from the cupboard and pours himself some cereal, cursing when there's not quite enough milk left in the carton. Dan watches him eat, and Chris eventually says, "Karl and Molly wanted to talk to you, find out if you have any preferences for the service or whatever."

Dan shakes his head. "I don't think I care. It doesn't really matter, does it?"

Chris shrugs. "I don't know. I think they're trying to make a point; do it right this time." He seems to know he's on shaky ground, but Dan doesn't want to start that fight up again. He's tired, and Chris is all he's got left of Justin.

"Are you going to talk to them today? Could you just tell them I don't care?"

"Yeah, I can do that." Chris finishes his cereal and sits back. "But you're going to have to talk to them sometime."

Dan would rather not think about that. "Yeah, sometime." He squints at Chris. "That's not one of them downstairs, though, right? That's Robyn?"

"I dunno, probably." He stands up and takes his bowl and Dan's to the sink, then comes back and sits down. "They were pretty messed up yesterday. Like, medicated."

Dan nods, and wonders why that option hadn't been made available to him. Some drugs could have been just what he needed. Then he thinks of the Wild Turkey, and his stomach churns a little.

"How was California?"

The question startles Dan, and it takes him a moment to even understand what Chris is talking about. "It was all right. Nice place, nice people."

Chris nods. "Jeff seems like a good guy... seemed concerned about you yesterday."

Dan feels like a bit of an idiot. "Yeah. I kinda... I might have screwed that up a little. I fell apart a bit, I guess. Not exactly the ideal house guest. Or the model employee."

Chris shakes his head. "I'm sure they understood. They know the situation."

"Yeah, but it's not their problem. I shouldn't have dragged them into it."

"Cut yourself some slack, Dan. You don't have to be Captain Control all the time."

Dan thinks about his behavior the day before, thinks about how he can't even remember what happened between going to lean on the boulder and submerging his face in the basin of water. "Yeah, I kinda do," he says softly.

Chris shakes his head. "Dude, trust me... you really don't." Then he swallows the last of his coffee. "I'm gonna go home, get some clean clothes. I'll call Karl and Molly from there, tell them you don't care about the service... if you're sure that you don't care?"

Dan shakes his head. "I've never even been to a funeral before. And... that's not Justin, right?" He finds himself tearing up again, but this time it feels okay, doesn't feel like he's on the edge of an abyss like it had the day before. "I mean… when I remember Justin, I'm gonna remember him outside, racing our horses across the hills in the back or swimming in the pond or…." He takes a moment to recover his voice, and then he grins through his tears. "Either that or in bed, and I really don't think any of those things is gonna fit into a funeral service, right?"

Chris grins a little as he says, "Not a traditional service, no." He nods his understanding and heads for the door, but when he gets there he pauses and turns around. "Hey, Danny?" Dan looks up, and Chris says, "Justin was my best friend for my whole life, for thirty-four years." Dan nods, and Chris continues, his voice cracking and low. "And out of all that, when I remember Justin… I'm gonna remember him with you." Chris turns and heads down the stairs, and Dan stands in the apartment thinking of how much he has lost, but also of how much he has managed to retain.

chapter 14

DAN eventually makes it down the stairs and finds that it *is* Robyn doing the chores. She tears up a little when she sees him, but she gets by with a quick hug, and then they both distract themselves with the horses. For once in his life, Dan doesn't really feel like riding, but he wants to stay busy and useful, so he lunges a couple of the young horses in the corner of the dressage arena. It feels better to work with them than with any of the older horses, the ones he and Justin had trained together.

His phone rings around lunchtime, call display showing the Brown Hotel, the same place Jeff had stayed the last time he was in town. Dan flips the phone open. "Hello."

"Hey, kid, it's Jeff." Dan wonders if his response is somehow Pavlovian. For a while, hearing Jeff's voice was making him think of sex, but now it just makes him want to cry.

"Hey, Jeff. How're you?"

"I'm good." He sounds a little cautious. "How about you?"

Dan tries to make his voice sound light. "Hung over and generally fucked up, but, you know… I'll be fine. I'm really sorry about yesterday, man. I can't… I can't really explain it."

"Dan, you don't have to. It's not a big deal."

Dan laughs a little bitterly. "Yeah, I'm sure it happens every day in the Happy Land of Kaminski."

"Careful, Dan… they've lost people, too, remember."

Dan immediately feels terrible. "Shit, I know, I'm sorry. I'm just… I don't know. Sorry." He searches for a topic change. "But I just lunged Kip, and he didn't seem sore at all, so at least we don't have to worry about shipping a lame horse out to California."

"Yeah, good. Listen, I was thinking of coming out, having a look at the horses. Are you going to be there? I could pick up something for lunch."

Dan doesn't think that sounds like a good idea. He's got a nice pattern of distraction set up, and Jeff would just get in the way of that. Jeff would make him start feeling again. "Oh, thanks, man, but I've already eaten."

"Oh… I was talking to Chris earlier, and he said you didn't have much food in the fridge."

So Chris is reporting to Jeff, now? "I had stuff in the cupboards." Dan doesn't like lying, especially to Jeff, but he doesn't need a nursemaid. "Thanks for the thought, but I'm fine, really."

Jeff doesn't sound convinced, but he lets Dan off the phone, at least.

Almost immediately, the phone rings again; this time it's the Archer house. Dan doesn't want to answer. He thinks about letting them leave a message. They might be just as relieved to avoid the contact as he would be. But Chris is right; he's going to have to deal with them eventually, so he flips his phone open. "Hello."

There's a pause, and then Karl's voice. "Dan, it's Karl. How are you?"

Karl doesn't make it sound like a casual greeting, he makes it sound like an invitation to bare his soul, and Dan feels a flash of anger. It's none of Karl's damn business how he is. But he puts a lid on that and makes his tone neutral. "I'm okay. How are you? And Molly?"

"We're both… as well as can be expected." Karl sounds old and tired, and Dan is annoyed again. These people shouldn't be his problem— how did he get himself in a position where he is supposed to care about them? But he knows he isn't being rational and tries to think of something to say that won't show his feelings.

"Is there anything I can do?"

"Oh, no, Dan, nothing for you to worry about." There's another pause. "We spoke to Chris earlier, and he said you didn't think you had any preferences for the funeral. Is that right? No favorite Bible verse or anything?"

Dan almost snorts. Has he ever said or done anything that would make Karl think he knew a single Bible verse, let alone had a favorite? "Uh, no, not really."

Karl continues, and Dan feels like bashing his phone against the wall of the barn. He wonders if Karl is still drugged, if that would explain his slow speech and apparent inability to accept that Dan doesn't care about any of this. "We thought we'd go with the Twenty-third Psalm. We know it's overused, but it's beautiful.'"

"Okay." Dan doesn't know how much of this he can take. "Have you got a time set for it yet? Do you know where it's going to be?"

"Oh, yes, we've got the schedule here somewhere...." There's the sound of rustling papers, and then Karl's voice calling to someone.

There's a rattling sound, and then Chris's voice. "Danny? Listen, let me call you back—a bunch of aunts and uncles just arrived, and everything's a bit crazy."

"Sure, fine," Dan says, and clicks the phone shut. Chris is over at the house again. Chris is taking care of everything. Dan feels a flash of resentment before he settles into being ashamed. Is it any wonder the Archers didn't trust Dan with being part of the earlier decision when this is how he acts when something bad happens? He'd melted down the day before. Today he's hiding in the barn, avoiding taking any responsibility for anything. He decides he should be grateful for Chris. Let him take the heat and deal with them all. Molly and Chris's mom are close, so she's probably involved, and the woman has never been a big fan of Dan's. She'd once called him an "opportunistic drifter" when she didn't know he could hear. And Chris knows all the relatives, has a knack for keeping track of cousins and grandparents that Dan would just as soon forget about. Family comes easy to Chris, so let Chris deal with the family.

Dan helps Robyn clean the remaining stalls and then heads upstairs. He hunts through the kitchen for food, wishing that there really was a secret stash in one of the cupboards. He knows he should just go and buy groceries or at least pick up some takeout. He knows he should have just let Jeff come over. But he feels like he's walking a fine line of control, and somehow being with Jeff makes it harder to maintain the facade of calmness, makes it more likely that he'll wobble out of balance. He remembers his little display the day before and grimaces. He knows he can't blame Jeff for it, but thinks maybe he would have managed to get it together faster if Jeff hadn't been so understanding and gentle. And Dan knows that Jeff doesn't have any business in Kentucky, knows that he seemed so weak that Jeff thought he needed to be baby-sat. The fact that Jeff is still here is embarrassing evidence of Dan's inability to make himself appear normal and in control. He thinks guiltily of Jeff's actual business, in California, and of the upcoming art show that he had said he'd need to spend a lot of time preparing for. Instead of doing any of that, he's hanging out in a Louisville hotel worrying that Dan is unable to even feed himself.

Dan's stomach growls as if echoing Jeff's concern. He looks at his phone, thinks about calling Jeff and taking him up on his offer, but it's too pathetic. Then there's the sound of footsteps on the stairs and a knock at the door, which Dan has left ajar, as usual. Dan is only a little disappointed when the door is shoved open to reveal Chris's face.

Chris pushes the door the rest of the way open with his foot, and Dan notices that Chris is carrying a lot of stuff. It's mostly in bags, but there are a couple of boxes, some Tupperware… Dan's stomach growls again, this time in delight. Chris has brought him food.

Chris takes everything over to the kitchen table and manages to set it down without dropping anything. "They're drowning in casseroles over there—I said I thought I knew a good home." He pokes around a little. "I tried to pick the good stuff." Then he opens up one of the bags and pulls out two cartons of milk and another bottle of Wild Turkey. They hadn't finished the one from the night before, but apparently Chris wants to be prepared.

Dan closes in on the table. "Is there anything that doesn't need to be heated?" He finds a Tupperware container filled with little sandwiches and eats one as he walks over to the cupboard. "You want a plate?"

"Yeah, sure." Chris is still sorting, putting things in the fridge or over on the counter. He pulls out one glass casserole dish. "His Aunt Debbie's mac and cheese—trust me, man, this is excellent. I'm putting it in the fridge, on top—you should have that for dinner." When Chris is done fussing, he takes the plate from Dan and they both take a few handfuls of the little sandwiches. They go to sit on the couch.

After a few moments of silent eating, Chris pulls a sheet of paper from his back pocket. "This is the schedule. There's visitation tomorrow, 4 p.m. to 8 p.m., that's at the funeral home—Wilsons', on Broadway, by the mall?" Dan nods blankly. He's not altogether sure what a visitation is, but he supposes he can find the place if he needs to. "Then the funeral service is the next day at one, at St. Andrew's United." Dan nods again. He knows he'll have to go to the funeral. Chris looks a little uncomfortable about the next part. "And then… they want to have him cremated. I know you said you didn't care, but I thought I'd run that by you."

"Cremated? Damn, they just can't get rid of him fast enough, huh?" Dan doesn't think that's what he meant to say, but he's not sure.

Chris looks a little pained. "Apparently it's a family thing—they're just not into graveyards."

Dan isn't too clear on all this. "So, then… where do the ashes go?"

"I guess they go wherever people want. You can scatter them, or keep them in an urn or something…."

"I thought they were trying to get away from keeping Justin in storage."

Chris gives him a level look. "Do you actually object to this, or are you just being pissy?"

Dan sighs and runs both hands through his hair. "I don't even know." He eats two more little sandwiches before he says, "I guess it's no worse than having him in the ground, right? I mean, either way…." Dan is proud that he said all that without crying. It's a lot easier to be irritable than to be honest, but Chris is doing a lot, and he deserves Dan's best effort.

"Okay. I'll let them know… but, Dan… the visitation tomorrow, that's going to be pretty public. Do you want that to be the first time you see Karl and Molly, or do you want to come back over to the house with me now?"

"Am I supposed to go to the visitation?"

Chris looks surprised. "Well, yeah. I think Karl and Molly were thinking you'd stand next to them."

"Stand next to them? Chris, what the hell's a visitation? And does it really last for four hours?" Dan is beginning to wish he had a bit more experience with funerals.

Chris snorts. "Feels like four years, usually. It's for people to come through and pay their respects, give their sympathy to the family." Chris scratches his nose. "Usually the coffin's there so people can say bye to Justin, and then there's a kind of line up that they go through, giving condolences. I don't know. I've been to ones that are less formal, just sort of a gathering of people. It's supposed to be a chance for people to talk one-on-one."

"I'm supposed to talk one-on-one with Justin's family? About what?"

"About Justin, mostly. But, honestly, the way Molly's going, I think practically the whole family is going to be in the damn receiving line, so you won't really have to talk to them."

Dan's mind is whirling. "Okay, wait, walk me through this… I show up at what time? At four?"

"A little before, probably. I can pick you up if you want."

"Okay, and then what?"

"Then you get in a line with the rest of the family and stand there and feel awkward as people come through and say nice things to you."

Dan tries to collect his thoughts, then shakes his head. "But I'm not part of the family. Why am I there? Do *you* have to do this?"

Chris smiles gently. "Karl asked me, but I said I might be more useful in the background, helping out. And it's not family like there's a blood test. It's family like people who cared about him."

"But then why don't you have to do it?" Dan is starting to panic. He'd thought the funeral would be bad, but this is sounding a thousand times worse.

"Dan, chill out. You don't *have* to do anything. It's just—you and Justin were together for a long time. People know you. You know people. They'll expect you to be there." Chris pauses, and seems to be searching for more ways to convince Dan. "There'll be a lot of horse people, probably. Justin was a pretty big deal around here—people will want to say goodbye. You can just talk shop with them."

"For four hours?" Dan's mouth is dry.

"For, like, a minute each person. And you can take breaks if you want to. Look, man, I'm not saying it's going to be a good time, but you might be glad you did it—it can help remind you that a lot of people care."

"Oh God."

"It'll make the funeral seem easy by comparison—does that help?"

"No, you sadistic bastard, that doesn't help!" Dan is half-laughing, half-crying. He feels like he might be getting a little over the edge. He sees yesterday's bottle of Wild Turkey on the table. He thinks for a second, and then leans over and picks it up, opens it and takes a swallow. It burns, but he waits a moment and then takes another. He offers the bottle to Chris, who considers it briefly and then stands up and goes to the kitchen, coming back with two glasses. Dan is already feeling better, the burn in his throat and stomach dispersing into a warm glow, but he takes the glass Chris pours for him anyway.

"Can I be drunk for it?"

Chris grins. "You probably shouldn't be falling down, but I bet half the people there will have a flask."

"Can I be drunk after it?"

"I dunno. Do you want to be hungover for the funeral?"

Dan doesn't think it would make things any worse. "I was hoping to be drunk for the funeral too."

"Damn," Chris says mildly. "I should have bought more than one extra bottle."

Dan lets out a deep, shaky breath. "This is really happening, huh?"

There's a long pause, and then Chris drains his glass. "Yeah, it really is."

They sit in silence for a moment longer, and then Dan reaches over and grabs the bottle, refills his glass and Chris's. "Okay. What else do I need to know?"

DAN doesn't make it over to the Archer house that afternoon. It's not that he thinks it's a bad idea, exactly, but when he looks at the amber liquid in his glass and realizes that finishing this drink will make him too drunk to impose himself on a grieving family… he finishes the drink. And then a couple more. Chris is being more restrained, and when Dan's eyes start drifting shut, Chris puts him to bed. Dan tries to resist, tells Chris that it's only mid-afternoon, reminds him that he wanted Dan to have Aunt Debbie's mac and cheese for dinner, but Chris dumps him on the bed, and Dan decides to stay there. It's comfy and warm.

When he wakes up, it's to the sounds of the horses being brought in and fed. The sun is going down outside his window. He doesn't feel hung over, so he thinks he must still be drunk, but he pours himself another glass just to make sure. He wonders briefly if this is becoming a problem, this alcohol thing, and then decides that for the next few days, it's allowed. For the next few days, anything that keeps him from screaming is allowed.

He gets up and goes to the kitchen, finds the casserole dish in the fridge and reads the directions on the attached Post-it note: *Oven, 350 degrees, for an hour*. He can do that.

While he's waiting, he paces around the apartment. Chris had said the funeral home was looking for photographs and mementos to place around the room during the viewing, so the two of them had gone through the boxes and found whatever Dan had. He didn't have much, really. Justin's parents had been the chroniclers of his career, and Dan had never been much for photographs. When Dan had moved out after hearing about the sale of the farm, he'd packed Justin's things along with his own, so he and Chris had unpacked almost everything Dan owned when they were looking for Justin's stuff. It's still spread all over the living room, and Dan thinks about picking it up. Instead, he picks up his phone. And then sets it down again. He's a strange mix of drunk and hyperactive, and it's driving him a little crazy.

He wants to call Jeff, but he's starting to feel really weird about the whole thing. He doesn't want Jeff's pity, and doesn't want to make himself look pathetic. He's also feeling a little guilty. He's not really thinking of sex, not anymore, but he can't deny that he's attracted to the man, and it seems wrong to want to talk to him now, so soon after Justin's death. And the drunken haze is making things alternately seem much simpler and much more complicated.

In one of the moments of seeming simple, he picks up the phone and finds the hotel number, hits send. He decides that it's like fate. If Jeff is in the room, Dan will talk to him. If Jeff isn't, he won't leave a message.

Jeff picks up on the second ring, and Dan almost hangs up the phone. When Jeff says "Hello?" for the second time, Dan finally kicks himself into gear.

"Jeff, hey, sorry. It's Dan."

"Hey, kid, how are you?"

"I'm okay. A little drunk, again. But I think that's good, really… or at least not bad." Dan decides to go for it. "Do you like macaroni and cheese?"

Jeff doesn't seem fazed by the topic shift. "I like homemade, but not from the box."

Yeah, Dan could have predicted that. "I've got some in the oven. It's supposed to be really good. Have you had dinner yet?"

"No, not yet."

"It's almost nine o'clock. Why haven't you had dinner yet?" Dan feels like turnabout is fair play. If Jeff can inquire into his meal planning, Dan can inquire into his.

"I had a late lunch." Dan can hear a smile come into Jeff's voice. "And I was talking to Chris this afternoon, and he said you had Aunt Debbie's macaroni and cheese, so I was holding out for an invitation."

Dan thinks about getting irritated. Is he really that predictable? And why are Chris and Jeff talking all the time, and do they have some sort of plan to manipulate him? But it all seems too complicated, and Dan doesn't have the energy to care.

Jeff notices the long pause. "Dan? Everything okay?"

"I was just wondering whether I could eat the whole thing before you got here. It's a pretty big dish, but I think maybe I could do it."

"I'm on my way. Should I bring anything?"

"If you want something to drink besides Wild Turkey or milk…."

"Okay. I'll see you in twenty."

Dan thinks about showering, and then kicks himself. Is he sprucing up for a date or something? He starts to pick up the crap in the living room, because that's not sprucing up, it's just good manners. But he gets a little sidetracked when he comes across a book on *Conditioning the Equine Athlete*. He and Justin had both started reading it and had squabbled over it on the few occasions that they had wanted to read at the same time. But then they'd started writing notes to each other in the margins, and it had turned into a game. It had begun quite innocently, with Dan highlighting something they should try at the barn, but by the end the comments had gotten pretty explicit, with each of them suggesting things that they should try in bed, or in the shower, or against the wall in the kitchen… Dan is glad that he stumbled across the book now, rather than remembering about it after he had lent it to someone. He has a quick flash of Tatiana reading the book and squirms. He doesn't want to throw it out, but he needs to find somewhere better to store it. He thinks briefly about contributing it to the display at the funeral home.

There's a knock on his door, ajar as usual, and Jeff is there. He sees Dan sitting on the floor surrounded by stuff, and walks over to stand above him. "So? Is there any left?"

Dan grins. "I may have exaggerated the threat level a little. It's still not done cooking."

Jeff cocks an eyebrow. "I was talking about the bourbon." Dan starts to get up, but Jeff stops him. "Don't worry, I can get it myself. Glasses are…?" He walks into the kitchen, and Dan directs him to the cupboard, and then to the bottle on the kitchen table. Jeff fills his glass and brings the bottle over to top up Dan's.

Jeff sits on the couch Dan is leaning against, and Dan thinks that if he shifted over an inch, his shoulder would be touching Jeff's leg. He doesn't do it. Jeff looks at the book Dan's holding, and then the piles of belongings all over the room. "Getting organized?" he asks mildly.

"We were looking for stuff. For the visitation. Have you been to one of those before?"

Jeff looks a little surprised. "Well, yeah. You haven't?" Dan shakes his head, and Jeff frowns. "You're in the receiving line tomorrow?"

"I guess. It sounds kinda weird. I just stand there and people file by and say nice things about Justin?"

Jeff grins and then scootches off the couch to sit next to Dan on the floor. Their shoulders are definitely touching now. Dan is careful to neither increase nor decrease the pressure, and as a result he sits almost completely still. "Pretty much. Usually visitors will know some people in line better than others, so they'll save their best stuff for the people they know. Like, if I didn't know you, I'd walk up and shake your hand and say, 'I'm Jeff Stevens. I do some business with Justin's parents. I'm sorry for your loss.' And you'd say…." Jeff cocks an eyebrow expectantly.

"I'm Dan? Justin and I…. Jesus, do I have to give us a name? Like, boyfriends or life partners or some crap? Can I just say we used to fuck?"

"Yeah, you can. That'd be great. If I'm gonna go through this line and make awkward small talk with strangers, I at least want the entertainment of seeing people's faces when you introduce yourself that way." Jeff nudges Dan's shoulder a little, disrupting his careful balance of pressure. He finds that he doesn't mind.

Dan nudges back. "Yeah, okay. Then I'd have another damn funeral to deal with, after Molly keeled over with a heart attack."

Dan can feel Jeff's laugh through their joined shoulders. It feels good.

They drink quietly for a bit, and then Jeff says, "I've only been in the receiving line once. For my father's funeral."

"Was it bad?"

"No, not terrible. We weren't close, so… you know, there's always regrets, like some Springsteen song, but… it wasn't a huge thing, really."

Dan waits, but Jeff doesn't say anymore. Dan says, "My father's still alive, as far as I know. And I didn't find out my mother was dead until eight months later, so… not a lot of formalities there."

Jeff is still and then asks quietly, "How did that come about?"

Dan isn't sure why he's doing this. He likes Jeff, wants Jeff to know him, but he doesn't know why he's telling him the worst stuff first. He continues anyway. "My mother got cancer when I was a teenager. A sick wife, a gay son—it was a lot for my father to take, so he didn't. He took off. So that's why I don't know about him." Dan takes a deep drink. "My mom got better, got remarried—but the new guy wasn't crazy about the gay son, either, so… I left. I came back through town a while later, but they'd moved. I asked a neighbor about it, and she told me about my mom. I guess the cancer came back."

The timer on the oven dings, and Dan scrambles to his feet, incredibly glad for the interruption. "Do you want to eat here or at the table?"

Jeff looks up at him. "I'm really pretty comfortable here."

"Do you want ketchup with it?"

"God, no. Not with homemade, you animal!"

Dan holds up his hands to ward off the criticism and goes to the kitchen. He uses a dishtowel to take the casserole out of the oven, and then a large spoon to dish it up onto two plates. Even with generous portions, there's still a lot left over.

Dan grabs forks, and then goes back over to Jeff. Jeff takes both plates while Dan sits down, and then they both balance their plates on their knees while they eat.

After the first bite, Jeff grins. "God bless Aunt Debbie—this is good."

"God bless Chris, he's the one who stole it for us."

Jeff waits until he's finished chewing his second mouthful. "He seems like a good guy. You going to miss him, if you go out to California?"

Dan shrugs, then grins. "Why, you gonna cook up some imaginary job for him too? Lure him out there?"

Jeff shakes his head. "Like I have money for that. Don't get me confused with Evan, kid. Besides, if you think your job is imaginary, you're gonna have a big surprise on your first day of work." Jeff looks at Dan out of the corner of his eye. "You are gonna come out, right? You're going to take the job?"

Dan shrugs. "I don't know. I mean… I'm definitely getting the hell out of here. I've been in Kentucky for five years already, and that's way too long." He doesn't say it, but he knows Jeff hears the silent, *And there's nothing keeping me here anymore.* Out loud, he adds, "And the job sounds good, and you all seem real nice."

"So, why wouldn't you come?"

"I don't know." Dan is a bit frustrated that this is the best answer he can give. "I mean, like I said, it was nice, and everybody was nice, but it's just—I don't really know how I'd fit in there. You know? Like, am I the barn help? Then what am I doing eating at the main house? Am I a friend? Then why am I taking money?" Dan looks at Jeff quizzically. "You never felt like that at all?"

Jeff shrugs. "It was a bit different for me—I mean, I was a friend of the family first, and I was never an employee, exactly. I was more like a contractor—I gave Tat lessons, but that was about three hours a week. It wasn't my full-time job. And I never lived on the property. But, yeah, I see what you mean." He takes his last bite of macaroni. "Would it be easier if it was just a job? If you didn't hang out with the family, just did the work and went home?"

Dan thinks about this. "Yeah, maybe. I mean, I wouldn't want to be rude about it—I like them both. It's not like I don't *want* to be friendly. It's just—weird." Jeff nods, and Dan continues. "Even with you, does it never bother you? I mean, I'm sure you're doing fine, but Evan's richer than God. He could buy and sell you with his pocket change, right? Doesn't that bug you?"

Jeff looks at his hands. "I'd like to say 'no'. I'd like to say he can't buy me, because I'm not for sale. And that's true, but… yeah, it bothers me a bit. Money's not a limitation for him at all. For me, it is. It's hard to draw a line sometimes, to figure out what it's okay for him to spend money on and what it's not." Jeff looks thoughtful, like he's trying to decide how much of this he wants to share. "Honestly, it's a pretty big reason why we keep things casual, at least from my perspective. I care about him, but I can't let my life get totally wrapped up in his, you know?"

"Yeah, I get it." Dan shifts a little, wanting to look at Jeff. It moves their shoulders apart, but brings their thighs together. Dan is temporarily distracted by the new sensation, the new heat, but then manages to ask, "And from his perspective? Why's *he* okay with it being casual?"

Jeff grins. "From his perspective? Best of both worlds—he gets me for security and someone to come home to, and he still gets to chase shiny things when he sees them." Jeff smiles wolfishly, reminding Dan that he was one of the "things" Evan had chased.

Dan feels his body respond a little to the look, and his voice is a bit lower when he asks, "And you? You don't like shiny things?"

Jeff's eyes are intense, and his voice has lowered as well. "I'm not blind, Dan. Of course I like shiny things. And I like them even more when I find out that they're not just pretty on the outside." Jeff stares at Dan for a minute, and then pulls his legs away and climbs to his feet. He takes their plates off the coffee table and carries them to the kitchen. As he moves, he says, "But I try to be a bit more responsible about it. I try to make sure I'm not taking advantage of someone at a bad time, and I try to make sure that relationships aren't going to get more complicated than they need to be just because of me."

Jeff comes back halfway, stands by the door. "And I try to protect myself a little. If there's someone I think I might care about, I try to make sure he's going to be able to care back before I dive into anything. I'm too old to think a broken heart is romantic."

Dan hadn't thought about Jeff's perspective on all this before. Truthfully, he hadn't given that much *thought* to his own perspective. He'd just been operating on an instinctive level, his body responding to the stimulus of Jeff's presence. Jeff is watching him, seeming to understand that Dan is digesting his words.

"Yeah, I can see that. I guess… I guess it's good that you've got your head on straight, that you're… being responsible." Dan knows he should leave it there, for so many reasons. But somehow, he just can't help himself. "Still… sometimes, don't you just want to forget it all, just do what feels good at the time?" Dan brings his eyes up, lets them blaze with all the heat he's been feeling in Jeff's presence.

Jeff's body actually sways a little toward him in response, but his feet stay firmly on the floor and his hand continues to grip the door frame, albeit a little more tightly. "Damn it, kid. You've got no idea," he growls, and then he's out the door and into the night.

chapter 15

DAN sleeps through most of the next morning, until Chris calls to arrange to pick him up for the visitation. Dan finds his only suit in the closet, and hopes that it's appropriate. It's dark gray, but should it be black? He doesn't know, and really, he doesn't care too much. Justin had been with him when he'd bought that suit, so that's enough for him. He puts minimal effort into shining his shoes and finding an appropriate tie. He ends up wearing one of Justin's. He guesses they're his now.

He heads downstairs to wait for Chris, and Robyn comes out to keep him company. She says she's going to finish up at the barn, then go home and get changed and go to the funeral home. He nods. It'll be good to see someone he knows, but otherwise he doesn't really see what Robyn is going to say to him or to Karl and Molly that she couldn't say at the barn. This entire ritual is beyond his understanding.

Chris arrives, and Dan climbs into his truck, waving goodbye to Robyn. They drive to the funeral home in relative silence, and then Chris parks and walks in with Dan. Dan balks at the front door. Chris stands quietly until he collects himself, and then they go in together. They're in a central hallway, with rooms to the left and to the right. There are some people Dan thinks he recognizes as Justin's extended family in the room to the right, but Dan's eye is drawn to the room on the left, where there is a display of flowers arranged around a coffin.

Somehow, this hadn't occurred to Dan, and he's not sure he can handle it. He looks at Chris. "Is that"—he nods toward the coffin—"is that Justin?"

Chris looks like he isn't sure how to answer. "It's his body."

Dan nods. Maybe it's easier to pretend that he and Justin had some sort of purely spiritual relationship, but truthfully, Dan loved Justin's body along with the rest of him. He loved the broad shoulders, the strong hands, the muscular limbs, the tight ass, the enthusiastic cock…. Dan steps into a little alcove and grabs for his flask. He'd thought he would try this without alcohol, but that was just foolish. He needs something to numb him a little.

Two big swigs, and even before the alcohol hits his bloodstream Dan is a little distracted, a little calmed. The burning in his throat spreads down to his stomach and then out to his arms. Chris stands and watches him quietly.

"Do you want to go see him?" Chris asks.

"I don't know if I can," Dan almost whispers. "I mean, I don't know if I can do the rest of the visitation if I do."

Chris nods a little. "So, *fuck* the rest of the visitation. Dan, what do you need to do? Do you need to say goodbye to him now? 'Cause if you do, that's cool, we can keep the doors shut forever if that's what you need."

Dan turns to Chris, and he can hear the emptiness in his voice. "I can't have what I need."

Chris breaks, just a little, but then he pulls himself back together. Dan sees it, and he tries to emulate Chris's strength. "Will he still be here after? Can I go and do the line, and then see him after, before he goes?"

Chris nods. "Yeah, you can do that." He pulls his own flask out of his breast pocket and takes a drink. Dan wonders how anyone gets through one of these things sober.

"Okay, let's do that," Dan says, and he and Chris go into the room to the right. Karl and Molly are there, and they both break off their conversations when they see Dan come in. He's tempted to leave again, but he presses on, walks toward them as they walk toward him. Molly gets to him first, and her eyes are dry. She takes his hand, and Dan focuses on resenting her, because if he lets himself care then he knows he'll fall apart. He tries the same treatment with Karl, tries to feel contempt for the man as he grips Dan's shoulders, but he can't help remembering how Karl had been with Justin, how proud he'd been of his achievements, how much true joy he'd taken from seeing Justin happy. Dan knows that these are the people who loved Justin, and he knows that Justin loved them too. Dan has no words for them, but when they hug him he hugs them back, and hopes that they understand.

The funeral director comes out and arranges them in a line. There are indeed a lot of members of Justin's extended family included. The line ends up wrapping around two full walls of the room. Dan knows that the only people in it who Justin saw more than a couple times a year are Molly, Karl, and himself. Molly is at the end of the line, gripping tight to

Karl's hand, and Dan is beside Karl. Chris comes up and says a few quiet words to each of them, and Dan marvels again at how good the man is at all this. He decides that if the law thing doesn't work out, Chris has a bright future in the funeral trade.

Then the doors are open, and people start spilling in. Dan recognizes most of them, but a few he doesn't, and he turns to Karl and Molly in panic. "I forgot—I don't care what I call myself—what do you guys want me to say?"

They look at him blankly, and Dan smothers a giggle when he realizes that they think he's just asked if they want him to use an alias. "I mean in terms of my relationship to Justin," he clarifies.

"Oh." Karl and Molly exchange a look. "Well, honestly… when we refer to you, we usually call you Justin's friend." Molly smiles. "I mean, everyone who knows Justin can figure out what that means, and if they don't know Justin it isn't really any of their business."

Dan doesn't really like it, but he doesn't argue. He just needs to get through the day, and he *had* told them he didn't care, after all. And he doesn't have a lot of time—the visitors have worked through the extended family quickly and are almost to Dan.

He recognizes them, at least. They're local eventers. Justin had competed against them when he was younger, and Dan still sees them when he takes horses to schooling shows. He holds out his hand, and Travis shakes it, but Natalie moves in for the hug, and Dan lets her. She's crying a little when she pulls away, and Dan has to fight his own tears. He's going to be a mess if this sets him off.

"We're really going to miss him, Dan. I mean, we already were, but now…." Natalie trails off.

"And I know it's not a fair trade, but at least people seem to be really looking at the safety issues now. We saw a demonstration on frangible jumps last week, and they looked really good." Travis seems sincere, and Dan agrees that the new materials make sense.

And then they're gone, moved on to Karl and Molly, and Dan faces the next person, an elderly woman he doesn't recognize. He sees Chris hovering in the background in case Dan messes up. He extends his hand and remembers to be gentle when he shakes hers, and then says, "I'm Dan, Justin's friend." The "we used to fuck" line is on the tip of his tongue, but he fights it back.

"His friend?" She looks at his placement in the line, and then smirks. "Oh, is that what they're calling it these days? Well, I'm sorry for your loss especially, then. Lord knows he was a fine-looking young man. So tall...."

The woman's companion, equally old and delicate, has finished talking to Justin's uncle, and now she joins the conversation. "Broad shoulders, and such a handsome face," she says, and both women nod. Dan finds himself nodding along with them, but they look at him as if waiting for his contribution.

He's tempted to let loose with a rhapsody to Justin's dick, but he's pretty sure that would bring Chris down on him, although he's not sure the women themselves would object. He just says, "Yeah, I'm really going to miss him," and the ladies move on.

The afternoon continues in a similar vein. Dan finds that he's too busy trying to find small talk to really feel sad, and the few times people break down in front of him he's working too hard trying to comfort them to join in. And Chris was right; it is sort of gratifying to see how many people were affected by Justin's life.

He takes a few breaks, goes and has a drink or two with Chris in the back hallway, but overall the afternoon is more aggravating than painful. Still, he's relieved to see the grandfather clock's little hand approaching the eight.

He doesn't realize how closely he's been watching the door until he finally sees Jeff's face appear, and he doesn't realize how attached he's gotten to the man until he feels the stab of disappointment when Jeff turns and smiles quietly at Evan as he and Tatiana follow Jeff in. Dan knows he's been playing with fire, knows he's not thinking as clearly as he should be due to the combination of grief and alcohol, but he had been looking forward to spending some more time alone with Jeff. Not thinking that anything would happen, necessarily, just basking in the glow of Jeff's warmth, like a cat in front of a fire. But now Evan is here, and Dan has the uncharitable thought that he's here more to emphasize his claim on Jeff than to offer condolences.

As soon as Evan is in front of him, Dan feels bad for being so petty. The guy is so genuine, so... Dan wants to call him wholesome, although that doesn't seem quite right given Dan's firsthand experience with his pick-up techniques. But even then, he'd seemed sincere, too intense, but not sleazy. And he's the same way now. Just the fact that he's here is too much. It's insane that he flew half way across the country to pay his respects to a man he never met, all because of a man he's only spent a handful of hours with. But Dan isn't arrogant enough to think that he could be an actual threat to Jeff and Evan's relationship, even if he wanted to be, so he knows Evan isn't really here to lay claim. He's here because he's Evan. He's over-sized in every way.

Evan seems to be trying to hold back from hugging Dan, but it's so clearly what he wants to do that Dan just gives up and leans in for it. He's been hugged tonight by people he's never even met, so Evan makes sense by comparison. Evan pulls back and looks him in the eye, saying, "Really, so sorry for your loss, Dan. I never got to meet him, but Tat's such a fan that I feel like I did. I wish I had."

Dan nods. He's got his own set of wishes about Justin, and they're no more likely to come true than Evan's is. "Thanks for coming, man. It's a long trip."

Evan shrugs. "Well, maybe we'll visit the horses while we're here. Apparently Tat's developing a bit of an interest in Sunshine." Evan smiles and moves over to speak to Karl and Molly, but he keeps a watchful eye on Tatiana as she approaches Dan.

"I hope it's okay that we came. I realized… I realized that I never told you how I got interested in eventing. It was…." Tatiana seems nervous, looks to Evan, who smiles back gently until she continues. "It was Rolex two years ago. I was watching on TV, and"—she shrugs self-consciously—"well, obviously Justin caught my eye because he was so good-looking, but what made me want to try the sport was how happy he looked. Not just when he won, but all through. It looked like he really loved every minute of it. Even when they went through that gully, and his face got all splashed with mud, he was smiling the whole time." She stops, and looks as though she's torn between the embarrassment of having spoken and the remembered joy of the moment. "He just looked like he was doing exactly what he was meant to do."

Dan can't believe it. He's made it through almost four hours of this shit with his dignity intact, and now some fifteen-year-old is going to break him down? Dan takes a deep, shaky breath. His eyes are filled, but they haven't spilled over yet, if she just moves on he might be okay.

She's on her way, her feet are moving, and then she looks back and says softly, "You were so lucky to have known him," and Dan is done. He's just crying now but he can feel the sobs building and knows he needs to get out of there. Karl is looking concerned and is guiding Tatiana away, and Dan heads out. There's hardly anyone left in line but he doesn't care anyway. He gropes his way to the back hallway but that's not far enough away, so he keeps going, finds the back door and pushes through it. Once he's outside he turns and slams his body into the side of the building, raises one hand over his head and punches the brick wall, sobs wracking his body. Justin is gone. Dan *was* lucky to have known him, lucky to have loved him, incredibly lucky to have been loved back, and now it's all over, and Dan is alone, and he doesn't know if he can stand it.

He's crying so hard his whole chest hurts, and he wants to stop but he can't. Justin is gone; his smile is gone; his laugh is gone; his stupid little smirk that made Dan so mad is gone. He hits the wall again, and he can hear himself making a strange sound, a sort of whining growl. Justin's never going to kiss him again, never going to get that mischievous look as he runs his hands down Dan's stomach, never going to touch Dan again, and he really doesn't know how he's supposed to accept that. Dan's sobs are almost gasps for air, and he feels his knees giving out, and he just doesn't care, letting himself slide sideways down the wall. He doesn't get that far, though, before he feels strong hands catching his arms, gently lifting him up. Dan almost fights them, wants to hit the ground and wallow there and wait until his heart finally explodes and kills him so he can be with Justin, but he's too tired to fight. He just slumps, instead, and the pain is still there and the sobs are still coming, but Dan can feel warm bodies on both sides of him, can feel his arms being propped across their shoulders as he is walked over to a windowsill and sat down on it, the bodies quickly turning and sitting on either side of him, propping him up.

Dan doubles over and braces his elbows on his knees, his forehead against his arms, and he keeps crying. There is a soothing hand rubbing his back, and then he hears a crunch of feet and something cool and damp is draped over his neck. A couple of times he thinks maybe he's done and takes a deep breath, but then the sobs build again, and he's back at it.

Finally, it's over. He feels exhausted, but his control is back. Something is pressed into his hand, and he hears Jeff's voice saying, "Okay, kid, take a drink now." He's still bent over, but he sits up a little and obediently lifts the bottle to his lips. He chokes when the cool liquid runs over his tongue.

Chris is there, too, and he laughs a little. "He was expecting bourbon."

Jeff's hand stops rubbing his back and starts patting a little. "Let's take a little break from that, kid. You can only put things off for so long." He guides Dan's hand so the bottle comes to his mouth again, and Dan obediently takes another sip. Now that he knows what's coming, the water is welcome. He reaches one hand up and finds the handkerchief that someone had soaked and put on his neck, and he pulls it around to wash over his face. The cloth isn't cool anymore, but it's still better than nothing. When he's done he just holds it in his hand, but Jeff gently takes it and the bottle from him, pours some more water on and wrings it out, then gives it back to him. This time it *is* cool on his face, and he almost starts crying again in gratitude.

The three of them sit there like that for a while, and then Dan feels a little better and sits up straight, but Jeff keeps his arm around Dan's shoulders, and Chris is still a solid presence on the other side. After another little while, Dan recovers enough to be embarrassed.

"Shit, guys, I'm sorry—" he starts, but he doesn't get any further.

"Shut up, Danny."

"No, but...."

"Danny, I'm serious, I don't want to hear it." Chris's voice is firm, but he's got tears in his eyes. "Justin was my best friend, and you and him were great together. You melting down a little? That's the absolute *least* that his memory deserves."

Dan hadn't really thought of things from that perspective. But then he still shouldn't have dragged Jeff into it. He turns to Jeff's side, opens his mouth to apologize, and Jeff hold up a hand to cut him off. "I consider the mac and cheese to be adequate payment for my part here." He smiles and runs his hand along Dan's shoulder to grip his neck, and shakes him a little.

Dan manages a smile and a nod. His composure has returned just in time, apparently, because the funeral director pokes his head out the back door and looks like he has something to say. Chris goes and talks to him quietly, and then comes back to crouch down next to Dan.

"Danny, they want to close up for the night and put the coffin away. If you want to see him, now would be a good time." Dan looks up at him shakily, and Chris says, "But it doesn't have to be now. They've got a schedule, but we can change things however we need to, if you aren't up for it yet."

Dan considers it. He's tired, but he also feels cleansed somehow, as if the crying had washed away some of the crap that was getting in the way of his feelings. It actually seems like a pretty good time to say goodbye. He stands up and tries to straighten his suit. "No, I'm good. I should do it now."

Chris and Jeff both look a bit doubtful, but Dan heads for the door, and they follow. He works his way through the back hall and pauses outside the room where Justin is. Jeff and Chris come up behind him, and the funeral director approaches. "Mr. and Mrs. Archer have already gone home for the evening, so please take your time."

Dan nods, and then steps into the room. He hears the soft sound of the doors sliding closed behind him.

He looks around. This is the room they displayed most of the memorabilia in. There are photos of Justin at all different ages on a variety of horses, and Dan traces his fingers over the image of Justin and Willow working in the dressage ring at the barn. Tatiana was right; even just during a regular work out, Justin looked happy. He looked like he was doing what he was meant to do. Dan looks at some of the other photos, and is surprised by how many of them he sees himself in. There's one he's never seen before, although he remembers the day. They'd been at a friend's summer cottage with the Fosters. Chris had gone back into town for work, but Dan and Justin had stayed behind and had been swimming and boating all day. The picture was taken just as the sun was going down, with Dan sitting on the ground by the lake, half-reclined against a huge driftwood log, and Justin leaning back against his chest, Dan's hand playing with Justin's hair, his other hand laced with Justin's. They're both facing the sunset, and their faces glow with reflected light. Justin is looking out at the lake, but Dan is looking down at Justin, and the love in his eyes is clear. Dan wonders who took the photo, and why whoever it was had never given him a copy. He also wonders why Justin's parents would have Dan call himself Justin's friend at the same time that they're displaying a photograph that shows so clearly how much more he was.

But all of this is just a distraction from the main event. Dan's eyes are drawn to the coffin in the corner. He knows he needs to do it soon. His crying fit might have cleaned him out temporarily, but he can feel it all building up again, and he wants to be as pure as he can be for Justin. He takes a deep breath and crosses the room.

He feels the breath go out of him a little when he looks into the casket. Justin looks more alive now than he has for the past year, and it's enough that Dan has to quickly quell the tiny, irrational hope that somehow his miracle has occurred. Once Dan looks a little closer, it's clear that the makeup hasn't been enough to give more than a thin illusion of life. Justin is gone. Dan thinks about touching him, but decides not to. He touched Justin all the time in the hospital, always hoping for some reaction, never getting one. At least there, Justin's skin had been warm. Dan doesn't want his last contact with this vibrant, hot-blooded man to be the chill of a funeral parlor and the waxy feel of mortuary cosmetics. Dan takes one last look at Justin's body, and steps away. He doesn't need to say goodbye to that; it's not Justin.

He doesn't leave, though. Instead he walks back to the photograph from the lake, and reaches out to touch it instead. He doesn't have any words, but he feels all the love in his heart and tries to pour it out through his fingertips, send it along through the photograph to wherever Justin is now. He's crying again, but he knows it's okay, knows that he's not going to lose control. He smiles a little, too, thinking of that day and of all the other beautiful days they'd shared. There should have been more, but he's glad he had as many as he did, and he knows he's found an answer to the question he'd had at Monty's stall the other night. Yes, it's worth it. The pain of sorrow is terrible and hard to bear, but the joy of love makes it worthwhile. Dan will never be sorry for having known and loved Justin, even though that love was taken from him far too soon.

He wipes his tears away and takes a moment to collect himself. Then he picks up the photograph in its cheap wooden frame. He walks over to the doors and slides one open, stepping outside where he's not surprised to find Chris and Jeff hovering. They're watching him closely, and Dan manages a smile.

Jeff walks up beside him. "You all right, kid?"

Dan turns to him and smiles a little. "You need to find another nickname." Jeff gives him a blank look, and Dan smiles a little more. "Evan is 'kid'. You can find something else for me, and you can call me Dan until you do." Then he turns to Chris. "I don't know whose this is"— he holds the photograph up—"but I'm taking it." Chris just nods with a half smile. Dan looks through the glass front doors. "It's almost a full moon, lots of light—you guys feel like going for a ride?"

Jeff looks at him from under raised eyebrows. "You're sure you're all right?"

Dan's smile is a little fragile, but it holds. "Nope, I'm pretty fucked up. But I don't think going for a ride is going to make it worse." He turns and looks at Chris. "You in?" Chris nods wordlessly, looking amused, and Dan's eyes shift back to Jeff. "If you're feeling your age and need to get a good-night's sleep, we understand. Really. I'm sure Chris and I will be like that in another ten or fifteen years. It's fine."

Jeff's grin is growing. "You give me that speech, and I can't call you 'kid'?" He shakes his head. "All right, *Dan*, let's go. Let's ride."

They head out into the parking lot, and Jeff grabs his overnight bag from his rental car before all three pile into Chris's truck. The moon is bright and the air is warm, and they drive with the windows down. It's not perfect, but it's good, and that's all Dan needs for now.

chapter 16

JEFF looks a little surprised when Chris doesn't turn the truck off at the farm. Dan hops out and then turns to Jeff. "I'm just going in to change— do you want to get changed here?" Jeff looks back at Dan blankly. "Oh, Chris is going over to his parents' place to get the horses." Dan grins. "You were gonna let us risk the eventers? Nah, the Fosters keep Quarter Horses—way better for this sort of thing."

Jeff nods, looking a little relieved to hear that Evan's horses aren't going to be used. "Yeah, if you don't mind. I've got jeans in my bag…."

Dan's already half way to the barn door. "Yup, that's good."

Chris pulls out, then stops and calls back—"Jeff, you do want a saddle?"

Jeff looks a little unsure. Dan grins, and softly says, "It's okay, Jeff, as you get older your legs just lose a bit of their strength, and your balance—"

"Whatever you guys are doing is fine!" Jeff calls over Dan's needling. Chris waves an acknowledgment and pulls away.

"What is this, then, punishment for the 'kid' thing?" Jeff asks. He's trying to sound crabby, but mostly he seems relieved that Dan is up to joking.

Dan pulls the door to the stairs open and heads up, unlocks the apartment and heads inside. He finds his flask as he shrugs out of his suit jacket, and considers it briefly before setting it down. He expects he'll come back to it later, but he just doesn't need it right now. He finds the original bottle and waves it questioningly at Jeff, but he shakes his head. Dan feels a bit awkward. He's not normally too concerned about nudity taboos, but after the scene last night, he supposes he should make it clear that he's not planning a seduction. He loiters around a bit, feeling like an idiot. "I'm just heading in there," he indicates the bedroom, "you can change out here or in the bathroom, or you can wait 'til I'm done. Chris's quick, but he'll have to get changed and get the horses and ride them over, so there's no real rush."

Jeff nods and starts rummaging through his bag as Dan leaves the room. Dan strips out of his suit pants and hangs them with the jacket on the door. Once he's changed, he'll put them in the bathroom. Hopefully the steam from the shower will take out the worst of the wrinkles, because he's got to wear it again for the funeral. He's got an extra dress shirt, though, so he throws the one he was wearing in the laundry hamper and pulls on jeans and a T-shirt, then a hoodie. Then he feels a bit awkward again. Is Jeff changing in the living room? Will it be weird if Dan walks out and finds him half-dressed? He paces around a little, feeling oddly like a prisoner in his own bedroom. Then he hears the TV turn on and takes it as a signal. Surely nobody goes to a guy's house and gets half-undressed and then starts watching TV before getting dressed again. Or at least surely Jeff doesn't do that. Still, Dan is careful to make a little noise as he opens his door, and he walks straight to the bathroom with his suit without looking into the main room.

When he comes back out, Jeff is talking quietly into his phone, fully dressed in jeans and his dress shirt, untucked. Checking in with Evan, Dan is sure. He knows he has no right to feel jealous, but he lets himself go with it a little anyway. He doesn't want to wreck his fragile good mood, though, so he tries to catch it before it goes too far. He reminds himself of how generous and kind Evan is. When that doesn't work, he reminds himself that for tonight at least, Dan has Jeff and all Evan has is a phone call. That does the trick, and he sits down on the couch with a much sunnier frame of mind.

Jeff clicks his phone shut and sits down at the other end of the couch. "Evan's jealous," Jeff says, and it mirrors Dan's thoughts so perfectly that he swivels his head to stare at Jeff. "He says we need to get some Quarter Horses for California so he can screw around at night too."

Dan doesn't make the catty comment, doesn't say that Evan seems to manage to screw around at night just fine without horses, but he smirks a little, and Jeff sees him. Jeff smirks a little, too, but he says, "Careful, now, boy."

Dan looks Jeff up and down. "'Boy'? Is that what you've come up with? I'm really not sure you can carry that off."

Jeff laughs out loud. "No, I'm not sure, either, but I thought I'd give it a try." They're both smiling at each other, and it feels so good, so natural, and all Dan wants to do is crawl down to the other end of the couch and bend Jeff's head back and kiss him, line up their bodies and grind in, make him groan…. Jeff feels it, too, Dan can tell, and the air in the room is crackling. They both gradually lose their smiles but keep staring until the only decision left to be made is who's going to break first, who's going to make the first move, and Dan's pretty sure it's going to be him because he doesn't think he can stand it for another second. They both jump when Chris's voice calls up from the bottom of the stairs.

"Guys, you ready? The cavalry is here!"

Jeff's eyes widen a little, and he's up off the couch in a flash. He calls, "We'll be right down," and the words are fine but his voice is a little high and strained. He shakes his head. "Jesus, Dan, do you bathe in fucking *pheromones* or something?"

Dan stands up, too, just as freaked out. He's not going to do this, not going to commemorate Justin's life by fucking some other guy. "Trust me, man, it's not just you." He looks around a little wildly, and then snaps back to the present. "Okay, horses and Chris, downstairs."

Jeff nods, and on his way out the door he grabs his overnight bag, leaving it at the bottom of the stairs. It feels like Jeff is making sure he can escape from Dan's lair, and Dan almost laughs. Then he remembers how close he'd just come to making a huge mistake and decides that caution is probably not a bad idea.

They go outside and Chris is still on horseback, holding the reins of one other horse and a lead rope attached to the halter of the third. He shrugs a bridle off his shoulder and passes it to Dan, who takes it over to the unbridled horse. Chris hands the reins of the other horse to Jeff. "That's Ranger. He's a good old guy, nothing too fancy—he'll be an angel as long as you don't try to take him away from the other horses." Jeff nods and looks like he's trying to remember how to get on a horse bareback.

Dan has already slipped the bridle onto Smokey, and he looks over at Jeff. He hands Smokey's reins up to Chris and walks over next to Ranger, cups his hands to give Jeff a leg up. Jeff hesitates, but then rests his knee in Dan's hands as Dan gives the traditional one, two, three bounces, and then Jeff is up and finding his balance. He grins a little. "Damn, it's been a long time since I rode bareback." Chris raises an eyebrow but doesn't comment, and Dan just shakes his head.

Dan heads over to his own horse and hauls himself onto his back. Dan's been riding Smokey since he came to Kentucky, and he's got the scrubby little trail horse as finely tuned as any of the well-bred eventers. He may not have the same natural ability, but he's got a damn fine attitude, and Dan's really enjoyed working with him. He's going to be sorry to leave him behind.

They head out of the yard toward the back of the farm. The moon is still bright, but the riders give their horses lots of rein anyway, trusting the horses' night vision more than their own. They just walk for a while, but the horses are feeling good and want to run, and none of the humans seem to object. They come out into an open field with a wide band mowed along the side, and they all move to canter almost side by side.

Dan loves riding at night. He wishes it was a bit darker, but he just closes his eyes and gets the same effect. Without vision to get in the way, and with his sense of hearing compromised by the wind whistling by, he relies almost entirely on feeling the horse, sensing Smokey's movements before he even makes them. He also has the opportunity to focus on his own body, finding his perfect balance and degree of contact with the horse. Justin used to say that Dan was a good lover because he was so used to being in tune with another body. It sounded uncomfortably bestial to Dan, but Justin seemed to think it made sense, and Dan didn't really worry about it.

Dan feels Smokey's weight shift a little before they actually start slowing down, and he reluctantly opens his eyes. They're at the bottom of the big hill, and Chris is looking over at him questioningly. Dan understands the look. The top of this hill was a favorite spot of the three of them, and it might be a bit weird to take someone else up. But it doesn't feel weird, really. Dan thinks that he might avoid the spot if it was just him and Chris, because Justin's absence would be so obvious, and he might avoid it if the third was someone else, but with Jeff it feels okay. Jeff takes away the emptiness without trying to take Justin's place, and Dan's fine with it. He shrugs, sending the question back to Chris, and Chris answers by steering his horse up the path.

It's single file most of the way, with the horses picking their way over roots and rocks and twists in the path, but it opens up near the top, as the trees fade away and the hill opens into a broad crown, sloping gradually up to a peak at the far end. Dan and Chris put their horses into a gallop as soon as they're out of the undergrowth, and they don't pull up until they're at the very top. Jeff joins them a little late, having understandably been a bit more cautious on the unfamiliar ground.

They're up high, and they can see the lights of Louisville sparkling. If they turn away from the city's glow, they can see the stars and the moonlight shining down on miles of farmland and forest. Dan sighs. It's not just Smokey that he's going to miss. He thought that all of his ties to

Kentucky were to Justin, but it turns out that he's a bit more widely invested than he'd thought.

Jeff speaks quietly. "It's beautiful up here. This is still the Archer property?"

Dan nods and points to the trees on the far side of the hill. "The property line is in there somewhere."

Jeff nods. "So what are they going to do with this when the subdivision gets built? I mean, they aren't going to build on a hill this steep, right?"

Chris shakes his head. "Nah, they're in talks with the city. It's probably going to get made into a municipal park."

Dan hadn't known that, but he's glad to hear it. It's nice to think that a little bit of Justin's land won't be lost. Nice to think of future generations of brown-eyed boys scrambling up the hill, laughing with their friends, and then maybe growing up a little and coming up here and making love under the stars. And… he's crying again. He swears softly and reaches up to scrub at his eyes with his sleeve.

Chris shakes his head. "Jesus, Dan, are you drinking lots of water? 'Cause I'd be worried about dehydration if I was you."

That makes Dan laugh, and he stops crying about the same time he tells Chris to go fuck himself.

They stay up on the hill a little longer, enjoying the view and each other's company. Just as Dan had thought, Jeff isn't intrusive; he's just a comforting presence. They head back down when the horses start getting restless, and the ride back to the barn is even quieter than the ride out, but it just feels peaceful, not sad. They pull up in the yard at Dan's, and Jeff looks over at Chris.

"Are you driving back into town tonight?" Chris nods, and Jeff continues. "Do you think I could catch a lift in with you?" Chris nods again, but he cuts his eyes over to Dan.

"You gonna be okay on your own tonight, Danielle? I can stay if you want, and Jeff can take the truck."

"Okay, I'm not actually a little girl. I'll be fine." He swings off Smokey and gives the horse a grateful pat before he slips the bridle off and puts the halter and lead rope back on. He hands the bridle and the end of the lead rope to Chris and then goes inside and grabs Jeff's bag. He walks over to Ranger on the far side, the side Chris can't see, and as he hands the bag up he grips Jeff's calf. It's not sexual, but it's a message, and Dan hopes Jeff understands it. "I really need to thank you, Jeff. I mean… for a lot of stuff. I've been a bit of a mess, and you've been putting up with way more than you should have had to." He releases his grip and shrugs, feeling a little foolish. "I just… wanted you to know that I appreciate it."

Jeff smiles and nudges Dan in the chest with his knee. "It's no problem, k—" He catches himself. "—Dan."

Dan smiles. "Gave up on 'boy', then, did you?"

Jeff shakes his head ruefully. "It seemed a little dangerous." Their eyes meet, and suddenly it's all back again, as strong as it was on the couch earlier, both of their eyes flaring wide in recognition and apprehension. Dan knows that if Chris wasn't there he and Jeff would be going upstairs together, groping and undressing each other in the stairwell, probably not even making it all the way to the bedroom…. But Chris is there, and Jeff's horse shifts a little in response to the tension in the air and in Jeff's body, and they both manage to snap out of it. "Shit," Jeff breathes, and Dan backs away.

Chris gives him a look like he knows something happened but didn't quite follow what it was, and then he's riding off with Jeff, and Dan is alone and reeling.

He heads up the stairs, peels his clothes off, and climbs into the shower. He needs to get cleaned up, likes to shower before bed, but he's not fooling himself. He was hard before he undressed, and it's only a minute or two of work before he's groaning and spurting his release into the warm water. He leans his head against the cold tiles and tries not to think about the face that he'd seen as he came. He resolves that he's not going to feel guilty about it. It was so much better than the trouble he'd almost gotten himself into that night.

He climbs out of the shower and pulls on a pair of sweatpants before collapsing on his bed. It's been a long day, and when he wakes up he'll be facing Justin's funeral. He reaches his hand over and feels the other pillow, thinks of the way Justin would always sleep on his side facing Dan, how Dan would wake up and know that Justin was watching him, just willing him to wake up so they could make love, or even just so they could talk. Dan remembers being a little crabby about it, remembers propping an extra pillow up on end between them so he wouldn't be able to feel Justin's eyes trying to wake him. Tonight is different, though, and Dan calls up his memories of Justin lying there and staring at him, recalls the love that was in his gaze, and he uses the power of that remembered look to soothe himself down into a deep sleep.

DAN wakes to the buzz of his alarm. He'd told Robyn that he would take the morning feeding and clean the stalls. She's been working overtime to cover for Dan *and* the Archers, and she deserves a break. He stumbles out to the kitchen, puts the coffee on, and then stares at the wall while it brews. His eyes eventually move to the couch, and he thinks of Jeff the night before, the pull between them… and then he jerks his mind back abruptly. He is not going to start the day of Justin's funeral thinking about another man. He goes into the bedroom and trades his sweatpants for the jeans he'd worn the night before, then finds a not-too-dirty sweatshirt and some clean socks. The phone rings as he's heading back to the kitchen, and he picks it up without checking the caller ID. "Hello."

"Dan? Hey, it's Robyn. I just wanted to check that you're okay to do the horses."

"Yeah, I said I would. God, I'm not that much of a flake. Go back to sleep."

"You're sure, Danny? Seriously, it's not a big deal."

Dan puts the phone next to the coffee pot, waits for it to gurgle, then brings the phone back to his ear. "Hear that? The coffee is almost done. Hear this?" He grabs one of his boots and clomps it on the floor. "Boots going on. And the next sound you hear will be the dial tone, 'cause I'm hanging up. Okay?"

"Yeah, okay."

Dan hangs up the phone, pulls his boots on and pours the coffee into a travel mug. As soon as his hand touches the barn door the horses start rumbling, weaving back and forth in their stalls and tossing their heads. "You guys are such fakers." Dan tells the barn in general. "Acting like you're starving to death." He wheels the hay cart out and starts at the far end, tossing a few flakes into each stall, offering each horse some friendly words. After the hay, comes the sweet feed, the stuff the horses are *really* after. The walls of the stalls flip up in little portals right above the food buckets, so Dan is able to give each horse its proper amount without going into the stalls, and it doesn't take long to zip down the aisle.

Once the horses are fed, the excited rumblings are replaced by peaceful chomping sounds. The half-hour or so that it takes them to finish their breakfast is usually downtime for the person looking after them. Supplies can be checked and replenished. The day's riding can be planned, but there's nothing directly horse-related to be done. When Dan and Justin were on morning-feed duty, this became their time to make out. Not trying to get anywhere, no big sex scene in mind, just standing up against the wall, leaning into each other, relearning the feel of the other's body, the taste of each other's mouths. They'd take breaks to talk and laugh, and Dan used to like to nuzzle in to the crook of Justin's neck and just breathe him in, the faint scent of his skin somehow more powerful than the stronger smells of the barn. Sometimes they'd get carried away and things would escalate, change from peaceful and quiet to intense and heated, but mostly they'd just have one last kiss and then separate, getting back to the ordinary world that existed around their little bubble.

Dan isn't sure what he's doing, doesn't know if it's self-indulgent to let himself get sad again. He knows he could put it out of his mind if he really had to. If he wasn't alone, he wouldn't do this. But somehow thinking about it all, sad as it makes him, almost feels good, like pressing a bruise or wiggling a loose tooth. He leans up against the wall, arches his head back into it, and thinks of Justin's face, so close he's blurred, nuzzling and touching, hands roaming everywhere, knowing that Dan's body was his, and that his body was Dan's. They'd almost seemed to melt together sometimes, so tangled up that they couldn't be sure where one began and the other ended.

Dan's crying again, and he thinks of Chris's warning about dehydration and smiles a little. He runs a hand across his neck and down over his chest, slow and sure, just the way Justin would have, but it's not the same. Of course it's not the same, and it's never going to be the same again. He knows he's still good-looking, and recent events with Jeff have made it all too clear that he's still capable of wanting someone, but he's not stupid enough to confuse love and lust. He'd truly loved Justin, and he knows that people are lucky to find that kind of thing once in a lifetime. He really doesn't think he's special enough to be the one to find it twice.

A horse down the aisle kicks his stall door impatiently, and Dan glances at his watch in surprise and then smiles. That's how things usually ended with Justin, too, with one of them unable to ignore the horses any longer. "Back to work, baby," Dan murmurs, and then he pushes off the wall and gets on with his day.

chapter 17

DAN has to hurry to finish the barn work and get himself showered and dressed in time for Chris to pick him up. He'd planned it that way, hoping that the tight schedule would keep him from having time to think about what was about to happen.

His suit isn't exactly crisp after his abuse of it the day before, but the steam from the shower has made it wearable, and Dan isn't too worried. Justin had liked him a little rumpled. He fills his flask and puts it in his suit pocket, then pulls it out and takes a healthy swig, then another. He refills it and puts it back in his pocket and is just heading down the stairs when Chris pulls up.

Chris's eyes are a little red, and Dan is disgusted with himself. He's been so busy with his own grief that he really hasn't been the friend Chris deserves. Justin was part of Chris's life for a long time before Dan had shown up, and Dan's been acting like he's the only person who's lost someone. He's not really sure how to make it better.

"Hey, Chris, how're you doing?" It sounds fake to Dan, and from the look of things, it doesn't sound any better to Chris.

"What?" Chris makes an impatient face, and Dan recognizes the irritability defense. He's been using it a fair bit himself.

"I just meant, you know… you've been really great for all of my shit, and, you know, if you need to… I don't know—" Dan breaks off, then tries again. "You must be feeling terrible, too… obviously." This is getting ugly, and Chris is just staring at him. "I suck at this."

Chris nods. "You really do." He puts the truck in gear and they pull out.

They're on the highway heading for town when before Chris talks again. "How's Jeff?"

Dan frowns. "I dunno. Last I saw of him he was riding Ranger back to your place."

"You haven't heard from him today? I thought you guys were in pretty close contact."

"What are you talking about? You're the one who's calling him up to tell him about macaroni and cheese." Dan knows what Chris is getting at, but he's not sure he wants to acknowledge it.

"Yeah, okay." Chris is good at making his opinion clear without using a lot of words. Dan's never seen him in a courtroom, but he bets he's pretty impressive.

"Chris...."

"He seems like a good guy, Danny. That's all I'm saying."

Dan can't really argue with that. "Well, yeah."

They're pulling off the highway and heading into town now, and Dan is starting to feel a bit shaky. He pulls out his flask for a quick swallow.

Chris glances over. "You'd better not finish that before I get parked."

Dan sloshes it, letting Chris hear how full it still is. Chris is apparently satisfied, and they finish the drive to the church without further conversation. They park, have a drink, and head in. The guy who'd handled them at the funeral home is somehow involved in this stage of the proceedings, too, and he'd asked them to arrive about a half-hour before the service. Chris and Dan had decided on their own to shorten that to fifteen minutes. There was only so much standing around and thinking about things that either one of them wanted to do.

They're greeted at the front door by the anxious funeral director. He's doing a good job trying to remain pleasant, but Dan can tell he's upset as he charges ahead of them and leads them to a room in the back of the church. Dan glances at Chris, who shrugs back, and whispers, "It's not like Justin's got something else scheduled."

Dan rolls his eyes, and it probably isn't good that they're both snickering a little when they're escorted into the room where Justin's parents are sitting with the pastor, surrounded by all the aunts and uncles. Molly gives them a stern look, but Karl smiles as he stands to introduce them to the pastor.

"Paul, this is Chris, and Dan. They're Justin's friends." Karl seems to realize that the terminology isn't quite adequate to the situation, but for once, Dan kind of likes it. It might be ambiguous, but it eliminates the strange hierarchy of grief that he'd been thinking about, makes it clear that Chris has just as much reason to be sad as he does. Dan may never have another lover like Justin, but Chris will probably never have another friend like him, either.

The pastor nods in a friendly way and then touches Dan's arm. "I couldn't make it to the visitation last night, but I was there in the afternoon, and I saw some of the photographs. You were obviously a very loving couple." Then he turns to Chris. "And I saw a few of you, too, I think… were you the little hellion in the soccer uniform, with the eggs?"

Chris grins. "Justin started that…."

The pastor nods in exaggerated understanding. "Oh, I'm sure he did." Then he smiles a little and gets down to business. He goes over the order of service and what will be expected at various times, and Dan nods when it seems expected, even though he isn't really listening.

He knows Justin grew up coming to this church, at least occasionally, but he hadn't ever been since Dan knew him. And Dan had never really gone to any church at all. It seems like a strange blend, all these practical considerations of who sits where and when, combined with the casual talk of God's love and life everlasting. Dan wonders if God really cares who sits in the first, second, and third rows. He's pretty damn sure Justin doesn't.

He's a bit relieved to hear that there won't be pallbearers, since there are too many stairs in the church. But the rest of it just sort of drones through him, and he doesn't even try to pay attention. If he needs to do something, he's sure he'll be reminded.

Finally, the pastor is done, and the funeral director starts arranging people. He places Dan in line and reaches out to straighten his tie, and Dan just stares at him. He wonders if the guy has a weird perspective on humanity, if he's gotten so used to seeing everyone at their worst that he just thinks that people are permanently weepy and dazed. The order of the lineup is about the same as at the visitation, except that Chris is next to Dan, which makes things infinitely better.

Dan can hear music being played somewhere, slow, dragging organ music that has nothing to do with Justin. The pastor stands by the door as the funeral director herds them all out, and his face is kind. He looks like somebody that Dan could talk to, if he had anything to say.

They file into the sanctuary and everyone turns to stare at them. Karl is right in front of Dan, and he's pretty big, so Dan tries to walk really close to him and scrunch down a little. They get to their seats, and Dan is glad to be in the front row if only because then nobody can see his face.

The casket is there, but Dan doesn't feel any more attachment to it or its contents than he had the night before. If Dan wants a physical memento of Justin's life, he knows he'll be more likely to find it at the barn somewhere. He thinks of the jumps he and Justin had built, the fences they'd repaired, the roof they'd put on the Archer house three summers ago. But all of those things are going to be torn down soon, lost to the developers' bulldozers.

Then Dan thinks of the horses. He thinks of all the hours he and Justin spent with each one, building their muscles with exercise, developing new neural pathways with training, making them into the highly developed athletes they've become. The horses wouldn't be what they are without Justin's sweat and skill and love, and that makes them more a part of Justin than the empty body lying at the front of the church.

And the horses are being sold, just like the farm itself, but they're being sold together, and they're going to a good home. Robyn's going with them, and Dan knows that she'll make sure they're taken care of, but he's not sure that's enough. He and Justin worked together on those horses. They built them from raw materials. The horses are theirs, his and Justin's, and they're Justin's living memorial.

Everyone around him has their heads bowed, and Dan realizes that they've been asked to pray, but he keeps looking straight ahead, staring at the casket. He's never been religious. He's not going to start now, just because it would be comforting. He thinks about the horses, and he smiles a little.

Then the prayer is over, and Chris is standing up and moving to the front of the sanctuary. He takes a minute to collect himself, and then he looks out over the assembly and starts talking. His voice is relaxed and doesn't seem loud, but Dan can feel the words in his bones.

"I was honored when Karl and Molly asked me to speak about Justin, but I was also a bit intimidated. I know how important Justin is to me, but I also know how much he means to so many other people, and I don't know that there are enough words in the world for all that love. But I'll do the best I can, and then at the end there's gonna be some time for you all to come up here and try to fill in the gaps.

"I've never been as involved with horses as Justin was, but I spent enough time around him and his that I learned a lot. And one thing I learned from listening to them is how important it is for a horse to have heart. I've seen Justin and Dan ripping their hair out over a horse that has everything going for him but just doesn't seem to care enough to be the best, and I've seen them both light up when they're riding a horse that doesn't have all the natural gifts of the other, but that has heart enough to try, no matter what.

"And then sometimes, so rarely, they'd come across a horse that had both, a horse that had all the gifts, but also had the heart to make it all work. And I think Justin was the human equivalent of that horse. He was good-looking, smart, athletic… but he also had a huge heart. He lived with intensity and passion, and he got everyone around him caught up his enthusiasm. But he wasn't flaky about it. He wasn't just charisma with no substance. He'd put the work in too. He'd have the big ideas, and then he'd work his ass off to make them into reality. Karl and Molly know about this. They know how driven he was to be the best." Chris pauses and smiles down at Justin's parents, and they nod back up at him before he continues. "People talk about law being a demanding profession, but I know I'd call Justin in the morning when I got to the office, and he'd already have been working for a couple hours, and I'd drop by the barn after work, and he'd still be going strong. He knew what he wanted. He knew how to get there, and he wasn't going to let anything get in the way."

Chris takes a little break, has a sip of water from the glass the pastor had given him. "You guys might remember him applying that philosophy to his personal life too. Do you remember when he and Dan started up?" Chris's eyes are wet as he grins down at Dan's blushing face. "D'ya remember, Danny?" Chris looked back up at the rest of the audience. "They'd gone out, maybe, what? Twice? And Justin said I had to meet him. So we went out for beers, and we were sitting there, and Justin started going on about all these plans he had, all these things they could do together once Dan quit his job and started working with Justin, and how they'd be a great team, and Dan could move in with him, and it'd all be excellent. And Dan was just sitting there staring at him like he was a lunatic. And so was I, 'cause I'd been friends with Justin forever, and I'd never seen him be anything but totally casual about anybody. But he was right, wasn't he, Danny?" Chris is tearing up again, and he takes another sip of water before he almost whispers, "'Sometimes you just know.'"

Chris takes a deep breath before continuing. "And them being such a great team was a big part of what got them to Rolex. Justin had been talking about that damn competition since I can remember, and for him to get to ride there and do well and have Dan, his parents, and all his friends there with him… it was just… golden." Chris pauses again, but this time it's like he's enjoying a happy memory. But then he continues. "And the next year, it all fell apart. But even then… I know people have second-guessed every damn thing about that day, about that jump, but… I really think it was just Justin riding the way that he lived, with effort and commitment and *heart*."

Chris needs another break, but then he looks up and seems to have himself under control. "So, that's how I'm going to remember Justin. That's how I think he'd *want* to be remembered. And now it's your turn—I know Karl and Molly have talked to several of you who would like a chance to speak. I think I'm just going to turn it back over to the pastor to handle that."

Chris comes down from the podium and sits down next to Dan, and Dan reaches his arm out and wraps it around Chris's neck. When Chris's head slouches down toward Dan's shoulder, he bends his arm at the elbow so his hand can come up and rest on Chris's head. They're both crying, but they're okay.

Nobody really wants to follow Chris, but eventually a few volunteer, and Dan sits and pretends to listen to them, and he's sure they're saying nice things, but he doesn't really pay attention. He's got his own memories of Justin. He doesn't need to hear somebody else's.

Eventually there's a hymn, and a closing prayer, and then the family is being escorted out, returned to the little room in the back of the church. Dan and Chris duck into a side hallway on the way to have a quick drink and try to brace themselves for the next step. Dan thinks they're in trouble when Molly appears, having come back to look for them, but Chris wordlessly extends the flask in her direction, and Molly just nods and takes a deep pull. She shakes her head as if to clear it.

"You doing all right, Molly?" Dan knows he can't make up for neglecting everyone, but at least he can show a little concern.

"As well as can be expected, I guess." Molly shakes her head again, and Dan notices how much she has aged. "I wanted to find you, Dan. We haven't talked much, since… well, maybe we've never really talked all that much. But I wanted to tell you; I wanted to make sure you knew…." She's still holding the flask, and she takes another drink. "Karl and I weren't sure, when you first came around. I mean, it was like Chris said, it just all happened so fast, and Justin was so sure, and he didn't seem to be seeing any possible downside, and we didn't know much about you, and… we just didn't want to see him get hurt."

Dan nods. This is nothing new. But then Molly continues. "But I wanted to make sure that you knew, because I don't know if we ever told you… we're happy that Justin had you in his life. Chris talked about how intense he was, and he's right, that was a great thing, but sometimes…

sometimes it seemed like it was maybe a little much. But with you, he just slowed down a little, and he enjoyed things a little more. He seemed... content. He was still driven in every other way, but he seemed to know he'd found what he needed in you, so he could stop looking; stop working so hard." She smiles, and squeezes Dan's arm gently. "You were really good for him."

Dan doesn't really know what to say. And damn it, he's crying again. But he brings his hand up to hers, and he tells her, "We were good for each other."

She nods. "Yes, I think you were." Then she shakes her head once more, and the softness falls out of her tone. "All right, then. Enough of this hiding. We're supposed to be in the church hall by now. And Karl will think I've gotten lost." She starts of down the hallway, and Dan and Chris follow in her wake.

They make it to the church hall and find people standing around in awkward clusters. Molly finds Karl and loops her hand through his arm, and he smiles bravely at her.

Dan sees Jeff, Evan, and Tatiana near the door, looking like they might be on their way out. He heads over to them, Chris trailing behind, and he tries to smile when he gets there. "Thanks again for coming all this way, guys." He feels a bit awkward, but he continues. "Jeff, again... I'm sorry I've been such a mess, but, seriously, thank you for everything." Jeff shakes his head gently, but Dan isn't quite finished. "And, Evan, uh, I know I've been a total pain about it, and if you've reconsidered I totally understand, but if the job's still open—I'd like to take it." They all turn to him in surprise, even Chris, and Dan shrugs a little. "I decided during the service. I want to stay with the horses... if that's all right?"

Evan's quick to reassure him. "Yeah, man, that's great. I was really not looking forward to having to find someone else. And, you know... Jeff and I have talked a bit, and... we can make things work, in terms of whatever divide you need between your job and your personal life." He grins a little. "Seriously, I can learn boundaries if I concentrate... they just don't seem to come naturally to me."

Dan smiles back. "Yeah, I'm sure it'll be fine. I was thinking I'd start setting up the horse transportation now, and maybe aim at getting them out there in about two weeks. Does that work?"

"Sure, yeah, that's fine. Coordinate through Linda once you've got details and everything, and if you need someone to help figure out estimates or whatever, you've been dealing with Becky, right?"

"Yeah, that's right." Dan is a little suspicious of how smoothly this is coming together. He'd half expected Evan to have changed his mind, decided that he was too high maintenance or something. He still isn't looking Jeff in the eye… better safe than sorry… but things seem to be working out.

Evan says that they have to go to catch their flight back home. He and Jeff shake Dan's hand goodbye, and Tatiana gives him a tentative hug and whispers that she's glad he's coming, and then they're gone. Dan stands there and looks at Chris, and Chris looks back at him. "You're moving to California, Danielle."

Dan nods. "Yeah, I guess I am." Chris seems a little lost for a second, and Dan remembers the feeling of being left behind, remembers how much easier it is to be the one to go than the one to stay. "But not… I mean… you're my best friend, Chris. Pretty much ever, if you don't count Justin. I'm not… trying to get away from you. I'm not really trying to get away from anything. I'm just looking for a change."

Chris nods. "Dude, yeah, it's fine. You've gotta do what's right for you; I get it. It's not like I need your whiny ass around anyway!" Chris grins. "And, hey, holiday spot in California, that could be all right."

"Absolutely. Or, hell, maybe you'll get sick of this place and come out yourself! They must need lawyers out there too. Maybe Evan could hook you up."

Chris just smiles. "You're pretty quick to be offering his services. What was all that about a division between your job and your personal life?"

Dan shrugs. "Well, it's not like you'd need his help anyway. You're Christopher Foster, damn it!"

"That's right. I'm Christopher Foster, and you, Dan… you are moving to California."

Dan smiles. He's feeling the tug of sadness already, but it no longer feels like it's going to drag him under. He knows that he'll never forget Justin, maybe never really get over him, but he feels good about the new start. Justin will always be a part of him, a big, good, important part, but Dan isn't dead, and needs to find a way to move on. He's not sure if California will work for him. Maybe he'll be back sleeping on Chris's couch before the end of the summer, but at least he'll have tried. He knows Justin would have expected him at least to try.

Part 2

chapter 18

DAN is tired. It's his second straight day of driving, and he'd spent a good part of the night before walking the horses to let them stretch out a little and then getting them safely settled in their temporary accommodations. His own rest and comfort came after that. The tractor-trailer that's hauling the horses has two drivers, but Dan's following along in his own truck, so he has to do all the driving himself. He wonders if he's getting old. There was a time when he did this sort of thing for weeks on end, but now he's tired after two days. Either old or soft; he doesn't know which would be worse.

He's more than ready to stop when he sees the stone gates welcoming him to the Kaminski property. He knows he's still got a lot to do once he arrives, but at least the end is in sight.

One of the drivers jumps out of the truck and opens the gate to the barn area, and Dan follows the trailer through before the driver closes the gate behind him. Dan takes a minute to look around. The construction all seems to be done, and the place is looking good. He sees a couple of the horses that had come out with Robyn a few days earlier, and they seem calm and happy in their new home. He hopes he can adjust as well as they have.

The trailer pulls up in front of the barn, and Dan parks a distance away—his truck may not be a prize, but he still doesn't want it kicked by a horse who's crabby after too long on the road. He sees Robyn come out of the barn to greet them, followed by Tatiana, who is dressed for work and looks almost grubby. Dan is really relieved to see that. He's worked for rich people before, and some of them seem to have trouble distinguishing between a trainer and a personal slave. He doesn't mind helping somebody out, but he's happy to see a rider who looks willing to do at least some of the work herself.

He pulls himself out of the truck and is in the middle of a big stretch when Robyn practically tackles him with a hug. "Dan! You're here!" She looks over her shoulder and smiles at Tatiana, and then excitedly whispers to Dan, "I love her, and I love it here, and I love you for making this happen!" Then she grabs his hand and drags him over to Tat.

Dan and the girl exchange a friendly but more subdued greeting, and then all three walk over to where the drivers have got the gate of the trailer open. Dan reaches inside the door and finds the lead ropes he stashed. "How about if I bring them out of the trailer, then you two take them into the barn? You'll have a better idea of where they're going anyway." The girls agree enthusiastically. Seeing them so excited has given Dan a burst of energy and makes it much easier to coax his body back to work.

Bringing a horse out of a trailer safely takes a certain amount of care and finesse, and Dan really doesn't want to have brought these horses three quarters of the way across the continent just to see them injured once they arrive, so he works pretty slowly, and either Robyn or Tat is always ready and waiting for a new charge by the time he's got the horse down the ramp. Monty is the second to last to unload, and Robyn takes him, and then Dan goes back for the final horse, the one that means the most to him.

Unlike the other horses, Smokey isn't used to the fancy shipping boots that he's wearing, and he walks with his knees brought exaggeratedly high, as though he's wading through a swamp. He's steady, though, pricking his ears in interest at the new sights and sounds but not even thinking about spooking or acting up. Tatiana almost claps her hands when she sees him.

"I was so happy when your friend called and asked if we had room for another horse! And he's such a sweetie!" She comes forward eagerly, and Smokey extends his nose in polite greeting.

Dan is almost reluctant to hand the lead rope over to her. He's been working with horses since he was thirteen, but he's never owned one before. When Chris had brought Smokey over on the last day in Kentucky and said he'd heard there might be room in the trailer for one more, Dan hadn't understood at first. He'd thought maybe Evan was taking steps in his ambition to have his own Quarter Horses to "screw around on", but he hadn't seen why he'd need to ship them in from Kentucky... and then Chris had told him, "Happy Birthday," and kept talking over the part where Dan pointed out that his birthday was in December. Chris had said that he'd already called California to make sure there was room and that they didn't mind a scrubby little trail pony mixing with their high class eventers. Chris had covered Smokey's ears for some parts of that speech. The shipping company had also been consulted and the drivers had some papers for Dan to sign, and then Smokey was getting his boots velcroed on and was loaded into the trailer, and Dan was left to say thank you and goodbye to his best friend. Chris hadn't let him say much, just handed him a box of Kleenex and a six-pack of water ("'Cause I can see you tearing up already, you little suck, and you know you're not going to make it out of state without blubbering.")

And now Smokey is about to start living the high life in California, and he seems to be fitting in just fine. He stands politely while Dan takes his shipping boots off and then follows Tatiana into the barn like a big, friendly dog.

The drivers are unloading the equipment that had come with the horses, and Dan helps them and then gives the trailer a quick check to make sure that nothing's left behind. He signs the necessary papers and sees the truck pull away, and then he picks up a couple of saddles from the pile and heads into the barn. It's strange to see the familiar horses in their new surroundings. Dan had arranged for a load of their regular Kentucky hay to come out with them. The California prices were so much higher that the shipping cost wasn't prohibitive, and he wanted to be sure their digestive systems didn't get a shock. And the equipment almost all came with them too. It feels a bit like an elaborate April Fool's joke, where the contents of one barn have been transferred to another. Right down to the staff, Dan thinks, as Robyn comes in from outside with her own armload of equipment.

They all work together to get everything put away and make sure the horses are settled, and then Tatiana reluctantly says she has to go up to the house for dinner. Dan isn't exactly expecting an invitation, but he wouldn't have been shocked to get one. He's a little surprised that neither Jeff nor Evan has been down to say hello yet. But no invitation or explanation is offered, so Dan is left to his own devices.

Robyn says that she's on duty for the evening, with feeding and putting the barn to bed. She's moved into one of the apartments upstairs, so it's quite convenient for her. She shows him the schedule she's set up for the staff to be in charge of the barn chores, subject to his approval, and she seems pleased when he says it looks good and asks her if she'd mind keeping the scheduling as one of her responsibilities.

Dan takes his truck over to the guest house and starts moving boxes and bags inside. He doesn't have much, and he doesn't feel like actually unpacking more than the necessities, so he decides to take the truck into town to pick up some groceries and maybe start scouting around for places that serve takeout. He has a quick shower to wash off the grime of the road, burrows through his bags to find some clean clothes, and then heads out. He stops off at the barn on the way to see if Robyn needs anything, but she doesn't—she says she loves the little town so much that she's happy to run her own errands. Dan wonders how long that will last.

There's no big grocery store in town, but there's a mom-and-pop operation that has everything Dan needs. He eats a lot of frozen meals, so he's gotten used to shopping with a cooler in the truck. He loads the frozen stuff and the milk in there and knows it should be fine for a couple of hours. He asks the man at the cash register about finding somewhere to get takeout meals, and he's told that he can get diner-style food from Carla's, good Italian from Zio's, or bar food from the Fireside Bar and Grill. Dan remembers Evan mentioning Zio's and the Fireside when he'd driven Dan through town on his last visit. A burger sounds good, so he heads for the bar-and-grill.

He'd somehow forgotten that it was Saturday night. It's still fairly early, so the place isn't packed, but Dan gets the feeling that it's going to be. He heads for the bar and a pretty brunette in a tight, low-cut T-shirt comes to take his order. He explains that he just wants takeout and a beer while he waits, and she touches his arm and tells him she can take care of that for him. She asks if he's sure he doesn't want to eat at the bar, and he smiles as he pulls his arm back out of her reach and says takeout is fine. She gets the message and takes his order, and he finds a seat at the end of the bar to drink his beer and watch the crowd.

There's a band warming up, and Dan remembers Evan had said something about him and Jeff coming here a lot for the music. Dan scans the crowd but doesn't see them. There's a huge fireplace along one wall, but it's early June and the air is warm, so the fire isn't lit. But at least Dan knows the place has its name for a reason. Most of the patrons are dressed casually, but it's the kind of casual that probably cost more than Dan's entire wardrobe. Dan isn't really sure about the economic base of this town, but at least some people are obviously doing pretty well. He wonders how many of them keep horses.

He's about half-done with his beer when he hears a familiar laugh from the direction of the door. He turns with a smile and sees Evan holding the door for Jeff and two other people: a tall blond man and a woman with her dark hair pulled back into a bun so tight it seems like it's pulling at her eyes. She looks like a slightly aged ballerina, even in her jeans and suede shirt. Evan is laughing at something the blond man said, and Jeff is watching him in amusement. The humor fades from Jeff's eyes when he looks over at the bar and sees Dan, replaced by a quick flash of something Dan isn't sure about, and then by a careful neutrality.

Jeff touches Evan's arm and nods toward the bar, and Dan has a moment of discomfort. Something seems wrong, or different at least, but he can't quite put his finger on what it is. Evan smiles in Dan's direction, but instead of charging over as Dan had expected, he waves and then turns to the couple they're with, obviously explaining Dan's identity. They look over without much interest, and Evan nods as they head for a table by the window, and then Jeff and Evan come over to the bar.

Dan hops off his stool and shakes Evan's hand, then Jeff's. "So you made it safely? The horses and everything are all fine?" Evan inquires.

Yeah, everything went smoothly. Hey, I haven't had a chance to thank you for finding room for Smokey—I really appreciate it." Dan smiles a little as he thinks of his horse.

Evan smiles back, but Dan doesn't really feel the warmth like he has before. "Well, Jeff said it was pretty standard for a trainer to be given a stall for his own horse, and we've still got lots of room. Don't worry about it."

There's a bit of a pause, and Dan turns to Jeff, who seems to be staring somewhere around Dan's ear. "So it's another couple weeks until your show, right? Is everything going well for that?"

Jeff nods. "Yeah, it's a lot of work, but I'm enjoying it."

Dan sees a flash of movement in his peripheral vision and is relieved to see that the waitress has returned with his meal in a brown paper bag. He's not used to carrying conversations, and he's especially thrown off that he's being forced to do that when he's talking to Jeff and *Evan*. He doesn't know if he's caught them at a bad time, or if this is their attempt to help him with the division between work and play that he'd mentioned to Jeff. Whatever's going on, he's too tired to deal with it. He thanks the bartender for the food and then turns back to Jeff and Evan, waving the bag as his excuse. "Well, I'd better get out of here, let you get back to your friends." They nod and step aside for him to get by. "Thanks again for the stall space, Evan."

"No problem, man. I'll try to get down to the barn in the next couple days, but if you need anything, give Linda a call, all right?"

Dan smiles his understanding and heads out the door. He walks past the bar's window on his way to the truck, and, despite his efforts, his eyes turn to look inside. He sees Evan and Jeff both looking out at him, both with unreadable expressions on their faces. He sketches a half-wave and then keeps walking. He has no idea what has happened to the relaxed, friendly men he'd spent time with on his last visit or during their time in Kentucky. He wonders if they have just gotten tired of worrying about needy little Dan, and are trying to make it clear that their babysitting days are over. That seems fair. Jeff had gone above and beyond any duty he owed to a casual acquaintance, and even Evan had been really generous with his time, especially considering how many other commitments he must have.

Dan is a little insulted that they think that he would keep imposing on them and a little worried that they might be questioning his professionalism, his competence to do his job. He decides that he'll be careful to display his own ability to be businesslike and certainly not show any sign of weakness that would make them feel awkward or suggest that he's looking for their pity.

He tries to ignore his own sense of disappointment. He'd moved out to California for a job and for an opportunity to keep working with the horses that he and Justin had worked so hard on. Spending time with Jeff, or even Evan, would just get in the way of that and would make things more complicated than they need to be. He should be grateful that the other two have apparently made the decision for him so that he won't have to worry about insulting them.

The horses have been without one of their trainers for the last year, and their training had been further disrupted by the drama of the past month. It will be a lot of work for Dan to get them back to where they should be, especially as he'll be working with two new assistant trainers. And he's never been in charge of a barn before. He isn't sure exactly what his duties in the new position will be, but he knows he'll have a lot to learn. He resolves to give the job all of his attention, all of his energy. If he can manage to tire himself out, maybe he'll be able to forget the hole in his life where Justin used to be, and maybe he'll be able to keep Jeff and those few electric moments out of his mind as well. He's not actually confident that this will work, but he knows he has no choice in the matter with Justin, and based on the scene at the bar, he doesn't have a choice with Jeff either. At least this way, he can tell himself that his isolation is all his idea.

chapter 19

WHEN Dan's alarm goes off, it interrupts a good dream. He tries to remember the details as he wakes, but they're already fading into the distance and the harder he chases them the faster they run away. He remembers a mood, mostly, remembers feeling safe and warm and loved. He's heard some people say that they can go back to sleep and pick up their dream where they left off, but he's never been able to do that, and besides, he has work to do, so he gets up.

He has cold cereal for breakfast and pulls on riding clothes. He has to hunt around a bit for his boots, but finally finds them tucked into one of the boxes. He looks around the guest house carefully to be sure he's leaving it in reasonable condition. He's never lived anywhere so nice, never had so much space all to himself, and it still feels like he's just visiting. His whole life out here still feels like he's just visiting.

He heads out of the house, down the short lane and onto the main drive. An unfamiliar dog appears and barks at him a couple times. She looks like a pit bull cross, and Dan is a little cautious, but he crouches down, and she comes over and meets him. She stops barking after that, but she still escorts him to the barn as though she thinks it's her job to keep an eye on him. As if she agrees that he doesn't quite belong.

That feeling continues when he gets to the barn. One of the new hires is there, just finishing the feeding. Dan can't remember the girl's name, and can't get over the feeling that she has more of a right to be there than he does. She seems surprised to see him, which doesn't really help.

"Oh, hi! Mr. Wheeler! I didn't know you'd be here this morning." Once Dan realizes that she's nervous, he feels a bit more comfortable himself. And a quick glance to the schedule Robyn had posted shows that 'Sara' is assigned to this shift, so....

"Sara, right?" She nods, and he smiles. "'Dan' is fine. And sorry to interrupt—it can be kind of nice to have the place to yourself, can't it?"

She smiles back. "At least you didn't catch me singing to the horses, or something." She's just fed the last horse, and she frowns. "The last stall—that horse isn't on the list. I gave him a couple flakes of hay, but I didn't know how much feed he'd want."

Dan snorts. "He'd *want* the whole bucket. But he barely needs any at all." Dan feels a little thrill of pride when he says, "He's mine," and the feeling isn't diminished at all when he adds, "He's just a trail horse, not an eventer. He doesn't need too much of the high energy feed." Dan ducks into the tack room and finds a pen, then comes back and adds Smokey's name to the feeding list. He pauses when he looks at the turnout groupings. They've kept the same divisions as they'd used in Kentucky, but Smokey had never been turned out with the Archer horses there. "His name's Smokey—let's turn him out on his own for a couple days, let him get used to the place. Then we'll try to find a group for him to make friends with." Sara nods, and Dan adds a note to the page. "I'm gonna take him out for a ride now... go up and check out the cross-country course. Can you leave Monty in? I'll ride him when I get back, and he's a pain to catch from the paddock."

Sara nods again. She's in that awkward time when the horses are eating and there's nothing else to do with them, and the barn is so newly organized that there are really no other chores. Dan remembers the solution he and Justin had found to fill the time, and wonders idly what Sara would do if he suggested that they make out. Wonders what he would do if she accepted the offer. Instead of finding out, he goes and gets Smokey's tack and grooming kit, and gets to work. The horse hasn't had much chance to get dirty yet, so the grooming consists mostly of Dan running his hands over Smokey's body to check for any hidden injuries or sore spots, without much need for brushing. Then he saddles up and leads Smokey outside, hops on, and heads out along the fenced path that leads to the cross-country course. It's the most convenient route, so Dan doesn't even need to think of it as a sign of weakness that it also manages to avoid taking him along the hillside where he'd gotten the call about Justin.

The dog from earlier meets him part way and continues along with them. She seems well behaved and politely puts her nose up for a sniff when Dan gives Smokey enough rein to put his head down, so, as long as everyone's getting along, Dan doesn't mind the extra company. The three of them head up the hill and through the woods. Dan stops a few times and jumps down to check the footing and construction of the jumps, and is happy to find that everything seems to be in good shape. There's a mulched, groomed track along the outside of a bit of a plateau, so Dan lets Smokey have his head, and they both enjoy the speed and the wind in their faces. The dog gives up trying to follow after only a couple strides, but she seems to guess where they're going and takes a shortcut across the middle of field, and she's sitting and waiting for them when they finish their little circuit.

They all head back to the barn, and the dog accompanies them most of the way before disappearing into the brush around the main house. Dan and Smokey continue on, and when they get to the barn Dan takes Smokey's saddle and bridle off while they're still outside and turns the gelding into one of the empty paddocks. Smokey takes a few trotting steps before deciding that he'd rather explore the taste of the grass than the corners of the field.

Dan brings the saddle and bridle inside, but he stops when he gets to Smokey's stall. All of the eventers have brass name plates on their stalls, their stable names in bold and their registered names underneath. On Smokey's stall, Sara has tacked a piece of cardboard, with "SMOKEY" in bold, and underneath, in smaller print, "Sir Smokes-a-Lot?" Smokey is mostly Quarter Horse, but he's not registered, so he doesn't really have a formal name, but that doesn't mean he should be left out. Dan grins, and when he drops the tack off, he finds a pen and comes back to the stall. He adds "Smokey the Bear?" underneath Sara's suggestion and then returns the pen to the tack room while he collects Monty's equipment.

He spends the rest of the day riding various eventers, getting them used to their new home, making sure they don't have any aches or pains from the travel. He rides Sunshine after Monty, and she seems fine, so when Tatiana wanders down in the early afternoon, he suggests she give the mare a try, and she does. Judging by the look on her face, she's pleased with the experiment, and so is Dan. He wishes Evan had come down with her. He's feeling a little uncomfortable with having so little contact with his employer, and he's not exactly sure what the rules for Tatiana are. She's only fifteen, and Dan knows that the whole barn is there essentially for her enjoyment, but he's not really sure what boundaries, if any, he's expected to enforce. He decides that's probably a question worth contacting Linda about, although he thinks it would probably be best to wait until Monday.

Tat hangs around for the rest of the afternoon, watching Dan work the horses. At first he's a little uncomfortable, thinking about what Evan had said about the girl's crush, but she starts asking questions about what he's doing, and it soon becomes clear that she's genuinely interested in learning more about training the horses. He ends up enjoying the afternoon, starts getting used to *explaining* instead of just *doing*, and a few times he hops off and puts Tatiana on the horse, because there's some things about horses that you have to feel to really understand. Robyn wanders down from the apartment while Tat is riding Kip, trying to feel the different degrees of collection, and she stands beside Dan, leaning on the fence and watching.

"She's going to be pretty good, isn't she?" Robyn asks.

"I guess... if she sticks with it. She's only fifteen, though—next week she could decide she wants to spend all her time playing the flute or something."

"Or chasing boys," Robyn agrees.

Dan grins. "God knows that was a bit of a distraction for me."

Robyn smiles back and looks around. "Jeff and Evan haven't been down?"

"No. I ran into them last night in town, but I haven't seen them since then."

"Huh." Robyn seems a bit surprised. "They were practically living down here the last few days, seeing all the horses arrive, helping them get settled. Maybe they were just keeping an eye on things, and now that you're here they can take a break."

Dan nods. He guesses that's as good an explanation as any, although it doesn't really help him understand the coolness he'd felt the night before. But he's not great at reading people, so maybe he had misinterpreted that. Tat pulls up beside them and starts asking questions, and Dan brings his focus back to the task at hand.

He works until dusk and then goes back to the house and heats up one of the frozen dinners. He eats it while reading one of his business books and then takes a notebook and a beer out onto the porch. He tries to put together a list of questions to ask Evan or Linda or whoever's available. He writes down a list, adds a few notes, and then reads a bit more. It's not exciting, but it's peaceful, and he feels like he's put in a good day's work. Everything still feels a little weird, but he's hopeful that it will get better and seem more natural in time.

He calls Linda the next morning, but only gets her voicemail, and he realizes that he doesn't even have a number to call Evan. He adds that to his list of things to ask about. He doesn't plan to harass the man, but if Tatiana is going to continue spending so much time at the barn, he'd like to at least have an emergency number.

He spends the day working with the horses and the new trainers, and when Tatiana comes home after school, he spends some time with her and Sunshine as well. She's only got one week of school left, so she's buzzing with excitement about all the things she'll do at the barn once she's got more time, and Dan appreciates her enthusiasm. He also appreciates it when she goes home for dinner and gives his ears a break.

Dan goes home for his own dinner and then sets up on the porch again, working out the conditioning schedules for the horses. It's a bit hard to do without knowing what Evan's priorities for the barn are, but he thinks that two calls in one day might be a little much. It's good to stay busy, though. He's not missing Kentucky too much, not missing Justin—at least not when he's not thinking about it.

The sun is just going down when the old Jeep Cherokee pulls into the guest house drive and Evan climbs out. He's wearing business clothes again, and he looks a little rumpled after a long day, but still pretty sharp. When he gets a little closer Dan notices the weary set to his shoulder and the bags under his eyes. It looks like maybe he's had more than one long day. He climbs halfway up the porch steps and smiles at Dan, although it's not one of the full-body smiles that Dan has seen in the past.

"Hey, man," Evan starts. "Sorry I didn't return your call. It was a busy day."

"No, no problem. There's nothing super-urgent, if this isn't a good time…."

"No, Linda told me what you wanted to talk about. You're right. We should get that stuff sorted out. Do you have a little time now?"

Dan nods, and Evan comes the rest of the way up onto the porch and settles into the other chair with a long sigh. Dan raises his half-empty beer bottle. "Want one? Or do you want some coffee or something?"

Evan looks like he's fighting some sort of temptation before he gives in with a sigh. "A beer would be perfect, man. Thanks."

Dan goes to get the beer and then comes back and settles into his chair and pulls out his list of questions. He doesn't know whether he should push Evan to get things resolved quickly so he can go get some rest, or give the poor guy a chance for a little break. Evan takes a long swallow of his beer and then sits forward and says, "Okay, let's get started," and Dan realizes that he was silly to think he'd be the one to determine the pace of the conversation. Evan's a powerful man, and he's not going to let his employee run a meeting.

"Yeah, okay. I think the big thing I need to know is how fast you want the horses turned over. I mean, the basic business is to buy cheap, untrained horses, train them, and sell them as valuable, trained horses. But 'trained' isn't an absolute term. We can sell them half-trained for a bit of a profit and then give our energy to another horse, or we can hold onto them for longer and train them more and sell them for more of a profit. You know—sell more moderately priced horses or fewer expensive horses." Dan glances over and sees that Evan is paying close attention. There's something a bit unsettling about it, as if Evan is actually paying *too* much attention or something. But Dan's always found Evan a little intense, so he just continues. "So I kind of need to know what kind of approach you're looking for. And I need to know how aggressively you want to be marketing things, how much time you want spent on showing and other promotional-type activities compared to active training. Stuff like that."

Evan nods thoughtfully, and they talk business for a half-hour or so. Evan takes off his tie part way in, and when he finishes his beer Dan goes and gets another for each of them. After a while, the conversation peters out, and they're both left sitting and watching the night settle in. It's peaceful, and Dan likes it more than the night before, when he'd done the same thing but been all alone. After a while Evan's eyes begin to drift closed, and Dan finds himself watching the man rather than the night. Dan's always known that Evan is good-looking, and Lord knows his body is a thing of beauty, but his face is so active that Dan's never really had a chance to see it for itself, without the ever-changing expressions. Half-asleep, Evan looks young, and peaceful. The lines in his wide forehead smooth out, but there's one tiny one left, and Dan's fingers want to reach over and smooth it out.

After a few minutes Evan snorts a little, and his eyes open, and Dan quickly looks out at the mountains again, pretends he was unaware of Evan's little nap. Evan takes a minute to collect himself and then rubs the back of his neck and says, "I'd better get home. Is there anything else we need to cover?"

"Uh, just… Tat." Evan raises an eyebrow, and Dan hurries to clarify. "She's great, and she's got a lot of potential as a rider, and I'm really happy to have her as a part of the barn. I'm just wondering how to treat her, I guess. What the priorities are in terms of balancing Tat's enjoyment of the horses with running the place as a business."

"Okay… I think I get what you're saying, but can you give me an example?" Evan's back in business-man mode, but the edge is gone, and it feels like they're colleagues rather than employer and employee.

"Well, I'm assuming that Sunshine isn't for sale right now, since she seems to be the horse Tat's settled on showing. But is she *never* for sale? Right now, Sunshine knows a hell of a lot more than Tat does. If she's only going to be Tat's horse, there's no real reason to put much energy into her training, at least for a while. You know?" Evan nods, so Dan continues. "And Tat's interested in riding more over the summer, which is great. But she really hasn't got the skills yet to be a whole lot of use as a trainer. She could do okay as an exercise rider, though. So if she was just another employee, I'd have her riding the horses up and down hills, stuff like that—stuff that's good for the horses but isn't really going to teach Tat much as a rider. But she's not just another employee, not an employee at all, so maybe I should be focusing on having her do more schooling-type riding, where she'd learn more even though she's not really the best rider for the job, you know?"

Evan smiles a little ruefully. "I hear what you're saying. I…." He leans back a little and now his smile seems a bit sad. "As far as I'm concerned, the whole Kaminski business 'empire' is only useful insofar as it makes Tatiana happy. I mean, I don't need a lot of money, and we're the only ones left in the family… so pretty much everything I'm doing is for Tat, so that when she gets old enough there will still be a business for her to choose to get involved in or to choose to ignore." He plays with his beer bottle a little, peeling the label off thoughtfully. "But, I dunno… it's probably not a good idea for a fifteen-year-old to realize that she has that kind of clout, you know? Seems like it would be hard to grow up normal knowing that a good-sized chunk of the world actually does revolve around you."

Evan pauses, and Dan jumps in. "For what it's worth, man, I think you're doing a great job so far." Evan glances over in surprise, and Dan blushes a little. "I mean, I'm not a psychologist or anything, but… she's a great kid. She's been working really hard at the barn, and Robyn and all the rest of the staff love her. She doesn't seem spoiled at all."

Evan's smile finally has the warmth that Dan remembers. "Thanks, man. That means a lot. She's... she's my most important job, you know? And I really have no idea what I'm doing. Jeff helps...." And then Evan's smile is fading, although Dan isn't sure why. He hopes there isn't trouble between the two, at the same time as a tiny part of his brain jumps to attention at even the hint that Jeff could someday be single again.

Dan squishes that thought down as hard as he can and tries to get back to Evan's conversation, tries to get back to the friendly, relaxed atmosphere of moments ago. "I'm not sure anyone really knows what they're doing. There's lots of kids from parents who should be experts who turn out bad. And like I said... so far, Tatiana seems like she's turning out great."

Evan smiles again, and it's almost at full power. "Yeah, she really is pretty excellent." He pauses for a moment. "So, in terms of the barn—can I ask you to just use your judgment? I'm not trying to unload my responsibilities onto you, but I just don't know if I've got an answer. I want her to be happy, but I know that she won't be happy long-term if she gets everything she wants all the damn time. So—maybe a mix? Have her do some stuff that's good for the barn, but try to work in some stuff like the training that's good for her. Does that make sense?"

Dan nods. It's not crystal clear, but at least it's a general guideline, and at least the issue has been raised.

"And I'll try to check in more regularly, without you having to chase me down. From the sound of things, Tat's looking to spend most of her summer at the barn, so you'll probably be seeing more of her than I do. So... I guess I'll be looking to you for updates on my sister." He smiles a little ruefully and then continues. "And I wanted to thank you for what you've been doing so far. She came home last night just about floating off the ground, totally thrilled with everything you'd been teaching her. And she texted me at work seven times today, babbling about how excellent everything at the barn is... so, whatever you're doing seems great... as long as she doesn't get spoiled."

Dan's a little embarrassed, but Evan is standing up and getting ready to go, so there really isn't a chance to dwell on it.

"Okay, so, thanks for everything. I'll try to drop by the barn and see what's going on, but I'm sure you've got it all under control." He smiles and scratches his stomach a little, and Dan's eyes are caught by a little flash of skin showing when his dress shirt rucks up a little. Dan tears his eyes back to Evan's face, but it's too late; Evan has noticed. The man's smile gets a strange little edge to it that Dan can't decipher, but he doesn't say anything, just sets his empty beer bottle on the table and heads down the stairs. He turns at the bottom and looks back up, and his eyes are a little warmer than they were before, a little more focused. "So, I'll be in touch. Let me know if you need anything."

He turns the Jeep around and heads out, and Dan sits back down on the porch. The meeting had gone well, and Evan had been friendly. So Dan figures he should be happy, should be satisfied that things are going smoothly. And he is, really. He just can't quite shake a little feeling like he's missing something, something that might be important. He tries to let his mind relax, and let it come to him, but all he gets is flashes of Evan's tanned stomach and peaceful sleeping face, mixed in with Jeff's gentle smile and hungry eyes. That's not at all helpful, he decides, and goes to have a shower before bed. When he gets in the shower and finds the same images going through his mind as his hand wanders to his cock, he tries not to worry about it too much. Fantasies are totally natural. He just has to make sure they don't get in the way of reality.

chapter 20

DAN quickly settles into a routine around the farm. He's working a lot, more than he did in Kentucky, even, but it's not like he has anything better to do. He can only ride so many hours in a day before even his work-hardened legs give out, and the barn is well-staffed so he doesn't have to worry about chores. But there's still lots to keep him busy, and most of it takes longer than it should because he's doing it for the first time and figuring it out as he goes.

He and Evan had agreed that the horses should be competing, if only as a way to build up the reputation of the stable. There's no hurry to sell, which is refreshing—Dan doesn't want to see Justin's horses going for a bargain price to someone who might not even appreciate them just because the economy's bad. But they're going to want to start selling eventually, and the Kaminskis are starting a new barn, so they need to get a name for themselves, and competitions are the way to do it. But Dan has never really been in charge of picking the shows before, or registering or arranging transportation or any of the other little details. And he's not really familiar with the California equestrian scene. He thinks about getting in touch with Jeff, but he feels like that would be imposing. Jeff was an incredible help to Dan in Kentucky, and he'll never forget that, never stop being grateful, but Jeff's making it pretty clear that whatever Dan might have thought was happening is not going to carry over to California, and Dan has to respect that. And if there's no personal connection, then there's really no excuse for Dan to expect his boss's boyfriend to help Dan do the job he was hired for. So Dan consults with Michelle, the other assistant trainer, and even with Tatiana, since she's done at least some showing in the region. It's not ideal, but he is doing the best he can.

On the first Saturday morning, a week after he arrived, Dan reaches the barn at his usual time and finds Tatiana already there, helping with the feeding. She beams at him when she sees his surprised look. "It's the start of my summer vacation! So I wanted to come down early and see the horses first thing. I want to spend the whole day here, so I can really understand what happens in the barn. You know, *everything*."

She sounds like she's anticipating some sort of high drama, and Dan hopes she isn't disappointed. "Well, live it up. Your brother isn't going to miss you?" Dan hasn't seen Evan since his visit on Monday night, but he remembers Evan saying that he tried to keep his weekends mostly free for family stuff.

Tatiana just snorts. "He probably won't even notice that I'm gone. He's super busy at work, and then he's over at Jeff's all the time, trying to get ready for his art show, or, you know… whatever." She blushes a little bit, and then brightens. "But that's okay, because I've got twenty-four new friends at the barn!" She cuts her eyes to Dan. "Is it okay that I counted Smokey? I know we don't *own* him, but he's still a friend, right?"

Dan just grins at her. "It's fine that you included Smokey, but I'm a little insulted that you didn't include any of your new *human* friends in the total." He looks over at Robyn, who shakes her head sadly.

Tat's eyes widen. "Oh, of course I count you guys! So… twenty-nine new friends! Who needs a stupid old brother?" She heads off happily to help Robyn take the horses outside, and Dan remembers back to his own teenage years. He figures that the fact that she can chat and joke about her brother probably means that she's actually pretty secure in the relationship, even if Evan does occasionally get preoccupied.

A couple of hours later, Dan's riding Chaucer, and Tat is on Sunshine, and both are working in the dressage ring. He's pretty much on autopilot with Chaucer, just working through transitions and trying to get the horse to pay closer attention to him, so he has some extra attention to spend on giving Tat advice. Between the two horses, though, Dan is pretty focused, and he doesn't notice their audience until Tat does, and waves. Dan looks over to see Jeff and Evan standing by the rail.

Tat trots to the fence and starts raving about Sunshine, and offers to show Jeff what she can do. Jeff nods and stands back to watch, and Dan flashes back to the first day he'd met these three, not that long ago but somehow in a different lifetime. It throws him off a little, thinking about all the changes since then, and he decides that Chaucer's had enough training for the day. Maybe he'll take Monty out. He's challenging enough that he'll keep Dan's mind from wandering.

Dan cools Chaucer down at the far end of the arena while Tatiana shows Sunshine off, and then when Tat pulls her up and starts talking, he takes Chaucer up to the gate, near where the others are standing. He sees a tension between the three of them that he's never noticed before, and just sketches a wave and jumps off to open the gate, hoping to not interrupt. But he's not that lucky.

"Dan!" Tatiana sounds upset. "Dan, Evan and Jeff can stay in the barn today if they want to, right? They wouldn't be in the way?"

Dan doesn't know what's going on. "Uh, I think it'd be fine?"

"See?" Tat spits at her brother. "If you don't want to hang around with me, that's fine. But don't make excuses. I'm not stupid."

Evan tries to sooth her. "Tat, we didn't say we didn't want to spend time with you. We just thought you might want to do it somewhere else. Like shopping, or… or anything, really."

Dan hears the "*anything but this*," and he's almost as confused as Tatiana. But he's quieter about it. She's almost yelling. "Yeah, great! So you know exactly what I want to do, and then you say you don't want to do it, 'cause you know I'll stay, and then you can have the day to yourselves. Nice." She shakes her head. "You know what? Fine. Go ahead. I've got stuff to do here, and I've got twenty-nine new friends to do it with."

There's only one reason Dan can think of for Jeff and Evan not wanting to be in the barn. Robyn had said that they spent a lot of time there while the new horses had arrived, but this is the first time all week that they've been down. The first time since Dan got here. He doesn't really know what he's done to make them feel that level of distaste for him, and he's not really sure he cares. He knows he was going to be businesslike, wasn't going to try to drag them back into his personal drama, and if they think he's that weak, he guesses that's their problem. He's almost to the barn now, and he can't hear what they're saying. He thinks about calling back to them, saying that he was going to take the rest of the day off, but that might make things more awkward, so he keeps going. Let them sort out their own issues. He's just going to do his damn job.

He leads Chaucer down the aisle and the sign on Smokey's stall catches his eye. People have been adding names to it as they think of them: there's "Smoke on the Water," "On Top of Old Smokey," and "Smokin' Hot." There's also "Smoke Frog," which Dan doesn't really get.

He hopes it's not some California drug reference that the guardian of a fifteen-year-old might not appreciate. But in general, the new names calm him down a little. At least some people have welcomed him and his horse into the barn and are making them feel at home.

He pulls Chaucer's tack off and runs a hand down his chest to check for heat. The barn's hot-walker is still on order, one of the few things that isn't complete yet, but it's a warm day out with hardly any breeze, and Chaucer isn't really hot, just warm, so he should be okay out in the paddock. Dan thinks about taking him outside. He's not sure whether the Fighting Kaminskis are still at the dressage arena or if they might have moved. He sneaks up to the door a little and tries to peer out, and jerks his head back quickly when he sees all three of them on their way in, not ten feet away. He scurries back to Chaucer and grabs the lead rope, busying himself with putting it on. He's sure that Jeff at least saw him sneaking— not really the way to impress someone with your "strictly business" attitude. Damn. He turns Chaucer around and heads for the doorway, and the three visitors stand to the side for him to pass. Jeff isn't looking at Dan, as usual, but he's pretty sure he can see a little snicker twisting the corners of his mouth.

Chaucer gives a celebratory buck when he's turned out with his friends, and Smokey trots over to greet him. The little cow horse has made friends with the big geldings easily, and seems to have appointed himself the social convener for the group. Tatiana thinks it's adorable, and Dan thinks it's nice that the little guy has got something to do. And nice that he, at least, is able to get along with everybody.

He heads back to the barn with some reluctance, not wanting to deal with the tension in general or Jeff's opinion specifically, but when he gets there things seem to have calmed down. Tat is showing Evan how to groom Sunshine, and Jeff is looking over some papers in the doorway to the tack room. It seems idyllic, but Dan feels a lurch in his stomach when he recognizes the papers. They're his rough notes for the competitions, and he'd had them at the barn because he was working on them and trying to get people's advice, not because he thought he was done, not because he'd wanted anyone to judge them.

Jeff looks up and sees him staring at the sheets, and says, "I saw these on the desk, thought I'd have a look…." He trails off as he sees Dan's frozen expression, and slowly lowers the sheets. "I can put them back if I'm stepping on your toes or something."

"No, it's fine." Dan tries to smile in a professional manner. "They're just really rough, still. I mean, we're coming into the season halfway through…." Evan has looked up, apparently monitoring the conversation, and Dan speaks to him a little. "We talked about that, remember? Said this year we could just feel out the competitions. We're not going to be winning any championships or anything starting this late, so it would just make sense to poke around a bit, see what's out there?" Dan can see the confusion on Evan's face and knows that it's more in reaction to his tone than to his words. Fuck! Professionals do not act like this. Professionals are not insecure. They're confident, and they don't freak out because somebody is looking at a few sheets of paper!

Evan shrugs calmly. "Yeah, man, I remember that. It's fine." He turns to Jeff. "Right, Jeff?"

"Yeah, no problem." He holds the papers out to Dan. "I was just going to say that it looks good. Looks like you've hit all the big competitions and found a couple interesting smaller ones."

Dan nods, but doesn't go any closer to pick up the sheets of paper. "Yeah, okay, thanks." He looks at the three of them, so peaceful before he'd arrived, and knows that he'll just ruin things if he stays. He can already see Evan watching Jeff closely, as if he's waiting for a sign that Dan is dangerously deranged rather than just painfully awkward. "So, you guys are fine here, right? I was thinking I'd go have some lunch. If that's okay."

Tat looks disappointed. "Already? It's only eleven! I thought we were going to do jumping. You said I could ride Kip." She catches herself, and Dan can feel her trying to sound more mature, less spoiled. "I mean, are you coming back after lunch? We could do it then, if that's better for you."

Dan doesn't really feel like spending the rest of the afternoon confirming his employer's low opinion of him. But he also doesn't want to look like he's ducking out of work, or breaking a promise to Tatiana. "Well, if Jeff's staying, you could ride Kip for him. I'm sure he'd have more to say about the riding side of things than I do. No point in having two teachers for one lesson, right?"

Evan breaks in. "Dan's not your personal slave, Tat. He's allowed to have time off." He turns to Dan. "She's been going on about what you're doing every day this week. Have you had a day off since you got here?"

Dan shrugs. "I like the horses, so I don't really need time off. I'd just sit at the house and wish I was at the barn." He catches himself. "But today I've got stuff to do. Laundry, and... house... stuff." He struggles a little. "Groceries? And... errands." He's done.

Evan gives him an odd look. "Yeah. Uh, are you getting out at all? You know, having fun?"

That's none of Evan's business, but Dan isn't quite sure of the polite way to say so. "I'm fine, thanks." He turns to Jeff. "Are you okay working with Tat this afternoon?" Jeff nods, but as usual he's looking somewhere over Dan's shoulder. "And, Tat, you can ride with Jeff, right? You've got all summer to work with me." He smiles at her, and after a momentary pout she smiles back.

"Can we go to the cross-country course?" She bargains. "Tomorrow, maybe?"

Dan grins at her and nods. "Yeah, that sounds fair. First thing, before it gets too hot?" She smiles back, and Dan heads out of the barn, on his way back to the guest house. He's halfway to the gate when he hears a voice calling out from behind him, and when he turns he sees Jeff jogging after him. Evan is standing in the doorway of the barn, watching them but not coming any closer. Dan stops. Did he forget something? He turns and waits for Jeff to catch up.

"Hey, k—" Jeff catches himself. "Dan. Can I just.... Can we just talk for a minute?" And then he looks Dan in the eye. There's no heat, but there is warmth, and Dan finds himself relaxing a little.

"Yeah, sure. What's up?" Jeff seems a little uneasy, and Dan's in the unusual position of trying to help Jeff relax. Unfortunately, he really has no idea how to go about doing that. Well, he has lots of ideas, but he doesn't think any of them are really appropriate for the current situation.

Jeff sighs. "Dan, look... I just wanted to let you know... I mean...." He sighs, and then smiles ruefully. "Sorry. I just wanted to apologize—for not being a better friend since you got out here."

Dan frowns. "Jeff, you've got nothing to apologize for. I mean... you were great in Kentucky, but honestly, man... we barely know each other. I'm not expecting you to be my best friend or something." Dan remembers Evan's question in the barn, asking if he'd been getting out. "And I'm not totally pathetic. I *can* make my own friends. I've only been here for a week, and I've been busy." Dan puts as much warmth as he can into his smile. "Seriously, man, it's not your job to baby-sit me, and I never expected you to do it."

"Dan, come on. It's not babysitting. I enjoyed spending time with you in Kentucky. I mean, it wasn't the best circumstance, but I enjoyed getting to know you." Jeff frowns. "But things got a bit complicated out here. You know?"

"Yeah, man, sure. I mean, this is your real life." Dan wonders whether he's really getting what Jeff's saying. It seems like there's more to it, but Jeff isn't really being clear, and Dan doesn't want to make things more awkward than they already are, so he doesn't want to ask a lot of questions. "It's fine, seriously. I came here for the job, for the horses, not…. I wasn't expecting anything." He glances back over at the barn, sees Evan still in the doorway, looking down at the ground and scuffling his feet. "Is Evan afraid I'm going to make a nuisance of myself? Is he… I'm doing the best job I can, and I think I'm learning about the business stuff. Is he thinking he should have hired someone else?" Now that the idea's in his head, Dan wonders if it makes the most sense. Evan's a nice guy, he wouldn't want to fire someone, but he'd probably been expecting someone who could be a little more self-starting, and would know more about running a barn.

Jeff jumps in. "No, Dan, not at all! Seriously, he's thrilled with how much Tat's enjoying herself, and he said you seemed to have a good grasp on how to make things work, business-wise. There's no problem with your work at all." Jeff looks at Dan again, and his eyes seem to be sincere. "We're just… he and I are working some things out between us, and we're just trying to make sure that nothing spills out of that. You know?"

"Uh, no, not really… but look, man, I probably don't have to, right?" Dan knows that complicated emotional situations are not his strong suit, and he'd rather avoid them if he can. "I mean, your business is your business. I don't need to know everything."

Jeff sighs. "No, you're right. There's no reason to go dragging you into things."

That doesn't sound quite right. "I don't mean I'm not happy to help…. I mean, I owe both of you. A lot. So if you need something, I'm there—no problems, no questions. I just meant… if you don't want to talk about it, that's fine too."

"I think… I think we're going to have to leave it like that for a while." He looks like he's thinking about something, and then nods decisively. "It's just a lot easier for everybody. All right?"

Dan nods warily. He's still not exactly sure what's going on. Jeff had chased after him to apologize for something that he had no reason to feel bad about, and then told Dan that he liked him fine but didn't want to hang out with him, even though he felt bad for not hanging out with him… Dan gives up. He's beginning to feel like he's listening to Tatiana talk to one of her friends. "So, everything's okay?" he asks cautiously.

Jeff looks a little frustrated, like he knows he hasn't got his message across but doesn't want to be any clearer. "Yeah, man, we're good. Sorry for all the drama."

Dan grins a little. "No, it's great. It's nice to be able to sit back and watch stuff happening without being in the middle of it!"

Jeff looks like he's thinking about arguing that point, but he lets it go, and Dan sketches a wave to Evan and heads back out toward the guest house. He glances back when he gets to the main road, and he sees Evan leaning back against the side of barn, Jeff standing in front of him. It looks like they're having a pretty serious conversation, and Dan is glad that he can't hear what it's about. He still doesn't know exactly what's going on with those two, and he guesses he'll probably never know.

He goes into the house and looks around. He wasn't lying, he does need to do laundry, and he really should get some groceries. He throws in a load of wash and then thinks about heading into town. Maybe it's time to make some new friends. If nothing else, he can hope that Jeff and Evan will calm down a little if they see him spending time with someone else.

chapter 21

DAN showers and pulls on jeans and a snug black T-shirt. He checks his face and hair in the mirror and shrugs. Dark brown hair, lean face with a dusting of stubble, green eyes… he looks like he always does, and people don't usually complain.

He drives into town and finds a parking spot on the main street. He seems to know what he's doing, but he isn't quite sure *why* he's doing it. Or isn't sure how much of it he's going to do. Or whether he really wants to do it at all. Or… or maybe talking to Jeff has fried his brain, and he should stop thinking and start acting! He can always play it by ear.

It's almost lunchtime now, so he heads for the Italian place, Zio's. It has a fair size patio, looking out over the street. Dan finds a table where the sun shines on his face, adjusts his sunglasses, and reads. When the server comes Dan orders a beer and a panini, and then goes back to reading. He can keep an eye on things over the top of his sunglasses, and he knows he's already picked up some interest. Most of it's female, but if he sends the first few girls away, it won't be long before a guy tries his luck. Dan's lived in small towns before, and he knows that they just pretend to be conservative and slow-paced. It seems like the less fresh meat a place sees, the more interest there is in any that does appear. And the small town sharks don't waste time before snapping up their prize. They never know when a bigger shark might come and take it from them.

Dan's mind starts racing, but he makes sure that his face stays calm. He wonders how far he is going to go with this. It's been a long time since anyone but Justin, and even before him Dan wasn't exactly a fan of quick pick-ups. There had been times when he'd just wanted an easy release, and there had been times when the thought of spending the night in a clean, dry bed had been more attractive than the guy in question, but generally Dan preferred to know somebody before he slept with him. He assumes that five years with a boyfriend haven't changed his tastes much. Which makes him wonder just what he's doing on the patio. Is he honestly just trying to prove something to somebody? And is that somebody himself or

Jeff or Evan?

He pushes his book away from him in an angry gesture, and almost knocks the plate that the server is in the process of placing in front of him. "Shit, man, sorry." Dan blushes, but the waiter just laughs.

"Don't worry about it—no smash, no foul."

Dan glances up. He's not sure he even looked at the waiter when he came in, which should have been an early sign that his head wasn't in the game. Waiters are often hot, and, in Dan's experience, often slutty. This one has longish blond hair pulled back in a ponytail, and a pleasant smile. Seems a bit too nice for what Dan's looking for, though. If he's actually looking.

"Yeah, thanks. It smells good—I'm glad it's not on the floor." The waiter nods and heads off to another table, and Dan takes a bite. The panini is incredible, with pesto and cheese and tomatoes and flavors Dan isn't even really sure of, and he feels his eyes roll back in his head a little. When he comes back to himself, he glances around and sees three sets of eyes on him, enjoying his little display. Damn, he hadn't even been trying. The sandwich was just that good. He takes another bite and tries to make his body language a little less welcoming. There's no one on the patio right now who could ever tempt Dan to risk his relationship with the panini.

The waiter drops a plate off at a nearby table and then returns to Dan. "Everything good here?"

Dan almost groans. "Damn, it's better than good. This sandwich is...."

The waiter nods his head. "Orgasmic, I know. I've heard."

"Wait a second, you've *heard*? Are you saying you haven't even tried it?"

"Gluten intolerant, man. I can't eat bread."

Dan takes a moment to explore the enormity of this. "Would you actually *die*? 'Cause otherwise, I really think it might be worth it."

The waiter laughs. "I'll think about it. Do you need another beer?"

Before the sandwich, Dan had been thinking about heading out, going back home and getting his head on straight. After the sandwich, he's thinking about ways to stay on the patio forever. "Sure, yeah, thanks." He's only halfway done with the first panini. He wonders how long he'd have to stay for his stomach to have room for a second.

The waiter returns with a beautiful amber beverage, and Dan trades his empty glass for the full one before having a terrible thought. "Wait a second... is there gluten in beer?"

"Yeah, most beer." The waiter shakes his head sadly but then grins. "Don't worry, I've found other ways to make myself feel like shit the morning after."

Dan nods. "Well, that's something at least." He's got one bite of panini left, and he wants to save it forever but he also wants to eat it before it gets cold. He pops it in his mouth and chews reverentially, and when he looks up the waiter is still looking at him. And maybe he doesn't look *quite* so nice anymore.

"You were at the Fireside last Saturday, right?" The waiter's voice is still friendly, but it's pitched a little lower, maybe just a bit husky, and Dan can feel his body reacting a little. This is what he came out for, after all.

"Uh, yeah, for about five minutes." Dan plays it cool. He'll wait and see where this guy is going.

"Yeah. I play in the band there." The smooth pick-up line is clearly weakened by the current setting, and the waiter has the sense to see it and laugh a little. "Obviously we're not exactly setting the music world on fire."

"Yet," Dan says. He likes it that the guy can laugh at himself, and he likes the smile his comment earns him.

"Yeah, yet." He wipes his hand on his apron and holds it out. "I'm Ryan. You just moved to town?"

Dan checks for panini drool and then takes Ryan's hand. "Yeah. I'm living on a farm a little east of here. I'm Dan." They shake hands, and then Ryan sees a customer looking for him and ducks back to work.

Dan wonders what he's doing. Ryan seems like a nice guy, albeit with some tragic food issues. And nothing's exactly happened yet, but he can see the potential. The thing is, it's been a long time since Dan's needed to see potential, and he's not sure he's really ready for this. Ryan seems a bit too nice for the quick-fuck approach, and Dan really doesn't think he's looking for anything more than that. Then he tries to pull himself together. He's not even sure Ryan's gay. Dan's not known for his precise gaydar, and Ryan hasn't done anything totally overt. Nothing has happened, and nothing needs to happen. He could just talk to Ryan. Maybe they've got stuff in common. "Friend" doesn't have to just be a euphemism. Dan thinks of Chris, and has a sudden flash of missing him. If Chris were here, he wouldn't let Dan get away with over-thinking every damn thing. Dan needs to make a little puppet Chris. He could sit on his shoulder and whack him upside the head whenever he starts getting too stuck in his thoughts.

Dan is actually looking at his paper placemat and wondering if he could fold it into a human shape when a shadow falls on him, and he looks up to see two young women standing in his sunlight. He smiles cautiously, and they smile back, and then one of them puts her hand out. "You're Dan Wheeler, right?"

Dan wasn't expecting that, but he extends his hand as well, and they shake. "Yeah, hi. I'm sorry, have we met?"

The other one laughs, and puts her hand on the chair opposite him. "No, not really. Do you mind if we sit? We can explain." He nods, and the first one pulls a chair over from an adjacent table while the second takes the chair from Dan's. They both look athletic and well-dressed and, well, rich. These are the type of girls who expect men to approach them, not the other way around. At least according to Dan's somewhat limited understanding of the rules of heterosexual dating.

"I'm Tamara," the first one explains from behind her designer sunglasses, "and this is Victoria. We used to take riding lessons from Jeff Stevens, you know, back in our horse-crazy years." She waves a hand dismissively, but Dan would be shocked if either of them is much over twenty-one. Their horse-crazy years can't be that far behind them. "Anyway, our parents are still pretty active in the equestrian community, so we're still up on all the gossip."

Victoria breaks in, and brings a perfectly manicured hand over to rest on Dan's wrist. "And you, Dan Wheeler, are gossip!" Dan appreciates their honesty, at least. And he adds a note to his mental collection of strange things about women. These two would never have approached him if they'd only been looking for sex, but add gossip into the mix, and all of a sudden he's irresistible. It's a bit invasive, but he doesn't really mind. He'd pretty much decided against going for a cheap pick-up that afternoon anyway, so if he's not looking for sex, he might as well talk to these two; give them something to chatter to their friends about. He'd rather talk to Ryan, but Ryan has work to do. Dan wonders if he should try to find a couple shifts bartending somewhere in town. He doesn't need the money, but it might be a good way to meet people. Then he realizes that he's already met two people and they're happily chatting away while he ignores them entirely.

Ryan comes over to take the new arrivals' drink orders, and raises an eyebrow at Dan. Dan just shrugs a little and tries to concentrate on what the ladies are saying. So far they've caught up on what a few of the girls they used to ride with are doing, but then they turn the conversation to Jeff, and Dan's ears prick up a little.

"Do you remember how mad your dad was when he found out that Jeff was dating Evan Kaminski?" Victoria swivels her head in Dan's direction. "You knew they were together, right? We didn't just spill some big secret?"

Dan smiles. "No, I knew."

Tamara almost snorts. Dan bets that if you got her really laughing, she'd sound like a pig, and it makes him like her a little more. "They're not exactly subtle about it! Which is a bit weird, because my dad says that Jeff used to be friends with Evan's father. I mean, isn't that a bit skeevy? The dad dies and the friend swoops in on his innocent young son?"

Dan isn't sure he likes where this is going. "Do you guys know Evan?" They both nod, and Tamara blushes a little when Dan adds, "Because he really doesn't seem all that innocent to me." Dan decides to gamble a little. "Did he seem innocent to you, Tamara?"

Victoria's head spins toward her friend, and Tamara blushes beet red. Victoria's eyes widen with the triumph of the gossip victor and she says, "Excuse us, Dan. We just need to run to the ladies' room." She almost yanks Tamara out of her chair toward the bathroom, and Dan feels bad for a minute, then shrugs it away. She shouldn't have called Jeff skeevy.

Ryan pops back over with a beer for Dan, telling him, "It's on the house. If you're going to deal with those two, you need alcohol." He takes a quick look over his shoulder. "Seriously, man, be a little careful of them. Their dads combine to own half the damn valley. They're not evil, they're just…."

"Thoughtless?" Dan supplies. He knows the type. Anyone who's worked in the horse world knows the type.

"Yeah, good word. Listen, man, I'm not gonna interrupt when they come back, and I'm off my shift in half an hour. But if you're looking for something to do tonight, come by the Fireside. I can introduce you to some more *thoughtful* people, you know?"

Dan nods. "Yeah, thanks, I might do that."

Ryan returns to his work, and the girls eventually come back from the bathroom. They both look a little high. Dan has no idea. It could be coke, or it could just be the excitement of gossip. Either way, he's not interested. But the girls have different ideas.

"So, Dan, tell us about you." Tamara leans forward and rests her hand on his forearm. Her chest is tanned as far down as he can see, and he can see a long way.

"Uh, there's not really much to tell, sorry. I'm just working in the barn."

"But there's more to you than that!" Victoria looks to Tamara for reinforcements, and gets a nod. "When Evan told us about you, he mentioned that you'd been competing at Rolex. And, well, that's a name dear to our hearts." The girls giggle and hold out their watches. Dan bets that either one would cost more than his truck. "So we Googled you. It really was quite a story. I mean...." Victoria stops. "Oh. Would you rather not talk about it?"

Dan manages a nod. "Yeah, maybe not." Dan can see them trying to decide how to play this. It's frustrating to not get any fresh information, but....

Tamara leans forward and rests her hand on his arm. "That's okay, we understand. It must be really hard. If you need anybody to talk to, or anyone to help you through this, please, think of us." Dan realizes that these girls are officially the only people in the state who seem to care about his crap, and he finishes his beer in two swallows.

"Yeah, thanks. I've actually got to head out now. I've got some things I need to do this afternoon. But it was really nice meeting you both." He smiles as sincerely as he can, and works his way through their protestations and insistence that he stay.

He catches Ryan's eye, and meets him at the bar near the cash register. "Please, Jesus, let me pay you here—do not make me go back to that table."

Ryan laughs. "So they got a little beyond 'thoughtless'?"

"I don't know. Probably not, really. I'm just never sure when my tolerance for that crap is gonna wear out, you know? I thought I had more to go, but then, bam! I was out. Had to leave before things got nasty."

"Yeah, good call." Ryan totals up Dan's bill and hands it over to him, and Dan sends it back with the total plus twenty percent. Ryan takes it without looking, and then calls over to the woman at the bar. "Debbie, we've got two tables, just drinking. Can you cover them for me if I duck out a bit early?" She waves a hand in the affirmative, and Ryan takes off his apron. "I'm supposed to be helping a friend build a deck. If you want to start meeting folks now, he and his wife are good people." Ryan seems totally casual about the whole thing.

"I don't know. I don't want to just invite myself over…."

"Dude, they're *building a deck*. The more muscle the merrier, you know?" Ryan grins. "But don't worry about it if you've got something else to do. Come by the bar tonight, or any Saturday… it's pretty much the same people every week."

Dan knows what Puppet-Chris would say. "No, sure, if you could use a hand, I'd be happy to help."

"Great." Ryan pauses. "I was gonna hitch out, 'cause my car's taking a little break. Have you got wheels?"

Dan nods and pulls his keys out. "It's just your car taking a break, not your license?" Ryan grins and nods, so Dan tosses him the keys. "You drive, then. I pretty well chugged that last beer to get away from the Troublemint Twins."

Ryan catches the keys and they head for the truck. Dan gets a different perspective from the passenger seat and spends half the trip picking up bits of garbage and tidying the glove box. He looks up eventually and sees Ryan smirking a little. Ryan sees him looking and says, "I might need directions. I didn't realize we were gonna stop off and pick up Martha Stewart on the way."

Dan shakes his head and digs his drawl up from wherever it hides. "Shoot, son, I'm from Texas. And in Texas, a man's truck is his castle."

Ryan shakes his head. "Well, your castle's fan belt sounds like it's on its last legs."

Dan gets serious. "Shit, I know. It's been bad for a couple weeks—I better get it changed before it strands me somewhere."

"Donny, the guy whose deck we're building? He's a mechanic. He'll get you a good deal."

"Wait a second. If your friend's a mechanic, how come your car isn't fixed?"

Ryan just laughs. "I said it was a good deal, I didn't say it was free. I'm working on his deck to trade off the labor, and then I've gotta find the money for the parts. I was hoping to apply your work to my labor bill, but now you want some fancy 'fan belt' for your castle, so I guess I won't be able to claim it." Ryan grins. "Then again, by the time I have enough money for parts, I'll have enough labor time saved up to build a whole new car, so don't worry about it!"

Dan laughs along with Ryan, but a part of his brain is thinking about Evan, about how he and Ryan would probably really get along. They're both nice guys, pretty laid back, good sense of humor... but Evan and Ryan could never have this conversation with each other. How could Evan understand the concept of saving up to pay for something as basic as car repairs? Dan finds he has a better understanding of Jeff, and his decision to maintain a certain distance between himself and Evan. It would be too easy to get sucked into the world of easy money, and once you're part of the world, once you're addicted, you're under the power of the one who has the cash. Dan doesn't think Jeff would do well being under someone else's control like that. Even someone as well-meaning as Evan.

They pull into the yard of a small but well-maintained house. Two people are already at work on the deck, and they watch the unfamiliar truck pull in and then smile when they see Ryan climb out of it. He calls, "I brought extra hands. This is Dan," and they wave at him before the woman points toward a cooler by the house. Ryan helps himself to a rum cooler and points a stern finger at Dan to discourage mocking, and then pulls out a beer and hands it to Dan.

They get to work, and it feels right. It feels right to be working under the hot sun with a beer close at hand, and to be part of a team, working with people who don't know or care where he came from or what he's lost. They're screwing the top boards onto the deck when Nikki goes inside and starts putting food together, and then Donny wanders over and fires up the barbeque while Dan and Ryan finish the last few boards and start cleaning up. They have grocery-store burgers on grocery-store buns, cheap beer and homemade potato salad, and it's a good meal. Nikki asks Dan a few questions about himself, but she doesn't pry, and when she sees that he'd rather be quiet, the conversation goes on around him without excluding him. They sit at the picnic table until the sun starts going down and Ryan looks at his watch.

"Damn, I've gotta go. Dan, do you mind giving me a ride into town?" Dan nods in agreement, and they say goodbye to their hosts, accepting thanks for their efforts and giving thanks for their dinners. Dan's shirt is still damp from sweat and it sticks to him a bit as he drives, but he feels good. Ryan needs to go home to get cleaned up, so he directs Dan down a backstreet to his apartment above somebody's garage. He climbs out of the truck and then peers back in, and smiles.

"You gonna come by tonight?" The softness is back in his voice, and Dan wonders if he could record it and play it for Chris; get his help in determining the degree or likelihood of gayness. But possibly that's a little impractical, so Dan just smiles back.

"Yeah, I think so. Gotta get cleaned up a little, but… yeah, I might come by for a drink."

"Well all right, then. I'll see you later." He looks like maybe he's going to say something else, but he doesn't, just shuts the door of the truck and bangs on the roof when Dan drives away.

Dan heads out onto the highway that leads to the farm. It's still warm out and he has the windows rolled down. He thinks about how easy the afternoon was. He'd made a friend. Made three friends, maybe, if he wants to count Donny and Nikki, and he thinks he does. He doesn't know if Ryan is looking for something more, and he doesn't know if he is himself. It doesn't really matter. Maybe he'll never see any of them again, and he'll still have a good memory stored away.

He thinks about Jeff and Evan, and how awkward things have gotten with them. He doesn't really know why, but maybe he doesn't need to care. Jeff is great, and Evan's sweet, and they're both hot, but… Dan doesn't need them. If they don't want him, he doesn't need to care about why, because whatever it is will just be their problem. He doesn't know why they keep popping into his head, but he's sure that will fade. Overall, it was a good day, and he drives through the falling darkness with a fresh sense of confidence and the idea that someday, somewhere, he might find a new place where he belongs.

chapter 22

WHEN Dan gets back to the house he has a shower and pulls on fresh jeans and a moss-green button down. Justin had given him the shirt and had said it brought out his eyes. Dan wonders what exactly he's planning on doing, and whether it's tacky to wear a shirt Justin had given him, if he's going out to do what he thinks he's going out to do.

He thinks about Puppet-Chris again, wonders what he would say, and then laughs at himself a little as he picks up his phone and calls the real Chris.

He hears the phone ring a couple times, and then there's a rattling sound and Dan pulls the phone away from his ear as Chris yells, "Danielle!" into the other end of the line. It's three hours later in Kentucky, and it sounds like Chris is well into his Saturday night.

"Hey, man, are you out?" Dan asks.

"What? Hang on a second, man, I'm at a club. Let me get outside."

Dan waits for Chris to come back on the line, wondering if he misheard his friend.

"Hey, Danny, sorry. It was a bit loud in there."

"Did you say you're at a club?" Dan tries to keep his voice neutral.

Chris laughs a little uncomfortably. "Yeah, well, some people from work were going, I thought I'd tag along...."

"To a club? Chris, man... are you looking for a new gay friend? Are you, like, a male fag hag? You can be honest with me, Chrissy."

Chris tries not to laugh. "Straight people go to clubs, Dan. Don't be so prejudiced." He puts a bit of a lisp on the last word, but Dan can't tell if it's on purpose or not. Chris could just be drunk.

"Yeah, straight twenty-year-olds. Paint the picture for me, man... are you the oldest person there?" The silence tells Dan all he needs to know, and he laughs. "You gotta come out here, Chris. I'm going to a bar and grill tonight—big old fireplace, people drinking draft, live band playing songs using actual instruments, songs people over thirty will have heard of...."

Chris groans. "Yeah, that sounds all right." He pauses a bit, then asks, "You going with Jeff?"

Dan thinks of what a logical question that is from someone in Kentucky, and how absurd it seems now that he's in California. "No, man, I haven't really seen much of him. He's got his own stuff going on out here."

"Huh... so, then, who are you going with?"

"Just meeting some people. One of the guys in the band was a waiter at the place I had lunch today. And that reminds me, man, the panini I had... it alone is worth the airfare. Seriously." Dan pauses for a second, and Chris seems to know there's more coming. "Look, man, I just wanted to ask... you know all those times you told me I should be hooking up... were you serious about that, or were you just saying it 'cause you knew I wouldn't?"

Chris sighs, and Dan can almost see him leaning against the wall of the building, rubbing the back of his neck. "You got your eye on someone, Danny?"

"No! Not really. I just... you know, in general terms. Do you think it's okay for me to start thinking about it?"

"God, Danny, it's been well over a year with nothing but your hand—I'd be surprised if you could think about anything else!"

Dan snorts a little. "Yeah, okay. But, you know. Thinking about *doing* something about it."

"And this isn't with Jeff?"

"Jesus, Chris! Get Jeff out of your head. There's nothing happening there. He and Evan are all wrapped up in each other, having some kind of intense relationship experience or something. This is... like I said, it's mostly just in general, but any specific there is would be someone else."

"The guy in the band?"

Dan is starting to regret making this call. "Shit, Chris, does it really matter?"

Chris's voice is surprisingly forceful. "Yeah, Danny, it does. I know you think you're all cool, and you can handle anything, but I gotta tell you… you've softened up in the last few years. You're not the same guy you used to be, and I don't think that's a bad thing. So if you're thinking of going out and picking up some stranger… I dunno, maybe the old you could do that with no problem, but I think the person you are now would regret it." Chris waits for a comment, but Dan doesn't know what to say. "I know you're not looking for some big thing, but I think if you found someone you like, maybe someone you care about a little… then, sure, maybe it's time." There's another pause. "Danny, you still there?"

Dan finds his voice. "Yeah. Sorry… I was just… I was looking more for Justin's perspective. Like, do you think it would be okay with Justin?"

"Fuck, Dan!" Chris sounds angry, and then Dan can hear him taking a deep breath before he starts talking more softly. "Justin's dead. He doesn't have a perspective… He was my best friend, and I loved him, but he's gone, and I can't worry about him anymore. I'm worrying about *you* now."

Neither of them says anything for a moment, and then Dan says, "Next time you're at a club and you get a phone call from me, you're not gonna pick up, are you?"

Chris just laughs. "Danny, I think you'll understand how much fun I'm having tonight when I tell you that this call has actually been a highlight."

"Damn. That's kinda sad."

"You're telling me." Dan can hear Chris's smile. "Seriously, man, you've got better sense than you give yourself credit for. Just take things easy; see what happens—you don't need to have a master plan for everything. You can see how things go; see how you feel." Dan can hear the smirk creeping back into Chris's voice, and he braces himself. "Remember, Danielle, if he really loves you, he'll wait."

"Yeah, thanks, I'll keep that in mind. Look, I'll let you get back to your club—I bet they're about to play the hot new dance track everybody just loves!"

"Fuck you, Danielle."

"Yeah, that'd solve one of my problems…." They're both laughing when they hang up.

Dan looks at himself in the mirror, looks at the shirt, and can almost see Justin hanging over his shoulder the way he used to, his arms wrapped around Dan's chest. He savors the memory for a moment, then unbuttons the shirt and takes it off, and hangs it carefully in the closet. He finds a deep navy Henley instead, and pulls it on. He has no idea where this shirt came from.

On a whim, he picks up his phone again. He tries to remember the barn schedule as he dials.

"Hello?"

"Hey, Robyn, what's up?"

"Dan, hey! Not much. How 'bout you?"

"Actually, I was just going to go into town, get a drink and hear a band. You doing anything?" There's a pause. "My treat…."

"Wow, Mr. Moneybags boss man!" Robyn's tone is light, but the words still sting a little. Dan *has* been finding it a little awkward to be around Robyn now that he's formally her boss. Back in Kentucky, it hadn't really mattered, because they'd both been minions of the Archers. But out here, where Dan is more or less in charge, it feels… weird. But he knows that's stupid, knows he just has to make sure it isn't allowed to get in the way of their being friends. He knows that's not the only reason he's been avoiding her, knows he'd also had some urge to leave his painful past behind and start fresh, but he doesn't like that idea any more than the first. Robyn isn't a reminder, she's a friend, and he should value her as such.

"That's right, I'm a big spender. You in?"

"Yeah, sure. I'm just out of the shower, but I've got to get dressed. And if I'm gonna be seen with you, I might want to go crazy and put on a little makeup. Can you give me ten minutes?"

"Absolutely. I'll swing by in ten."

"Great! I'll see you then!" She sounds really happy as she hangs up, and Dan kicks himself. Once again he'd let himself get so caught up in his own drama that he hadn't taken any time to think about other people. Robyn's new to the place, too, and Dan had checked that she was fitting in with the other barn staff and knows that they'd all gone out for dinner a couple times, but he should have done more. He thinks of the Chris puppet again. It could be a tiny head with a big arm for slaps upside the head and a big boot hanging down behind for kicks in the ass.

He feels good about calling Robyn. It's like an official proclamation that he's not going out to pick up, he's just going to meet some new people. He gets a little worried that Ryan might be offended but then catches himself. Ryan didn't seem like the type to be easily offended, and Dan's not even sure he's gay. Hell, maybe he and Robyn will hit it off. But if Ryan is gay, and if he is interested… has Dan been leading him on? Is he going to seem like a tease? Dan checks his reflection again. He looks casual, but the Henley is pretty fitted. It's snug across his chest and shoulders, and then just kind of clings to his waist. Dan's always liked guys in Henleys… maybe they're sexier than he's giving them credit for. He swears to himself as he heads back to the bedroom. He's changing into his third shirt, and he's not even going on a date? Maybe he should call up Tat. They could do each other's hair.

He throws the Henley on the bed and pulls out an old black T-shirt, faded almost to gray, with the logo of a saddle manufacturer on it. There— he's officially a guy casually hanging out. He hears a knock at the front door and heads down the stairs, opens it to see Robyn.

"Hey! I know you were gonna come by, but I took less time than I thought so I walked over. Maybe I can sneak a peek at your place?"

"Oh, sure, yeah… it's…." He grins a little bashfully. "It doesn't really feel like mine, to be honest. So feel free to poke around the Kaminski guest house all you want. I'm just gonna go find my keys."

He turns and heads down the hall, hoping his keys are in the kitchen, and Robyn calls after him, "Damn, are those new jeans? Your ass looks fantastic!" He pauses for a moment, but there is just no way he's changing again. Especially since he's probably making up the whole Ryan thing anyway.

They drive into town with Robyn filling Dan in on all the barn gossip. He's surprised by how much there is, really, with only three other people, but he guesses he needs everyone's back stories, and that takes a while. Robyn's good about gossip. She keeps it chatty and light, nothing vicious, and Dan's pretty sure that if any of her subjects overheard her they'd be more flattered by her interest than offended.

The bar is busier than it was the previous Saturday. Dan figures that he's an hour or so later, and apparently that makes all the difference. Ryan is on stage, playing guitar and singing, and there are no tables or seats at the bar available, so Dan and Robyn order drinks and then stand around against a wall. It's not ideal, but there's a table that looks like they're gathering stuff up, so maybe it'll be available soon.

The band seems to play mostly covers, but they play one of their own at the end of the set and Dan tries to pay closer attention to it so he can say something about it to Ryan if he talks to him. As the song is ending, somebody nudges his shoulder, and he turns to see Evan standing there. "Hey, guys! You're getting out a little, huh? We should have warned you that you need to come early if you want to get a seat. Sorry." He glances to the side, and Dan follows his eyes to see Jeff sitting at a table, watching them. "We've got room, I think. We can borrow a couple chairs…." Evan seems a little vague, and Dan realizes that he's pretty drunk. That would explain the unexpected friendliness.

"No, man, that's fine." Dan doesn't want to speak for Robyn, but he also doesn't want to impose on Jeff and Evan. "We've got a line on a table over here, I think. Don't worry about it."

Evan looks doubtful. "Are you sure?"

Dan sees Ryan working his way through the crowd. "Yeah, Evan, no problem." Ryan arrives and reaches out and gives Dan a one-armed hug in greeting, and he feels like he's in the middle of too many people. "Hey, Ryan, how's it going? We just got here, but what we heard was great."

"Thanks, man. Glad you could make it." Ryan seems nice and relaxed, which is more than Dan can say for himself.

"Uh, Ryan, this is Robyn, a friend of mine, and maybe you already know Evan? He's my boss."

Evan is giving Ryan a pretty heavy look, and Dan has no idea why. He wonders just how drunk the guy is, especially when Evan throws an arm over Dan's shoulder and leans forward to talk to Ryan. "His friend too."

Dan heaves Evan off a bit and smiles apologetically at Ryan. "My friendly boss."

Evan looks at Dan and seems to be working up something to say, but then Jeff's there, and it seems like he brings calmness with him. "Hey, guys." He smiles at Dan and Robyn, nods politely at Ryan, and then turns to Evan. "Our food just got here. You ready to eat?" Evan looks like he's going to argue, but Jeff raises an eyebrow, and Evan seems to reconsider.

"Yeah, okay." Evan looks back at Dan, then shakes his head a little and heads back to his table. Jeff smiles politely and follows Evan.

Nobody says anything for a moment, and then Ryan breaks the

silence. "So, the great Evan Kaminski. You didn't say that he's who you work for." Ryan looks a little cautious as he continues. "He seems a bit… protective."

Dan shrugs bemusedly. "I have no idea what that was about, man."

Robyn is looking at him curiously. "No idea? So you never… anything? With either of them?"

Ryan is following the conversation pretty closely, and Dan realizes that if Ryan had any doubts about Dan's orientation, they're pretty much gone after that. And he hasn't even answered the question yet. "What? No. I mean… when would I have?"

"I don't know. I hadn't worked out precise schedule. I just thought, you know… you all seemed pretty cozy, and then you all seemed pretty weird."

"Yeah, well, what can I say? Every now and then I can manage to screw things up even without having sex with anyone."

Ryan smiles at him, and Dan thinks maybe there's just a little more warmth there than there was before. "So, we've got room at our table. Come on over and have a beer, meet some people." Ryan herds them over with a hand in the middle of Dan's back, but when they get there he takes it away, and Dan can feel a cool patch where his skin had gotten used to the warmth. The band is at the table, along with about five other people, including Donny and Nikki, and introductions are made as Robyn and Dan are given glasses from the table's pitchers.

The conversation is lively and Robyn gets involved quickly. Dan mostly sits back and listens, and a few times he glances over and sees Ryan's eyes on him, and he thinks he kind of likes it. Jeff and Evan are farther away, and the bar isn't well lit, so Dan can't be sure, but sometimes he thinks he feels their eyes on him, too, and he really doesn't know what to make of that. The band gets up for another set and the table mostly just enjoys the music, although they still talk a little. There's another break, and another set, and before Dan knows it the band is thanking the audience and saying good night.

Ryan comes back over to the table for last call, and takes his seat beside Dan as usual, but this time his chair is twisted around a little so he's looking almost straight at Dan. Dan figures it's time to stop pretending there's any ambiguity. Ryan is interested, and Dan likes him. He's just not really sure what he wants to do about it.

Ryan smiles at him. "So, you had a good time tonight? I told you I knew some good people."

"Yeah, I'm glad I came. Good music too." He smiles back, but doesn't look right at Ryan. He thinks back to Chris's words: *"See how things go; see how you feel."* Yeah, that's great in theory, but he's feeling about fifteen different things simultaneously. *Thanks a lot, Chris.*

Ryan is still watching him assessingly. Dan knows he can end it now, grab his keys, wrangle Robyn, and get the hell out of there, but he's not sure if that's what he wants. He knows he doesn't want anything tonight, but someday, maybe… and if he leaves now, without saying anything, is he shutting that door?

Robyn slips into the seat beside him and snuggles in under his arm, and then speaks softly in his ear. "Jeff and Evan are still here. I can get a ride home with them, if…."

"No." Dan isn't loud, but he's emphatic, and he knows Ryan notices. He decides to get it over with and he turns to face Ryan directly. "We're gonna head out, I guess. But, thanks, seriously, for inviting me. It, uh…." He doesn't really have any words, so he just smiles at Ryan, hopes he understands. "I'm glad I came."

Ryan pauses, then nods. "Yeah, I'm glad you came too. And you know pretty much all the places to find me—here, home, or the restaurant—so if you want to do something sometime, let me know." Dan nods and they both stand up, and Ryan gives him another hug, and then looks at him with warm, sincere eyes. "I hope I'll hear from you."

Dan nods. "Yeah, absolutely. My schedule's still a bit up in the air, but… yeah. I think you will." He grins a little, and Ryan grins back, and suddenly everything seems just a little bit more clear. Robyn tucks herself back under Dan's arm and they work their way out of the restaurant. They glance over at Jeff and Evan on the way, and Robyn gives a little wave, which Jeff returns. Dan doesn't even want to start thinking about them tonight. He just wants to feel good for a while.

They hit the sidewalk and head for the truck, and Robyn keeps looking at Dan. He tries to ignore it, but eventually he cracks. "What?" he growls.

"Nothing." She makes it three more steps before she says, "I like Ryan."

"Yeah, I like him too."

She nods, and just before they get to the car, she says, "Seriously, though? Nothing, ever, between you and Jeff? *Or* you and Evan?" Dan sighs and shakes his head. "Huh." Robyn's mouth twitches a little, and she says, "I've gotta say, the barn gang is going to be a little disappointed to hear that!"

Dan's head swivels toward her, and she laughs as she says, "What, you thought you were magically immune to being gossiped about? Please! But that's all right. You should hear all the great stuff I got tonight! I swear, living in a small town is brilliant—everybody knows everybody! By the time I get done passing all this along tomorrow, we might not even have time to get to your sorry lack of a love life."

Dan stares at her, and he can tell she's starting to think she went a little too far. Then he shakes his head in exasperation. "Okay, then, tell me what you got." And the rest of the ride home is filled with happy chatter about people who Dan doesn't know, and whose problems he doesn't have to care about. It turns out to be a really, really pleasant drive.

chapter 23

DAN wakes up with the sun the next morning. He's only been in California for a little over a week, but already his body has adjusted to the time change and re-established its old patterns. He puts the pillow over his head and tries to get back to sleep, but it's no use, and eventually he gives up and just lies there. He's been trying to avoid having any downtime. When his mind isn't occupied, it always seems to go back to Justin, and there's no point in dwelling on things that he can't change.

But this morning he lets his mind go there. He doesn't want to spend the rest of his life searching for ways to distract himself. He wants to be able to just *be*, at least sometimes. So he lies there in bed, and he lets himself think about Justin. And it isn't as hard as he'd thought it might be. It still makes him sad, and maybe he's crying a little bit by the end, but he remembers a lot of good times too. He's never understood people who like watching sad movies, but he thinks maybe he's starting to get it. He thinks maybe it's possible to be sad and happy at the same time.

But he can only handle it for so long, and then he hauls himself out of bed and into the shower. He runs the water cold for a while, hoping it gets rid of any puffiness around his eyes. He's not vain, but he doesn't really feel like advertising his emotional frailties.

He gets dressed, finds some breakfast, and then heads down to the barn. He still hasn't worked out any system of days off for himself, but he doesn't really think he's going to take many. He truly does enjoy his job.

Tatiana is already there when he arrives, helping Devin with the chores, but she abandons that as soon as Dan appears. "Morning! Ready for the cross-country course?" she chirps, and Dan groans. He's glad he'd had to stay sober enough to drive home the night before. Tatiana must be pretty hard to take with a hangover. But he had promised her.

"Yeah, okay. You're going to take Sunshine?" She nods and goes to get the mare out of her stall. Dan is tempted to take Monty, but this is Tat's first trip up the hill on horseback, so Dan decides that he'd better make sure he's not being too distracted by his own horse.

He heads over to Smokey's stall, and checks out the additions to his name plate. "Smoke and Mirrors," "Smoke Gets in My Eyes," "The Big Smoke," "When Smokey Sings," "Smokin' Tails"... the poor horse is going to have an identity crisis. But he seems to be handling the pressure all right, and ambles out of the stall and into the crossties. He nuzzles affectionately at Dan, who's just about to be flattered when Devin strolls by and gets the exact same treatment. The little horse is just friendly.

Dan and Tat saddle up and head out along the path up the hill. When they get near the house, the pit bull comes out again. She's made a bit of a habit of joining Dan for his morning rides, and it seems like she was waiting for him.

"Oh, Lou! Hi, sweetie!" Tatiana coos, and Dan is a little disgruntled. He'd known intellectually that the dog must belong to somebody, had thought she was likely Jeff's, but he'd started to think of her as his own little friend. Tat turned to Dan. "Is it okay if she comes with us?"

"She's never been a problem before. Just give Sunshine a chance to meet her, make sure she's okay with it." Tat loosens her reins and the mare extends her nose down, and then tries to sneak a bite of grass while she's down there. "Yeah, she's fine," Dan snorts.

They head on up the hill and onto the course. Dan finds his stomach knotting up a little. He doesn't really like the feeling of being responsible for someone else's safety, especially not for a fifteen-year-old's. "Okay, so this is your first time around. We're not going to do the whole course. We'll just look at each obstacle, you'll tell me what the challenges are, how you'd handle it. If it sounds good to me, you'll give it a try." Tat nods seriously, and Dan continues. "Your focus will be on precision and control. If the horse starts getting worked up, the jumping is over, and we'll head back down to the barn. If *you* start getting reckless, the jumping is over, and you'll *walk* back to the barn. All right?"

Tat nods and tries to look serious, but Dan can see her eyes dancing. He remembers the feeling, and doesn't want to discourage it. He just wants to make sure she's safe.

"Okay, we're not gonna do any of the tricky ones today. Let's start with four—it's just a brush jump, like you've seen in stadium jumping. What's going to be different when you're doing it out here?"

They follow Dan's cautious approach for several jumps, with Dan and Smokey standing at a distance from the jump with Lou, and Tat discussing the jump, trying it, getting feedback, and trying again. Dan's impressed with her focus and ability to analyze what she's doing wrong and what she's doing right. She really does seem to be taking this seriously. Toward the end of the session he has her take a few jumps in sequence, and she's clearly thrilled. He's just about to suggest a break when he sees a man's head rise over the top of the hill. Lou is taking off toward him, barking happily, before Dan's even sure that it's her owner.

Jeff greets Lou and walks over to join Dan, and Tat trots Sunshine over happily. "Jeff, this is so incredible! We're doing really well, and Sunshine is awesome, and I'm not, but I'm learning! You should see us!" She turns to Dan. "I know you said that was our last trip, but can I do just one more? I'm not tired, and Sunshine is fine…."

Dan smiles, and nudges Smokey to move forward to stand next to Sunshine. "You can do one more if you chill out a little. It's good to be excited, but you've got to keep it under control, or your horse will feel it and things will get crazy. Do a couple big circles, get yourself calm, make sure Sunshine's good, and when you're ready, do one more run."

Tatiana beams at him and pulls Sunshine away, heading out to the track of the large circle they've been riding. "This job would really suck if she wasn't a sweetheart," Dan says mostly to himself, but Jeff's rumbling laugh isn't unexpected.

"A lot of things would be a lot more difficult if she wasn't a sweetheart. She could have made things hell for me and Evan."

Dan glances over at Jeff. He hadn't thought about that, but it's a good point. Tatiana is old enough now to know what people are saying, and to know that her brother and his older male lover aren't exactly standard issue. Dan thinks of the girls at the restaurant the day before and winces to think of Tat having to deal with that.

Jeff sees Dan's agreement, and continues. "He's having a bit of a tough time, lately. I hope he wasn't a problem last night at the bar?"

"No, not really. Just a little drunk, a little random. No big thing."

Jeff's looking at him. "Seemed random, did it?"

"What? There was a reason?" Dan is confused, as usual. "You mean, like, his employees aren't allowed to hang out in the same bar as him or something?" That doesn't sound like Evan, but Dan has to remember that he doesn't know the guy too well.

Jeff laughs a little as he shakes his head. "No, Dan, I don't think that was the problem." He looks over at Tatiana, who is lining Sunshine up to start jumping. Both men watch her quietly as she approaches the first obstacle and takes it cleanly. Dan is just thinking that he needs to talk to her about keeping Sunshine straight for a little longer on the landing when Jeff mutters, "Straighten her out a little," and Dan feels reassured. He's used to training horses, not riders, so he's glad Jeff agrees.

Dan bobs his head and practically jumps with Tat as the second and third jumps also go well, but when Dan glances over at Jeff to see if he's pleased, he finds that the man is looking at him, not at Tatiana. Dan gives him a questioning look, and Jeff smiles a little. "I think… I think Evan and I haven't been as clear as we should be. You're a part of Tatiana's life, now… a good part. Hopefully you're going to be around for a long time. And what Evan and I are trying right now isn't really working." He pauses, and then smiles brightly at Dan. "And you're really, really terrible at reading people."

Dan barks out a quick laugh. He hadn't realized his problem was quite so apparent. "Yeah, I kinda am." He glances almost shyly at Jeff. "I have no idea what's going on with you and Evan. But, seriously… I'm not nosy. I don't need to know everything, if you'd rather not explain yourselves… 'cause you're right, I'm really not likely to figure it out on my own."

Jeff smiles at him, and Dan almost feels like they're back in Kentucky. The heat isn't there, and, all things considered, Dan is thankful for that, but there is warmth, and the feeling that Jeff actually cares about him. He feels like a cat basking in the sunlight. Jeff shifts, almost reaches out for him, and Dan can practically feel the heavy hand sitting on his knee, but then Jeff pulls back, and says, "I'm gonna talk to Evan, okay?"

Dan shrugs. "Okay." Jeff could tell him he was going to build a new barn out of oatmeal, and that would be okay by Dan.

Tatiana pulls up on Sunshine, and Dan and Jeff both congratulate her warmly. Dan feels a bit like he and Jeff are parents watching their child perform, and it strikes him as odd that none of them are actually related. They set off down the trail to the barn, Tat and Dan riding on the outside, Jeff and Lou walking together in the middle.

Both horses prick their ears forward as two large dogs appear off to the side of the path, and Sunshine dances a little as Trapper and Copa approach. They aren't quite as well-behaved as Lou around the horses, and when Evan appears they act up a little more, as if they are protecting him from the horrible equine monsters. Jeff quiets them down pretty well, and when Evan meets the riders on the path the dogs settle completely with his hands on their foreheads.

Evan smiles a little tentatively at them all, and then addresses Jeff and Tatiana. "Tia sent me out to find you. She's got brunch just about ready." He turns to Dan. "I'm sure there's lots, if you haven't eaten yet."

"No, thanks, I did eat. I can take the horses back, though. Tat, I can ride Sunshine back and lead Smokey, if you want to head straight to the house."

Tatiana looks shocked, and maybe a little offended. "But you said that a true horse-person looks after the whole horse, not just the riding part!"

Dan smiles at her. "Yeah, I did. But a true horse-person is also happy to trade chores with another horse-person. It's no big deal, seriously."

She shakes her head stubbornly. "No, Sunshine did her job on the hill, now I should do mine in the barn."

Dan sees Jeff and Evan both smiling at her, and for a second it's like they're *all* fond parents. "Okay, then," Jeff says, slapping Sunshine on the shoulder. "You take care of your responsibilities. We'll keep brunch warm for you."

"And save me some bacon!"

Evan shakes his head. "It's every man for himself with bacon, you know that."

"Jeff—can you ask Tia to save me some bacon?" Tat asks sweetly.

"I'll see what I can do, sweetheart."

Tatiana smiles smugly at Evan and then nudges Sunshine forward. "Let's go, honey—we'll find some brunch for you too!"

Dan has a quick urge of irrational jealousy as he watches Jeff bring his hand up and rest it on Evan's neck as they turn and walk back to the house. He needs to get a lid on that. Whatever Jeff may or may not want to talk to him about isn't going to be any easier to understand if he's still harboring some stupid crush.

Dan and Tatiana head back to the barn with the horses, and when they get there Robyn is waiting for them, looking a little excited. She lets Tatiana take Sunshine into the barn and then grabs Dan's arm. "It's about time! Hurry up!"

"What are you talking about?"

"We're going to Santa Cruz." She gives Dan a pleading look. "Please, please, please, we're going to Santa Cruz?"

"Wait, who's 'we', and why are we going to Santa Cruz?" Dan has only a vague idea of where that even is.

"You, me, and some people from last night. Scott called about half an hour ago, asked if we wanted to go with them."

"Scott the drummer? You gave him your number?" Dan gives Robyn a long look, and laughs when she blushes.

"Okay, yes, I'm weak! Are you happy? But I don't want to go by myself, and you were invited, too, so… please, Dan? He's really cute, and I think he was pretty nice."

Dan shakes his head, but he's not saying no. "Yeah, he seemed all right… who all else is going?"

Robyn makes a face. "Okay, will it make it *more* likely or *less* likely that you'll go if I say Ryan is going?"

"It'll make me less likely to dump a bucket of water on your head if you just spit it out."

She looks at him skeptically, and then says, "Okay, fine. He's going. But so are Molly and Nikki, but without Donny because he has to work, so it's not like a date unless you want it to be."

"I don't know, Robyn. I've got a lot of work to do around this place. I can't just keep taking off every afternoon."

"It's not every afternoon! It's two afternoons this week, and you worked fifteen hours every other day. I don't think anyone's going to accuse you of shirking."

"She's right." It's Tatiana, looking out at them from the door of the barn. "Sorry to eavesdrop, but… if you want to go, you should go. You've been working really hard, and Santa Cruz is pretty fun. It's less than an hour's drive, and there's lots to do there." She looks a little sad, and Dan finds himself unable to read another Kaminski. "I mean, if you don't want to go, that'd be great—you could stay and hang out with Jeff and Evan and me. But if you want to go… you shouldn't stay just because you think you're supposed to work."

"Please, Dan? I'll be your slave for a week," Robyn pleads.

"You're already my slave, stable girl." So much for not letting their new work hierarchy change their relationship.

"Yeah, but for a week I'll actually listen to you. And… I won't gossip about you at all, for a whole month. Please, Dan?"

Dan honestly isn't even sure what he wants to do. He isn't against the idea in general, it just all feels a little… rushed. Rushed to get ready today, but also rushed that he hadn't even met Ryan twenty-four hours earlier, and now he's thinking about going on his second semi-date with him. Third, if you count the deck building… and, hey, there'd been dinner. But Robyn's really excited, and Dan still feels a bit guilty for neglecting her all week. Her phone rings, and she looks at him imploringly as she picks it up. He nods resignedly, and then watches as she puts her game face on to be cool for the phone call.

While Robyn is sorting out details, Dan leads Smokey into the barn and pulls off his tack. He's carrying it to the tack room when he notices Tatiana looking at him a little shyly. "You okay, Tat?"

"Yeah. I just… this Ryan guy… do you really like him?"

Dan really hopes this isn't more of that crush that Evan had teased him about. He really hasn't seen much sign of it, though, so maybe she's just curious. He decides honesty is the best approach. "I don't really know, Tat. I mean… I don't really know him."

"But you like what you know."

"Well, yeah, I guess so. It's really not… I dunno, Tat. When you're a teenager, everything's intense, and that's great. But when you get older—sometimes it's nice to just relax a bit, without the huge roller coaster. Does that make sense?"

"So Ryan's not a roller coaster, he's just…."

Dan runs a hand over Smokey's body to check for dampness, but he hadn't really done much work, and he's bone dry. "I don't know, Tat. Honestly."

Tat doesn't seem to want to let this go. "But is there any other guy that you might be interested in? Maybe?"

Dan's mind catches on the word "guy." That doesn't sound like she's holding onto her own crush. But then what *is* she talking about? "Uh, not really, I guess?" He doesn't think he'll give her the rundown of his lustful thoughts about Jeff, or the flashes of attraction to her own brother. He doesn't want to scar the poor kid for life.

Robyn breezes in then, thankfully. "We're supposed to meet them in town at eleven thirty. That gives you forty minutes to shower, shave, dress, and drive us in. Are you up for the challenge?"

"I think I can handle it. Tat, are you okay putting Sunshine out in the paddock?"

"I think I can handle it," she mimics.

"Okay. And then you're down here all day tomorrow? Sunshine should do flatwork tomorrow, but we can find lots of horses for you to ride down here, and then we'll take Sunshine back up on Tuesday. Sound okay?"

"Yeah, sounds good." She smiles at him, but he's still not getting the full enthusiasm out of her, and he doesn't like it. But with Robyn staring at him, he doesn't have time to worry about it, so he takes Smokey out to the paddock on his way back to the house.

He showers, then pulls on jeans and the Henley that he'd rejected the day before. He doesn't really worry about looking too good today. He's back at the barn at eleven fifteen, and follows the sound of voices inside. He realizes his mistake when he sees no sign of Robyn, only Tatiana looking sullenly at a helpless Jeff and a frustrated Evan. "It's really, really not something for you to be getting involved in, Tat," Evan is saying, and Dan backs out carefully. He turns and almost runs into Robyn.

"I wasn't eavesdropping!" she hisses before he can even speak. "I was just trying to intercept you before you blundered into it."

"Good work with that. What happened to their damn brunch?" He shakes his head. "Are you ready to go?"

"I think so… but now I feel bad leaving when Tat's upset. What if she needs someone to talk to?"

Dan shrugs. "She survived up until last week without your advice. I expect she can make it a little longer. But, hey, if you don't want to go—"

"No, I want to! I just—" Robyn breaks off as the door of the barn opens and Jeff, Evan, and Tatiana come out. Evan's got his arm around

Tatiana's shoulder, and her other arm is looped through Jeff's.

Dan takes a look at them as they walk over, and then smirks at Robyn. "Amazing—they solved it without you!"

She doesn't have time to respond before the others are within hearing distance. They're looking a little strained, but they aren't fighting, at least.

"So you're heading down to Santa Cruz?" Jeff offers.

"Uh, yeah, looks like." Dan turns to Evan. "I'm gonna start keeping track of my hours. I can just keep a list in the tack room or something. I mean, you shouldn't just have to hope that I'm putting in the time."

Evan just shakes his head. "You don't have to do that, man. I trust you, remember? It's one of the reasons I was so hot to hire you."

Dan shrugs. "Well, I'll do it anyway. Make myself feel better, even if no one else ever looks at it."

"Whatever works for you." Evan smiles awkwardly. "Look, do you guys know when you're getting back tonight?"

Dan looks at Robyn. He really has no idea about their plans, so she takes over. "They were talking about getting dinner some place down there, so, I don't know… it might be late-ish."

"Yeah, okay. Okay. Well, hey, have fun, all right?" Evan seems a little uncertain.

"Sure, yeah." Dan looks over at Robyn, who's standing by the truck but not getting in, obviously as hesitant as Dan. "Look, it's no big deal, today. If there's something you need done…."

Jeff steps forward. "No, Dan, it's fine." He looks over at Evan. "There's no rush here. We can wait." Evan almost says something, but then he nods, and Dan and Robyn warily climb into the truck.

They pull out and head down the driveway, then out onto the main road. They're halfway to town before Robyn finally says, "On the plus side… Evan looks really hot when he's all brooding." Dan gives her an incredulous look, and she laughs. "What? I hear he dabbles in women… and even if he's out of my league, he's still nice to look at." She leans over on the seat and pushes Dan's shoulder a little. "Don't even tell me you haven't noticed that he's hot. Good face, *rockin'* body, and the money doesn't hurt. And Jeff's beautiful, too, with those eyes and that voice… yummy! I seriously don't know, Dan… if you got your choice, which one would you pick?" There's a bit of a strange edge to Robyn's voice, as if her questions are somehow more significant than she's letting on, but Dan doesn't want to play.

"Honestly, we're on our way to reunite you with the drummer of your dreams, and this is the best thing you can find to think about? Why don't you concentrate on Scott? Or Santa Cruz?"

"Yeah, okay, Danny, if you're afraid to answer."

They drive on in silence, and Dan thinks about Justin, wonders what he would say about Dan going off with some new guy like this. Justin could be jealous, even a little possessive, but Dan had never really minded because he'd liked the feeling that someone valued him enough to want to keep him. But he wonders what Justin would think about Ryan. He remembers Chris's words: Justin is dead. He doesn't have a perspective. But Dan isn't sure that's true, because Justin is still a part of him, so doesn't that mean Justin's perspective is the same as his? So when he's wondering what Justin would think, is he really wondering what he thinks himself? Dan doesn't like these sorts of thoughts. They always make him feel like the high school dropout he is. He wishes sometimes someone would explain it to him, because he really doesn't feel equipped to figure it out alone.

He sighs a little when he pulls into Ryan's street, and then he looks ahead and sees a few people already standing outside the apartment stairs, sees Ryan raise his hand to wave a greeting.

"Ready or not, here it comes," Robyn says, and Dan thinks that's true. It's coming, and he's really not sure he's ready.

chapter 24

THERE are six of them going on the trip, and there's really only room for four in Scott's car, so Dan says he'll drive, and Ryan offers to ride with him to help navigate. The truck has a good-sized back seat, so there's lots of room for Robyn and Ryan both, but Dan isn't surprised when Robyn decides she'd be more comfortable riding in the car. Dan reminds himself that he'd spent a good part of the previous day with Ryan and had enjoyed it, but his hands are still a little sweaty when he climbs back behind the wheel. Ryan seems relaxed, though, and makes easy conversation as they drive, and Dan calms down pretty quickly.

It's a beautiful day and the drive takes them through some scenic countryside, so a lot of the time they're both just looking outside and appreciating the view. They tend to talk more when they drive through the fingers of urban sprawl that stretch out from the city. Ryan tells Dan about his musical ambitions, and Dan explains the basics of eventing and how he earns his living. There are no huge revelations, but by the time they pull in beside Scott's car in the Santa Cruz parking lot, Dan at least feels a bit more confident in his assessment that Ryan is a good guy.

The Californians have been to the seaside town before, and they already have somewhere in mind for lunch. Dan and Robyn are happy to go along. After the meal, they all walk down along the boardwalk, but it's really too crowded for a group of six, so they divide up with plans to meet for dinner, and again Dan finds himself with Ryan. It's neither unexpected nor unwelcome. He thinks briefly of the electricity he'd felt from Jeff that night in Kentucky, but then remembers how quickly that seemed to have faded into nothingness. He might not feel a fiery passion for Ryan, but he is developing a gentle affection, and maybe that's better in the long run. It's certainly less confusing.

They spend a couple of hours on the boardwalk, poking around in the touristy shops. There are rides, but Dan isn't a big fan. He's not afraid of speed, but he'd rather be at the controls than sitting passively. And Ryan doesn't seem to care too much one way or another, so they don't bother.

They run into Robyn and Scott a couple times, and see Nikki and Molly in the line for salt water taffy, but otherwise they're on their own.

They make it to the far end of the boardwalk and find a little niche where they can take a break, leaning with their arms braced on the railing, looking out at the ocean. Dan takes a deep breath of the salty air, and lets his shoulders relax. He looks over and sees Ryan grinning at him.

"Not a huge fan of the crowds?"

Dan laughs a bit sheepishly. He must come across as totally neurotic. "Nah, I'm fine. Just… no point in going to the beach and not breathing sea air, right?"

"Makes sense. Hey, there's a harbor, for boats. Wanna go have a look at them?"

Dan has no idea why anyone would want to look at boats, but he doesn't object. Maybe he'll be surprised by how interesting they are, and at least it sounds like it should be less crowded than the boardwalk. "Sure, all right."

They walk over toward the harbor, but when they get to the mouth of the inlet they see a restaurant with patio, and they grin simultaneously. "Or we could get a drink," Dan suggests as Ryan nods happily.

They find their way onto the patio and discover that they have a good view of the yachts coming in and out of the harbor, so—as Ryan says as he happily sips the gluten-free beer that he found on the menu—it's the best of both worlds.

Most of the boats are pretty small, essentially just motor boats, but there are a few that look big enough to live on. "What do you say? Would you ever want to leave it all behind, sail around the world?" Ryan asks.

"I dunno… there might be room for the horses, but there wouldn't be much space to ride them."

"So, the horses—they're really that important, are they? I mean… they're more than just a job?"

Dan considers it. He knows that they are, but he doesn't know how to explain it. Part of it is wrapped up in Justin, but Dan loved horses long before he moved to Kentucky, so there's more to it than just that. Ryan isn't pushing, and Dan knows he could just laugh him off, but he's interested himself, now. And he feels like Ryan might appreciate a bit of actual openness from him. "Yeah. They're a lot more than a job."

He shrugs. "I started riding when I was a kid… a teenager, I guess. My mom was sick and there was no one to take care of us, and I got put in foster care. And, I dunno, I was angry, and a bit of an asshole, and I got kicked out of a couple places. The social worker told me I was one step away from a group home, and she put me with this family on a farm. They were super-religious, and I thought I was gonna hate them, but… they had horses." Dan cuts his eyes over to Ryan. He could stop now, doesn't want to be boring, but Ryan smiles encouragingly.

"So I guess it just sort of clicked. The horses didn't care if I was scruffy, or if I did bad at school, or…. They didn't care if I was gay." Dan grins a little self-consciously. "Although I really didn't advertise that to the family—they wouldn't have been impressed." Dan's looking out at the harbor now, but he's seeing the dry farm in Texas more than the ocean in California. "And then when I got better, figured out how to ride, how to work with them… it was nice to be good at something. Nice to be able to do something that people wanted. And horses are… I don't know. I understand horses. People…." Dan thinks back to his conversation with Jeff that morning. "People confuse the hell out of me." He smiles shyly, surprised at how much he's just said. "I dunno. I guess that was a pretty long way of saying I don't really want to live on a boat."

Ryan laughs gently. "Okay, no boat. Check."

"What about you? You like the idea of being that rootless?"

Ryan shrugs. "Kinda, yeah. I mean, seeing new things and new people every day, not getting stuck in the same old job… it sounds pretty good to me."

Dan nods. He's not surprised to hear that about Ryan. He seems like a traveler. "So how come you're not doing it? I mean, not on a boat, maybe, but how come you're stuck in a little town?"

"Stuck?" Ryan feigns disbelief. "Oh, I'm not stuck, I'm planning!" He grins. "I met the guys from the band, they're almost all from the area, and we decided to stick around there until we got our shit together, got a good sound and were ready to tour. We've been trying to get some sort of a recording deal, too—get some help with expenses on the road. And it's almost coming together, really—it won't be long now!" Ryan's as excited as Dan's seen him, and Dan can't help smiling. It's nice to see someone with dreams. Then he realizes that it reminds him of Justin, of how sure he was that they were going to the top, that Willow was only the first in a long string of exceptional horses that they'd develop together. He realizes that the smile must have faded from his face when Ryan leans toward him in concern.

"Shit, man, I'm sorry. I mean… were you thinking that…." Ryan stumbles, and Dan can't help him because he has no idea what the man is talking about. "I mean, I'm really enjoying spending time with you, and obviously you're smokin' hot…." Dan stares at him. These are nice things to hear, he supposes, but why is Ryan….

"Oh! Oh, no, man, sorry! I'm not looking for anything serious either! Like, probably not anything at all, I don't know…." Now it's Ryan's turn to get a strange expression on his face. "No, not because I don't like you, just because…." Dan is almost panicking. Things have gone really wrong really quickly. He takes a deep breath and starts again.

"I was seeing someone, back in Kentucky. Pretty long-term." He really doesn't want to get into details, so he leaves it there. "So I'm just sort of… unsure about dating in general. Or, not dating, even, just… everything. I'm sort of unsure of everything." Ryan is looking much calmer, and not offended, as far as Dan can tell. That's an improvement. "So you being excited about traveling—seriously, man, it's not a problem."

Ryan nods, and then laughs a little. "Yeah, okay, that makes sense." He looks a little sheepish. "Sorry."

Dan just shakes his head. "No, it's good to get it out in the open. I mean… 'casual if anything'… it's good to get that clear."

"Okay, well, as long as we're getting things clear…." Ryan leans in a little bit, bringing his face close to Dan's. "Casual's great, but I'm really hoping that there's something."

Dan glances around nervously, but no one seems to be paying any attention to them, and he brings his hand up and finds Ryan's, rests them both on Ryan's knee. "Okay," he breathes, and then he leans the little bit closer and brings his lips up to Ryan's. It's barely more than a peck, just a brush of lips, a little puckering motion, and then pulling away, but Dan's heart is racing, his face is burning, and he yanks his hand back from Ryan's as if he's been burned. He knows he's overreacting, knows he must seem like a freak, but… he hasn't kissed anyone but Justin in a long time. This is a lot more than just physical, and he's not sure if he's ready to go ahead with it.

Ryan seems to be taking it all right, though. He looks curiously at Dan and says, "You all right?"

"Yeah, sorry. Just… like I said, I was with one guy for a long time."

Ryan shakes his head a little. "He really did a number on you, huh?" He brings his hand up to where Dan is gripping the arm of his chair and gently works his fingers loose. He brushes his own fingers along Dan's lightly before bringing his hand back to his own side.

Dan tries to relax. Their server comes over and takes orders for refills, and Dan welcomes the distraction. By the time that's dealt with he's back to normal, more or less, and he's able to go back to having a casual conversation. They end up phoning the others and suggesting that they meet at the restaurant for dinner, so the only moving the two do for the next several hours is over to a larger table.

They're walking back to the cars after dinner when Nikki's phone rings. She answers it and has a short conversation, and then turns to Dan. "Donny says he can fix your fan belt tomorrow if you drop the car off tonight. I can run you out to your place after if you want…."

Ryan jumps in. "Or if you don't mind me driving your truck, I could ride out with you, drop you off, and take the truck back into town with me."

"Oh, uh… I appreciate the offers, and I do need to get it fixed, but I really don't want to be a nuisance."

Nikki talks into the phone. "Yeah, okay, book him for tomorrow." She hangs up and smiles at him. "It's not like you live that far out."

They sort it out that Ryan will do the errand-running, so Robyn climbs into the truck with Ryan and Dan so they can go straight to the farm without going through town. Ryan insists that she take the front seat, but when he leans over from the back to talk to them, he rests his hands on their seats, and his fingers brush Dan's shoulders a little too often to be accidental. Dan feels a bit like he's back in high school. It's sort of fun.

When they get to the farm Dan drives Robyn down and drops her at the barn, and Ryan whistles between his teeth. "Man, this barn is about ten times nicer than my apartment."

"You should see Dan's house!" Robyn chirps, and then looks a little awkward, as if she's making a decision on Dan's behalf.

Ryan just ignores the comment, though, and gives Robyn a good-night hug before climbing into the front seat. Dan pulls away and drives the short distance to the guest house, and then leaves the engine running as he climbs out. Robyn's suggestion or not, he's not inviting Ryan in.

Ryan doesn't seem surprised or disappointed. He just gets out of his own side and walks around the truck, but when he gets to the driver's side, instead of going around Dan he stands in front of him, so they're standing facing each other, lined up against the side of the truck.

Ryan smiles gently at him. "Thanks for coming out today. It was a good time."

"Yeah, it was. Thanks for inviting us." Dan looks at Ryan and tries to decide what to do. Tries to decide what he wants.

Ryan moves forward slowly, carefully, and brings his right hand up to nestle in Dan's hair at the base of his skull. Dan lets it happen, and he lets Ryan bring Dan's head forward, bring their mouths together. The kiss is still gentle, still not much more than a brush of lips, but it lasts a little longer this time, Ryan tilting his head and applying a gentle pressure, and Dan kisses back. Ryan moves in a little closer, then, and Dan pulls away. Ryan lets him go without protest, but Dan still feels like he has to explain.

He looks down at his shoes for a second, and then turns and leans his back against the side of the truck, looking out into the night. "The guy from Kentucky. The one I was with for a long time?"

Ryan nods and smiles ruefully. "Yeah. The guy you're getting over."

"We didn't break up." Dan takes a quick breath. "He died. He got in a riding accident, and he died." He looks down at his shoes again. "Justin."

Ryan freezes for a second, and then nods. "Okay. Yeah. Shit, Dan, I'm really sorry."

"No! No, man, don't be sorry. It was nice to have someone to just hang out with, without thinking that you were feeling sorry for me, or afraid that I was gonna break or something." He sneaks a peek at Ryan. He isn't running away, at least. "I just... I thought you should know, because... I don't know, I'm kind of freaking out about all this." He looks at Ryan again, and doesn't see anything but warm concern on his face. "I feel like I'm cheating on him. You know?"

Ryan doesn't say anything for a minute. "Well, I don't *know*, but, yeah, I can see how it'd be weird." He turns and leans his back against the truck, too, so they're both looking out into the darkness. They stand quietly for a minute before Ryan starts talking again. "Okay, here's the thing… I like you. Totally apart from sex." He looks over at Dan. "When I first met you, I wasn't sure you were gay, and I still thought you'd be a good guy to hang out with. I mean… I *hoped* you were gay… a lot. I hoped a lot." His smile is self-deprecating. "But, you know, even if nothing happens, you're still a good guy, we can still hang out. Right?"

Dan isn't sure if he can believe this. "Wait. So, you're okay with this? I mean…." He laughs a little. "Do I have to choose? I mean, I'd totally understand that, if you didn't want me being a cocktease…."

Ryan laughs. "Let me put it this way… if I ask you to choose, you'd say just friends, right?"

Dan shrugs uncomfortably, then nods. "Yeah, I think so."

"Well all right then. You don't have to choose. At least this way I have a *chance* at some action."

"Seriously?"

Ryan pushes himself off the truck and stands in front of Dan, legs slightly spread, arms out to the sides. He's laughing. "Here is my body. You can use it, or ignore it as the whim takes you."

Dan laughs and looks away, then looks back. He grins a little. "You know, you're really a very good waiter." Ryan laughs. "No, I mean it, this is some exceptional service. I feel bad for only giving you a twenty percent tip."

Ryan puts his arms down and moves around Dan, heading for the driver's door. "Well, now I just feel cheap—" he begins, and then Dan is wrapping his fist in Ryan's shirt and pulling him in for another kiss. It's a bit rougher this time, a bit more needy, but it still doesn't last long, and it's still Dan who pulls away first. Ryan just grins at him and gives his lips a quick lick and then gets in the truck and shuts the door. "I'll call you tomorrow about getting the truck back to you," he says and backs it up.

As the truck turns, its headlights catch three dogs trotting down the lane toward Dan, and farther behind them, Jeff and Evan standing by the side of the road. They look as though they'd been coming down the driveway and stopped. Ryan drives out carefully, making sure to avoid people and pets, and Dan raises a hand in greeting to Jeff and Evan. He's a bit embarrassed, and wonders how much they saw. Wonders if they'll judge him, thinking he's forgetting Justin or moving on too soon.

He crouches to ruffle the necks of the dogs, and lifts his chin up to avoid the worst of their licking. Jeff and Evan seem to be talking about something, and Dan isn't sure whether they're planning on coming the rest of the way down or not. He stands up just as they start walking toward him.

Evan looks frustrated, almost angry, but Jeff is the picture of calm. Luckily, he's the one who speaks. "Hey, Dan. It's pretty late. You heading to bed?"

"Uh, yeah, I was going to. But if you guys need something…."

"Nah, don't worry about it," Jeff replies. "We can always—"

Evan breaks in. "Actually, if you don't mind giving us a few minutes… that'd be great."

Jeff and Dan both look at him, and he raises his chin a little defiantly. Jeff is frowning a little, and Dan groans to himself. What are these two going to try to drag him into now?

chapter 25

DAN leads Jeff and Evan up onto the porch, and then turns to look at them. "Is this… do you want to go inside, or stay out here?"

Evan looks a little less sure of himself than he had just been. "Uh, out here is fine, I guess." He looks to Jeff as if for confirmation, but Jeff just raises an eyebrow at him. Jeff hadn't wanted to do this now, so apparently he's letting Evan take care of it his way. Dan isn't sure he likes that idea.

"Okay. Uh, do you want beers or something?"

Evan seems almost pathetically grateful for the delay. "Yeah! Yeah, a beer would be great!" Jeff smirks, and then nods solemnly at Dan. Beers all around, apparently.

Dan gestures to the big wooden chairs on the porch. "Okay, well, make yourselves at home." He smiles awkwardly at Evan. "Which shouldn't be too hard since it *is* your home."

Evan shakes his head. "Nah, Dan, it's your home. I'm just the landlord."

"Okay, well… I'm just gonna go get the beers…." He ducks inside and can hear hushed voices start almost immediately outside. He doesn't know whether to hurry up so he can get whatever it is over with, or to slow down and give the other two a chance to get a bit more organized. He decides to do neither, and just goes to the fridge at his normal pace. When he returns to the porch, Jeff is sitting and watching the night, while Evan is pacing around like a caged animal. The dogs have settled themselves on the ground at the bottom of the stairs. Dan hands the beers around and sits at one end of the porch bench. And waits.

Evan takes a swig of his drink as if for courage, and then turns to Dan. "Okay, here's the thing." He stops himself and then pulls up a chair and sits in front of Dan. "Okay, so… you know Jeff and I have a bit of a… non-traditional… relationship, right?" Dan nods cautiously, and Evan continues. "So, it works because other people are just fun, just sex. You know? We're both happy to fuck around a little, and neither of us cares if the other is doing it, too, but we make sure that we come home to each other."

Dan nods again. He knows all this. He begins to get a weird feeling in the pit of his stomach, combined with a tickling in his brain as if he *almost* understands what's going on. It's aggravating.

Evan is playing with his beer bottle. The label is peeled almost all the way off already, and now he's rolling the bottle back and forth between his hands. He looks at Jeff for help, but again Jeff just nods at him. "Okay, so the thing is… when we came back from Kentucky… after I'd seen Jeff with you… I got a bit worried. A bit jealous, I guess. I mean, I'd come on to you myself, I couldn't blame him for wanting you. I'm not that much of a hypocrite. But—" He breaks off again and sends a pleading look to Jeff, who finally takes pity on him.

"But he thought maybe I was getting a bit involved emotionally, thought it wasn't just physical." Jeff's voice is calmer than Evan sounded, calmer than Dan feels. "And I had to admit that he was right. And we wanted to protect what we had, weren't sure how to deal with that sort of situation, so… that's why we avoided you for the first week or so." He looks over at Dan. "I'm really sorry if that made things awkward or confusing for you."

They both look at Dan for his reaction, and he's happy to give it. "Okay. No big deal. I mean, obviously you guys have to look after each other. That's cool. Like I said, it's none of my business—no hard feelings."

Jeff frowns a little. "How is it none of your business?"

Dan's stymied. "Well, I mean… everybody's eye wanders sometimes, right? It doesn't mean anything. But you guys—what you have means something. But it's *your* thing, not mine. So… none of my business." It seems pretty clear to him. He wonders if he's still missing something.

Evan shakes his head. "Yeah, okay, maybe that would have been true if we'd left it there. If avoiding you had worked."

Oh. Dan guesses that's what he was missing.

Evan continues. "But we still saw you, and every time we did, I could tell that Jeff was still… interested. And that would have been bad enough, but—" Evan breaks off and stands up, walking over to the top of the porch stairs.

Jeff continues for him. "But Evan started to see my point. He started to get interested himself, in more than a strictly physical way." Dan can't quite believe this. He's trying not to react, trying to sit still and see what happens, waiting for the punch line.

Evan crouches down next to him now, tries to catch Dan's eyes. "It's not like a creepy stalker thing, it's just—spending time with you, even on your last visit... the first part....." Evan almost quits there, as if appalled by his lack of tact, but fights through it. "And seeing you with Tat, and with the horses, and even the dogs... you just... fit in. You make things better."

Dan's surprised to hear himself speak. "I make things better? Jesus, Evan, that's my job! If I made things worse, why would you pay me to be here? Linda makes things better, Robyn makes things better, Tia makes things better—we all make things better." He stares incredulously at the other man. "That doesn't mean that you're... *attracted* to me...."

Evan groans and buries his head in his hands. "Okay, maybe that wasn't a good explanation. But you're still missing... the problem isn't that I'm *attracted* to you. Dan, I'm attracted to a *lot* of people—believe me, I know what that feels like. This is more. I'm... interested. And so's Jeff. Attracted, *too*, obviously, but... more."

Dan looks over at Jeff, who grins a little sheepishly, but doesn't say anything. Apparently it's Dan's turn. "Okay... okay. So... what do you want me to do about that? I mean... I know I'm not great at the job, but I like it, and I'm working to get better, I don't really want to quit...."

Jeff and Evan both jerk their heads toward him. "Shit!" Evan exclaims. "Shit, no, Dan, I was gonna say that first... shit. Okay, no, none of this is at all to do with your job, and I love what you're doing there, and we absolutely want you to keep doing it forever. And whatever we cnd up doing, it is completely my responsibility to make sure that you aren't uncomfortable at your job or...."

Jeff starts up as Evan trails off. "Really, we aren't expecting you to do anything. It's not your problem, it's ours. Seriously, we'll figure things out, one way or another." He smiles a little at Dan, and he looks sincere.

Dan stands up. He needs to move around a little. He rubs his damp palms on the sides of his legs. "Okay. So... if you don't want me to do anything, why did you tell me?" He looks from one to the other, sees them exchange glances as if trying to figure out how to proceed.

Jeff's smile is sheepish again. "Okay, well... having it be our problem, and just having us figure out a way to get past it... that's absolutely an option. It's... from our perspective, it's the second best option." He shrugs a little and looks down at his hands before looking back at Dan. "But we thought... we thought we owed it to ourselves to at least mention the possibility of Option A."

"Which is still pretty poorly defined," Evan contributes. "I mean, it's not so much poorly defined as it is totally flexible, dependent on you." He looks over at Jeff. "We've talked about it... a lot... and we think it's worth a gamble, worth trying whatever you want to try."

Dan feels like there's too much happening. He's getting tired of feeling that way, tired of always being just a little behind everything. "What do you mean, whatever I want to"—*hic*—"try?" The hiccup catches him by surprise, but the question is still pretty clear.

"Well, pretty much anything," Jeff says. "We talked about it, and we're willing to find a way to work around you trying pretty much whatever you want, with either one or both of us." He grins a little as Dan hiccups again. "We understand that you're maybe not looking for anything serious, and... we know we're not exactly the only option that you've got open to you right now." He glances at Evan, who is glowering just at the thought. "We just thought... Jesus, Dan. Do you want a glass of water or something?"

The hiccups are coming fast and hard, and Dan is having a little trouble concentrating on what Jeff's saying. "No, I'm"—*hic*—"I'm fine," he manages. "I"—*hic*—"I just don't quite"—*hic*—

"Oh, for Pete's sake." Evan heads for the door. "I'm gonna get you a glass of water." Evan heads through the door toward the kitchen, and Jeff just sits back in his chair and tries not to react to Dan's problem.

"Don't laugh,"—*hic*—"man. It's not funny."

Jeff doubles over, and Dan guesses that maybe it is a little funny. Evan comes back with the glass of water, and hands it to Dan. "You gotta drink out of the wrong side, man."

"I"—*hic*—"I know how to"—*hic*—"get rid of hiccups!" he says, and leans over to drink out of the far side of the glass. He tries to ignore Jeff and Evan, who are both pretty amused by the whole situation. He hiccups in the middle of the first sip and sends some water up his nose, which of course sets Jeff and Evan off even more. Finally he gets a proper swallow down, and cautiously brings himself back upright. He seems to be back under control, and Jeff and Evan sigh as they calm down. Dan grins a little. Even if he's the butt of the joke, it still feels pretty good to hear them laugh.

They sit quietly for a moment, and then Evan giggles a little. Jeff brings his hand over to Evan's neck in that familiar grip, but this time Evan leans into it, all the way over until his head is nestled into Jeff's shoulder. And then he giggles again. Jeff raises his eyes to Dan's in amusement, and Dan is almost frozen with how good it feels. He wonders for a moment if this is what they could possibly mean, if they could be suggesting that Dan could have this, could be part of this circle of affection and warmth. Jeff's watching him, seems to be reading his reaction, and Dan wonders what would happen if he went over and sat on Jeff's other side, maybe down on the porch floor so he could lean back against Jeff's leg. Maybe one of Evan's big, strong hands would come down and rest on his shoulder, or run through his hair….

Jeff moves a little, and Dan is afraid that he's going to hold out his hand to invite Dan over, and equally afraid that he isn't going to. It breaks the spell, and Dan snaps almost to attention. "Okay, so, uh… I don't really know where to go from here. I mean… it's a lot. You've… I'm not quite sure what… yeah." He sits down on the top step and leans against the porch railing, facing the other two men. "Can we just sleep on this or something? I mean, I think I probably have questions, but I don't even know what they are."

Jeff runs his arm up around Evan's shoulder and nods. "Yeah. You're right, it is a lot. But, seriously, Dan… it can be whatever you want it to be. As casual or as serious as you want." He shakes his head a bit. "And it can also be nothing at all. That's… that's obviously an option. We're just hoping you'll give us a chance."

Dan frowns even as he nods. He still can't quite wrap his head around exactly what Jeff and Evan are thinking of, how they think things might work. He thinks of Justin, thinks of how quickly he'd known what was right and how long it had taken Dan to catch up, but this isn't like that. He and Justin had been a regular couple, not… whatever it is that Jeff and Evan are thinking of. And then Dan remembers Justin's parents, how they'd tried to persuade Justin to slow down, remembers Chris's mother calling him an opportunistic drifter, thinks of the dirty looks they'd gotten sometimes for being too obviously together in public, the hate mail after Justin had kissed him at Rolex... maybe that relationship hadn't been exactly traditional, either.

Lou has seen Dan sitting on the floor and rouses herself to walk up the stairs and climb over his legs and then collapse next to him, nuzzling her chin into his lap. He obediently lifts his hand and starts petting her, and she groans a little and nestles in, reaching her legs out straight behind her in an ecstatic stretch.

"Jesus, Jeff, your dog is such a slut," Evan murmurs.

"Don't tell me you're getting jealous of *her* now, kid," Jeff replies, and brings his hand up to ruffle Evan's hair.

Evan snorts a little and nuzzles in more, and Dan can see that he's kissing Jeff's neck, and then he sees the skin stretch a little bit as he nips. Jeff doesn't stop him, just leans his head back to give him more room, and when Dan's eyes go to Jeff's he sees that the other man is watching him, seeing his reaction. Dan blushes and looks down at Lou, but then he can't help looking back up, and Jeff smiles a little when he does, angles his head to give Dan a better view of the spot where Evan is working his mouth, and Dan feels a stir of heat when he realizes that Evan is sucking on Jeff's neck, marking him. When Evan is satisfied, he pulls his head back a little and gives Jeff's neck a quick lick, then a soft kiss, and then he turns his head, and *he's* looking at Dan as well, and the two of them together, their eyes blazing with controlled fire, staring at Dan as if they're daring him to do something, they're sin and comfort wrapped up in one bundle, and it's too much, much too much.

Dan almost kicks Lou he climbs to his feet so quickly. "Okay, I've gotta get up tomorrow. I'm gonna go to bed now... go to sleep... you guys are welcome to stay out here if you want, I'll just...."

But Jeff and Evan are standing up, too, Jeff maybe looking a little apologetic but Evan still burningly, challengingly sensual. "That's okay, Dan. We should be going." Dan's amazed that Jeff can sound so calm. "Thanks for listening, tonight. We're happy to talk again, if you want clarification or have any ideas or anything." He smiles. "Ball's in your court."

And then Evan's pushing forward a little, and he's quiet, but there's too much tension in his voice to call him calm. "Are you going to see Ryan again?"

Dan isn't sure how to answer that. "Well, yeah—he's got my truck."

"I'll buy you a *new* truck," Evan practically growls, and Dan can see Jeff's hand sliding up his back, trying to soothe him.

Dan just looks at him for a second. This is too much, too intense. "I like my old truck. And, yeah, if he's still into it... I'm gonna see him again." Evan's face darkens a little, and at first Dan thinks that it's anger, but then he realizes that it's disappointment or even hurt.

"Are you gonna think about us? Consider it?" Dan thinks that Evan is trying for the challenging tone again, but there's too much else in his voice to really carry it off.

Dan looks at them both, sees warm, gentle Jeff and hot, passionate Evan, and he gives the honest answer. "Yeah," he says. "I'm going to think about you both." And then he turns and goes into the house and shuts the door carefully behind him.

chapter 26

DAN doesn't know what to do with himself once he's safely inside. He's not sure what just happened, and he needs some time to process it. Maybe a lot of time. He wishes he had a dog, someone to talk to, to recount the conversation to without having to worry about the response. He thinks about opening the door back up, walking outside, grabbing Lou and coming back in without an explanation. He thinks that wouldn't leave Jeff and Evan any more flabbergasted than they've left him.

He knows he should go to bed. He has a lot to do the next day and would prefer to be well-rested while doing it, but he also knows there's no way his brain will stop racing long enough to get any sleep. He wishes he could call Chris, but it's pushing midnight in California, which means that it's almost three a.m. in Kentucky. Besides, maybe Dan needs to figure things out for himself for a change, instead of running to Chris all the time. And what would Chris think, anyway, with a phone call one day about one guy, a call the next day about two others? What kind of way is that to honor Justin's memory?

Dan goes up to his bedroom, and looks at the photograph on his bedside table: Justin and him at the lake, the picture he'd stolen from the funeral home. He reaches out and touches it, and then, feeling a little foolish, he begins to talk. "Hey, baby. Did you hear any of that? It's a bit crazy, right?" Dan looks at himself, talking to a photograph, and wonders if he's really in any condition to judge "crazy." He keeps going anyway. "It seems like things are happening really fast, Justin. I mean, for a year it was like everything was frozen, and then everything just went nuts." He pauses for a second, decides maybe Justin needs a bit more background information. "I went out with a guy today. I mean, we kind of went out yesterday, but today... yeah, today was a date." He pauses, almost expects the glass in the picture frame to crack or something, but there's no reaction to his news. He's not sure if he feels relieved or disappointed.

"He's a good guy, I think. And Jeff and Evan are good guys too. I'm pretty sure. It's just—I don't want new people. I want you." Dan thinks for a minute. "I mean, I *want* them, I guess. You know. It's been a long time. And, I don't know, sometimes I want more than just the sex, I guess. I don't know. I just—" Dan breaks off. He's talking to a photograph. He needs to get a grip.

He toes off his shoes and shrugs out his jeans, climbs into bed in his Henley and underwear. He doesn't think he's going to be able to sleep, but he's tired, so he wants to give it a try. He thinks about Jeff and Evan, wonders what the details of their plan might be. Their relationship seems confusing enough with just two of them in it. Dan can't imagine adding a third.

Then he thinks about Ryan. Is there any way that he's for real, that he's really that laid back and happy with whatever Dan can give him? It seems unlikely, but the guy really appears to be genuine. Dan thinks about kissing him. Thinks about kissing Justin. He and Justin had been together for a long time, and they'd gotten a little casual about their kisses, maybe. They were great, from comfortable greetings to passionate explorations, but they had been totally secure, nothing tentative about them. It had been beautiful to feel so safe, but maybe there's something to be said for being a bit nervous, a bit unsure. Maybe adrenaline adds an interesting flavor occasionally.

Dan doesn't feel himself getting sleepy, but the next thing he knows the early morning sun is shining through his window. He lies in bed for a few minutes and thinks about the previous day, and then he rolls over and grabs his phone. Chris will be at work by now, but he never seems to care if Dan interrupts him there. Sometimes Dan isn't sure Chris is really a lawyer; he never seems to do much that seems like law to Dan.

Chris picks up on the second ring. "Danielle. I was gonna try to call you later today. How'd it go Saturday night?"

"Saturday night?" Dan honestly has to search his mind a little to remember what had happened Saturday night. It seems like it was about seven crises ago. "Oh, yeah, with Ryan. It was good."

"Yeah? Like… how good?"

"Good enough that I spent most of yesterday with him as well." Dan just lets that sit there for a while. He needs a minute to decide how to bring up the more pressing matter.

"Really? Huh. And you had fun?"

"Yeah, I guess. I mean… he says casual is fine, we can take it slow, all that stuff. I dunno… it seems good….”

"Did you tell him about Justin?" Chris sounds like he's trying pretty hard to keep his voice neutral, but Dan has no idea what emotions his friend might be trying to hide.

"Yeah. Eventually. It just…. I was being a bit mental… it seemed like he deserved an explanation." Dan pauses. "But that's not really what I wanted to talk to you about." He waits again, but Chris just makes an inquisitive humming sound. "So…." Dan almost laughs. "Do you remember when we were in JP's that night and Jeff and Evan came over, and you said they'd been checking me out?"

There's a pause, and then Chris says, "Yes…."

"So, uh… maybe you were right, a bit."

"Danielle, of course I was right." Chris sounds like he hasn't really heard the content beyond the admission of his correctness. Then he catches himself. "But what happened? A day and a half ago you jumped on me for asking about Jeff, and now… what'd he do?"

"He didn't *do* anything. He didn't even say much, really. It was more Evan. And he just… I don't know, I guess he just suggested… shit, I don't know, really. He just said they were interested, and I should think about it, and the ball was in my court."

There's silence for a moment, then, "Are you shitting me?"

"Uh, no. I don't think so." Dan has a flash of doubt, wonders if he could possibly have misinterpreted something. It had seemed pretty clear the night before, the big picture if not the details. Could he have gotten it that wrong? Then he remembers Evan sucking on Jeff's neck, remembers Jeff's eyes burning into his as it happened, and he knows he got the right idea.

"Well, shit, Dan. I mean… okay, let me be a lawyer for a quick second, okay? He's your boss, and that's a pretty kinky setup. If he puts any sort of pressure on you, or hell, even if he doesn't but you think that maybe you'd like a little extra money—you let me know, and we'll sue his ass, okay?"

"No, man, it's not like that." Dan isn't quite sure why it isn't, but he knows that doesn't sound right. "I mean, he made it really clear that it wasn't connected to work at all."

"A gay threesome? Dan, I don't care how clear he made it—if you want to, we can make a stink about it. He'd settle out of court to avoid the publicity. How'd you like to own those horses instead of riding them for somebody else?"

"Jesus, Chris, no." This is a whole layer of complications that Dan doesn't want to get into. Maybe calling Chris was a bad idea. "I don't... I don't feel harassed. I mean, I'm a bit freaked out, but I don't think he was abusing his power. Okay?"

Chris sounds a bit grudging. "Okay... but if that changes at any point, you let me know."

"Yeah, okay. Thanks, I guess."

"Well, I guess you're welcome." Chris seems to be coming down a little bit, less lawyer-protector and more curious friend. "So, what are you thinking? Are you into it?"

Dan sighs. "I don't think so. I mean, they're both hot, but... it'd be pretty intense, right? I mean, they said I could just hook up with one of them... I think. But even that would be too many strings, right? I'm not even sure I'm up for something with Ryan."

"Okay. That makes sense. Are you comfortable telling them that?"

"Jesus, Chris, stop making it sound like I'm a little girl!" Dan catches himself. "I mean, *obviously* I'm not comfortable telling them that, but... I can do it."

"Yeah? Okay. And... how hard do you want to shut the door?"

"What?"

"Are you not into it because it's too soon, or are you not into it at all?"

Dan takes it back—Chris might just be a pretty good lawyer. His cross-examination technique is gentle, but effective. "Shit. I don't know."

Dan can hear Chris's smile. "Damn. You're a kinky bastard, aren't you, Danny?"

Dan laughs, and he can feel the tension flow out of his shoulders. "Shut up, Chris." Calling Chris was a good idea.

"Hey, I'm just saying—maybe you can tell them 'not now', instead of 'not at all', you know?"

"Yeah, but then won't it just be hanging over us all the time? I mean, maybe it'd be a better idea to just shoot it down hard, and not have to think about it again."

"Yeah, maybe." Chris doesn't sound convinced. "But, seriously, Dan... isn't it kinda fun to have something like that hanging over you? I mean, the possibility of a hot threeway isn't exactly a terrible thing. And you know your brain is gonna find *something* to be uptight about... it might as well be something hot."

"Jesus, Chris, could you be any more into this? I half expect you to fly out and volunteer to take my place."

Chris laughs a little. "No, man, I'm just saying—if I was offered a threeway with hot members of the gender of my preference—I'd be pretty damn tempted."

"Okay, yeah. But... okay, this part's a little fuzzier... but they said they weren't just attracted; they said they were *interested*. Like... I don't know...." Dan can feel his face going red and is glad that Chris is far away. "Like it's more than just physical. Or something."

There's a pause. "Huh. Okay. So what do you think that means?"

"What do you mean, 'what does it mean'? It means... I dunno, they *like* me."

"Now who's making you sound like a little girl?"

"Fuck you, Foster. But you know what it means. So, does that change anything?"

"I dunno, Wheeler, you tell me." He just sits on the phone and waits.

Maybe calling Chris *was* a bad idea...

"I mean... it doesn't make me any more likely to want something right now. Makes it less likely, I guess. But, I dunno, in the future? What do... what do you think that means? Like, do they want to... I dunno, *date* or something?"

"What'd they say they wanted?"

Dan wracks his brain. "I don't know—I think they said it was flexible, it was up to me... but, you know, I'm sure there's parameters on that. I just have no idea what they are."

Chris snorts. "Well, if you decide to get into this as more than a one-time thing, you damn well need to figure that out. I could help you—we'd draw up a contract."

"You're a freak, Chris. I'm not having a dating contract."

"I dunno, man… something like this, you'd want to make sure everyone's expectations are crystal clear—that sounds like a job for a contract."

"Okay, well, you're not writing a dating contract for me and my boss and his lover. Okay?"

"First thing we'd work out would be titles. If you're all in this, it wouldn't get to be 'your *boss*' and '*his* lover', it'd be 'your lovers'." Chris sounds like he's enjoying himself. "I should jot down another few notes, do a bit of research, maybe check for precedents. This could be an important document for future gay threesomes."

"You're a menace to the legal profession, Chris." Dan thinks for a moment. "I guess it doesn't really matter for now, right? I mean, either way, I'm not into it right now, probably not ever. So if I shut the door, but don't slam it, then I'm covering all the bases, right?"

"Sounds safe. Just make sure you're not being a tease, Danny. You like these guys. You don't want to lead them on if you're absolutely not into it."

"No. I won't. I'll just… try to be honest." Dan thinks that might be easier to say than to do, but he figures he can give it a try.

"Well, all right. Have you got any other bombshells to drop on me, or can I get back to work?"

"Your important 'gay threesome' research?"

"I'm not at liberty to discuss the details at this time."

"Yeah, that's what I thought. If you need any terms explained… don't call me, please."

They laugh as they hang up, and Dan does feel a bit better. He hasn't come up with a long-term solution, but he knows what he's thinking right now, and that's better than he's usually been doing lately.

He finds clean clothes and some breakfast and heads down to the barn. Tat, Sara, Michelle, and Robyn are already there, and Dan feels like a bit of a slacker, but he checks his watch, and it's not even seven thirty yet. Seems like everyone just wants to get an early start on the week.

Sara gets left behind to do the chores, but the others saddle up and go up the hill to the cross-country course. Dan puts Tat on Chaucer and tells her that she can only ride on the flat until she gets used to him, but the three actual trainers give their horses a good workout over the obstacles, and then all four go for a little hack along the back property line. Dan's on Monty, and he's reminded again how much he loves the big gelding's power and heart. Smokey treats everything he sees as if it's expected and kind of interesting. Monty acts like everything's a total surprise but shows no fear, only a determination to overcome the obstacle. Dan finds himself trying to compare the two to Jeff and Evan, and cuts off the train of thought. Horses are horses, and Dan knows he loves them. He doesn't want to start confusing them with people in his mind.

They go back down to the barn, and Dan spends a little time talking to everybody, figuring out training goals for each horse for the week. He's registered several of the animals in a horse trial the next weekend, so the barn's priority will be to work with them and make sure any kinks have been worked out. It feels good to be back with the horses, back where he's confident in his abilities and his role. He can't totally keep his mind off other things, though, and when he's talking to Tat about Sunshine's training, his mind wanders to her brother more often than it should.

"So, you understand what we're trying for there?" he asks. "Sunshine is registered *hors concours*. That means that she's competing at a lower level than she should be, so she won't be eligible for any prizes. We're treating this as her introduction to California, and as an opportunity for you to get some experience. She's ready to go quite a bit higher as soon as you are, so most of our training is going to concentrate on getting you up to her level. Does that make sense?"

Tat nods, but looks a little pensive. "Is it bad that I'm holding her back? I mean, is she losing important opportunities or something?"

Dan grins and resists the urge to ruffle Tat's hair. "No, she's fine. She's probably happy to take it easy for a bit. Top-level eventing is really hard on horses. It's pretty rare to find one that retires because of old age rather than injury. So you're essentially giving her body a bit of a break, and that could be good in the long run."

Tat nods but still looks worried. "But then, should I *never* compete her at the higher levels? If that's going to hurt her?"

That's a tougher question. The ethics of his sport are not crystal clear for Dan. "I don't think so. Wait until you see her next weekend; she'll be so alive, so enthusiastic. Good eventers are competitive—if they don't want to win, they don't do well." Tat is looking at him like he holds the answers to the universe, and it's a little unsettling, but he tries to find something intelligent to say. "It's like… do you remember what you said about Justin?" He's proud that he's saying this without having to fight back a huge rush of emotion. Maybe things are getting better. "You said that he seemed so happy when he was eventing, like that's what he was meant to do." She nods in recollection. "That's what a good eventing horse is like too—it's like they've found their place in the universe, and they *have* to give it all they've got. You know?" Tatiana is smiling now. "Wait and see her on Sunday, and then you can figure out what you think she'd want to do."

Tatiana nods and starts to move away, but Dan can't help himself. "Hey, Tat? Is your brother around, do you know? I have some stuff to go over with him."

She shakes her head. "No, he left just after I got up this morning. Said he had a big day at work, probably wouldn't be home until late."

Dan feels a bit foolish. Had he expected Evan to abandon his multi-billion-dollar business just to sit around and wait for Dan to want to talk to him? "Oh, yeah, okay. Uh, what about Jeff?"

"He left with Evan. But if there's something important, you could give them a call. I'm sure they wouldn't mind."

"No. There's nothing important. I can just catch up with them later." She grins as she heads back to work, and Dan is left feeling a bit foolish. He had been dreading the conversation with Evan and Jeff, expecting awkwardness and embarrassment, but now that he knows it isn't going to happen for a while, he feels a bit let down. He shakes his head and focuses on his work. It seems like horses are about the only thing he understands these days.

chapter 27

DAN rides three more horses that day, and the last of them, an off-the-track Thoroughbred called Winston, has such a bad day and is so stubborn about not leg-yielding that Dan's muscles are almost shaking by the time he finally gets the beast to behave. They manage one properly rounded trip around the ring in each direction and then Dan hops off quickly, grabbing the opportunity to end the training session on a positive note. Winston's still a little hot, and once he's got the rider off his back he's a total sweetheart, with none of the pigheadedness he'd been showing under saddle. So Dan pulls off his tack and walks him with a lead rope and a cooler for a while, then takes him out to the side of the barn and hoses him off. The cool water feels good on Dan, too, and he's not exactly careful about keeping himself dry.

He's just finished rinsing his head under the end of the hose when he hears Robyn's voice. "Oh, *there* you are!" Dan looks up and sees her just as she finishes stating the obvious. "Ryan's here." She gives Dan a quick look-over and then says something under her breath to Ryan. He just grins at her and nods in agreement, and she turns and heads back the way she came.

Ryan holds up Dan's car keys in one hand, and takes a couple cautious steps forward before coming to a reluctant halt. Dan can't figure out what the problem is, and then realizes that he's standing next to twelve hundred pounds of restless animal. Winston is a teddy bear, nudging Dan a little to get back to the bath time, but apparently Ryan isn't a big fan. Dan grins. It's nice to see someone else's vulnerability for a change.

"He's okay, man. He's really friendly." Ryan nods, but doesn't come any closer. He is *looking*, though, and Dan remembers that he's soaking wet from the waist up, and more than a little damp lower down. He holds out his arms in mimicry of Ryan's move from the night before. "See something interesting?" he asks teasingly. "Wanna come over and have a closer look?"

Ryan chuckles nervously, his eyes cutting from the horse to Dan and then back. "Is there any way you could get rid of the audience?"

"Who, Winston?" Dan shrugs his shoulder in under Winston's chin, draping one arm up and around his head. "Nah. Winston likes to watch." Dan grins then but tells himself to stop teasing. Ryan is being a good guy about Dan's issues, and Dan shouldn't be working him up unless he's willing to do something about it. He takes hold of the end of the lead rope and walks toward Ryan, leaving the horse behind. When Dan gets to the end of the rope, he's still a couple of feet away, but Ryan makes up the difference, stepping forward and eagerly meeting Dan's mouth with his.

Dan's feeling a lot more relaxed today. When Ryan brings a hand up to cup his head, he goes with it, and when Ryan's other hand brushes gently against Dan's torso, knuckles running along his abs through his soaked shirt, Dan leans into it a little, deepening the kiss and bringing their bodies into contact. He's vaguely aware that there's no longer any tension on the lead rope, but he doesn't think much about it until he feels warm, sweet breath on his cheek and finds Ryan jumping backward in alarm.

Ryan looks like he's been nuzzled by a bear rather than a horse, but Dan tries to keep a straight face. "Seriously, man, it's okay. Come on, you should meet him. This is…. You not liking horses is like if I was scared of guitars or something…."

Ryan shakes his head, trying to relax. "What am I supposed to do?"

"I dunno. Come over and say hi?"

"Yeah, he already said hi, thanks!"

"Come on…. Look, I'll hold his head really snug, okay? So he can't move. You can just come up and pat him on the neck, or the shoulder." Dan tightens up the lead rope as promised, and Ryan takes a tentative step forward, then another when Winston doesn't react. He works his way around to the side, and reaches out to touch the horse's neck with the tips of his finger.

He jerks them back quickly, and looks at them. "He's wet."

"Yeah, dude, we were having a bath." Dan smiles a little. "Okay, now bring your hand back, and rest the palm of it on his neck for five seconds. Okay?"

"Five seconds." Ryan looks a little dubious, but he leans forward and puts his hand on Winston's neck. Dan moves then, one arm still reaching back to hold the lead rope, the other pulling Ryan's face around for another kiss. Dan puts some effort into this one, working their lips open and bringing his tongue forward to meet Ryan's eagerness. Ryan's spare arm wraps around Dan's back, pulling him in tighter, and Dan doesn't resist. He does notice when the hand from Winston's neck moves over to his own, and he pulls his mouth away a little in protest. Ryan seems to know what he's going to say, and murmurs, "It's been way more than five seconds," before finding Dan's lips again.

It's not long before Winston gets restless and moves a bit, and Ryan's attention is distracted long enough for Dan to remember where he is, and remember why making out at work is an *especially* bad idea given his current circumstance. He pulls away a little, and Ryan lets him go, his eyes running over Dan's heated face and down over the wet shirt clinging to his body. He shakes his head. "Damn, Robyn was right."

"Yeah? What'd she say?"

"She said you oughta be illegal," Ryan rumbles, and Dan ducks over to the other side of Winston before he gets dragged back in.

"Well, illegal at work, at least," Dan says, as much to himself as to Ryan. Ryan seems to take the warning, though, and takes a step back.

"I brought the truck back out… new fan belt and Donny did a couple other things as well—none of it cost much, and he said you definitely needed it done."

Dan sighs and nods, has a quick flash back to Evan's offer to buy him a new truck. He knows it hadn't been meant seriously, at least not entirely, but he wonders what it would be like to have that kind of money. Thanks to the back pay from the Archers and the generous moving allowance to get to California, Dan has savings in the bank for pretty much the first time in his life, but he's been poor too long to take it for granted, and he doesn't want to blow it on a new truck. Or on truck repairs, really, but at least they're cheaper. "Okay, yeah. Is there a bill?"

Ryan nods. "I left it in the truck. I was hoping I could get a lift back into town?"

"Yeah, absolutely. Thanks for helping out with this." Dan looks down at himself. "Are you in a hurry? I should probably change."

Ryan checks his watch. "I'm supposed to be at work in about an hour, and I need to put on my work clothes. So maybe if we left here in forty minutes or so?"

"Yeah, that's good. Let me just dry Winston off a bit, and then he can go in the pasture and I can get a quick shower and we'll go."

"A shower, now? Jesus, you were just about killing me with the 'changing' talk, and now there's a shower?" Ryan's voice is teasing, but there's heat in his eyes.

"Well, if you want to drive into town with someone who smells like a horse, I guess that's your call."

Ryan grins. "I wouldn't mind the drive, but I was gonna ask if you wanted to have dinner at the restaurant. Mondays are slow, so I'll probably have a bit of spare time. And the paninis miss you."

Dan can feel his mouth starting to water. "Damn, absolutely. Bring it on!" A part of his head reminds him that this is three days in a row that he's spent time with Ryan, and that's not exactly casual, but he ignores it in favor of thinking about the paninis.

Dan runs the sweat scraper over Winston and puts some oil on his hooves to help deal with the dry California climate, and then turns him out in the paddock and calls in to tell Robyn that he's leaving. She nods and waves, and he and Ryan pile into the truck for the short trip to the guest house. Dan's mostly dry by now, but one good thing about having a cheap old truck is the vinyl seat covers. He really doesn't need to worry about wrecking the upholstery.

It's a bit awkward when they get to the house. Obviously Dan's not going to ask Ryan to wait in the truck, but he doesn't want to make it seem like he's inviting him *in*, either. Ryan solves the problem by commenting on the view from the porch, and asking if he can sit out there while Dan cleans up. Dan doesn't know if Ryan's being really tactful or just likes looking at mountains, but he doesn't complain either way, and promises to just be a couple minutes.

He barely rinses himself off in the shower and then pulls on clean clothes and heads down the stairs. When he gets to the bottom he hears voices on the porch, and proceeds a bit more cautiously. He looks out through the window and sees Ryan talking to Jeff. They both seem relaxed. It looks like Jeff is telling a story, and Ryan is listening happily, interjecting comments now and then. Dan has no idea how his life got so complicated, and he almost wishes that other people could be a bit more uncomfortable about things, to keep him from feeling like quite such a spaz. But it's Ryan and Jeff, so expecting them to be anything but laid back might be asking a lot.

He waits until there seems to be a pause in the conversation, and they both look up with smiles when he opens the door and steps out.

"Hey, Dan," Jeff says. "Evan's working late, so I just dropped by to see if you wanted to get some dinner, but it seems like I'm a little too late." As usual, Dan has trouble reading his face.

"I said he should come with. I'm gonna be working most of the time, so it'd be good for you to have some company," Ryan volunteers.

"Yeah, that'd be great," Dan says. He thinks he means it. "I guess you've probably already had the paninis at Zio's?"

Jeff nods. "Yeah—they're worth the trip, no doubt. But I don't want to intrude." Jeff gives him another unreadable look, and Dan sighs internally. If the man is honestly trying to communicate with Dan, what happened to his realization that Dan can't read people?

Dan glances at Ryan, who gives him a laidback shrug in return. Jesus, enough with the body language. Dan decides to lead by example. "I'd be happy to have you along, if you want to come." There. Clarity.

Ryan nods. "And you'd get to ride in that fine piece of American craftsmanship—they don't make 'em like that anymore." He nods at the truck, and Dan gives him a cautious look. Is he making fun or being genuine? Ryan grins and holds his hands up in a 'don't shoot' gesture. "Seriously, man—it's a great truck."

Dan's still suspicious, but he lets it go and turns to Jeff. "If Evan's working late, should we bring Tat?"

Jeff nods. "But you've got to go to your place first, right?" he asks Ryan, who agrees. Jeff turns to Dan. "Why don't you drive Ryan in, I'll go and see what Tat's up to, and we'll meet you there. 'Cause God knows she's not going to appear in public straight from the barn." He glances at Dan's freshly washed self and grins at Ryan. "It's always the pretty ones who end up getting vain."

"Oh, excuse me for not wanting to track horse shit all over your restaurant—" Dan begins, but the other two just laugh at him. Dan is starting to wonder whether it's a good idea to let Ryan and Jeff spend any more time together.

They need to get going, so Jeff heads off to see what Tat's up to—he's got Dan's cell number if they decide not to meet them. Dan and Ryan drive quietly for a while, and then Ryan clears his throat carefully.

"So—*really* never anything between you two?" He doesn't sound threatened, just interested, and maybe a little skeptical.

Dan isn't sure how much he's allowed to say. He doesn't really want to violate Jeff and Evan's privacy. "Not really. Lots of... I don't know, not *flirting...* just sort of an awareness, you know?" Ryan nods. "But nothing's ever actually happened."

"Yet," Ryan adds, and again, he doesn't sound upset by the idea.

"Why, did he say something?" Dan doesn't think Jeff is the 'staking a claim' type, but he's been surprised before.

"Nah, just... I was aware of the awareness, you know?" Ryan shrugs.

"Yeah." Dan doesn't really think he has much to add, so if Ryan's okay with this, he's happy to let it go. They're almost in town before Ryan speaks again.

"I don't really feel like I've got any right to say anything about that," he says softly. "But, you know—keep me in the loop, okay? No surprises?"

Dan wants to deny it all, wants to tell Ryan that there's nothing to worry about. But he also wants to be honest. "Yeah. Yeah, I will. If there's ever anything." He glances over, and Ryan just smiles.

They park behind Ryan's apartment, and it's the same awkward situation as at Dan's house, only this time it's Ryan, so it's not awkward at all. "Hey, come on up for a second. You can see how the other half lives."

"Shit, man, I *am* the other half. I just got a good rental."

Ryan nods as if he's humoring him. "Yeah, okay."

They head up the stairs and into the apartment. It's about what Dan expected, and a hell of a lot nicer than a lot of places he's lived. There's a living area and a bathroom and a bedroom. The only things that look like they're worth anything are the stereo and the guitars. Ryan says, "Make yourself at home. I'll just be a minute." He heads into the bedroom, and Dan flops down on the couch. It's ugly but pretty comfortable.

Ryan is out in just a minute, pants changed, buttoning up a white shirt. It looks beautiful against his golden skin, and Dan has a sudden urge to stand up and try to persuade Ryan to change directions, start undoing buttons instead. Ryan catches him looking but just smiles a little. "Don't you go starting something," he warns. "I've got places to be."

Dan grins and looks at his watch. "Come on, now, we've got a little time...."

Ryan bites his lip a little as he walks over and holds both hands out to Dan. Dan grabs hold and Ryan hauls him to his feet, and Dan tries to keep leaning into him, but Ryan holds him off. "Oh, no. No way. I want more than a *little* time with you."

Dan gives Ryan his best seductive look, and judging by the way Ryan sways toward him, it's pretty good. "Maybe a little now, a little more later...." He's joking, teasing, but he finds that he means it too. He's not quite sure what happened. Maybe the more outrageous suggestion from Jeff and Evan had made the simpler relationship with Ryan seem safer. One way or another, he seems to have gotten over most of his concerns about getting physical. Of course, he has no idea whether that will continue or if he'll have another little freak-out, but he's feeling pretty damn frisky right now.

Unfortunately, Ryan seems to have a little more self-control, or he's a little less interested. Dan chooses to ignore that possibility, but he can't ignore the way that Ryan is working his way toward the door. "Seriously, not even a little?"

Ryan pauses and looks at him, and Dan seizes the opportunity. He surges forward and grabs hold of Ryan, pushing him back against the wall as their mouths join together. Dan works to loosen the carefully tucked in shirt and then his hands are on Ryan's stomach, his chest, and he can feel Ryan's sudden gasp. Ryan tries to turn his head away to lower the intensity, but Dan gets one of his hands up there, holds his face and gently brings him back, slows a little, makes things deeper but less frantic. Ryan is still breathing in short little hitches, but his hands are up and on Dan, running under *his* shirt, along his back... then Ryan's hands come between them, and he's easing Dan away, pushing his forehead against Dan's to separate their lips, and they both stand there for a minute, breathing heavily, not moving.

Ryan finds his voice first. "That was not a *little*." He doesn't sound too upset about it, though.

"Shit. It really wasn't." Dan looks at Ryan a little sheepishly. "I don't know what to say—waiter kink?"

Ryan laughs and pushes him away, tucks his shirt back into his pants. "Excellent, I'm all for it. Usually I get the musician kink, so at least you're original."

"Fuck, yeah, I forgot about that. Damn, get back over here." Dan pretends to reach out for Ryan, but he's just playing. The intensity of his response has left him a little freaked out, and he's not really sorry that they have to go out in public now.

Ryan grins at him as he backs up a little farther. "Not that I'm complaining, but what happened to taking it slow?"

Dan just shakes his head. "Fuck if I know." He shakes his head. "But I don't think I'm complaining, either."

"Good. But, seriously, I do have to go to work. If I'd known I'd have such a good reason for being late tonight, I wouldn't have been late all those other times... but as it is, I'm pretty much on my last chance with them."

Dan nods his head ruefully, but then perks up. "Hey... panini!"

Ryan just laughs as they head out the door and down the stairs. "Man, you're a cliché—the way to a man's heart is through his stomach."

"Dude, I don't mean to be crude, but it wasn't my *heart* that wanted to keep us in that apartment."

Ryan laughs and they drive the few blocks to the restaurant. Ryan goes in and gets to work. Dan goes out and finds a table on the patio. He's not there for long before he's joined by Jeff and a freshly scrubbed Tatiana. Tat seems to be in a bit of a mood. Jeff catches Dan's eye and makes a sort of warning face.

"Hey, Tat, glad you came," he ventures. "Piper didn't take too much out of you this afternoon, then?"

Tat looks like she's torn between sulking and talking about horses. Luckily for everyone, the horse talk wins. "No, she was good. She's really fast, isn't she?"

Dan grins. "Yeah, she is. Thoroughbreds—they're made for speed. But you've got to work on controlling her and making sure she only uses the speed when you want it." Tat nods seriously. Dan nods to indicate Jeff and Tat together. "Are you two still going to do lessons? I can help with the horse end of things, but I honestly don't know that much about training riders." Tat gives Jeff a bit of a dirty look, and Dan begins to sense the general source of the sour mood, if not the exact cause. "I guess Jeff might be getting pretty busy with the art thing—your show's in less than two weeks, right?" Jeff nods, and Dan continues, "But you should probably be taking lessons from somebody."

Tat looks like she might be gearing up for something to say in that area, but then Ryan comes over to take their order and she pours the full weight of her disapproval onto him.

"Hey, guys, can I get you something to drink?" Dan already has a beer, so Ryan's talking to Tat and Jeff.

"Yeah, a beer would be good, thanks," Jeff says, and they all turn to Tat.

"Is your Diet Coke from a can or from a fountain?" she asks in a tone that Dan wouldn't have thought she knew. He wonders if they teach that tone at rich-kid school. He wonders if Evan would mind if he washed Tat's mouth out with soap until she forgot how to use it.

"It's from a can." Ryan's smile is friendly, and Dan wants to stand up and protect him. Had he not heard the tone?

"Is it *really*, though? Or is that just what you're trained to say?" Dan wants to smack her, but Ryan still smiles.

"I can bring you the can unopened with your glass, if you'd like."

Tatiana doesn't really have a comeback for that. "Please do," she says as if she's the queen, and then turns back to her menu. Dan gapes at her in astonishment before turning apologetic eyes to Ryan, who just smiles back.

"Comes with the job," he says softly and then heads to the kitchen, Tat glowering after him.

Dan sits for a minute, but doesn't think he can let this go. "Hey, Tat?" he says softly. She looks up at him, rebellion burning behind her innocent expression. "Tat, I consider you a friend of mine. And I think you know that Ryan's a friend of mine." He tries to catch her eyes, but she's staring over his shoulder. "But that shouldn't really matter, because I don't think anybody deserves to be talked to that way. And it makes it really hard for me to keep thinking of you as a friend when I see you treating someone like that." She just stares at him, and then she stands up.

"I need to go to the bathroom." And she heads off through the restaurant. Dan stares after her helplessly, and it's Jeff who breaks the silence.

"God knows she'd better not have details... but she's picked up on Evan's interest in you." He looks a bit apologetic. "And maybe she's got the idea that Ryan's a threat to that somehow." He shrugs. "I was going to call Evan, and see if he wanted to come meet us here when he's done work, but maybe it's not a good idea. Maybe one hostile Kaminski is enough for one night."

Dan wonders why he and Jeff haven't sat down and talked before this. "I... I don't really see the two things as being connected. I mean... I thought about what you guys talked about last night, and... that's really not something I'm ready for right now. I mean"—he looks around almost furtively—"I mean, if it was just you, that'd be one thing. And I respect what you've got going on with Evan, but... I'm really not up for all that jealous, possessive crap. Not right now, maybe not ever." Jeff is looking at him intently, and Dan looks over to make sure that Tat's not coming back. He feels like this is his opportunity to get things straightened out.

"And I don't really understand the exact mechanics of whatever you were talking about, and, you know, if it ever came down to it we'd definitely have to work out some details." The word "contract" dances through his head, but he suppresses it. "But... me and Ryan... we're right now, not down the road. I don't think we're long-term or anything, but... we're good for now. You know?"

Jeff nods, then looks up at Dan, and his eyes are riveting. "So are you saying you might be interested in something else eventually?"

"Might be? Eventually?" Dan shrugs his shoulders. "I can't say there's no attraction. But... I'm a pretty simple guy. Gay thing aside, I'm pretty traditional, I think. I mean—"

But Ryan arrives with the drinks, and then Tatiana comes back from the bathroom, eyes possibly a little red, but she's polite to Ryan the rest of the night. Jeff and Dan don't really have another chance to talk, but that's okay with Dan. He doesn't really have that much more to say, at least for now.

Jeff and Tat go home as soon as they're done with dinner, and Dan follows soon after. He thinks about sticking around and waiting for Ryan, but they're both tired, and Ryan's scheduled to work until midnight.

Dan reminds himself that his priority is the horses—his and Justin's horses—and he hauls himself home to bed.

chapter 28

DAN spends the next day working, and when he goes home for dinner, showers, reads for a while, and gets ready for bed, he realizes that he's spent the entire day without any contact from Ryan, Jeff, or Evan. He thinks about calling Ryan, but decides against it. Maybe it would be good to take a day off. But he feels a bit like he's going through withdrawal. He's gotten used to a certain level of attention, and apparently he misses it.

The next day starts the same way, but around lunchtime Dan gets a call from Ryan, and he sounds excited.

"Dan, man, you'll never believe it. We got a call yesterday from a record label—Good Dog Records—they're not huge, but they're a fair size, big enough to really help us out. And they had our demo, and they're interested! They're coming down tomorrow night to hear us play live!"

"Holy shit!" Dan doesn't know much about the music industry, but he knows that Ryan's been working for this for a long time. "Congratulations, man! That's incredible."

"Yeah, no kidding! We're gonna be crazy busy getting ready—we don't normally play on Thursdays, so we've got to call around and get people to come, *and* we've got to get the band as tight as it can be. But I wanted to give you a call." His voice softens a little, and Dan wonders if there are other people in the room. "Wanted you to know I'm thinking about you—a lot. I just... I've gotta go for this a hundred percent right now."

"No, absolutely you do. And I can come tomorrow, and I'll try to get some other people to come too. It'll be great."

"Thanks, man." Ryan hesitates a little. "Listen... I can't be.... If it was just me, I'd say the record company should take me as I am, but... there's the whole band to think about. And I don't really know if the company will care about me being gay, if it'll decrease marketability or something... but I can't really take that chance, you know?"

Dan's stomach has tightened up a little. "Yeah, okay. So... do you not want me to come?"

"Shit, no, of course I want you there. I just mean—don't be offended if I don't… you know… if I don't act like a boyfriend."

"Yeah. No, we're not really at the boyfriend stage anyway, right? Just casual." Dan knows that Ryan's got a good point, that it would be insane for him to risk something he's been dreaming about for years over a person he's known for less than a week. But it still feels a bit weird—a bit wrong.

Ryan can obviously sense Dan's feelings on the matter. "You understand why, right?"

"Yeah, Ryan, I'm not an idiot. It's fine." Dan tries to put a lid on things. Ryan had sounded so excited when he called, and Dan doesn't want to be the one who kills that excitement. "So, is there anything I can do to help you get ready? I mean, I don't know anybody out here, and I don't know anything about music, so probably not… but if you need someone to carry heavy things or something…."

Ryan laughs a little. "No, I think we're good. Thanks for the offer, though. It's… I don't know, it's almost too much, you know? It seems like things are happening really fast."

"Well, you deserve it, man. Seriously. You guys are really good, and you've worked hard, and it's about time somebody took some notice, right?"

"Well, yeah, when you put it that way…." Dan can hear Ryan smiling over the phone. Then he hears a voice in the background, and Ryan says, "Okay, I've gotta go now. Scott just got here, we're gonna start rehearsing. But you'll come Thursday, right?"

"Yeah, absolutely. You'll be great, man."

Ryan sounds a little overwhelmed. "Yeah, thanks. Bye."

Dan waits until Tat is on a horse before he tells Robyn the news. Tat's been better about Ryan, but she's still obviously not a huge fan, and there's no point in starting a scrap about nothing. Robyn is excited and starts imagining all the perks of knowing a star, and Dan leaves her to it. The barn is going to its first horse trial on the weekend, and he's driving himself crazy trying to make sure they're as prepared as they can be. He knows it's important to stay flexible, remembers that Karl and Molly used to make changes at five in the morning before leaving for an event, but he's not quite that confident yet. He wants everything totally planned, and he wants it to go smoothly.

Devin is a bit of a music fan, and when he hears the news about the record deal he gets excited even though he's never met Ryan. So he's in for Thursday night, and Michelle and Sara decide they'll come along as well. Dan feels like he's doing his part to fill the seats and make it a good show. He thinks about calling Jeff. He might like to come, but he'd probably bring Evan, and Dan doesn't really think that having a huge rich guy glowering at him would help Ryan put on a good show. Devin is asking for details about the situation, and Dan is trying to explain the few he has, when Tatiana comes in from riding.

"Good Dog Records, he said. Said they were medium size, big enough to be useful. Seriously, man, that's all I've got." Dan holds up his hands.

Tat looks over with interest. "Good Dog Records? Why are you guys talking about them?"

Dan looks at her in some confusion. "What, you've heard of them?" He hadn't really thought that Tat was into music.

"Yeah, we own them." Tat frowns, and then corrects herself. "Well, The Kaminski Corporation owns a majority share of their parent company." She rolls her eyes as if she's trying to remember. "I think that's it. Evan made me learn all this last summer, but I've forgotten some of it. But that was definitely the name, because every time we talked about it Evan would say the 'good dog' part really loud, and the dogs would get confused."

Dan freezes a little. He's not sure what that means, not sure if it means anything. No one else seems to think it's more than an interesting coincidence, but Dan's got a weird feeling.

He heads outside where he can get some peace, and pulls out his cell phone. He doesn't like the idea of calling Evan at work, and he isn't sure if he wants to know the answer to this anyway. If it's a good thing for Ryan, should it matter if it came about in a non-traditional way? But he decides that he does need to know, and he dials the number.

He has Evan's office number, but also his cell, and that's the number Evan had told him to call if he actually wanted to talk to him in person. Apparently the office number would take him through at least a secretary and Linda before he got to talk to the man himself. So Dan calls the cell.

"Hey, Dan, how's it going?" Evan sounds completely innocent, and Dan has a flash of doubt.

"I'm good, thanks. Listen, I'm sorry to bother you at work."

"Nah, don't worry about it. What's up?"

"Okay, uh…." He's starting to feel pretty stupid, but he decides to just get it over with. "Okay. Ryan…" and he's stuck already. Does he need to explain who Ryan is? Surely not, but it seems strange to just leave it like that.

Evan prompts him. "Ryan…."

"Ryan's band got a call from a record company, and they're coming up to hear them. And the company is called Good Dog Records, which Tat says you guys own." Dan leaves it there for a second.

"Well, they're a subsidiary of a company in which our family company has a majority share."

Dan can't tell if Evan is hedging, or if that's actually an important distinction.

"Yeah, okay… what I want to know is… did you have anything to do with him getting the call?"

There's a pause. "How would you feel if I did?"

Dan huffs out a little. "I don't know, man. Did you?"

Evan sounds reluctant to answer. "Okay, yes, I did, but not in some sinister get-rid-of-the-competition way. Seriously. I told you that Jeff and I go there a lot to hear music, and we both really like Ryan's band. So the other day I was looking over some papers and the Good Dog name caught my eye, and I was thinking of Ryan a bit at the same time, because… not in an angry way, just sort of a what's-he-got-that-we-haven't-got kind of way. You know?"

"Okay…."

"Okay, so I just thought, hey, I should mention his name to them, maybe they'd be interested. So I did. And that's it. I got a call from their president yesterday, and he said they'd found a copy of their demo—so Ryan sent the demo in himself. It wasn't something they had to ask for—and had a listen, and they were sending people out to see them live. That's all I did." There's dead air while Dan thinks, and then Evan fills it. "It could work out totally against me, really, because maybe they'll give him some money to stay in one place for a while and get better, rather than going on the road. Or maybe they won't like him at all, and I wouldn't interfere with that. I just made a little suggestion."

Dan sighs. "Yeah, okay, but if the owner of your subsidiary or… whatever, if the top guy makes a suggestion—it's a little more than a suggestion, isn't it? I mean, if you suggest that I look at a new source of sweet feed, I'm gonna look at it. You know?"

"So what am I supposed to do, not speak? And there's nothing wrong with having them look, right? As long as I don't pressure their decision? Like, if I suggested the new food, and you looked at it and decided that it wasn't right for your horses, I'd accept that. And if these guys go see Ryan, and they don't like him… okay."

Dan doesn't really know how to deal with this. Evan's right, it is a good thing for Ryan, and he's right that there's no guarantee that they'll send Ryan out on tour right away, assuming that Evan is telling the truth and isn't telling the company exactly what to do….

"Dan?" Evan sounds tentative. "Hey, are you mad?"

"I don't know… no. I'm not mad. I just… do you understand how fucked-up this is, that a little word from you can change somebody's life like that?"

"But in a good way, right? I mean, it's not like I said they *shouldn't* sign him, just 'cause I was pissed off at him. And it's not like I went and told him that I'd get him a recording deal if he stopped seeing you… right?"

"Jesus, Evan, those are both really nasty options!"

"Yeah, but they're what I *didn't* do! I did the good one!"

Dan laughs a little. "Yeah. I guess." There's a pause, and then Dan continues. "Listen, a bunch of us are going to hear them on Thursday. Do you want to come with us?" Then a thought hits him. "Wait, would the record guys know you by sight? Like, would they be weird about you being there? Would it influence things?"

"Nah, I don't think so. Well, I don't know. I wouldn't have met them, but… they might recognize me. But even if they did, they'd just know that I liked the band. And that's true, so… would it be so bad?"

"I don't know. I think Ryan would probably rather know that he'd made it on his own."

"Well, even if they recognize me, Ryan wouldn't need to know, would he?"

"I don't want to start lying to him, or keeping things from him."

"So… things are still going well between you?" Evan sounds like he knows he's getting into a tricky area.

"Yeah, they are." Dan wants to sound confident, but he doesn't want to rub Evan's face in it.

"So… I *shouldn't* think of Thursday night as us going on a date?" The mischief is clear in Evan's voice, and Dan laughs.

"Uh, no, probably not."

"Damn. Hey, how about on the weekend? Tat wants me to come along, says she's nervous about competing. Can I consider *that* a date?"

"Dude, I'm gonna be working my ass off all day Sunday! If that's your idea of a date, we are *never* going out!"

There's a pause, and then Evan says, "But if I thought of something better, if I thought of something really good—maybe we would?"

Dan sighs. "Evan, it's… there's a lot of complicated stuff getting in the way of us going out. I like you, I do, and… you know, you're good-looking and all… but I'm not really looking for complications right now."

Evan sounds a bit tentative. "So… is it bugging you, me asking you out? Letting you know I'm interested?"

Dan gives it a little thought. "If it's just like this? Just joking around? Nah, that doesn't bug me. But… I can't handle the aggressive bullshit, man. If you're gonna be an ass around Ryan, or around anyone else that I might be interested in… yeah, that's gonna bug me."

There's silence, and Dan wonders if he's taken the honesty thing a bit too far. "Evan?"

"Yeah, sorry… I just… I honestly hadn't considered the possibility of someone else other than Ryan. I was just getting used to the idea of him… shit… but you're not actually seeing anyone else right now, right?"

"No, but, Evan… Ryan isn't what's keeping me from being interested in you and Jeff. You know?"

"Yeah—that's what Jeff said." Evan pauses. "But I bet if it was just Jeff, you'd be interested, right?" Dan's mind races. He'd essentially told Jeff that the night before, but would Jeff really have repeated it to Evan?

"I've seen the way you look at him, Dan."

"Yeah, okay, maybe. But he's with you, I know that. I'm not... I wouldn't... I mean, even if I could, which I know I couldn't, I still *wouldn't*."

Evan laughs softly. "Yeah, okay, chill out. I didn't mean to make you panic. I'm just saying... it's me that's the problem. It's good to know that, so I know what I can work on."

"Evan... seriously, it's not *you*. It's just.... I'm a pretty conservative guy. It could be Jeff and his identical-in-every-way brother, and I'd still be totally freaked out by the... the threesome aspect of things."

Evan sounds excited. "Okay, but that's what we were saying about flexibility... it doesn't have to be a full-on threesome. I mean, don't get me wrong; I think that would be *awesome*, but we could all just be, like a series of twosomes, you know? It could be me and Jeff, you and Jeff, and, I dunno, maybe you and me... right? Would that be less freaky?"

"Yeah, okay, but what if it ended up being you and Jeff and me and Jeff, and that's it? I mean, I'm last-man-in, and I think I'd have trouble with that situation. Are you saying you wouldn't?"

There's another pause, and then Evan's voice is somber. "Yeah, man. That'd drive me fucking nuts. But I could figure something out, you know? I mean, I could keep a lid on things. Handle it with a little more *savoir faire* than you've seen from me so far. And I'd figure out a way to put a leash on Tat, too—sorry about that. But... yeah, if you're just into Jeff, you should go for it. He's... he's a great guy."

Dan had thought this conversation was clearing things up for him, but now he's even more confused. "But... why would you let that happen? You know you could stop it."

"No. I don't know that I could." Evan sounds tired. "I mean, I could stop you and Jeff, yeah. You're both decent guys. You wouldn't do that if I said it wasn't okay. But... I can't... I can't keep Jeff happy forever. He's.... I don't know... restless? Maybe?" Dan doesn't like hearing Evan sound like this, doesn't like hearing him sound defeated. "I mean, don't get me wrong... I want you, Dan. I want you a lot. But I think maybe Jeff kind of *needs* you. You know? Or maybe not you, exactly—I swear, man I'm not trying to put more pressure on you—but he needs more than he's getting with me."

"Jesus... has Jeff actually said any of this?"

"Jeff? Oh, no, never." Evan sounds bitter now. "Jeff's all about everybody else's needs, making everybody else feel good, but he won't even admit to being in a bad mood, let alone having some sort of serious issue. I don't know if he thinks it makes him weak, or if he thinks he's imposing… but, no, he just brushes me off whenever I try to bring it up." Evan takes a somewhat shaky breath. "Shit, man, I'm sorry. I didn't mean to lay all this on you. You just called to find out about your boyfriend's band."

"He's not my boyfriend." The words are out before Dan even knows he's thinking them. "I mean… it's just casual."

"Yeah, okay. Sorry. Anyway, you just called about that, and I drag you into some big drama. Sorry."

"No, Evan, it's fine. I mean… it helps me understand, a bit. I can't— I don't think I can be everything you want me to be. But… I do really like *both* of you. I… I don't know. Do you think maybe we could try just hanging out a little, just… *not* dating, just—"

"Getting to know each other better?" Evan sounds a bit happier. "Yeah, man, we can do that, but I've got to warn you… to know me is to love me. There is only so much time you're gonna be able to spend with me before you're ripping my clothes off, you know?" Dan thinks of his plans to take things slow with Ryan, and wonders if there might not be some truth in Evan's teasing. But he knows that Puppet-Chris would be slapping him upside the head about now. Don't over-think, just *do.*

"Well, I guess I can take my chances, Evan."

"All right, then. Do you wanna come up for dinner tonight? We're barbecuing, and a couple friends of Jeff's… well, friends of ours, but, you know… friends of Jeff's… are coming over. Just casual. Hey, it'd be nice to have someone closer to my own age!"

"I don't know, are we gonna have to sit at the kids' table?"

"Shit, man, I hope so—that's where all the best action is!"

Dan laughs. "It wouldn't be weird? I mean… you're cool with just hanging out?"

"Yeah. I'm sorry I've been a bit tense. I just…. The situation with Jeff is making be a bit crazy, and I was kind of pinning my hopes on you. But, really, I'd probably do just as much good if I could just relax a little and go back to having fun, so… yeah. Bring something to swim in… and come up… I don't know. I'll be home early, five or so probably. Jeff'll be there by then, and his friends are coming at six or so, but it'd be good if you were there earlier, so we could swim without worrying about splashing the old folks."

"Jesus, is there actually gonna be a kids' table? Just how old are these people?"

"Not that old, but I like to bug Jeff about it, so I'm just getting warmed up. Anyways—come, yeah?"

"Yeah. Okay. Five thirty, maybe?"

"Perfect. I'll see you then."

They hang up and Dan wonders what the hell just happened. It had all made sense at the time, but… what happened to keeping a little space between him and Jeff and Evan? He puts his phone away and heads back into the barn. He may be taking a see-what-happens approach to his personal life, but he's still pretty uptight about his work, and he's got some show planning to do.

chapter 29

IT'S uncomfortable going up to the main house.

Dan knows he was invited, but it still feels like he's intruding on Evan and Jeff's private space. He's not sure that he's wearing appropriate clothes (Evan had said it was casual, so he's wearing jeans and a button down with his swim shorts on underneath). He's not sure he's at the right time (Evan had said five thirty was fine, but maybe he was supposed to add some sort of "stylishly late" half-hour to that). He's not sure if he should have brought something (actually, he's pretty sure that he should have, but he'd had no idea what to bring and had finally given up). All in all, he's really not confident in the whole situation. He feels like he used to when he was a teenager, unsure of how he fit in or how he was expected to act. Of course, as a teenager he'd been able to release his frustrations by picking a fight or breaking something. He doesn't really think those options would be appropriate anymore.

He's not sure if he should ring the front doorbell or go around back. He's hovering around the front walk indecisively when a Mercedes SUV pulls up, and Linda hops out of the driver's side. "Hey, Dan! Can you give me a hand for a second?" He heads over, and she goes to the back of the car and lifts the hatch. Dan looks inside and sees a strange shape covered in black plastic garbage bags. It's about the size and general shape of a small body, and Dan wonders if he's seen too many mob movies. Linda just shakes her head, and pulls back a bit of the plastic to display what seems to be an enormous stuffed fish. "Don't even ask," she says. "I really don't think 'fish wrangler' was part of my job description." She grabs one end of the fish, and he grabs the other, and they steer toward the front door of the house. It's opened before they get there, Tia sharing a look of amused disgust with Linda, and then Dan helps them get the fish into Evan's office. They're just trying to figure out where to set it down when Evan himself appears in the doorway, dressed in board shorts and a T-shirt.

"Hey, fantastic! Dan *and* my fish!" He smiles happily and takes Linda's end from her. "I'm not sure where he's gonna go yet. Let's put him over by the window for now." They carry it over, and Dan lifts each end of the fish as Evan peels the plastic away. Evan stands back and looks at it proudly. Dan stands up and exchanges doubtful looks with Linda.

"Uh... did you catch it yourself?" Dan asks.

Evan looks over at him. "Nah, I don't fish. I won him!"

"It... it was a prize?" Dan's still trying to figure this out, but Linda looks like she's just trying not to laugh.

"Yeah, kinda... it's a contest. My dad and his friends used to do it, and when my dad died, I got in. It goes to whoever's company has the best quarterly results. And I'm pretty conservative with the business, so I don't usually have the best quarterlies—I mean, if you looked at it for a year, or better yet, a five-year period, I'd do really well, but I don't have the same roller-coaster numbers that some of them have." Evan leans back against the desk and surveys the fish in satisfaction. "But this quarter, I kicked their asses! Mostly because the economy tanked so bad, but still... I won."

"Wow. Congratulations." Dan couldn't care less about the fish, but Evan seems really happy about it. Linda smiles indulgently at him and waves goodbye. Evan waves back and then returns to staring at his prize.

"What do you think, above the desk?"

"How do you even anchor that thing? It's gotta weigh one-fifty at least...."

Evan waves a hand. "Don't bother me with details!" He grins. "Somebody will figure it out. Above the desk or over by the window?"

Dan hadn't really expected to be consulting on home decor when he came over. "Uh... you seem to like looking at it... which direction do you look in the most?"

Evan nods thoughtfully. "Above the door it is, then!"

"Wait a second—what if it falls on somebody's head?"

Evan just shakes his head and pats Dan on the shoulder. "Dan, my friend, you have got to stop worrying so much! The fish will be fine." He smiles peacefully, and then his face gets more animated. "Hey, d'ya wanna swim?"

Dan nods cautiously. "You're not bringing the fish with us, are you?"

"Unfortunately, no. He'll have to stay in here where he's safe." Evan takes one more fond look at the trophy and then leads Dan out of the office. "Do you need to change?" Evan asks. Dan just pulls the waistband of his jeans out to show his trunks underneath. "Efficient. Do you want a beer? Jeff'll probably have wine when he gets here."

"No, a beer would be great, thanks." They head outside, and Evan pulls a couple of beers out of the fridge built into the barbecue cabana. He takes both lids off and hands one to Dan, then holds his out to clink the necks together in a toast. They both take long swallows, and then Evan sets his bottle on the counter and peels his shirt off, and Dan's glad there's no beer left in his mouth because he thinks he might have drooled it all over himself. He'd known Evan was fit, but the man's torso is a little bit unbelievable. Almost literally. Dan's lean and muscular because he has a physical job. Evan sits at a desk all day, or so Dan imagines, and he's….

"Wow." Dan supposes that isn't the smoothest thing to say, but he's impressed he's able to verbalize anything at all. "Shit, man, how much do you work out?"

Evan grins a little self-consciously, but he doesn't hide his body, so Dan's fine with it. "Pretty much every day. It's a good stress-reliever, you know?"

"Jesus. You must have a lot of stress."

Evan laughs, and then has another drink from his bottle before flipping his shoes off and diving gracefully into the pool. Dan just watches him for a second, admiring the lines of his arms as they cut through the water, the even golden-brown of his skin in the late afternoon sunlight. Dan has always known Evan is good-looking, but he hadn't really realized just how beautiful he is. Evan pops his head up and looks at Dan quizzically. "You coming in?"

"Yeah, sorry." He has another long swallow of his beer, almost finishing the bottle, and then unbuttons his shirt and peels it off. He's aware that Evan is watching, and is torn between a feeling of self-consciousness and a strange urge to put on a show. He hangs the shirt over the back of the chair and glances over at Evan while his hands go to the button of his jeans. Evan's eyes are running over Dan's body appreciatively, but when he sees Dan looking at him he looks him straight in the eye.

"Do you want me to look away?" he asks softly, a little purr in his voice.

"No," Dan says, but his voice is barely more than a whisper. Evan must read lips, though, because he doesn't turn away, and actually swims a little closer, treading water by the side of the pool. Dan toes off his shoes and bends over to peel off his socks. He has the somewhat irrelevant thought that he should get pair of sport sandals, and then his mind flashes back to the present. Evan smiles encouragingly, and Dan finds himself smiling back even as he blushes a little. He undoes the button and fly of his jeans and shimmies them off his hips, letting them fall around his feet. He stands there for a second in his swim trunks while Evan's eyes run down his body and then back up to his face. Evan smiles a little and raises his eyebrows, and Dan takes one big step and dives over Evan's head into the deep part of the pool.

He stays underwater for as long as he can, trying to get himself under control, but when he surfaces, Evan is right there waiting. Dan stays still while Evan swims a little closer, so close now that Dan can feel the currents of water shooting away from Evan's hands and legs, and Dan doesn't seem to be able to do anything but tread water and stare at Evan. Evan leans in so his face is right next to Dan's, maybe an inch away, and Dan can feel Evan's breath on his damp skin.

"Dan...." Evan murmurs. "Dan, you said we were gonna hang out as friends for a while." He looks him in the eye, and Dan can't look away. "I've got to say I'm a little disappointed with the way you've turned this innocent swim into some sort of a sexually charged situation."

Dan stares at him for a second. What? Then he sees the smirk starting to form at the corners of Evan's mouth. "I mean, this is my family pool. My baby sister could arrive at any minute. Is this really the time or the place for your erotic strip tease?" Evan's grinning openly now. He's obviously enjoying the chance to turn the tables on Dan. "Yeah, I'm really disappointed in you, Danny."

But Evan doesn't have a chance to continue because Dan has pushed himself forward and gotten both hands on Evan's shoulders, dunking his aggravating, smug face deep under the pool water. Evan comes up sputtering but laughing, and immediately seeks his revenge. They wrestle around in the water for a while, and strangely enough, this *is* innocent, despite the physical contact and exertion. This is just them being kids, and they both revel in it.

They finally break apart, both gasping for air and coughing up pool water, and they look up to see Jeff sitting on one of the deck chairs, watching them bemusedly. "Boys," he rumbles, and Evan surges over to his side of the pool, hauling himself out in one smooth motion and falling to his knees beside Jeff. He leans forward and kisses Jeff deep and sloppy, and Jeff leans into it, his shirt getting wet from the water dripping off Evan's body. Dan stares, and wonders what would happen if he got out of the water and joined them, knelt beside Evan and worked his way into the kiss. Or if he sat in the chair behind Jeff, his legs bracketing Jeff's strong hips. He could lean forward and take Evan's mouth, all the while grinding into Jeff's ass....

Dan isn't sure whether to be relieved or disappointed when he hears Tatiana's voice from the direction of the house. "Oh my God, could you guys please get a room?" She walks out toward the pool, and then notices Dan. He's stopped staring, at least, but Jeff and Evan have only pulled away a little. They're still face to face, both grinning a little and looking like they share the world's best secret. "Dan, hi!" She sounds a little surprised, but covers fairly well. "Are you staying for dinner?" At Dan's nod, she turns to Evan. "Does Tia know? Evan! Did you remember to tell Tia that we're having one more?"

Evan finally looks away from Jeff. "Yes, Tat, everything is fine. I called Tia this morning."

"Oh. Good." She still seems a bit discombobulated, and Evan finally takes pity on her. He puts a hand on Jeff's shoulder and uses it to bring himself to his feet, then he walks over to the bar. He looks at the beer bottles on top as if unsure of which belongs to whom and then shrugs as if it doesn't matter. He takes the closest one—*mine,* thinks Dan—and finishes it off before circling around and going into the little kitchen area. He pulls out a blender and a bowl of strawberries, and grins as Tatiana almost shrieks. "Strawberry mimosas, Evan?!" He leans down and brings up a magnum of champagne and a pitcher of orange juice, and Tat actually hops in excitement.

Jeff cuts his amused eyes over to Dan. "We weren't sure about giving her alcohol—and it may have been a mistake...." Tat is skipping over to Evan and doing a strange but amusing little dance all around him, darting her hands out to almost touch him and snapping her fingers, all while gyrating her body wildly. Jeff watches her for a second and then turns back to Dan. "We also weren't sure about the dance lessons—they may have been a mistake as well."

"Or maybe you should get her a few more," Dan suggests quietly, and he and Jeff share a quiet laugh. Dan pulls himself out of the water then, and he knows that both Evan and Jeff watch him as he crosses to the pile of towels stacked on one of the lounge chairs and takes the top one. He's never really been much of an exhibitionist, but as long as his nerve holds, he's kind of enjoying the attention. He scrubs his hair with the towel and then brings it down over his arms and chest, looking up as if he's just become aware that he has an audience. He catches Jeff's eye and then Evan's, but it's when he realizes that Tatiana is also staring at him that he gets a little awkward, and quickly throws the towel over his shoulder and goes back to sit next to Jeff.

"Good swim?" Jeff asks innocently.

"Uh, yeah, thanks. You don't swim?"

Jeff shrugs. "I swim, I just don't engage in aquatic warfare. I thought you two were gonna drown each other." He puts his hand against his heart melodramatically. "I wasn't sure which of you to save!"

Dan smiles. "Save Evan," he says softly. "I can look after myself."

Jeff gives him a quick look, and then Evan calls over, "Do you guys want mimosas?"

"I don't know," Dan replies. "Will there be any left after Tat's done?"

Evan looks at the huge volume of ingredients on the counter, and then at his slip of a sister. "I'm not sure," he laughs. "You'd better get yours first."

Dan grins and stands up, leaving the towel behind as he walks over and perches on one of the bar stools. "I shouldn't admit it, since I've actually been paid to work behind a bar, but I don't think I know what a mimosa is—I thought they were just orange juice and champagne."

"Oh, they're heaven!" Tat swoons.

A little more informatively, Evan points to the ingredients on the counter. "A basic mimosa *is* just OJ and champagne, but at Casa Kaminski, we like to spice things up a little." He grins. "We just add strawberries and ice, make it a blender drink."

Dan shrugs. "Sounds good. Get some vitamins, right?"

Tat looks at him in concern. "An alcoholic beverage should not be your source of nutrition! Robyn said you only eat cold cereal and frozen dinners. Is that right? Are you taking care of yourself? I see your lunches, and... frozen pizza is gross the first time around, you really shouldn't be eating it cold the next day."

Dan ruffles her hair, and she doesn't seem to mind. "Thanks, Tat, but I'm all right." He glances at Evan. "Normally I'd say I grew up big and strong eating that way, but around here, maybe I do look a bit stunted."

Tat shakes her head. "I'm gonna start bringing an extra lunch down for you, okay? Tia makes mine, and it wouldn't be any trouble for her to just double up."

"Yeah, sure, you get me all spoiled over the summer, and then you go back to school in the fall and I'm left with a lunch-dependency and no way to get a fix. Nah, I'm fine, Tat. Besides, I eat a lot of apples."

"No, you eat two bites of an apple and feed the rest to your horse." Tat seems to have been paying a little too much attention to Dan's eating habits.

"Okay, but I eat two bites of, like, ten apples a day."

"Wait a second," Evan interjects. "Doesn't the barn buy the apples? Those apples are for the horses, not for your greedy gut."

"Dude, it's quality control. I have to taste each one to make sure it's good enough for them!"

Evan grins and pulses the blender, and for a moment the rattle of ice being pulverized by an industrial-strength bar blender drowns out all conversation. By the time Evan is done making noise, Jeff has stood up and joined him behind the bar, pulling out a bottle of red wine and a corkscrew.

"Not the mimosa type?" Dan asks him.

Evan mouths the words with him as Jeff says, "It's a waste of perfectly good champagne." Jeff knows what Evan's doing, and gives him a mock elbow to the ribs as he reaches across to get a wine glass for himself. Dan feels it again, the sense of belonging, of being part of a family. It feels good, but it scares him a little. It would be too easy to get comfortable here and too hard when he has to leave. He wonders if he's not already in too deep, though, because he can feel himself relaxing as Evan pours the blender's contents into three big wine glasses and Tat garnishes each one with a slice of strawberry and of orange, and then gives each glass a straw. Evan doles them out, and they all raise their glasses, three pinkish monstrosities and Jeff's rich red wine, and they toast and drink and then sit happily together enjoying the evening.

Tia brings the first of the guests out, and Evan was right, they are a little older, older than Jeff even, but still healthy and vibrant. Dan takes the time when they're being greeted to pull his shirt on, although he doesn't get it buttoned, and then he's drawn over to be introduced.

Evan does the honors. "This is Dan. He just moved out here from Kentucky, so we're trying to get him adapted to the California lifestyle."

Dan raises his mimosa as he extends his hand for shaking. "They're doing a pretty good job of it." He notices that Evan didn't mention that Dan was his employee, didn't say why Dan had moved. He can't decide whether he likes it that Evan hasn't immediately slotted him into a social class, or if it's a slight, if Evan didn't mention it because he thinks Dan should be embarrassed by it. Puppet-Chris slaps him upside the head, and he tries to concentrate on the conversation at hand.

The new people, Will and Addie, are talking to Jeff about his upcoming show. Apparently they're collectors. They look rich, maybe not in the Kaminskis' class but well off at the least, and Dan wonders how that works. Do they buy Jeff's art, and if so, does he wonder if they're doing it because they really like it or just because they're friends? Dan can't even figure out whether he should be leaving a tip for Ryan when he eats at Zio's. He can't imagine having to make the decision on a much larger scale. But they seem to have figured out some way to deal with it, because he doesn't sense any tension coming from them or from Jeff when they discuss the likelihood of making sales at the show.

Another couple arrives, Jason and Liam, and Dan likes Jason immediately. He's a bit dumpy looking, sort of an Elmer Fudd type, and he has one of the most open, friendly smiles Dan has ever seen. Liam seems a bit more reserved, especially around Dan. When Dan goes to help Evan get drinks for everybody, Evan whispers, "Don't worry about Liam. He's just used to being the prettiest one in the room," and winks.

The final arrival is Natasha, who sweeps in dramatically, as if expecting an ovation. Evan, Tat, and Dan have retired to the bar, ostensibly mixing drinks but really just hanging out. Evan had grinned when he'd noticed how the crowd was divided, and said, "See? The kids' table." Now he watches the new arrival with amusement, then leans over and says, "She acts like an annoying flake, but really she's salt of the earth. She used to be an actress, then her husband died, and she took the money and opened up an after-school program for street kids. She teaches them drama. Jeff volunteers once a week teaching them art... a bunch of people help out. It's a really cool program."

Evan brings the drinks over, and Tat and Dan trail behind him. Natasha hugs Tat and then turns to Dan and almost purrs. "And who is this delicious newcomer?"

Evan's busy distributing drinks, so this time it's Jeff's turn to do the introductions. "Natasha, this is Dan. He's helping Evan train his new horses."

Dan reminds himself of her good work with the street kids as she looks him up and down like a piece of meat. And then Evan is there, an arm slipping possessively over Dan's shoulders as he leans forward to shake Natasha's hand. "Hey, Natasha, how are you?" The arm on his shoulders pulls him in tight against Evan's side, and Dan can't believe it. He stiffens and pushes away, trying not to be too obvious but definitely looking for a little space.

Natasha notices, of course, and raises an eyebrow as she responds with, "I'm fine, darling. Thank you so much for asking." She looks from Evan back to Dan, and then over to Jeff. "So, what's been keeping you busy these days?" she asks him, her tone making it clear that she thinks she already knows the answer. She takes his arm and walks with him over to the seating area, while Jeff casts a concerned look over his shoulder at Evan and Dan.

Dan just stares at Evan, who brings a hand up as though to hide his face. "Shit, man, I'm sorry, I did it again. I know. I just—"

"You just what, Evan?" Dan tries to keep his voice down. Everyone else is being pretty loud, so he's sure they can't hear him. "What are you thinking when you do that shit?"

"I don't even… honestly, I was fine, and then I saw her look at you, and… I don't know. Fuck!" He looks genuinely upset. "I can't believe I screwed this up again. It was going really well, I thought."

Dan wants to stay angry, but Evan seems genuinely upset. "Okay, dude, it's not the end of the world. I mean, you've got to figure out a way to keep a lid on that, but…."

Evan looks at him hopefully. "Yeah, I totally will. Seriously. It just caught me by surprise tonight. Now I'm on guard… I really didn't think I was going to have to worry about getting jealous of women." He peers questioningly at Dan. "Or are women a concern as well?"

Dan shakes his head in frustration. "Jesus, none of this should be 'a concern' to you." He takes pity again, though, and grudgingly adds, "But, no. Women are…. I've been with two women, both when I was a teenager. I'm not going back."

Evan nods. "Okay. And, hey, tomorrow night at the bar, Ryan can be all over you, and I won't even frown. I promise. I've already got myself totally psyched for it."

"Yeah, well, that's not going to be a problem." Evan gives him a strange look, so Dan explains, "Ryan's worried that the guys from your company might be homophobes, so he's playing it straight."

Evan frowns. "And you're okay with that?"

"Yeah. I mean, mostly. We've gone out, like, three times, and I've been the one saying I want to keep it casual. So, obviously he's not going to risk something this important. And we're not exactly PDA people, so it's not like I'll even notice the difference, likely."

"I don't know, man. I mean, if it was me, I'd dance right up to you in my tight black pants and unbuttoned black shirt and I'd say, 'Nobody puts Danny in a corner,' and then we'd dance and dance." Evan waves his upper body around slowly, and Dan just shakes his head.

"Yeah, we'd have the time of our lives, I'm sure. Jesus, you are so gay."

"Hey, you recognized it. And I've been with *lots* of women! So you're gayer than me!"

They don't notice that Jeff has returned until he interjects, "Sweet Jesus, I thought you two were over here having an actual argument. Let me settle this one for you: You're both plenty gay. Now get your pretty little asses over there and talk to some people."

Jeff swats them both, Evan hard on his ass, Dan lightly on his lower back, and herds them over to the crowd. The rest of the night passes pleasantly, but Dan heads home fairly early. Jeff and Evan both walk him to the side of the house—they would have walked him to the door, he supposes, but it seems stupid to go inside just to go outside again. All three pause at the corner, and Dan has a sudden urge to reach out for them, to kiss one or both, to….

He breaks off from the fantasy, but he thinks it might be too late. Jeff, at least, seems to be able to read Dan's every thought, and even Evan looks like he caught that one, judging by the way he's smirking.

"Yeah, okay, I'm off. Thanks for dinner and everything."

"You sure you want to leave so early?" Evan asks. His voice doesn't have the low rumble that Jeff's does, but it's got its own little purr that Dan is finding pretty damn effective. "You could stick around for a bit. We could drink a bit more, maybe have a soak in the hot tub…." He's smirking, clearly ready to leave it all as a joke, but Dan has no doubt that he'd follow through with it if Dan went along.

"Yeah, no, I really do need to get going." He stops himself just before he starts babbling. "Okay. But I'll see you both tomorrow at the Fireside?"

"Absolutely," Jeff answers. He smiles lazily and drapes an arm over Evan's shoulder, and for the first time in all of this Dan feels a little bit jealous over Evan, wishes that he were the one touching him. He waves quickly and turns to walk home. He doesn't think the jealousy can be a good thing, in any direction, but he's really not sure how to stop it.

chapter 30

DAN gets home from the barbecue and showers before bed. He tells himself that he's washing the pool's chlorine off, but he's hard before he's even gotten wet, and there's a jumble of images playing through his mind as he jerks himself off in long, slow strokes.

He's asleep as soon as his head hits the pillow, and when he wakes up the next day with morning wood, he goes again, this time focusing in on Ryan. Ryan's his current interest, Ryan's the one who makes sense and is simple, and Ryan's the one he imagines as he shoots all over his hand and bare stomach. But he's barely up and dressed before he's thinking about Jeff and Evan again. Then on the way out the bedroom door, his eyes fall on the photograph on the bedside table, and it's like everything else falls away.

A wave of guilt washes over him, and he actually feels a little sick to his stomach. He knows he hadn't forgotten about Justin, knows he never will, but how had he let himself be distracted from him? He knows the guilt isn't rational. There's nothing he can do to help Justin now, nothing he can do to change anything, but he still feels like he owes Justin more grieving time, owes their relationship more of a tribute. Puppet-Chris tells him that he doesn't have to be sad to remember Justin, doesn't have to deny his sexuality in order to honor their love, but Dan doesn't want to listen to that little bastard. What does Chris know about losing a lover? He takes the picture in his hands and leans against the wall, then slides his back down it until he's sitting with his knees drawn up, the picture resting on them.

He runs his fingers over Justin's face, and tries to channel all of his love and send it into the picture. Justin is gone, his body already probably being absorbed by the plants on the farm he had loved, but surely as long as Dan's thinking about him, a part of him is still alive. Then Dan thinks about the way they'd kept Justin's body around for too long after his essence had disappeared, and wonders if he's doing a similar thing by hanging on to the memory. He thinks maybe it would be a better tribute to only focus on the happy memories, and not carry this sadness around with him. But what if he can't do that? He rests his head on his arms and lets himself be sad for a while, and then he makes himself get up and put the picture back on the table. He goes into the bathroom and splashes some cold water on his face, then he heads off to the barn to look after Justin's horses.

He's a little subdued through the morning, but the training goes really well. The horses all seem to have settled into their new home and are starting to respond to the more regular training schedule. The afternoon is almost as smooth, although one of the young horses plows into a jump and sends Robyn flying. But it's a stadium jump, built to collapse under any sort of pressure, and Robyn is barely bruised. She gets back on the horse and takes him through his paces to make sure he's not injured while Dan rebuilds the jump. She goes over it, this time without incident, and gets a round of applause from Dan and Tatiana.

They quit for the day shortly after, and Dan heads home to get cleaned up and changed. He takes his time, but when he goes down to the barn to pick up Robyn and Michelle, they're still getting ready, so he sits on Robyn's couch and offers his opinions on her various outfits. She hasn't seen Scott the drummer since the trip to Santa Cruz, but she doesn't seem too upset about it. She says he was cute, but didn't really have anything interesting to say. She does want to make sure she's looking good, though—best to make it clear that *she* is the one who isn't interested.

Michelle comes in eventually, and Robyn settles on the clothes she's wearing, and they head out. They've planned to have dinner at the Fireside before the show, and run into a lot of other people who've had the same idea. Ryan is already there, fussing with the equipment, and when he sees them he comes over to say hello. He's actually nervous, and Dan finds it adorable. Seeing laidback Ryan all tense makes Dan feel better about his own neurotic moments. Michelle and Robyn go to join Devin and Sara at a long table near the stage, and Dan leans over to talk quietly to Ryan.

"It's really a shame you're not being gay tonight. I might have had an idea for how to help you relax." Ryan groans, and Dan leans back and smirks at him.

"Shit, Dan…." But one of the guys from the band is calling him over to deal with some amp issue, and Dan goes to join the rest of the table. Jeff and Evan show up shortly after, and Evan *is* on his best behavior, keeping his hands to himself and smiling at everybody. He really does look relaxed and friendly, but Dan reminds himself that Ryan hasn't gotten closer than twenty feet since Evan's arrived.

They order dinner, and drink a while, and then the band starts. The crowd is enthusiastic, and Dan looks around, trying to see if anybody seems less like a fan and more like an observer. He doesn't see anybody. After the first set, Ryan comes over and sits down for a beer, still careful to keep a certain distance away from Dan. He's discouraged, though.

"I don't know, man… we all talked, and someone in the band knows everybody in the bar except for those four old people at the back and the drunk kids by the door. I really don't think any of those are from the record company." He sighs. "I dunno—maybe something came up, and they can't make it."

Dan frowns, and his eyes cut to Evan. Evan looks back and then subtly holds up his phone, a questioning expression on his face. Dan doesn't like it, but he looks at Ryan and then back at Evan, and nods a little. Evan gets up and goes outside, and when he comes back he claps Ryan on the shoulder. "Hey, man, cheer up! If they came up all the way from LA, they're probably trying to see more than one band tonight. They're probably watching the first set somewhere else, then driving here, and they'll be here any minute." Ryan looks at him a little doubtingly, but Evan puts on his best smile. "Seriously, man! I'm the business guy, remember? I know this stuff."

Ryan looks encouraged and goes to share the idea with his band mates, but Dan feels a little like he just dug his own grave. After Evan's performance, it's going to be really hard to tell Ryan that Evan owns the record company and that Dan knew all along. Well, it would have been hard anyway, given that he's left it so long, but even harder now that Evan has been deliberately evasive. Dan knows he can't blame Evan for this one; it had been Evan's idea, but Dan's decision. He just hopes the record guys *do* show up, so at least the lie will have been worth something.

The band starts playing again, and after a couple songs the doors open and three people come in, two men and a woman. The woman and one of the men are young, thirty at the most, but the other man is older, maybe in his fifties. They're dressed casually, but they don't seem to be at the bar for fun, and while they order drinks, they only sip them. Dan exchanges a glance with Evan, who shrugs but grins. Ryan and the band have noticed them, too, and their energy increases dramatically. They finish the set and the younger man gets up and goes and introduces himself to Ryan and the band, and Ryan goes over to the table and talks to all of them for a while. He goes back and talks to the band again, and they look like they're sorting things out.

The final set is made up almost totally of the band's own songs, including some that had been played already that night. Nobody minds the repetition, though, and everyone makes sure to cheer enthusiastically. They wrap up that set and the whole band goes to meet the A&R team while the rest of the bar pretends to be busy with their own affairs. The band visits for a few minutes and then the record company people shake hands all around and head out. Ryan waits until they're safely away before he goes back to the stage and takes the mic.

"Okay, uh… first, let me thank you all for coming out on a weeknight and being such an incredible audience. I think that really helped. And, I don't know if it was you or something else, but something went right, because they're going to give us a call tomorrow to work out a contract!" The bar erupts into cheers, and Dan joins in happily. He hasn't known Ryan for long, but he likes him, and he's happy to see something good happen for him.

Ryan comes down off the stage to celebrate, and he stops by Dan's table, but he has a lot of people to visit. It makes it clear to Dan how little he knows the man. There are people here who've loved Ryan his whole life, and Dan is a johnny-come-lately next to them. When Dan gets up to tell him that the gang is heading out, he looks disappointed but not crushed. "We've all got to be up early for work tomorrow, so we need to go. But you have a great night celebrating, okay?" Ryan nods and gives Dan a hug, and Dan wonders if it's over, if whatever they might have had has flared out and gone. It makes him sorry to think so, but he realizes that it's nothing that he can't move past. He hopes it's not gone, but if it is, he'll be okay. He guesses he managed to keep it casual after all.

He spends the next day working, not thinking. He rides all of the horses that are going to the horse trial on the weekend and finds them all in good shape and totally ready for the level of competition they'll be dealing with. He's happy about that. Tat is going to be riding Sunshine, and he spends some time walking her through what to expect, then he gives shorter reviews to Robyn, who'll be riding Chaucer, and Michelle, who's taking Kip. Dan looks over his own strategies for Monty and Winston. Two of the horses, Sunshine and Monty, are competing well below their appropriate levels and will be entered *hors concours*, which means they can't win any prizes, and Dan is just taking Chaucer and Winston along for experience, and isn't sure if he'll take either on the cross-country course. That leaves Kip to represent the barn in the ribbons, and Dan really doesn't have a good enough idea of the level of competition out here to be confident about the results. Back in Kentucky he thinks he'd have done pretty well.

Ryan calls in the late afternoon. He's got a dinner meeting with the band, but wants to know if Dan's free afterwards. They agree to meet up at the Fireside at ten o'clock. Dan goes home shortly after the call and has a nap. He doesn't usually sleep during the day, but he's had a few late nights, and it looks like another coming up. When he wakes up it's fully dark outside, and he looks at the clock to see that it's nine thirty. He's slept almost four hours. He hurries into the shower and gets dressed. He's just about to head out the door when he stops and goes back and takes a long look at Justin's picture. He's really not sure what's going to happen with Ryan, but he can't shake the feeling that it all somehow comes back to Justin.

Ryan is waiting for him when he gets to the bar, looking a little flushed and very happy. He stands and gives Dan a bear hug in greeting, and Dan is happy to return it. They sit down and the waitress brings Dan a beer, and then Ryan just beams for a minute, until Dan breaks and says, "Okay, okay, give me the details."

Ryan just about explodes. "The contract is good—we ran it by a lawyer and she says it looks fair… not a lot upfront but a good share of any profits. There's support for touring and recording, and they want to get started right away." He sits back and looks a little less happy, but only a little. "The only downside is that they want to start *right* away. They had some other band lined up for a bunch of gigs, and they fell apart somehow, but the A&R guys say that our sound is similar enough that we can just slip into most of their shows."

Dan shrugs. "Well, that's not really a downside, is it? I mean, you've been waiting for this for a long time—why wait any longer?"

Ryan smiles a little sadly. "Well, I was kinda thinking maybe we had something good happening here. I know it doesn't make sense to try to go long distance after three dates. I just… you know."

"Wonder what could have been. Yeah, I know." He smiles. "But, seriously, man, this is a great opportunity, right?"

"Yeah, it totally is." Ryan starts to look happier again.

"When are you leaving?"

"Monday morning, first thing. We're in LA for rehearsals and set up for four days, and then, bam, on the road."

Dan nods. "And I'm leaving tomorrow before noon, and won't be back until Monday sometime." He looks at Ryan. "So this is it."

Ryan looks back at him. "I guess it is."

Dan takes a deep breath and looks at the table. He thinks about Justin, thinks about himself. Then he looks up at Ryan. "So, do you want to get out of here?"

Ryan looks a little surprised and smiles almost shyly. "What, you mean…. Do you want to go back to my place?" He sounds like he's not sure he believes it.

Dan shrugs a little. "Yeah, maybe. If you do…."

"Are you shitting me? I mean, yeah, I do. I absolutely do."

"Dude, you sound like we're getting married."

"Okay, I don't think 'are you shitting me?' is a traditional part of the wedding vows."

Dan laughs. "Maybe it should be." He pulls out his wallet and throws a ten on the table. "No guarantees, man… I could still chicken out at any moment."

Ryan stands quickly. "Okay, let's try not to let that happen." He looks at the ten. "Are you paying for my beer?"

"Consider it a Happy Contract present. Now are you coming or not?"

They walk quickly, neither saying anything, and Dan can feel his nerves beginning to build. He wonders what he's doing, wonders if he's ready. He wonders if he's even going to make it to Ryan's apartment at this rate. They're cutting through an alley behind a corner store, and Dan stops walking. Ryan turns and looks at him in concern, and Dan steps forward and brings their mouths together, a quick, nipping kiss. He puts his hands on Ryan's arms and pushes him gently backward until he hits the wall, and then he goes in for another kiss, slower and deeper this time. Ryan tastes good, feels good, soft lips and tongue, hard teeth, warm breath catching when Dan nips a little. He runs his hands down to Ryan's waist and then up under his shirt to find the warmth of his skin, and he feels Ryan's hands under his shirt, leaving a trail of goose bumps on his stomach and then up to his chest. They break for air for a second, and Dan runs his mouth down along Ryan's chin to his neck. Ryan lets out a shaky little groan when Dan's mouth finds the hollow above his collarbone, and Dan focuses there for a minute. He's never been much of a marker, but he likes the idea of sending Ryan away with a memento, so he sucks hard and nips a little. Ryan leans his head back against the wall, drops his arms to his sides, and just lets it happen. When Dan decides that he's done, he licks the reddish bruise, and has a flashback to Evan's quick pink tongue lapping at Jeff's neck that night on the porch.

Dan pulls Ryan's head forward and wraps his tongue around Ryan's, hears Ryan groan again as Dan licks at his mouth and then pulls away. "Okay, let's go."

Ryan's eyes are dazed when he looks at Dan. "What?"

"Let's go. That was just a refreshment break. We still need to get to your place, right?"

Ryan nods and stumbles away from the wall, and Dan remembers how much he used to like this, the sense of power that comes from driving somebody crazy. He walks alongside Ryan and reaches his hand out, tucks it under his shirt to touch the small of his back, and then dips it down to rest on the waistband of his jeans, fingers just tickling the very top of his ass. Ryan's body is warm, and Dan likes the feel of it.

They have one more make-out break before getting to Ryan's, this time up against a mailbox. When they get to the apartment, Dan grabs Ryan and eases him down on the stairs before they even get inside, one of Dan's knees taking most of his weight between Ryan's legs, grinding his cock down against Ryan's thigh, biting and licking and sucking now more than kissing. This isn't romantic. This isn't about love or even affection. This is just physical need, and Dan wants to keep it that way.

Ryan is writhing beneath him, trying to get more friction for himself, and Dan thinks about getting him off right there on the stairs, fully dressed. It's tempting, and he grinds his thigh up into Ryan's groin for a second, lets him rub along it. But Dan wants more, wants at least nakedness, and he pulls away and puts out a hand to haul Ryan to his feet. "One more stretch," he mutters and turns Ryan and shoves him up the stairs.

They get inside and Ryan turns as if he expects Dan to jump him right there, but instead Dan brushes by him, forces himself to look nonchalant as he crosses to the fridge and looks inside. He pulls out a bottle of water and crosses over to lean on the wall next to the bedroom door. He opens the bottle and takes a long swallow, then turns to Ryan. "You have too many clothes on, Ryan."

Ryan grins a little. "Yeah, you too."

Dan reaches down with one hand and casually pulls his T-shirt up and over his head, dropping it on the floor. Ryan starts undoing the buttons on his shirt, walking closer to Dan. He stops about a foot away and drops his shirt, and Dan has to grip his water bottle to stop himself from reaching out to touch. Ryan is darker than Dan but lighter than Evan, a delicious honey color that Dan wants to taste. Dan bends from the waist to pull his shoes and socks off, and he feels Ryan reach over the top of him to rub along his spine, then bend over to kiss each knobby bone. Dan waits until Ryan pauses before he sinks to his knees and brings his hands to Ryan's fly, his fingers loosening the button while his palms push against the hard bulge inside. Ryan is breathing quickly again, and Dan loves it. He undoes the zipper and runs his hands back over Ryan's ass, still on top of his underwear but beneath his jeans, and then he runs his hands down Ryan's legs, pushing the jeans with them. Ryan shifts his weight to let Dan pull his jeans and flip flops right off, and then Dan's attention returns to Ryan's cock.

Dan runs a hand up and over it, caressing it through the cotton of the underwear. He mouths along the outline of it, and he smiles as it twitches and Ryan takes a quivering breath. He gently pulls the fabric down, letting Ryan's cock bob out in front of him, swollen and hard and begging for attention. Dan breathes on it, gives it one or two almost experimental jacks with his hand, and then sinks his mouth as far over it as he can go. The taste and the weight on his mouth feel like favorite memories. Ryan gives a hoarse little shout and grabs Dan's hair, and Dan goes with it, bobbing his head a few times, sucking hard and using lots of tongue along the bottom. Ryan's breathing is ragged, and he's pulling at Dan's head, trying to get him to stop. Dan thinks about keeping on, bringing Ryan off right away, but he decides Ryan would be disappointed with that, so he eases off and rubs his body along Ryan's as he stands and brings their faces together.

"Problem?" He asks softly. There's a little mole on the left side of

Ryan's chin, and Dan leans forward to kiss it a little, then lick it.

"No problem, but I'm gonna be done pretty quick if you keep that up." Ryan sounds a little shell-shocked.

"Okay. I don't think I want to fuck, but... you can have my hand or my mouth."

"Oh, shit," Ryan almost whimpers. "Okay, I'm gonna be done pretty quick if you keep saying things like that too." He closes his eyes tight, and Dan wonders if he's reciting baseball scores, or thinking of kittens, or....

Dan grins and waits patiently for a minute. "You all right?"

Ryan nods. "Yeah, I think so." He looks down at Dan. "Hey. You've got too many clothes on, man."

"Well, no one's taken them off of me yet."

Ryan grins. "Sorry about that." But instead of reaching for Dan's jeans, he takes his hand, and pulls him toward the bedroom. "Come on. I want you horizontal."

Dan can't argue with that, especially when Ryan stops him by the side of the bed and eases his jeans and underwear off together, and then turns Dan and shoves him onto the mattress on his back, standing over him and looking down. "God, you are gorgeous."

Dan grins up at him and raises a hand. "Come down here." Ryan complies readily, stretching out on top of Dan, lining them up so their naked cocks rub together, smearing precome all over. He grinds down while he sucks on Dan's collarbone, leaving a mark to match the one on his own skin. It feels good, great even, warm skin and warm mouths, but Dan wants more. He grabs Ryan's hand and brings it down with his own, works them between their bodies and wraps their joined hands around their cocks, rubbing them both together. Ryan groans and thrusts even harder into the new tightness, and Dan picks up his rhythm and works with him. Ryan's mouth gets increasingly frantic, roaming from Dan's lips to his neck, all over his face and then down into the crook of his shoulder. It's there that he stays, burrowing in a little and moaning, as he makes a few final, wild thrusts and then spasms and spills all over their joined hands and onto Dan's chest. It feels like a baptism, like the start of something new, and Dan isn't sure how he feels about it.

Ryan only rests for a few moments, and then his mouth is back on Dan's, kissing deep and sloppy. It's a good distraction from Dan's thoughts. Ryan's hand takes up its rhythm on Dan's cock, but after only a few kisses he drags his lips down Dan's body to take him in his mouth. He's pretty good at this, and Dan looks down and enjoys the visual, the blond hair falling forward and brushing on Dan's sensitive skin, the hollowed cheeks and rounded mouth…. It doesn't take long before Dan's gasping and throwing his head back. "Shit, Ryan, I'm gonna come," he warns, but Ryan just hums a little and pulls off part way, working his tongue even faster and harder along the sensitive head. Dan feels the orgasm building and tries to hold off for a bit longer. Everything feels so good; he doesn't want it to be over. But it washes over him anyway, more powerful than the ones he gets by himself, and he feels his hips thrusting, feels Ryan's throat working around him as he swallows, and he's almost crying by the time his body relaxes, and he collapses on the bed.

Ryan worms his way up to Dan's face and kisses him, and it's a little too sweet, a little too real, and Dan doesn't know if he can handle it. He sits up, rests on the side of the bed, and Ryan sits up next to him. "You okay, man?"

"Yeah, I'm fine. Just… a little intense, you know?"

Ryan chuckles. "You're telling me." He brings a hand up to Dan's shoulders. "You want to get under the covers, sleep for a bit?"

A part of Dan really does, but he thinks that might be a little too much. "No, thanks. I mean—" He turns to look Ryan in the eyes. "Thanks. For everything. I guess this is pretty much it, and… you know…. I haven't known you for that long, but you've been… important." He squints a little, looking for understanding. "Does that make sense?"

Ryan smiles a little sadly. "Yeah, kinda. But my work here is done. Is that what you're telling me?"

"Well, that's what you're telling me, really. You know… you're leaving. Which is great. I mean, it's not great that you're leaving, but it's great that you're getting your shot. I'm happy for you, really."

Ryan looks like he's trying to decide something, and finally bursts out with, "Do you want to try to keep it going? I mean, keep in touch at least?" He reaches out and runs a hand along Dan's neck. "I just… I think maybe we could have something here. I know we said it was casual, and that's cool, but…."

Dan smiles at him. "Dude, you're going out on the road! You need your freedom. And I have no idea what I'm doing, but I don't really want to be sitting around pining after a guy who I only knew for about a week." The words are a little harsh, but he keeps his tone soft, and he thinks Ryan's okay with it. "I mean, let's stay in touch, absolutely. But... you know, let's do it as friends. And then if we ever end up in the same place again, and the timing's right... who knows?"

"Yeah. No, you're right, that makes sense." He smiles ruefully. "Damn, though. I really don't want to say goodbye."

Dan nods. "Yeah, me neither. That's kind of why I want to go tonight. It's just gonna be harder tomorrow."

Ryan grimaces. "Yeah. Okay. So this is it?"

Dan reaches down and finds his underwear and jeans, lines up his feet and pulls them on as he stands. "Yeah, I think so. For now, at least." He turns around and leans over, and this time he lets the kiss be as sweet and as real as it wants to be. When he pulls away, Ryan lets out a little huffing sigh.

"Okay. It's been great to know you, Dan, and I'll keep in touch."

Yeah. Great to know you too." It sounds wrong, sounds too distant, but he doesn't know what to say that would be better, and maybe a little distance is what he needs. He scoops up his shirt and shoes in the living room, but waits until he gets outside to pull them on. He doesn't want to take the chance that he'd change his mind if he stayed inside a minute longer.

He climbs down the wooden stairs and heads out into the night, taking deep breaths of the cool, dark air. He thinks of Justin, wonders what he would think, but he remembers his resolution from that morning and tries not to let himself dwell on that. Instead, he tries to think of a happy Justin memory. The first one he comes up with is about a time that he made Justin laugh so hard that tomato soup came out of his nose at his mother's dining room table. Not romantic, not poignant... but funny as hell. He laughs a little to himself, remembering Molly's reaction, remembering how Justin had tried to stop laughing, and it had only made him laugh more, until he'd had to get up and spit what was left of his mouthful of soup down the drain. He'd stood there over the kitchen sink, broad shoulders shaking, and Dan had come up behind him and hugged him as they laughed together. Dan thinks Ryan would have liked Justin, and that Justin would have liked Ryan. He isn't sure whether that makes what he did better, or if it makes it worse.

chapter 31

DAN doesn't sleep too well that night. He's not sure he left things with Ryan in the right way. He had thought it would be easier if he didn't stay any longer, but now it feels like he left too abruptly, and he wonders if he's somehow cheapened the memory of the whole relationship. And he's also still not sure how he should feel about moving on after Justin—Justin's been out of his life for over a year, but he only actually died a month ago, so maybe Dan's pushing on too fast. On a more concrete level, he's worried about taking the barn to its first horse trial the next day. He's been to plenty of competitions before, but he's never been in charge, and he really doesn't want to let Evan down. And that thought makes him anxious about Evan himself, and how things will be on the road with him. All in all, it's not as restful a night as he might have hoped.

Still, he's up with the sun the next morning, and heads down to the barn to start getting things ready. The horses were all bathed the day before, but they need to have their tack packed up and their shipping boots and blankets put on, and then Dan has to run over things with the riders and make sure that they're bringing everything *they* need, and there's a moment of panic when the shipping company calls to confirm a two-horse trailer when Dan had ordered a six. But it's a six-horse trailer that shows up half an hour later, and the horses all load smoothly. Dan tries to calm himself as he helps Evan and Robyn pile the last bits of equipment into the trailer and the back of Evan's Cherokee. Dan thinks about calling Ryan and trying to say a better goodbye, but he doesn't know what he'd say differently, so he doesn't call.

Tat is excited about riding in the horse trailer, so after Evan meets the driver and satisfies himself that he seems sane, Tat and Michelle climb up to the cab of the big truck, and Robyn and Dan settle in with Evan. Dan's in the back seat, and he feels himself starting to nod off before they even get to town. He has trouble staying awake in a moving vehicle at the best of times, unless he's driving, and this is not the best of times. Evan and Robyn are chatting happily in the front, and Dan doesn't really feel like his presence is required, so he balls his jacket up to use as a pillow, and drifts off to sleep.

He has weird dreams, filled with motion and sound. He wakes up from a vision of Evan swimming through the flooded hallways of what Dan thinks might be his own elementary school, only to find the car stopped and Evan turned around in his seat and staring at him. He blinks a little confusedly, and then remembers where he is. He brings a hand up to his face to check for drool, but luckily it comes away dry.

"What's up?" he asks, trying to sound somewhat coherent.

Evan grins. "Lunch break." He's looking at Dan fondly, and Dan bashfully smiles back. Justin used to say that Dan looked soft when he first woke up, as if he hadn't gotten around to putting his walls up yet, and Dan wonders if that's what Evan sees. He's surprised to find that he doesn't really mind if it is.

Robyn is already out of the car, stretching a little as she waits for them. Dan takes another second to wake up and then opens the car door and climbs out, indulging in a stretch of his own. The others are wandering back from the truck parked in front of them, and Dan finds the driver. "Can you open up the back for me? Let me give them a quick check while we're stopped?" He looks at Robyn, then at the highway McDonalds they're stopped at. "Can you just order me a Big Mac meal, with a Coke and an apple pie? I'll be in soon."

Tat's excited to check on the horses as well, so she gives her order to Evan and climbs up the ramp with Dan while the others go into the restaurant. Tatiana is peering around at the animals like she's never seen them before, and Dan tries to focus her a little.

"So, the first thing you want to check for is temperature. Too hot is worse than too cold, but neither is ideal, so you can change the vents if you need to. But I think we're okay today. And we're parked in the shade, so it shouldn't get too hot while we're sitting still. Then check each horse out. You don't need to go right in with them, just tap their butts and see if they turn around and look alert, make sure they're standing naturally. While you're at it, check their boots and their sheets, and make sure everything's still in place." He and Tat do this, and Dan resists the urge to double-check the horses Tat looks at. He figures it's important for her to think that he's trusting her with a responsibility, and that he won't automatically catch it if she messes up. But he sneaks a look when he can, and doesn't see anything amiss. "Then check their hay—it's not crucial on a trip this length, but having something to munch on can keep them calm." He watches her carefully peek at each animal's hay net, and grins. "They good?" She nods. "Okay, and we'll give them water when we come back out. They usually won't drink at the start of the break, but they probably will by the end. Everything make sense?" She nods, and they head out of the trailer and lift the ramp back up and bolt it shut. Dan checks the sight lines to be sure they'll be able to see the trailer from inside, and then he and Tat head over.

The others have already bought the food and found tables by the windows, so Tat and Dan take quick detours to the washroom and then join them. The truck driver is a story teller, and while Michelle looks as if she's heard about enough, Tat is still enthralled and gives the man a rapt audience. Dan catches Michelle's eye, and softly asks, "Do you want to trade seats, ride in the car the rest of the way?"

Michelle smiles warmly at him. "No, I'm okay. But thanks for asking."

They finish up the meal and tidy the table, and then Dan and Tat go out to pour water out of the containers they'd brought from the farm and offer it to the horses. They all have at least a little, and Dan goes back to the Cherokee confident that the horses are traveling well.

The rest of the trip is uneventful. Evan and Robyn try to get Dan to play stupid road games, and then to sing along to the radio. Robyn seems to hit her apex when she develops an epic game of "Would you rather...?" By the time the Cherokee pulls into the eventing grounds, she's found the ultimate question of "Would you rather cut off your baby toe or sleep with Amy Winehouse?" and Dan and Evan have both bowed out of the game citing car sickness.

The next hour or so is busy with getting the horses unloaded, checked in, settled in their temporary accommodations, and unpacking and sorting out the equipment. The most valuable stuff will stay in the back of the Cherokee, but there's still enough equipment of medium value that Dan uses bicycle locks to fasten the footlockers to the metal stall enclosures. It won't stop a determined thief, but it will keep things from being casually lifted.

At three o'clock the cross-country course is opened to allow the competitors to walk it, and they all go out and have a look at what their horses will be asked to do the next day. Dan encourages the other three to think out loud and try to figure out the challenges for themselves, only interjecting when he thinks they've missed something. He takes special care to point out a few dangerous spots to Tatiana, and works out possible strategies with her to ensure that she gets herself and her horse through safely. Evan has tagged along with them and seems to be listening carefully, occasionally throwing worried looks at Tat.

As they're walking back from the course, Dan tries to reassure him. "There's always an element of risk, but Sunshine's a really strong, sensible jumper, and there's nothing out there that will challenge her even a little bit. She'll take care of Tat." Evan nods and looks a little better, but still not exactly calm. Dan can't blame him. Eventing is a dangerous sport, and all the caution in the world can't change that. And it's one thing to take the risk yourself, quite another to see your beloved baby sister try it. Dan wonders if Evan's going to make it through the weekend without losing his mind.

There's a barbecue planned for that night for all the competitors and visitors, and people are starting to gather around now, but the crew decides to take a quick run over and get settled in their motel before coming back. That brings up the awkward division of rooms. They'd had only one room booked originally, for the three women to share. Dan had planned to stay on a cot in the tack stall, to be near the horses. Then Tatiana had gotten it into her head that it would be an adventure to stay on the site, but Dan had refused to let her stay alone, and hadn't really thought it would be appropriate for him to stay with her, so Robyn had volunteered, and Dan had booked another room at the motel so he and Michelle could have separate rooms. When Evan had decided to come, Dan had thought that it wouldn't really seem fair to book a separate room for him when he'd expected the three girls to all stay together in one. He'd asked Evan if he wanted his own space, and Evan had said he was fine with sharing, and it was up to Dan. So he hadn't added a room, and now he's sharing with Evan. He isn't worried about Evan being aggressive or inappropriate, he's relieved to find, but it's just… awkward.

Tat and Robyn stay on the site, Tat taking her responsibility so seriously that she can barely be dragged away from the stalls to eat. Evan, Dan and Michelle dart over to the motel and check in, throw their bags into the rooms, and drive back to the eventing grounds.

By the time they get back, the barbecue is well under way. They head over toward the food line, and they're just walking past a small group of people when a surprised voice says, "Dan?"

Dan turns, and Evan stays with him while Michelle goes to find Robyn and Tat. "Sean! Hey, how are you?" Sean had competed at the national level for years with his old ride, but Dan hadn't heard much about him since the horse had retired.

"I'm good, good...." Sean's suddenly looking a little awkward, and Dan knows what's coming. "I was, uh, sorry to hear—"

Dan cuts him off. "Yeah, thanks." Like most athletes involved in high-risk sports, eventers can be superstitious, and Dan knows that it seems like bad luck to refer to a fatal accident on the eve of a competition.

Sean looks surprised, and then grateful. "Okay, thanks, man." He gets a little more animated. "So, what are you doing out here? You're not competing, are you?"

"Yeah, kinda." He twists around to bring Evan into the conversation. "Evan, this is Sean Dubois. We used to ride against him. And, Sean, this is Evan Kaminski. He's brought the Archer horses out from Kentucky, and I'm training them for him now."

Sean looks impressed. "Kaminski? Wow. I, uh...." He raises his eyebrows. "I'd heard you were thinking about getting involved in eventing."

"Just starting up, actually. Dan's showing us the ropes."

Sean nods. "Yeah, great, no one better." He looks back at Dan. "So, what are you riding tomorrow?"

"Nothing serious—we've got a couple horses going *hors concours*, a couple just taking trial runs at beginner novice, and then one competitor at training level. How about you?"

"Uh, just one, at training."

Dan nods, and then looks over to the food line. "Well, we'd better go if we want any food. I'll see you tomorrow."

Sean nods, and Dan and Evan move off. When they're a safe distance away, Dan looks at Evan and says, "I'll bet you twenty bucks he's hitting you up for my rides by the end of the weekend."

Evan frowns curiously, and Dan explains. "He's a pro. Showing one horse at the training level—that's not enough to keep him fed. He must be looking for work, and he won't mind taking someone else's ride if he has to."

"Is that normal? I mean, to be that cutthroat? It sounded like you guys are friends."

Dan shrugs. "It's a business. Eventing is an expensive sport, and most of the people seriously involved are either rich"—he nods toward Evan—"or doing whatever they can to earn rides, just trying to have another season with the horses." He nods down toward himself and then adds, "Sean's not rich."

Evan looks a little incredulous. "But you don't do that... you don't act like that."

Dan shrugs. "I've got a sweetheart deal. I mean, I'm a kept man, to some extent." He glances at Evan's raised eyebrows and shakes his head with a little smile. "Not that way. I just mean most trainers are running their own barns, responsible for their own bills, and if they don't do well, if they don't produce winners, their business shuts down." They've arrived at the line now, and Dan turns to face Evan directly. "I don't mean that there's no burden on me to get the horses to perform, but you've got realistic, long-term expectations, and you've got the finances to give us a cushion. I don't hustle like that because I don't have to, but if I had to... I don't know. I know I want to keep riding."

Evan frowns. "It's—I mean, it's just a game to me, even to Tat...."

Dan nods and smiles again. "Yeah. I know. I think there's a lot of things I take seriously that are just a game to you."

Evan frowns, and looks a little hurt, and Dan shakes his head. "I didn't mean... I didn't mean personal stuff. I meant... I don't know, like that fish." It's strangely important to Dan that he make Evan understand this. "I'm not saying you shouldn't have fun, I'm not being critical of it, but... how much money are you talking about there? I mean, if you're looking at the whole quarterly profit of a company your size—you're talking about millions of dollars, right?"

Evan nods cautiously.

"So you'd think that making millions of dollars would be a pretty big rush, but you've got so much money that it doesn't even matter to you anymore. I mean, if I made... I don't even want to know, but let's say, what, a hundred million? In three months?" Evan shrugs his acceptance of that estimate, and Dan can't help but be a little shocked. He'd known the Kaminskis were loaded, but... wow. He tries to get back on topic, and explains, "If I made a tenth of that, it would change my life entirely. But for you, the money doesn't really matter, so you turn it into a game. You play with a bunch of numbers and take bets on a damn stuffed fish."

Evan looks thoughtful, and maybe a little sad. Dan tries to make it better. "I don't mean it as a criticism, man. It's just the way things are. It's different for you."

Evan nods a little. "Yeah, no... I get it. I was just.... Jeff used to talk the same way.... I was just wondering why he doesn't anymore." Evan's eyes lock with Dan's, fiercely intent. "Because I appreciate you saying it, I do. I mean, it's easy for me to just waltz around and ignore that stuff, and it would be easier for you to just dismiss me as some spoiled brat, and not bother trying to explain." He takes a deep breath, and then lets it out. "I wonder if Jeff has given up on making me understand."

Dan doesn't like the direction this conversation is taking. "Jeff loves you, man. I'm, like, the least perceptive person in the world, and I can see that."

Evan nods. "Yeah. But...." Evan doesn't finish the sentence, but he doesn't have to. The "what if that isn't enough" is clear on his face, even to Dan.

"Hell, maybe he doesn't talk about it anymore because *he's* gotten spoiled, too, you ever think of that?" Dan grins. "He seems pretty damn comfortable walking around your place and inviting his friends over for barbecues, and drinking the fancy wines and whatever. Maybe he doesn't bug you about it because he doesn't figure he's got the right!"

Evan grins a little, and then sounds like he's trying to stick up for Jeff. "He's really careful about paying his own way. I mean, anything necessary, he takes care of himself."

"Yeah, but he's happy to enjoy your luxuries, isn't he?" Dan raises his hands. "I'm not saying I blame him either. You guys are together. You don't mind sharing... great, why not? I don't think it's hurting anyone. But, lifestyle-wise—he's a have, not a have-not."

They're at the food service table now, and there's a pause as they load up on burgers and side dishes. They see the girls at a picnic table and start toward them, but before they arrive, Evan asks, "So how would it change your life? If you made ten million dollars?"

Dan grins a little at the idea, but then he stops walking and frowns as he thinks about it. "Shit," he snorts. Evan looks at him in surprise, and Dan shakes his head before he starts speaking. "If I had ten million dollars, I'd ride eventers all day. I'd live in a nice house and keep the horses in a great facility, with private riding rings and a beautiful cross-country course. I'd hire fun, talented people to work with... hell, I'd even have a hyper teenage barn rat running around to keep things interesting." He looks at Evan a little sheepishly. "I dunno, man, maybe I was wrong. If I made ten million dollars right now, I'd probably just put it in the bank."

Evan shakes his head. "Maybe you would, or maybe you'd take it and spend it on stupid stuff, and end up realizing that you were better off beforehand." He shrugs. "I'm not saying life isn't a lot easier when you have money, 'cause I know that it is. There's times when it's really, really useful. But... it's not all there is, you know? And it can buy you some security, but it can't protect you from everything."

Evan looks down at his plate, and then off to the darkening horizon. "Tomorrow's Father's Day, and I was so *fucking* glad when I heard that Tat was going to be coming to this thing, because maybe it'll distract her and keep her from falling apart the way she has every other year on Father's Day, and Mother's Day, and their birthdays." He looks back at Dan. "And, I know, we have money so we can pay for the distractions, and we have money so I can afford to be here in case she *does* fall apart, and all that's true, but it doesn't change the fact that she lost both her parents when she was nine years old. Money can't bring them back." Evan isn't crying, but his eyes are full.

Dan shakes his head. "No. It can't bring anybody back."

There's a quiet moment, and then Tatiana's voice cuts through the dusk. "Evan? Are you lost? Dan? Follow the sound of my voice! Don't be afraid!"

Evan shakes his head. "Money can't make it okay for me to muzzle her."

"Maybe it could buy you a really, really good pair of earplugs."

"Evan? Do you need help? If you need help, bark like a seal!" The girl is clearly enjoying herself.

Evan shakes his head resignedly, and they walk the rest of the way to the table, where Evan carefully puts his plate down and then leans his head over Tat's shoulder. "Aauurf, Aauurf," he barks in her ear, and as Tatiana shrieks with laughter Dan reflects that it really is a very good seal imitation. Maybe rich kids get special tutoring in animal voices.

The rest of the meal goes smoothly, and shortly after they're done eating, Robyn and Tat go down for a final check on the horses, and the other three head back to the motel. Evan takes first turn in the bathroom, and when Dan comes out the lights are turned off, but there's enough light filtering in through the window that Dan can make his way to his bed. He climbs in and lies there staring at the ceiling, listening to Evan breathe in the bed next to him. After a few minutes, Evan stirs.

"Dan?"

"Yeah?"

"Dan, sing me a lullaby," Evan whines.

"Go fuck yourself, Evan."

Evan snorts. "Well, since *you* won't…."

Dan doesn't respond to that, but a few minutes later he says, "Evan?"

"Yeah?"

"Are you still… I mean, okay, I wasn't loving the aggressive come-ons, but are you still… thinking in those terms?"

Evan shifts, and in the dim light Dan can see that he's turned on his side and facing him. "Yeah, but…."

Dan braces himself. "But…."

"But I want to do it right, now. You know? I want to do it like you said. I want us to keep doing this, getting to know each other, and hanging out, and… being sure." He shakes his head. "I know it sounds like I'm a little girl, but I want to take it slow."

Dan absorbs that information. "So, if I got up right now and climbed into bed with you, you'd turn me away?" He puts enough teasing in his voice to let Evan know that it's not going to happen.

Evan responds in a similar tone. "I don't know—why don't you give it a try?"

They both laugh a little, and then it's quiet again. Dan looks at the ceiling, and the way the lights from passing cars reflect off the panels.

"Evan?"

"Yeah."

"I'm sorry about your parents, man."

Evan lets out a deep breath. "Yeah."

They stop talking then, and Dan feels his body relaxing. He thinks briefly about how he didn't spend the night with Ryan, and how he now *is* spending the night with Evan. He thinks it should seem backward and unnatural, but somehow, it doesn't. Then he lets himself drift off to sleep, listening to the comforting sounds of Evan's soft breathing in the background.

chapter 32

THE alarm the next morning is early even by Dan's standards, and Evan just makes a strange groaning snort and buries his head under his pillow as Dan struggles upright and heads for the shower. He brings fresh underwear in with him to avoid the awkwardness of being totally naked in front of Evan, and even remembers to grab the white boxer briefs instead of his usual black. He sometimes can't believe that he has a job where he has to worry about his underwear showing through his white pants.

He showers and shaves, and then heads back out to the main room. He finds his dress breeches and pulls them on, and is just hunting around for the silk socks that work best under his dress boots when Evan sits up with a groan. "What time is it, man?"

Dan checks his watch. "Half past five. We need to be out of here in half an hour—I've got cereal, and there's milk and fruit in the mini-fridge, but if you want to go to the diner for breakfast you'd better haul ass."

Evan rubs his face. "Is there food at the site?"

"Yeah, there's a sort of lunch wagon. No guarantees, but they usually have donuts and stuff in the mornings, and then hot dogs and sandwiches for lunch."

"Okay. I'll have cereal and donuts."

Dan grins. "What, isn't Tat gonna make you have some fruit?"

"Yeah, you're probably right." Evan glances over with a smile, but his eyes catch somewhere around Dan's neck and the expression fades. He seems to have to shake himself back into gear. "Okay, right, I'm just gonna hop in the shower."

He almost bolts from the room, and Dan's hand goes to his collarbone, and he feels the bruise left by Ryan's mouth. Damn. He guesses he can't be too critical of Evan for *his* lack of subtlety, when Dan's parading around waving his exploits in Evan's face. Dan tries to get the situation out of his mind, and he tells himself that he definitely shouldn't feel guilty about the hickey itself.

He pulls on a white undershirt, and then checks to make sure that the rest of his clothes are ready to go. He's got a pair of light coveralls that he wears around when he's not actually riding. They make him look like he's going to work on a car, but they help keep his show clothes clean. Whoever thought up white pants for riding horses definitely had a team of grooms doing the grunt work.

By the time he's sure everything is set, Evan's out of the shower, and Dan busies himself with getting the breakfast food out to avoid staring at Evan as he dresses. There's a knock on the door from Michelle's room, and Dan glances over to make sure Evan's decent before answering it. If he doesn't get to look at naked Evan, then neither does Michelle.

She comes in dressed similarly to Dan, with her brown hair tied up in a tidy bun. She's a fairly stout woman, and her coveralls are a bright pink. She looks a bit like a lollipop, but Dan knows better than to say that. He's almost afraid to ask what she'll be wearing for the cross-country event. That's the only time there's any real room for creativity in the riders' wardrobes, although usually competitors try to reflect their stable's colors. But since the barn hasn't figured out colors yet (Tat had squeaked excitedly when Dan asked her to take care of that, but she hasn't actually produced a final decision yet), Dan had just told the girls to put together whatever they wanted. He knows Tat and Robyn had been poring over catalogs and had received several rush deliveries in the past week.

Dan offers a bowl of cereal to Michelle, and she accepts, and then Evan comes over for his, and the three of them slurp their breakfasts in companionable silence, Evan and Dan sitting on their unmade beds, Michelle on the room's only chair. They finish eating and run through a final checklist to be sure they've got everything, and then head off to the venue.

They're early, but by no means the first ones there. Evan parks, and they head toward the stalls. As soon as they're in sight, Tatiana is storming over, looking angry. Dan braces himself, but Evan is the one who she focuses on. "Evan! Could I talk to you in private, please?"

Evan actually hangs his head, looking like he's being called in front of the principal, while Dan gives him a sympathetic look and heads over to check in with Robyn. He and Michelle help her with feeding and watering the horses and then get started on braiding and grooming, but they also find time to ask her about Tat's mood.

"I'm really not sure," Robyn says. "Everything was fine, then we got up around midnight to do a quick check, and there were a couple guys out front." She frowns a little. "It was weird, because this is such a small show, you wouldn't think there'd be any super-valuable horses here—I bet Monty's got them all outclassed by a mile. But, honestly, they looked like security, like those guys we saw at Rolex. And she saw them and just got really quiet."

Dan thinks for a second, remembers the conversation he'd had the day before, showing just how much money the Kaminskis have. But he doesn't want to start speculating. "Well, I guess if it's any of our business, they'll let us know. Let's run through the schedule, make sure everything is on track."

Robyn and Michelle buckle down, and it's not long before Tat and Evan come back over. They both look a little tense, but it's easy to distract Tat with getting Sunshine ready for the dressage test. The lowest level, beginner-novice, runs first, and that's where most of the barn's horses are registered: Robyn riding Chaucer, Tat riding Sunshine, and Dan riding Winston. Dan doesn't expect much from either Chaucer or Winston. They have the skills, but this is their first event, and they will likely be too excited to do well, especially at dressage, where they need to be relaxed and attentive. And Sunshine has competed at a much higher level in the past, so she's not eligible to place at this level, and is only showing as a way to give Tat some experience.

Because Dan is riding another horse later in the day, he's the first of the team slated to ride, but all three are close enough on the schedule that they saddle up, put on their show jackets, and go to the warm-up ring together. Michelle and Evan follow them and stand at the rail watching as they run through some exercises and then the required test. It's a fairly basic pattern of movements, but the judges will be looking for how well the horses perform them, how balanced, flexible, and responsive they are. Dan watches Robyn and Tat warm up, and then focuses on his own horse. Winston's a bit of a mess. He's strung out from the excitement of his first show and is even more intent on ignoring Dan than he is at home. The energy will serve him well in the jumping portions of the day, but for dressage, he needs to calm down.

Dan is the third rider of the day, and when he sees the first two head over he takes a moment to run everything over in his mind and try to get Winston relaxed. He and Winston walk over to the ring shortly after, then his name and horse are announced, the bell is rung, and he's in the ring.

It's been over a year since Dan has competed, and he's a little nervous himself. It's not the riding that makes him uncomfortable; it's the audience, everyone staring at him. But he focuses on the task at hand and works his way through the test. Winston starts off terribly, fighting Dan every step, his whole body tense and rebellious. Dan has just resigned himself to muscling the beast through the test and then selling him for dog food when Winston finally seems to give up the fight. His whole body lightens, he bends his neck and curves his spine, and he performs the remaining moves as if he's dancing. Dan doesn't know whether to hate him for the first half of the routine or love him for the second. He salutes the judges and heads for the exit gate, and the man running it laughs a little as he passes. "Nice to see he's got the ability, but now you've got to work on the attitude, huh?" Dan nods and smiles back. He'd forgotten this, the sense of community. People are competitive, and for some of them it's big business, but they also love the sport. It's too much hard work and too much risk to take part if they aren't enjoying themselves.

Dan rides over to where Tat is waiting on Sunshine, Evan and Michelle beside her. She looks incredibly nervous, and Dan grins at her. "Did you see that, see what a bastard he was at the start?" Tat nods jerkily. "Yeah, you're lucky Sunshine won't pull that crap on you! You just get to go out there and trot around a little, make me look bad. She can do these moves in her sleep, and I bet you can, too, we've practiced them so much!"

Evan pipes up. "So, is that your advice? They should just go out there and have a nap?"

Dan nods thoughtfully. "You know, I think it is."

Tatiana looks at them in some disgust. "You're both crazy," she says, but her hands have stopped shaking.

Tat's name is called, and Dan thinks he notices a bit of a stir in the crowd. He wonders if the gossip of the rich new family has spread already, and hopes a little for Tat's sake that it hasn't. But then he's focused on watching her ride. She does really well. Sunshine is a dream, of course, but Tat does a good job of staying out of her way and of communicating clearly enough that Sunshine knows what's needed. Dan hasn't seen all the competitors, but from those he has seen, he thinks Tat would have won if Sunshine had been eligible. They leave the ring and Tat is so thrilled she's practically floating, beaming into Evan's video camera and almost squeaking as she tries to give them all a play-by-play of the ride.

Robyn does well, too, with Chaucer not exceptional but solid, especially for his first event. There's a bit of a gap then. It's not yet time for the low-level jumping or the higher level dressage. They untack their horses and have a snack, and after that the day is just a blur, Dan trying to coach the other riders while still being competitive on his own rides. He takes Winston through a clear round in the stadium jumping. The horse has kept most of the tractability from the second half of the dressage test, and he's obviously thrilled to be doing something where he's given a bit more freedom. And when it's his turn Monty waltzes through the dressage test and then takes each jump as if it were a mountain, building up to a huge takeoff and soaring over most of them at double the required height. It's a waste of energy and Dan knows Monty shouldn't be doing it, but it's kind of fun. And Monty's enthusiasm and love of showing off are big parts of what makes him such a great eventer. The other horses do well also, with Kip going clean after a strong dressage test, and Sunshine carrying Tat easily through the jumping.

Dan had debated whether to even enter Chaucer and Winston in the cross country phase. It's the last of the three disciplines at this trial, so he can always pull them out and cite fatigue. But they've both done so well on the first two stages that he decides to keep going, and he's glad of it. They both roar around the course like champions, fearless and strong and beautiful. And despite Evan's white knuckles, Tat and Sunshine come through safely as well, although Dan has to shake his head at Tat's orange and pink outfit with matching orange reins. Then the junior horses are cooled out and put back in their stalls for a well-deserved rest, and it's only Monty and Kip left. Monty's just running the course for fun, but Kip had a solid dressage test and a clean jumping round, so he's in third place going into the cross-country. If he goes clean, he'll be guaranteed to be in the prize money. Dan knows that it's a paltry amount compared to the expenses of even just the trip, let alone the enterprise as a whole, but he'd still like to see at least a start to the income that the stable should someday earn.

The course wraps around in big loop so the end is near the beginning, and Dan is able to watch the two horses ahead of Kip in the rankings come in with significant faults, opening the door for Michelle not just to place but maybe win. He sees Michelle bringing Kip home while he's waiting for Monty's start time. Evan, Tat and Robyn are even closer, the girls screaming encouragement as Evan films the action, and when Kip comes in on time and Michelle raises her arms to indicate that there had been no faults on the course, Dan feels not elation but relief. He hadn't realized how anxious he'd been about this day, about showing Evan that he's doing a good job and has found him good employees and brought him good horses, until just that moment. If he's honest, maybe it's not all about showing Evan. Maybe some of it is about showing himself. He'd worked with Justin for so long, it was hard to be sure if he was any good on his own or if he had just been riding on Justin's coattails. A win in a training level regional horse trial isn't his ultimate goal, but it's a start.

He barely even thinks about Monty's ride, just lets the big horse's talent and arrogance carry him over the obstacles as if they're beneath his notice. He rides clean, making Monty slow a little to make sure they don't come in under the minimum time, and then rides strong to the finish. His results don't matter, but the others have stayed behind to wait for him and cheer him on anyway, and it feels good. Monty and Kip get turned out together at home and are friends, and Kip even adds a greeting of his own, whinnying loudly when Dan takes too long to get Monty over to him. Dan laughs and lets the two tired, sweaty horses greet each other, and then he and Michelle ride back to the main area together, with the other three trailing behind on foot.

Usually the stadium jumping is the last stage of an event, and the results are available quite quickly. With cross-country last, it takes a little longer to compile the results, since judges have to come in from the course and then do the math, so the team untacks the horses and starts the process of post-event caring. Each horse gets walked until it's cool and dry, and then gets a massage and an anti-inflammatory lotion applied to its legs. Dan's responsible for two horses, and while he's already cooled Winston down, he's happy to have Evan work on him while Dan works on Monty. It's useful, and it's a good way for Evan to learn a bit more about his horses. After the lotion, they put stable bandages on the legs and put them in their stalls. They'll walk them again before bed, all in an attempt to keep them from getting too stiff.

This is a social time, too, with competitors touring around and chatting now that the competition is over. Because the Kaminski barn is new, they get a lot of attention, and Tat seems to find a few new friends in the younger visitors. Dan sees them exchanging phones and punching information in, and babbling about posting on each other's Facebook walls.

He also notices quite a few of the females casting their eyes toward Evan. There's one woman, a beautiful brunette, who apparently knows Evan a little from somewhere, and they have an animated reunion. Dan doesn't think the initial hug is especially comment-worthy, but he can't help but notice that the woman keeps touching Evan afterward, lots of little arm rubs and even a few playful leans and hip checks. Dan tells himself that he has work to do and goes to check on Sunshine's bandages, but when he finds himself peering out at Evan from under the horse's belly, he realizes that he may be in a little trouble. Evan is touching her back now, and Dan wonders how bitchy he would seem if he asked Evan to walk Winston a little more.

Evan does his own playful lean into the woman, and Dan stands up and tries to make himself talk to Tat. "Yeah, those are fine. They're a little on the loose side, but that's better than too tight, and they're not bad enough to re-do." Tat nods thoughtfully and reaches down to test the tightness, and Dan casts another look over at Evan. He's giving the woman the "look up through your bangs" treatment, and Dan is about done with this. Then Evan glances over at Dan, raises an eyebrow and smirks a little. Dan immediately shifts his eyes down, pretending he wasn't looking, but he knows it's too late—he's busted. He looks back up, and Evan's smirk widens, and Dan shakes his head a little ruefully, then tilts it in acknowledgment. Okay, yeah, Evan wins this round.

By this time, the results are available, and the brunette returns to her horse. Evan comes up beside Dan and gives *him* a playful hip check, which Dan repays with a fairly sharp elbow to the ribs. Evan grunts and laughs a little, and Dan says, "Yeah, okay, but at least I didn't run over and drape myself all over you!"

They all walk over to check the results. Dan takes a quick look at the board and grins at Michelle. "We'll just lead the other two out in coolers, but Kip won—do you want to saddle him up and ride him out?"

She looks tempted, but then shakes her head. "No, I guess not—he's all comfy now, and it looks like most of the rest of the people are just taking them out in show coolers." She brightens. "Besides, there'll be lots of other times for him to win, right?" Then she looks a little panicked. "But do I get to keep riding him?"

"Dude, you won. Why would I take your ride away when you won?" Dan grins at her look of relief, and then goes to get Winston ready for the ribbon presentation. He'd gotten sixth, Chaucer had gotten eighth, and Dan's thrilled with both of those results, considering that it's their first event. When Dan takes Winston out and the judges come by to award the ribbons, they're a bit chatty during the traditional handshakes.

"He was great all day, except for the first minute and a half," one of them tells Dan.

"Yeah, I know—it's his first event, and he's young, so... he'll get better."

The judges nod, and a different one says, "I saw Three Willows at Rolex a couple years ago. Your *hors concours* horse, Three Card Monte— he's her full brother?"

Dan nods. "I think he's as good as she was—different personality, but the same strength and courage."

The judges all nod, looking impressed. "Well, we'll look forward to seeing more of both of you—welcome to California."

They move on, and Dan looks at the green ribbon fluttering from Winston's halter. Winston doesn't seem too sure about it, and makes a few efforts to twist around to get a better look, apparently not understanding that it moves as he does. "You'd better get used to it, buddy—you're gonna be seeing a lot more of them," Dan mutters to him, thumping his neck.

They trail out of the ring and Dan sees Tat looking at the ribbons enviously. He thinks for a second, and then walks over. "You know, we could probably have you ride Sunshine *and* Chaucer in the next trial... as long as you work on your fitness, and we spend a lot of time training you and Chaucer together." He shrugs. "You probably won't be getting firsts for a while, but at least it would give you a shot at the ribbons—" The rest of Dan's words are buried under Tat's excited hug. He extracts himself eventually, and says, "So I guess that means you're interested?" She just nods, and then scurries over to Robyn to tell her the good news.

Dan swears a little to himself, and heads over to explain to Robyn why he just gave away her ride. He tells her, "You did great today. It was a fantastic introduction for him. You can switch over to Winston if you want—he's just a little too strong for Tat right now. Or you can bring up one of the younger horses." She nods, and he thanks his lucky stars that she's got enough self-confidence to accept that it's not a demotion.

There's a lot of work to do getting the horses cleaned up and relaxed and ready for bed, and it was already almost seven when the ribbons were awarded. Evan goes and picks up a few pizzas while the others are finishing off with the horses, and when he gets back everyone falls on him as if they're starving to death. Robyn peers at the boxes a bit skeptically until Evan nods her in the direction of the vegetarian option. They don't bother to talk; they just eat and then lie back, full and tired.

Evan sighs a little, and then says, "So, Tat... what d'ya say? Another night out here, or do you want to go back to the motel?"

Dan hadn't really thought of that, but it does seem fair to trade around. "Yeah, if you guys want to go back and sleep in a real bed, I'm fine staying out here."

Robyn shakes her head. "No way, man! This bed is fifteen minutes closer than the motel—that makes it mine." She glances over at Tat. "But it's no problem if you want to head back, sweetie. I'm good here."

Dan's chivalrous side has never really liked the idea of leaving a woman alone in the tack stall. The gate locks, but it's not as secure as a motel room, and part of the job is being ready to leave the stall to check on the horses. But he knows that lots of women do it, and that it's an important part of the groom's job at many barns. Excluding women from the task would mean making them less employable.

Tat looks at Evan a little sullenly, and then says, "No, I'll stay."

"You're sure?" Dan isn't quite sure what's going on between the two of them, still doesn't know what caused Tat's tantrum that morning, but Evan seems to be treating whatever her complaint is with some level of respect.

She nods, and when Evan looks at Dan and Michelle to see if they're ready, she stands with him and gives him a hug. Evan looks a little surprised, but wraps his arms around her immediately and hugs back. She looks up at him with her face still squished to his chest, and says, "Thanks for today, Evan. It was a good day."

He smiles a little sadly. "Do you want me to stay out here with you? I can fold up some horse blankets, make a little nest for myself."

She pushes him away firmly, and shakes her head. "No, I'm fine. I'm gonna be asleep as soon as my head hits the pillow."

Evan nods. "Your phone's charged?"

She rolls her eye now. "Go away, Evan! Dan and Michelle are waiting for you."

"Okay, okay." They smile at each other, and then Evan is heading toward the parking lot, Michelle and Dan trailing along behind him. Evan gets a call when they're almost to the car, and has to hang back to take it, and Dan reminds himself that Evan has a lot of responsibilities beyond his family. It says a lot that he's uncomplainingly sacrificed his weekend to sleeping in a room in a crappy motel and driving around with a bunch of horses, just because that's what his sister wants. Dan thinks about their conversation of the previous day, and realizes that one more thing money can't buy is time.

Evan returns, and they climb in the car, and even over the fifteen-minute drive Dan has to fight to keep himself awake. It's been a good day, but it's been tiring. He catches Evan watching him in the rear view mirror and smiles a little, and Evan smiles back, although he looks a little tense. Dan decides that he can wait and figure that out the next day. Things with Kaminskis really don't seem to stay buried for long.

chapter 33

THEY drive back to the motel quietly, then leave Michelle at her door and head back to their own room. As Evan follows him through the door, Dan says, "I'm gonna shower, so if you want the bathroom first...."

Evan nods, and grabs his toiletry kit before going to the bathroom. He's out a couple minutes later, and Dan goes in, letting the warm water of the shower wash away the sweat and grime of the day. He realizes when he's done that he forgot to bring in a change of clothes and he really can't face the idea of getting back into the dirty stuff he'd just dropped on the floor. So he wraps a towel around his waist, brushes his teeth, and heads out into the main room. He'd expected Evan to already be in bed, like he had been the day before, but he's not. He's sitting on the end of his bed, and it really looks like he's waiting for Dan. He turns his head toward the door as Dan hunts around for clothes, pulling underwear on under his towel and then putting on a pair of sweats. But when Dan turns to look at him, Evan leans forward a little.

"Are you super-tired now, or can I talk to you for a minute?"

Dan's tired, but he really doesn't think he's going to be able to sleep after that. "Uh, no, we can talk."

Dan remembers his hickey and pulls a crew neck shirt on, then walks over and sits on the corner of his bed, his legs angled toward Evan. Evan swings his own legs around so they're almost facing each other, and then he sighs. "Okay, I hope this isn't going to be a big deal, but, uh...."

Dan sighs and braces himself. He guesses he should have known that the weekend had gone too smoothly.

"Okay, you saw that Tat was kinda pissed off this morning?"

Dan nods. He'd figured he'd be hearing about this eventually. "Well, that was because she saw a couple of the guys who do security for us at the site. She knows they're necessary, but... she hates it. She just wants to be normal, you know?"

Dan nods. "How come she didn't know they'd be there?"

"I don't know—wishful thinking, maybe? I mean, she doesn't have them when she's at home, and as long as she's going somewhere totally unexpected she doesn't usually need to have them if she goes out. But something like this, where her name was on the registration list, posted on the internet? When she's going to be sleeping overnight on an almost abandoned site? She needed security."

"It's for kidnapping?"

Evan nods. "Yeah, essentially. I mean, they'll jump in if there's any sort of problem, but the real risk is kidnapping."

Dan raises his eyebrows. He guesses it makes sense, but he can't imagine living like that. "So, is there anything I can do to help? Like, things that I should be looking out for?"

Evan looks really uncomfortable for some reason. "Uh, just keep your eyes open, I guess. But, in terms of helping…." He gives his head a shake. "Okay, I'm sure it's not a big deal. I don't know if you remember, but when you got hired you filled out a lot of paperwork, and one of the things you signed was a permission form for the company to do an Investigative Consumer Report. Which is essentially a background check. I honestly don't even know what all they look at—lots of stuff, I guess." He looks over at Dan as if trying to read his reaction, but Dan keeps his face still. "Anyway, I trust you, so I didn't put a rush on it or anything, but I guess when they were lining up security for the weekend they finally got around to putting together everything they'd got for all of you guys, and they called tonight and said they had a few questions they wanted to ask you." Evan looks at Dan a little tentatively.

"Just me?" Dan asks quietly.

"Uh, yeah. I don't know what it's about, and I told them I don't want to know. I mean, I trust you. And I could just tell them to skip it and not bother, but… they're professionals, you know? They're not going to forget about whatever it is, and if they're busy being suspicious of you they're maybe not going to pay the attention they should pay to somebody else who might really *be* a risk, and… it's my sister, man. I can't do anything that will get in the way of them doing their jobs." Evan looks miserable.

Dan is really tired. "Yeah, that's fine. Don't worry about it. I… I dunno, but probably they found my juvie record."

Evan cautiously says, "You have a juvenile record?"

"Yeah." Evan hasn't asked, but Dan doesn't want to make him.

"Assault, vandalism, possession... theft... I was a pretty fucked-up kid." He sneaks a look, and sees that Evan doesn't seem too alarmed, so he continues. "The record's supposed to be sealed, but Chris said that a good investigator might find it, especially if he throws a little money at the right people." He grins a little bitterly. "I'm betting your guys had some money to throw."

Evan frowns. "I told them I didn't want to know, but maybe I should give them a call. I mean, if that's all it was, then they shouldn't need to talk to you about it."

"It didn't all stop when I turned eighteen, but at least I knew enough not to get caught anymore." Another look, and Evan still seems reasonably calm. "I... I was on my way to leaving it behind when I met Justin, and... I don't know, I guess he gave me something to lose, so I calmed right down."

Evan takes a deep breath. "Okay. I... I don't know how much they would have found if there's no formal record of the adult stuff—you never got arrested after eighteen, or you never got convicted?"

"Never arrested, after eighteen. Questioned a few times... I expect my name might be in a few reports somewhere."

Evan shakes his head. "Damn, Dan, I'm sorry they're dragging all this up."

"Like I said, don't worry about it. Do they want me to go somewhere to talk to them?"

"Uh, they said they could come out to the farm. Tomorrow afternoon, if that's all right."

Dan nods, and then shakes his head. "No, wait. It... it might be better to keep this out of the barn. Can I meet them somewhere?"

Evan shrugs. "You could go down to the office, I'm sure. But they'd be discreet. They could go to your house, or you could meet them at my place if you want—use my office."

"No, the guest house is fine. Do you know what time?"

"I can just call them and tell them when's good for you."

"It doesn't matter. We should be back by noon." He runs a hand through his hair. "Does it matter to you? If that's all they're worried about, is it a big deal?"

"A juvenile record? No, man, I don't care. I mean, they shouldn't even have had access to it, right? Those get sealed for a reason."

"Yeah, okay." Dan looks over. "Is that it?"

Evan seems to sense that Dan isn't taking this quite as well as he's pretending to. "Seriously, man, this isn't me. I mean, I trust you... remember, that's why I wanted to hire you."

"Evan, really, don't worry about it. You don't have to apologize for screening your employees, or whatever. I get it. Just because we're friendly doesn't mean I'm exempt."

"Friendly? Don't... don't downgrade us because of this, man. I mean... we're friends. Working on maybe something more? This is separate from that, right?" Evan looks at Dan almost pleadingly.

Dan takes a deep breath, and then blows it out. "I'm just tired, maybe. It's... right now, it's... you're my boss. I shouldn't be letting myself forget that. Like I said yesterday, this is pretty much my dream job, and I don't want to screw it up. And I could screw it up if I forget who my boss is."

Evan shakes his head. "No. I'm not your boss like *that*. I mean, I'm not your boss like I supervise you every day, or get you in trouble if you're late, or—"

"Evan. You're my boss." Dan knows he sounds testy, and he tries to modulate his tone. Tries not to snap at his boss. "Okay, I'm sorry. I don't know... I'm just being a pussy. I'll talk to the guys. It'll be fine, no big deal." Evan doesn't look even a little bit convinced by this, but Dan tries to ignore it. He doesn't know why this is bothering him so much. Maybe it's because he had been enjoying the fantasy, having fun thinking of Evan as just a guy, rather than his employer. So maybe it's a good thing that he's been brought back to earth now rather than later, when he'd have had farther to fall. "So, maybe I'll just get some sleep now, if we've covered everything...."

Evan nods reluctantly, and Dan resolutely stands up, pulls the covers back, and climbs in. Evan stays sitting on the end of his bed for a while, then gets up and turns out the light, and makes his way to bed himself. Dan doesn't get to sleep for a long time, but he doesn't say anything, doesn't want to resurrect the silly chatter of the previous night. He needs to re-establish some boundaries here, and pillow talk is not going to be the way to do it.

He finally drifts off, but wakes up before the alarm the next morning. He lies there, trying to get back to sleep, but as usual it's no use. He looks over at Evan, sleeping peacefully in the next bed, and rips his eyes away almost immediately. Employees shouldn't look at their bosses asleep, shouldn't want to touch their bosses' bare shoulders, or run their hands down under the covers....

He lifts himself out of bed warily, and scouts out his objectives before he moves. His shoes are there; his socks are there; and the room key is there... he'd slept in sweatpants and a T-shirt, so he can go outside without needing any new clothes. He carefully retrieves all the items and heads for the door. It makes a little brushing sound as it opens, the loudest noise he's made since he woke up, but he forces himself not to turn around and check on Evan. He squeezes outside and shuts the door softly behind him, and takes a deep breath of the cool morning air. It feels good to be free.

He sits down on the curb and pulls on his socks and running shoes. He thinks about Evan's workouts, the idea of exercise as stress relief, and he stands up and walks a few steps before he starts jogging. He'd worked hard the day before, and he hadn't slept well, so he doesn't have all that much energy, but it does feel good to be working at something. He heads out on the sidewalk and turns left. They'd come from the right, and he doesn't remember seeing anywhere all that running-friendly in that direction. Not that he needs anywhere special—at this time of day, the sidewalks are deserted, so he can get enough room anywhere. He stops after ten minutes and stretches, and then starts out again at a faster rate, pushing himself a little, trying to get into his non-thinking zone. He finds his rhythm, hears the slap of his feet on the pavement as if it's coming from inside him, somehow, and everything else fades away. It feels good.

Eventually, he comes out of himself enough to notice that traffic is starting to pick up a little. Still not exactly rush hour, but probably time to get back. They aren't on quite such a tight schedule today, but there's still a lot to get done. And Dan had told Evan that they'd be home by noon. With that thought, he feels all the tension he'd just worked out of his body come rushing back in. They'd be home by noon so Dan could go and answer a bunch of questions about some stupid stuff he'd done in what seems like another life. He believes Evan that a juvie record isn't a big deal to his current employment, but that doesn't mean he's looking forward to reliving it all, or being grilled on his life's mistakes by total strangers.

When he gets back to the motel, the room is empty and Evan's stuff is gone, although the Cherokee is still parked outside. Dan glances at the clock. He's tight for time, but not yet late. He hangs his sweaty clothes up to air out a little while he has a quick shower. Evan's still not back when Dan gets out, so he pulls on jeans and a T-shirt, finds his work boots, and packs up the rest of his crap. He knocks on the door to Michelle's room but there's no answer, so he eats his cereal by himself, then pours out the last of milk and packs up the food from the mini-fridge. He piles everything by the door and does a quick sweep of the room for anything left behind, then walks over to the diner that's attached to the motel. If Michelle and Evan are anywhere together, it's probably there.

His suspicion is confirmed as soon as he opens the door and hears Evan's loud laugh coming from farther inside. The two of them are in a booth by the window, Evan's back facing the door so Dan can only see Michelle's face. She looks pleased at having made Evan laugh, and Dan feels a moment of irritation. Obviously Evan isn't too worried about what he's making Dan go through today. But then, why should he be? People have their employees go through security stuff all the time, and Dan needs to make sure he doesn't forget that he's Evan's employee.

He walks over to the table determined to be civil. "'Morning, guys." They both look up, and Dan addresses himself to Michelle. "Are you out of your room? Can I go check us out?"

She nods. "Yeah, we put my stuff in the car. We're ready to go whenever you are. We were just waiting for you."

Dan glances at his watch. They're still on schedule, but he feels like Michelle is accusing him of something. Maybe he's just being paranoid, bracing himself for the accusations that will come that afternoon. "Okay. Uh, Evan, can I borrow the keys to the car? If I load my stuff I can check us out, and then meet you guys out there in a few minutes?"

Evan nods, and stands up to dig the keys out of his front pocket. "Sure, man. Do you need any help? Or do you want me to do that, let you get some breakfast?"

"No, I'm good, thanks." He's really not interested in owing Evan any favors.

A few minutes later when he walks out of the motel office, Evan and Michelle are both sitting in the Cherokee waiting for him, Michelle in the back seat. It's a fifteen-minute drive, so Dan doesn't bother trying to figure out a way to get her to trade positions.

Michelle has a few questions about the barn while they're driving, and Dan tries to drag them out, turn them into discussions for just him and Michelle. Sometime over the course of the restless night and short morning, Dan seems to have developed a bit of resentment toward Evan, and he's reluctant to talk himself out of it. It would be a lot easier to keep his distance from the guy if he weren't so damn likeable... and at least right now, he's not.

When they get to the site, Tat and Robyn have already fed the horses and are working on packing things up while the animals eat. Dan looks around for the horse trailer, and then looks quizzically at Robyn. "No transport yet?"

She shakes her head, and he checks his watch, then tells himself to calm down. The guy isn't even late yet, so why is Dan looking for trouble?

Someone is running a tractor with a low hay wagon behind it as a sort of equipment shuttle, taking stuff from the temporary stalls to the loading area. Dan flags the driver down, and they all start loading equipment. And then one of the site administrators comes over to settle up the final accounts. They'd brought feed and hay with them, but they'd bought bedding, and there's the prize money, meager though it is, to sort out. By the time that's taken care of the horse trailer has arrived, and everyone's busy loading equipment and then animals.

When everything's on board, the crew gathers. Dan looks at Michelle. "I wouldn't mind talking to the driver about some stuff, get his impressions on different events and things about the industry out here. Would you be okay riding in the car?"

She leans in to make sure the driver can't hear. "You don't have to... I've got a second wind for the stories, I'll be fine."

Dan makes himself laugh. "No, I seriously want to talk to him." She smiles, happy at her escape, and Dan turns to the youngest member of their band. "Tat, there's room for you in the car too...."

"No way! I want to hear about the events too!" She looks excited, as usual, and Dan groans to himself. Now he's got to come up with some actual questions to ask the guy. Still, better to make conversation with him than with Evan.

By the end of the trip, Dan isn't sure that was true. He'd run out of any possibly useful questions after the first half hour, and after that the driver had just taken the bit in his teeth and told story after story, almost all of them with no discernible point or ending. Even Tat is looking a little overwhelmed, and Dan feels like he's been to war. He jumps out of the cab before the truck has even come to a complete stop, and sees Robyn and Michelle notice and laugh at him. He rolls his eyes at Michelle, and she nods in agreement, and then they get to work with the horses.

Sara's at the barn looking after the animals that were left behind, and she comes out to help. Tat is game, but obviously dragging, and Dan would just as soon be rid of Evan. "Why don't you head home now, Tat?" She raises her eyes in protest, but Dan says, "Sunshine's unloaded and in her paddock, you've taken her tack inside, and you spent two nights on a cot… you've done more than your share, for sure." She looks tempted, especially when Evan smiles fondly at her and gives her an approving nod.

"Yeah, head up, brat. I've gotta sort a couple things out with Dan, and then I'll be up too. Why don't you see what Tia's got for our lunches?"

She nods, and then turns to Dan. "Are you gonna come up for lunch too?"

He's caught a little off guard, but manages a calm, "No, thanks, I've got some stuff to take care of down here."

She leaves, and Evan turns to Dan. "So, I talked to the security team. They said they'd like to get this cleared up as soon as possible, so they're gonna come by today at one, to your house. Is that cool?"

Dan looks at his watch. It's already half past twelve, and Evan grimaces. "Yeah, sorry, man. When they get something in their heads, they're pretty aggressive."

Dan doesn't want to hear any more apologies, doesn't want to pretend that this is a favor he's doing for Evan. This is mandatory; it's a term of his employment. If they say to be ready at one, he guesses he'd better be. "Yeah, okay, I'll just make sure everything's on track here and head over."

"Is there anything I can do to help? I mean, here, or…."

"No, not really. Everybody here knows more about horses than you do, so they can handle everything. It's fine. I'm gonna take the rest of the day off, probably. Did you see the sheet in the tack room for everybody to record their hours? I'll sign out in there."

Evan shakes his head impatiently. "Dan, I told you not to worry about the damn hours! I trust you, I know you're doing your job, you don't need to prove anything to me."

Dan snorts. "Well, apparently I need to prove things to somebody, right? I'll just hang onto the hour sheets in case payroll decides to launch their own investigation some day."

Evan looks like he'd like to answer that a little sharply, but after a brief struggle he holds his tongue. "All right. Let me know if there's any problems this afternoon."

"Evan, if there's problems, I expect I'll be the last to know. That's how it worked this time around."

Evan's face twitches a little, but again he doesn't respond, just raises a hand to wave and climbs into the Cherokee. Dan feels a little bad, but he resists that urge. Evan's the one who dragged him out here into this crazy world with its bodyguards and in-depth security checks, so why should Dan be the only one who's uncomfortable, while Evan cruises around consequence-free in his little bubble of wealth? He knows that's not fair, remembers that Evan and Tat have not been cushioned from all of life's blows, but he doesn't really care about being fair.

He goes over to the paddock where Smokey is grazing. The water trough has overflowed somehow and made a little mud pit, and Smokey's obviously been playing in it, with mud splashed all over his legs and up under his belly. When the little horse sees Dan he comes over to the fence to nose around for treats, and Dan pats his neck affectionately, fingers working loose some of the dried mud that had splashed up even that far. "You and me, Smokey… maybe we're a little too dirty for a place like this, huh? What do you say? Do you want to just run away, go live in the hills?" Smokey nods his head, but Dan isn't convinced. "Yeah, you say that now, but how about when it gets cold or if it rains, huh? And you'd miss all the apples you get down here, wouldn't you, and all your friends?" Smokey nods again, and then, apparently giving up on finding a treat, he turns and walks back over to where the other horses are grazing. Dan can tell that he's in a bit of a melodramatic mood because he actually feels betrayed by the horse's choice.

He shakes his head and walks over to the barn. He needs to make sure that everything's on track and then sign out. He doesn't want to be late for his own inquisition.

chapter 34

WHEN Dan arrives at the guest house, he sees a dark sedan already parked out front, and as he approaches two men climb out. They're wearing dark suits and sunglasses, and Dan feels dirty and underdressed. Not the best start to the meeting. Still, he has no choice, so he approaches them and holds out his hand.

"I'm Dan Wheeler. You guys are from the Kaminski security... thing?"

The older of the two men nods. "I'm Bill Albanese, this is Neil Dawson." They all shake hands, and then Bill says, "Do you mind if we go inside?"

Dan shakes his head and walks in front of them toward the stairs. He deliberately angles his body so they can't see his code as he punches it into the door. He knows they probably have easy access to that sort of information, but fuck them, why should he trust them when they don't trust him?

He doesn't really know what to do with them when they get inside. He drops his bags from the trip in a pile by the door, then turns to the men. "Uh, do we need a table for this, or do you want to sit in the living room?"

"A table might be useful." This time it's Neil talking.

"Okay, uh, let's go into the kitchen." They follow him down the hallway, and when they arrive in the sun-filled room, Dan wonders how much of a host he's supposed to be. "Do you guys want coffee or anything?"

Neil shakes his head, but Bill says, "If you're making some anyways," and Dan decides to like him better. He still doesn't like him, but... he's better. Dan wonders if they'll do a good-cop-bad-cop routine, and how much it would mess up the system if Bill turns out to be the bad cop. While he's having these thoughts, his body is automatically moving around the kitchen, pulling out the coffee and pouring water into the reservoir, settling the carafe in place, and checking the fridge for milk.

Luckily, he's got some, and he pulls it out and puts it on the table next to the sugar bowl. Then he gets mugs out. He's aware that the two men are watching him do all this, but he doesn't really see how much they could be picking up from his actions. Doesn't everyone make coffee about the same way?

With nothing left to busy his hands, he looks over to the table. It's got one end against the wall, and the visitors have seated themselves on either long side, leaving the end between them for Dan. He wonders if this is a psychological ploy, wonders if it would frustrate them to know that he usually sits there anyway. He wonders if maybe he's giving these two a little too much credit for deviousness.

He sits down and looks at them expectantly. There's a pause, and then Bill begins. "All right, well, as Mr. Kaminski has likely advised you, we ran the routine background check that we perform on all new employees, and then we ran an enhanced check due to your position of access to the Kaminski family. It was the enhanced check that raised a few... troubling questions."

Dan nods, but doesn't say anything. He's not going to do their job for them.

Neil pulls out a digital recorder and holds it up for Dan to see before turning it on. "For our record keeping and to avoid any confusion, we routinely tape all our interviews. Do you have any objection to this?" It sounds like he's said the same things a lot of times.

"What if I do object?" Dan doesn't really care, but again, he doesn't feel like making their lives easy.

"Then we would terminate the interview and advise Mr. Kaminski that you were uncooperative and that we recommend against your employment." Neil sounds like he's said that a few times as well.

"Can I get a copy of the tape?" Dan has no idea what he would do with a copy of his own interrogation, but....

Bill answers this one. "We'll provide you with a copy and a transcript. We've also brought a copy of the file we've compiled on you, for your records and review." Bill smiles a little. "We're not just being nice, California law requires this." Yeah, Bill's good cop.

"Okay, I don't object to the tape."

"All right, then." Bill's in charge for now. "The concerns that we have arise from a variety of smaller issues and one large one. For clarity, we'd like to just go through them all chronologically. For each issue, we'll show you documentation or present what we've found, give you a chance to review it, and then ask any questions we may have. If at any point you feel that we've missed something, please bring it up. And I need to remind you that you're not under oath, this is not a formal legal proceeding, but it is in your contract that your employment can be terminated immediately, without severance or other consideration, if you are in any way dishonest or evasive in any security-related matter. That's clear?"

Dan just nods, and Bill pulls the first document out of the folder. "We have two copies of each of these, one for us and one for you." He passes the sheet over. Dan has to look at it for a second to figure out what it is, but then he realizes that it's a list of all the school he ever attended. There's only one school for kindergarten to grade six, then three junior highs, then a long string of high schools. Dan has no idea what this is supposed to prove.

He looks up at Bill, who says, "We'd just like to confirm that these are the schools you attended." Dan nods, and Bill says, "We only have audio recording, so we need you to respond in words."

Dan rolls his eyes a little, then says, "Yes, these are the schools that I attended."

Bill hands over another sheet, a transcript from the last school on the list. "And this is your final transcript? It seems to indicate that you did not graduate. Is that accurate?"

Dan frowns. "I never *said* I graduated."

Bill nods. "No, we're not accusing you of anything. We're just trying to get our facts straight. So, could you confirm that you did not graduate from high school?"

"No, I never graduated from high school." The coffeemaker has stopped making noise, and Dan stands up and fills two mugs from it, bringing them over to the table and passing one to Bill. It felt good to stand up and get away from the two of them, and he's sorry he has to come back.

The next paper that gets passed over is what Dan was expecting. He wonders if the school stuff was just a way to get him off balance, put him on the defensive. He looks down at the arrest report in front of him, complete with his mug shot. Dan in the picture looks young and scared, trying to look old and mean. It's a little sad.

"This is a copy of an arrest report, showing a Class B Misdemeanor of possessing less than two ounces of marijuana. Would you like to explain anything about the charge?"

"Explain anything? Not really… I mean, I was in possession of less than two ounces of marijuana. I got charged." Dan pauses for a second, then adds, "I was fifteen."

"No extenuating circumstances, no claims that it wasn't really yours."

Dan shakes his head, then rolls his eyes and says, "No," out loud.

"And were you convicted of this offense?"

Dan is pretty sure that these guys have the court records that show his convictions, and they're just testing him. He doesn't really appreciate it, but this is their show. "Yes, I was."

"And what was the sentence?"

"Probation, and I think community service and a fine."

"You think?" Neil frowns at him.

"Dude, it was a long time ago. I know I did community service for a couple things, paid a couple fines. I can't remember for sure what was for what."

Bill says nothing, just pulls out the next sheet. It's another arrest report, this one for aggravated assault. Dan looks it over, and then Bill says, "You probably remember the questions. Do you want to just answer them all at once?"

A part of Dan doesn't want to, wants to make this as inconvenient for Bill and Neil as possible, but mostly he just wants to get it over with. "I plea bargained to regular assault. I think I did two months in juvie and some more probation."

Bill nods. "This one is of concern to us because it seems to show a temper problem and a propensity to violence. If there's anything more you could tell us about the circumstances, that would be very helpful."

Dan doesn't want to go back there, doesn't want to think about the person he was then. "I *used to* have a pretty hot temper. I was an angry kid. The other guy had been pushing me around and calling me a fag for weeks, and one day I'd had enough, and I fought back."

"And broke his jaw and a couple of ribs?"

Dan doesn't really have anything to say to that. "Yeah."

"Were you injured?"

"Some bruises, and I broke my hand."

"You broke your hand by hitting him?"

"Yeah." Dan doesn't like where this is going, but he doesn't really know what he can do to stop it.

"I'm trying to get a clearer picture—was the other boy larger or smaller than you?"

Dan shrugs. "I don't know... about the same size, maybe a bit bigger. He was on the football team, so it's not like I was picking on some little geek or something."

Bill nods. "Okay." He hands over the next report, and this is the one Dan's been waiting for. "So, a single arrest seems to have led to several charges here... and we're a bit concerned about these as well, so if you could run us through the situation again, that'd be great."

Dan looks at the mug shot on this one. He still looks young, but he's got a big bruise over one cheekbone, and his expression looks dead. He looks a lot closer to the 'old and mean' that he'd been shooting for in his first arrest photo. "I got in a fight with my stepfather, and it got physical. He called the cops, told me to get out. I left, but I took his car. Stupid, obviously. I went to a friend's house and we got drunk and smashed a couple windows at the school. The cops caught us. We got arrested." He glances down at the report. "My stepfather insisted that I get charged with the assault and car theft, and then obviously the cops weren't pleased with the vandalism. And resisting arrest... I'd forgotten that one."

Bill's face is neutral. "And the outcome of that?"

"The outcome? Uh, plea bargain, I think. I ended up doing another eight months in juvie, then probation."

"And you completed the probation?"

Dan hadn't thought about that. "I guess not, no. I went back to the house for about five minutes to get some clothes, but then I left town. I was supposed to do some community service stuff, I think, and report to a social worker or somebody." He shrugs. "But they sealed my records... theoretically, at least... so they must have forgiven the missed probation, right?"

Bill shrugs. "It seems like. So, this brings us to the end of our findings on your juvenile arrest record. Do you have anything you'd like to add or correct?"

"No, I don't think so." If that's all they want, Dan is relieved. But then he glances over at the file and sees that there's still quite a bit of paper in it…

Bill hands him several pages stapled together. "This is what we've come up with in regards to your whereabouts and activities from the present back to the time when you left the juvenile facility. Could you please look at it and see if there are any errors or omissions?"

Dan takes a few moments to shuffle through the sheets. "Jesus. You guys—how did you put all this together? I wouldn't have been able to remember all this!"

Bill smiles, and it looks genuine. "We are really pretty good at our jobs. And because of your unique position of access to the family—living on the property, working with Miss Kaminski unsupervised—we were especially thorough."

"Yeah, I guess!" He flips through the pages, a chronology of addresses, employers, even friends and lovers. He feels like his life has been laid out for everyone to see. It's a bit intimidating, and he supposes that's what Bill and Neil were shooting for. He looks up. "Like I said, I can't remember everything, but, yeah, this looks about right."

"There are several gaps in there, times when we weren't able to find an address for you, or any employment. Especially in the earlier years. Would you be able to fill in the blanks on any of those?"

Dan looks down at the sheet. This is like a twisted version of looking at an old photo album. Instead of making him remember good times and loved ones, he's looking at a record of the worst years of his life. His fingers unconsciously go to the first entry, seeking comfort from his most recent address: the apartment above the barn in Kentucky. They have Justin's name there, too, and two dates beside it. Dan immediately recognizes the day of the accident and the day of his death. Then Neil shifts in his seat, and Dan drags his eyes back to the older pages, looking for the gaps.

"I think for most of them I was moving around, or, you know, couch surfing, staying in shelters… if it was warm I'd camp out sometimes."

Bill nods. "And during those stretches with no recorded employment—how were you finding enough money to live?" His tone is carefully neutral, but Dan knows what he's asking.

"I never lived off crime. I… I dunno, I probably shoplifted a few things." Dan is going to say that he'd never actually taken money for sex but that he'd been happy to take meals and a place to stay from people that he'd slept with, but he decides that's more information than Bill needs. If he asks specifically, Dan won't lie. "It doesn't really cost that much to stay alive if you don't mind eating at soup kitchens every now and then."

Bill nods, and pulls out another page and passes it over. "This is a statement we took from Mr. Hugh Winters. In it he claims that you lived with him for a period of about three months, from December of 1997 to early March of the next year. He claims that you were verbally and physically abusive toward him, and that when you left you stole several valuable works of art. We'd like your response to these accusations."

Dan wants to respond pretty damn strongly, but he forces himself to calm down and read the statement. When he's done, he takes a moment to collect his thoughts, and then looks up. "Did you notice the dates there? He doesn't mention it in his 'statement', but I think you can figure out why a thirty-year-old closet-case would take in a seventeen-year-old street kid. And that was in LA, so the age of consent was eighteen. So if there was abuse, it wasn't me doing it. And the reason I left is because I found out he'd been taking pictures of me." Dan doesn't want to say what kind of pictures they were, and doesn't really think he has to. "When I was sleeping and with hidden cameras. So when I left, I erased his hard drive and took the prints. That's about all I have to say about him." Dan had started off calm, but he knows his voice was a bit strained by the end, and when he looks down at the paper in his hands, it's visibly shaking. He carefully sets the page down on the table and puts his hands in his lap, then forces himself to look Bill in the face. Bill just nods and maybe even looks a little sorry.

"Okay. Uh, there's one more area that we need to cover." He pulls out the remaining pages from the folder, but doesn't pass them over as he had with the others. "Before we get started, I'd just like to ask… your father, Richard Wheeler, and your sister, Krista Wheeler—when's the last time you saw them?"

Dan doesn't try to hide his surprise at the question. "Uh… since before I left Texas. Dick left when I was fourteen, and then… I haven't seen Krista since I left, when I was seventeen."

Neil jumps in now. "There's been no contact whatsoever since then? No phone calls, e-mails, Christmas cards—nothing?" He sounds skeptical.

Dan just shakes his head. "I wouldn't know how to start trying to find them, and I don't know why I'd want to, at least for Dick. Krista... I don't know, I've just never looked for her. I thought about it, but... she wasn't exactly sorry to see me go, when I left. And I guess she hasn't been looking for me, 'cause you can find me on Google." He grins a little ruefully at Bill. "But I guess you probably already know that."

Bill smiles. "Yes, we did check there. It's a shame you don't have a Facebook—they're often very useful for us."

"You seem to have done all right without it."

Neil is a bit impatient with the chatter, and shoots Bill a look. Bill goes back to the folder. "Well, we looked them up, and... we have some concerns about what we found." He hands the report over to Dan now, and he flips it open. The first page takes his breath away. It's a series of mug shots. The first one is of Dan's father, looking older and meaner than Dan remembers; the second is of a woman he has to squint at to recognize as his sister, although the name she's being booked under is Krista Russert; and the third is of a man Dan doesn't recognize, with the name Scott Russert beneath him. Dan supposes he's looking at his brother-in-law.

He looks up and sees the two men watching him, then turns the page and looks at the report inside. It's pretty scary reading. There's a summary of the lives of all three of them, showing how they'd gotten in trouble on their own, and then how Krista and Scott had joined up, and then a mysterious appearance by Dan's father. The story closes with all three of them wanted in connection with a series of armed robberies. Apparently they're still at large.

Dan wonders what happened to his little sister. They'd never been close, exactly, but she and he had banded together sometimes against their stepfather, had been allies if not friends. He wonders if all this would have happened if he'd been a little stronger, if he'd been able to pull himself out of his own anger and misery and found a way to help her out. He remembers Justin had suggested that they look her up, but that he had said he didn't want to. He hadn't wanted anything from the difficult past to touch his perfect present. He checks the dates with some trepidation, but is relieved to find that Krista had started getting in trouble shortly after he'd left. By the time he had been in a place to really help her, she had already been well down the road to trouble. Still, he should have done something....

He remembers his audience and looks up. They're still watching him closely. He's not sure what the appropriate response to this information would be, so he just goes for honesty. "Shit. I had no idea."

Bill nods. "The part we're most concerned about is... if you turn to"—he reaches over and leafs through the stack of papers in front of Dan—"this page, it shows a list of known associates of Scott Russert." Dan looks at the list of names, and then back up at Bill, and shrugs. "You may not recognize them, but a lot of law enforcement officers would. These people are members of organized crime families, in Texas, Nevada, and right here in California." He purses his lips. "These are the sorts of people who could actually have the resources and intelligence to plan a successful kidnapping attempt on Ms. Kaminski, or to be a threat to the Kaminski interests in a variety of other ways."

Dan feels a little sick. *He* might know that he has nothing to do with his family, but how can he prove it, especially to two people who are paid to be suspicious? He wonders if he's about to lose his perfect job just because his family is fucked up.

He feels tired, again. He looks up at Bill. "What can I say? I mean... I haven't seen either one of them in more than a decade. If they got in touch with me... I don't know. Krista's my sister, I'd try to help her, but in a 'turn yourself in, and we'll get you a good lawyer' way, not... I would never do anything to risk Tat's safety."

Bill nods. "I realize that it's a difficult situation." He pauses, as if being careful of his words. "Because of the nature of the work you're doing, we consider it necessary for you to have the highest level of security clearance. For that level of clearance, family is considered as a possible challenge to a person's loyalty, and in this case, your family is of serious concern." He smiles a little at Dan. "On a personal level, I believe you that you have had no contact with your family members, and I sympathize with your situation. I think it's admirable that you've been able to overcome some difficult beginnings and create a new life for yourself."

Dan steels himself. "But...."

"But we will have to review this situation very carefully, in consultation with our managers and our full security team. I can't say for sure what their recommendation to Mr. Kaminski will be, but… it would be very unusual for a person with that family background to be employed in an environment that requires such a high level of security." He sighs. "We'll be contacting Mr. Kaminski immediately, and advising him that our concerns are still not fully resolved. We may be able to find temporary measures that will satisfy the need for security while still allowing you to continue with your employment, but…."

Neil takes over. "When are you scheduled to work next?"

"I make my own schedule. I was planning to go down maybe this evening or for sure tomorrow morning."

Neil shakes his head. "We won't be able to have this sorted out by this evening. We'll contact Mr. Kaminski and advise him that you won't be able to work today, and that we've asked you not to return to the barn until further notice." He glances over at Bill. "We're also a little concerned about your living arrangements. This house is within the security cordon of the family property, so there aren't many barriers between it and the main house. Given the situation… I'm sorry, but we're either going to have to ask you to leave the property now, and we'll put you up in a hotel until this is dealt with, or we're going to have to put our security team on a heightened alert, which will likely be alarming and upsetting to Miss Kaminski."

"Are you… are you kidding me?" Dan turns to Bill. "Is this for real? I have to move out, or else I'm the sort of person who enjoys scaring a little girl? I've—" He realizes that he's practically yelling, and tries to calm down a little. "I've been working with Tat for a couple weeks now with no problems. I shared a room with her brother for the last two nights, for fuck's sake! If I wanted to hurt the family, I've already had plenty of chances."

Neil's jaw works a little. "There were some regrettable oversights in the security screening for this enterprise, and we are working very hard to determine why they occurred and to find ways to make sure they don't ever re-occur. At this point, I can tell you that if we had insisted on completing a full security check before you came onto the property we would have recommended strongly against your employment, at least in this capacity. As it is, your two weeks of service work in your favor, but are hardly enough to override the other concerns."

Dan shakes his head. "This is so fucked up."

Neil isn't giving him a lot of space. "If you'd like, we can give you a few minutes to decide how you'd like to proceed."

"A few—" Dan breaks off in disgust. "Yeah, sure, give me a few minutes. That'll take care of everything." He glances over at Bill, who's looking a little helpless. Dan goes back to the front hall and grabs his bags from the trip, then goes back through the kitchen, ignoring the two men, and heads into the laundry room. He takes the garment bag that carries his show clothes and hangs it next to the washer, then takes the duffel and upends it, scattering his dirty clothes all over the floor. There are some clean clothes folded and piled on top of the dryer, and Dan stuffs them into the duffel. A couple pairs of jeans, a few T-shirts, socks and underwear. He's ready to go. He just has no idea where he's going *to*.

chapter 35

NEIL and Bill watch wordlessly as Dan angrily stuffs his clothes into the duffel bag and grabs his toiletry kit from where he'd left it on the stairs. He starts toward the front door, then stops sharply and turns into the living room. He opens the door of the entertainment unit and pulls out a nearly full bottle of Wild Turkey, and stuffs it in his bag. Neil and Bill are watching this, too, of course, and he glares at them defiantly as he walks by them and out the door. He doesn't wait for them to catch up, just sets his bag in the bed of the truck and climbs behind the wheel. He starts the truck and backs it up to turn around, and is about to pull away when Bill appears beside him and taps on the glass of the window. Dan thinks about just peeling out, ignoring him completely, but he controls the impulse and rolls down the window instead.

"If you want to follow us into town, we can get you set up at a hotel and—" And Dan's had enough. He rolls up the window as he's pulling out of the driveway. He's not following anyone anywhere.

He gets a couple miles down the road when he starts to feel a bit stupid. The situation is fucked up, there's no doubt about that, but maybe he's being a bit of a baby about things. This is always his problem. He either over thinks or doesn't think at all. Either all brain or all heart, never a balance of the two. Then he thinks about losing the job he'd moved out here for, losing access to Justin's horses, all because of the stupid behavior of two people he has nothing to do with. He decides he's right to be completely pissed off. That doesn't mean that he's got to be stupid about it, though. Why pay for his own hotel when he could be billing Kaminski? It's not like his soon-to-be-ex-employer can't afford it.

Dan thinks about just driving, leaving the whole mess behind. He's got enough money. He could just arrange to get his stuff and his horse shipped to wherever he's going. Taking off is what he used to do when things got to be too much, and it worked pretty well, really. He'd settled down for a while in Kentucky, but that had been because Justin had made it worth fighting through the hard parts. There isn't anyone here with that kind of pull, and Dan had been stupid to pretend that there might be.

Then he thinks of Jeff. None of this is Jeff's fault. None of it's really Evan's fault, either, but Dan doesn't want to think about it in those terms. He'd rather think about Jeff. Jeff is so calming, so relaxing. He makes Dan feel like everything will be all right, even when Dan knows that some things will never be all right ever again. Dan thinks about calling him, but Jeff is part of Evan's world, and that's what Dan's trying to forget about. He curses the timing. If this had happened yesterday, he could have gone over to Ryan's, and had one more night of peace and easiness before he left. But yesterday Dan had been off at a stupid horse show, working his ass off so that Kaminski's business would do well, so that Kaminski's spoiled little sister could have a fun hobby. And Ryan had left this morning.

His phone rings in his jacket pocket, and he pulls it out and looks at the call display. Kaminski. No, Dan's not quite ready for that call just yet. He needs a glass or two of bourbon before he wants to talk to him. The problem is figuring out where to go. He thinks of his baby sister, on the run from the law. She must feel like this all the time, always trying to get away from her mistakes, never anywhere safe to go. Yeah, Dan's going to need that bourbon pretty soon.

His phone rings again, but this time the caller display shows that it's Jeff. Dan isn't stupid. The timing of that made it pretty clear that Evan had called his boyfriend to get him to deal with the situation, but Dan can't help himself. He wants to talk to Jeff.

He's on the edge of town now, and he pulls onto the side of the road before picking up his phone and flipping it open.

"Hello." He tries to sound chipper and strong. If Jeff's going to be reporting back, Dan doesn't want to give him anything to say.

"Dan, hey. Evan just called me in a bit of a fit. Can you tell me what's going on?" Jeff sounds more curious than alarmed. Dan can't say for sure whether it's an act.

"What, he didn't tell you? He just called you up, said he was in a fit, and hung up?"

Jeff laughs a little. "Pretty much, actually. He said there was some mix-up with the security clearances and that the guys had gone way over the line, and that he was on his way into a meeting with them, and you weren't picking up the phone. He sounded a bit worried."

"Did he?" Dan's in no mood to care about Kaminski's nerves. "Hey, Jeff, where are you?"

Jeff only sounds a little surprised. "I'm at my place. Why, do you want to come over?"

Dan knows that it's not a great idea, but he's tired of trying to do the smart thing, or the right thing. What good has that done him? He's worked his ass off to follow their rules, and now he's losing what he wants because of someone else's screwups. So, enough with doing the smart thing. If people are going to think that he's a no-good loser, then at least he can have some fun....

"Yeah, I do. Give me directions."

If Jeff is surprised by Dan's directness, he gives no indication. He gives Dan simple directions to his place, and then tells him that he's been painting all day and needs to clean up and take a shower. If there's no answer when Dan knocks, he should just come right in. Dan likes the sound of that.

He arrives at Jeff's place less than ten minutes after the call. It's a modest house, more of a cottage maybe, but it's on a good-sized lot, and there's a gate leading to a fenced backyard. That must be nice for Lou. There's a lot of natural wood, and some big windows. It looks like a good place for Jeff to live.

Dan heads up to the front door and knocks, but then barely waits before he pushes it open and goes inside. Lou greets him gently, and then goes back to lie down on her bed in the living room. Dan's got that feeling he used to get, animalistic, almost predatory. He feels like he's stalking his prey in its own den, and he likes the adrenaline. He likes the feeling of being the one to make things happen for a change, instead of just sitting back and waiting for everything to happen to him. He used to be like this, and he thought he'd left it behind, but apparently he's not allowed to leave things behind, and this is one aspect of his personality that he's glad to resurrect.

He hears a change in the sounds of the house, and realizes that he was hearing the shower when he first came in and now it's been shut off. That's too bad, a lost opportunity, but it's not the end of the world. Dan moves in the direction the sound had been coming from. He pushes open a door with his finger tips, and he sees a bedroom, lots of browns and deep reds, an oversize bed... clearly Jeff's room. This is confirmed when the door on the far side of the room opens with a cloud of steam, and Jeff appears, wearing a dark navy bathrobe. Dan approves of bathrobes. They're easy to open.

Jeff sees him and looks a little startled. "Hey, Dan! You made it in good time. Just give me a minute to throw some clothes on, and we can have a beer on the deck."

Dan doesn't say anything, just takes a step closer. Jeff notices, and he isn't stupid. He looks Dan in the eye, and shakes his head slowly. "No, Dan." He sounds regretful. "Not like this, man. Not when you're upset about something else or mad at Evan."

Dan smiles a little as he takes another step. "I'm not upset, Jeff. And I'm not mad at Evan." He takes another step. Jeff isn't moving closer, but he's not moving away, either. "It just seems like we've been dancing around this for too long, you know? Making it too complicated." Another step, and he's right in front of Jeff. "I want you, you want me… it's time to do something about that, man."

Dan reaches out and runs his hands under the front of Jeff's robe, feels the hair on his chest, still a little damp from the shower. Jeff's staring at him like he's not sure what to do, and Dan likes being the one with a plan. He runs his hands down along Jeff's skin, uses his nails to bring a little shiver, and then he's at the loosely tied knot of the robe, and he nudges it so it falls almost open. Dan can see the dark patch of Jeff's hair, and his cock nestled in it, already half hard. Jeff makes a sound somewhere between a moan and a gasp, and his hands catch Dan's wrists, holding them still. "Dan, this is not a good idea."

Dan just smiles again, and he does his best to put the promise of all kinds of wickedness in his look. "Jeff, this is the best idea I've had in a long time." He doesn't try to get his hands free, though, just lets Jeff hold him there as Dan spreads his hands out as wide as they'll go, his fingers reaching up along Jeff's belly and down into the very top of his pubic hair. Then he takes a half-step forward and falls to his knees, his mouth nestling through the opening in the bathrobe and catching Jeff's cock like they were made to fit together. It's a bit tricky to work a half-hard dick with no hands, but Dan feels like he's up to the challenge, and apparently he is, because it isn't long before Jeff's rock hard, and his fingers are tight on Dan's wrists.

Jeff tries once more. "Dan, seriously… please…." Dan can't imagine why he's bothering. If Dan didn't give up before, there's no way he's going to now, not when he's got Jeff's cock, hard and red and glorious, right in front of him. He does pull off for just a second, long enough to say, "If you want me to stop, move away," but then he's quick to get his mouth back around Jeff, swallowing him down hard, feeling his cock hit the back of Dan's throat and then press even further down, as Dan works his way right to the base. He slurps back up and then down and again, and Jeff isn't even pretending to object anymore. One of his hands releases Dan's wrist and goes to the back of his head, and Dan moans a little and presses back into it. This is what he wants, what he needs. Something mindless and primitive and pure.

Dan takes his free hand and uses it to take Jeff's other hand off of Dan's wrist, and guides it back to hold its side of Dan's head. The invitation is clear, especially when Dan changes his posture a little to improve the angle. Jeff's talking again, but he's not objecting any more, and the words coming out of his mouth turn Dan on more than anything else so far. Jeff's moaning. "Oh shit, babe, your lips, your beautiful lips wrapped around me, you feel so good. Yeah… oh, yeah, like that. That's so good, Dan, so perfect, so… oh, Jesus, you are good at this." He keeps going, his hips driving in long, slow thrusts, and Dan brings one of his own hands down and unzips his fly, pushes his jeans down enough to get his underwear down under his balls, and then he wraps his hand around himself and groans around Jeff's thick cock.

"Oh, yeah, babe, you're… oh, I need to see that… please," and Jeff's hands are pulling Dan's head away from him. Dan fights a little, doesn't want to let go, but Jeff's insistent. So Dan surrenders to the idea, straightening up a little and using his free hand to push his pants and underwear farther down, and then leaning backward, arching his spine and pushing his hard cock up in the air for Jeff to see. He keeps working himself, and uses his other hand to pull his T-shirt off over his head, giving Jeff a better view. Jeff's cock jumps a little at the sight, and Dan gives him a wicked smile, then levers himself back up. Just before he takes Jeff's cock back, he slips his middle finger into his mouth, getting it wet with spit.

Jeff sees him do it and his eyes go even darker. He practically grabs Dan's head and pushes his cock back in, moaning, "Oh, yeah, man, do it." Dan doesn't need to be asked twice, and he runs his hand back through the legs that Jeff spreads for him, finds his hole and runs the finger around the edge just once before pushing in firmly, driving in and rubbing until he finds the right spot. Jeff almost shouts, and his hips start moving faster and harder. He's hitting the back of Dan's throat every time now, and usually he slides past but every now and then the angle is wrong, making Dan gag. Dan loves the thought of choking on Jeff's cock, and increases the pressure and speed with his finger.

Jeff doesn't last much longer. He moans a little and releases Dan's head, giving him the choice to pull off if he wants to, but this is Jeff, and Dan doesn't know if this is ever going to happen again, and he wants every drop of the experience. He pulls away enough so he won't choke, and then takes the hand from his cock to Jeff's, working his balls and then bringing a finger back to work just behind them, so he's massaging Jeff's prostate both inside and out. That's what it takes and Jeff is coming, hard hot spasms into Dan's mouth, and it's perfect, it's what Dan came here for, and he brings his hand back down for two quick, hard pulls and then he's coming, too, shooting out all over his hand, the floor, Jeff's feet.

They're both quiet for a minute, breathing hard and coming back to reality. Dan's head is resting against Jeff's hip, but he pulls it away as he takes his finger out of Jeff's ass. Jeff still has his robe mostly on, and Dan reaches up and rubs his come off on the hem as Jeff watches. Then Dan takes the belt of the robe and pulls everything back together. He drags his own pants up as he rises to his feet, and then he finally looks Jeff in the eye. "So... I think you mentioned a beer?"

Jeff just stares at him for a moment, then laughs almost reluctantly. "Yeah, I think I mentioned putting some clothes on too."

Dan shrugs. "Seems like a shame, but I guess it's your call." He reaches down and pulls his T-shirt off the floor, but instead of putting it back on, he tucks the end of it in his jeans pocket. Dan's never really understood the psychology of it, but guys like guys with tails. He turns and saunters out of the room, giving his hips enough of a roll to make the shirt move a little, but not enough to seem burlesque or effeminate. He thinks.

Jeff follows him a minute later, and he's still in his robe. Dan sees it and smiles, probably his first real smile since he got here, and Jeff smiles back, laughing a little before getting serious. "Shit, Dan, what the hell are we doing?"

Dan shrugs. "You said I could have you if I wanted you. Didn't you?"

Jeff rubs his neck, crossing to the fridge and pulling out two beers. He takes the lids off and hands one to Dan. "Yeah, I did. We did. But… the idea wasn't that you'd use me as a way to say 'fuck you' to Evan."

Dan shakes his head. "That's not what this is."

"It's not. So you're not mad at Evan?"

Dan shrugs. "Not really. I mean, it's a fucked-up situation, no doubt, but… I see Evan's point. He's got to look after his sister, and there are bad people out there. Apparently I'm related to some of them."

Jeff frowns. "Okay, I'm gonna need more details. When Evan called he was just going into the meeting with the security consultants. He knew they had concerns about clearing you, but he didn't know what they were yet." He looks around. "Okay, beers on the deck is still a good idea. Let's go sit down, figure this out."

Dan snorts a little at Jeff's naiveté, his belief that everything can be figured out through talk. But, hey, Jeff's still in his robe, so…. Dan follows him outside.

The backyard is beautiful and secluded, a tall wooden privacy fence itself largely hidden by trees and tall shrubs. The screening gives Dan ideas, but he needs a little recovery time, and figures Jeff must need at least as much.

But that doesn't mean he wants to talk about the situation at the farm. Instead, he says, "So, your show opens this Friday, right?" When Jeff nods, Dan continues. "So, I don't really know anything about that. Is it…. Do you choose the paintings, and then they put them up and try to sell them for you? I mean, is it mostly about selling? Or just showing them to people?"

Jeff looks like he knows Dan's going for the evasion, but he lets him get away with it. Sort of. "It's a mix of the two, I guess. It'd be great if I got sales, but it's also about building a reputation, getting people interested in my work, even if they aren't looking to buy right now. It's sort of like a horse show, really—you might interest a buyer there, but really you're just showing off the animals and your training, so that when it is the time to buy, people will come to you. Evan said the trial went pretty well yesterday…."

Dan grins a little at Jeff's attempt to get them back to the Kaminski topic. "Yeah, it was pretty good. Kip won his level—the competition wasn't fierce, but it was solid. And Winston and Chaucer had a good intro. I guess it's funny, them having their first shows, you having your first show. Are you excited about it?"

Jeff drowns his laugh in a swallow of beer, and Dan relaxes a little. This is much easier than talking about anything serious. "Yeah, I really am. I mean, it's nerve-wracking, obviously. A lot of stress. I feel like I'm putting myself on display, sort of. But at least art is a *figurative* expression of myself, not a literal one. It's not like people came into my home and grilled me about my personal stuff. You must really have hated that."

Okay, that game's over. Time for a new one. Dan's shirt is still off, and he stands up and walks out into the middle of the yard, feeling the afternoon sun on his skin. He faces the back of the yard and lifts his arms up, stretching his back, letting his muscles roll. "This is a great yard, man. It's really… private." He looks back over his shoulder at Jeff, making sure he's sending the right signal.

Jeff just shakes his head. "Oh, no. You caught me by surprise last time, but I'm on to you now. I know your tricks." He's smiling, but there's a bit of a warning in there too. Dan decides to ignore it. Recovery time is over.

He smiles at Jeff. "Oh, no, you've hardly seen any of my tricks. I've got *lots* more to show you." He moves back toward the deck, sun still warm on his face, and high enough in the sky that it doesn't make him squint.

Jeff shakes his head. "No, Dan, come on, man. We need to sort this out. I mean, I understand if you don't want to tell me what the security team is worried about. It must already feel like a violation of your privacy, without dragging me into it. But—"

"But it's out of my hands now, so there's no point in worrying about it. Not when there's so many better things to do." Dan steps up on the deck, eyes locked on Jeff's. "I think I want to mark you."

"Dan…."

"What, am I not allowed to? Am I your dirty little secret?" Dan leans back a little and squints at Jeff. "Are you going to tell Evan about this?" It comes out a bit aggressively, and Dan deliberately softens his tone. "Are you gonna tell him how I sucked you off? How you fucked my mouth? Are you gonna tell him how it got me so turned on I barely needed to touch myself before I came?"

Jeff tears his eyes away from Dan's and looks out at the backyard. "I think I'll spare him the details, but, yeah... I'm gonna tell him the basics."

Dan shrugs. "So if you're gonna tell him, why are you being shy now? Can I mark you, Jeff?" Dan catches Jeff's eyes again, staring as he moves closer. "Can I?" He runs his fingers along Jeff's jaw line and down his neck, sees the goose bumps rise. "Right here, Jeff?" he whispers, and his fingers feel Jeff's convulsive swallow as he nods.

Dan doesn't waste any time. He swings a leg over Jeff's lap so he's straddling him, and Jeff's hands instinctively go to Dan's hips. Dan smiles at that and grinds forward a little. They're both still soft, but he doesn't think that needs to continue. He puts his hands on either side of Jeff's head and pushes him around a little, staring at his neck while he picks the exact spot he wants. He leans in and lays a wet kiss up underneath Jeff's jaw line, the stubble tickling his lips and tongue. "Hmmm...," he murmurs. "Good, but not quite—" He shifts over to the other side, to the little hollow just above Jeff's collarbone. He licks a little here, nips even. It's one of his favorite spots, the place that he and Ryan marked each other, and Dan feels Jeff's hand on his chest, pressing on the fading bruise.

"Find somewhere else," Jeff growls, and Dan smiles as he nips once more and then moves away. He's known where he was going to end up all along, and Jeff has known too. Dan brings his mouth down to the side of Jeff's neck, the exact spot Evan had chosen that night on the porch, and Dan goes to town. He puts his whole body into it, rubbing up against Jeff in a wave, thighs, crotch, belly, chest, and then starts over again, all the while sucking and licking and biting. Jeff has his head tilted way off to the side, and he's making a little rumbling sound that Dan *feels* more than he hears, the vibrations carrying through Jeff's throat to Dan's sensitive tongue. Dan doesn't stop until they're both hard, and then he pulls away and brings Jeff's head back to vertical.

He looks Jeff in the eyes and runs his fingers along his neck, rubbing along the purpling bruise. "I want to fuck you, but I don't want to get up to get the stuff." He leans down and nibbles again a little on Jeff's neck. Then he murmurs, "I want to lick you, and work you open, and then I want to fuck you slow, while you're on your back, so you can look at me and know who's inside you." Jeff groans a little and brings his mouth toward Dan's, but Dan pulls away just enough to avoid him. He's not sure why he's holding out on that, but he doesn't want to kiss Jeff. Not yet. "I want to be inside you while I jack you off. You can show me what you like, and the whole time I'll be fucking you slow and deep." He's making this up as he goes, but he's not surprised to find that he really does want to do it all. The description is getting him even more turned on than he already was. "Then when you come, I'm gonna pull out of you and lick you clean, and then I'm gonna flip you over and slam into you hard. You're gonna be all relaxed, and I'm gonna let loose. I'm gonna fuck you as hard as I can, just pound away. Make sure you feel it for a while. Make sure you remember me."

He leans down and sucks again on Jeff's bruised neck, and Jeff almost whimpers as he simultaneously arches his neck and his hips into Dan. "Do you want that, Jeff? Do you want to do all that?" Jeff nods, and Dan grinds down again. "The problem is, though… I just can't tear myself away from you for long enough to stand up and go inside the house. And the way I want to fuck you… we need lube for that. Lots of lube." And then the phone rings. Jeff jerks as if he's been shot, but Dan just shakes his head. "Ignore it, man. Unless it's a lube delivery service, it's nothing we need."

But the ring has broken Jeff out of the spell. "No, it's probably Evan. I need to get it… he was worried."

Dan brings his hands into it, running one down over the terry cloth beginning to gape below the tie of Jeff's robe, the other up to pull his hair a little. "You can call him back when we're done. Or tomorrow." And this time he's the one who goes in for the kiss, not because he really wants it, but because Jeff had wanted it earlier, and Dan is feeling a little desperate to get Jeff back under his control. And this time Jeff is the one who pulls his face away.

"Dan, wait. We need to figure this stuff out." Jeff's got his hands on Dan's arms again, but when Dan looks at him he can tell that it's not like in the bedroom, he's not going to be able to override Jeff's objections this time. The phone has stopped ringing, but Jeff is still gently pushing Dan away. "You know I want to, Dan, but… we need to do this right. We need to sort out what's going on, and all be in a good place."

"All?" Dan tries to keep his voice reasonably controlled, but he's not sure he succeeds. "There's no 'all', Jeff. There's 'both'. Two people, not three."

Jeff looks at Dan sadly for a moment, then shakes his head. "I can't do that, Dan. Not… not like that."

Jeff's already pushed Dan most of the way off of his lap, and now Dan takes the final step, standing up and backing away. He pulls his T-shirt out of his pocket and pulls it on. He's still hard, but it's going down fast. The phone starts ringing again, and Dan just sneers a little as he raises an eyebrow, looking toward the door expectantly.

Jeff stands up reluctantly. "We'll see what's up, maybe get him to come over." Dan keeps his face expressionless. "Seriously, I get that you're not happy about whatever it is, but Evan's a good guy, and we'll figure something out." Jeff backs toward the door, then opens it and goes inside, hurrying over to get the phone.

As soon as the screen door slams, Dan moves. He'd seen the gate on the way in, and he walks over and opens it up, heading out to the front of the house. His car keys are still in his pocket, and as he works them out, his dick gives an optimistic little twitch, as if hoping that maybe Dan *hasn't* just screwed up its chances. But Dan ignores its disappointment, and focuses on getting the hell out of there. He doesn't know what he's doing, knows he's running around like a bit of a maniac, but he doesn't seem to be able to stop. He thinks of the bottle in his duffel bag, and figures that if that doesn't stop him, it should at least slow him down. Now he just needs to find somewhere safe to lie low. He needs to spend a little time regrouping.

chapter 36

DAN just drives for a while. He's not sure where he's going. He's just going. He had tried so hard to have Jeff, just for a little while, but as soon as the phone rang Jeff had been back to Evan, back to their perfect couple. How can Dan ever hope to be a part of that? If Jeff will drop everything, literally push Dan away, just because the phone call *might* be from Evan, and Evan *might* have something to say—when Dan had been right there, on his goddamn *lap*, trying to say something of his own—yeah, Dan needs to consider Jeff's priorities as another good thing to understand. He's learning a lot today, and most of it isn't exactly welcome, he admits, but he tries to tell himself that it's better to know now than to find out later.

He thinks about calling Chris. Chris always makes things better. But somehow it seems wrong to be running to Justin's best friend with stories of how Dan's fucking up his life. Dan has the impression that Chris feels about him the same way *he* feels about the horses. They're all Justin's projects, tamed and gentled and made useful and healthy because of Justin's love and understanding. Dan knows how he would feel if somebody told him that the horses were running wild, losing all of the benefits of their time with Justin. He doesn't want to make Chris feel the same way.

He wishes Ryan were still in town. It would be beautiful to be able to spend some time with somebody normal and drama-free. Dan has a sudden flash of hope. Maybe Ryan hadn't left. Maybe there'd been some confusion. Hell, Ryan was going to work for Kaminski, so maybe he hadn't passed *his* stupid security test, either. Dan's on the edge of town now, and he pulls the truck to the side of the road and gets his phone out, selects Ryan's number. It rings twice, and then Ryan picks up.

"Hey, Dan?"

Dan fights to keep his voice normal. "Hey, man. Sorry to bother you. Is this an okay time?"

"Yeah, sure. We're just waiting around, actually. Supposed to be meeting with some songwriter, but she hasn't shown up yet. How'd the horse thing go?"

"Oh, that…. Yeah, it was good. Everybody did well, and we got home safely, so… yeah, it was good."

There's a bit of a pause. "You okay, man? You sound sad or something."

"No, I'm all right. Just tired, I guess, and it's been a really crappy day. So you're in LA, though? The trip went okay?"

"Yeah, it's been great so far. Listen, are you sure you're okay? How crappy a day are we talking about?"

Dan just sighs. "Pretty fucking crappy, really. I'm sorry, I shouldn't have called. I don't want to wreck your good time. I just—" An idea suddenly comes to him. "Hey, did you get out of your lease? Or do you have another thirty days on the apartment?"

"Another twenty-seven, now. Why, do you need a place to crash?"

"I…. Yeah, maybe. I don't really know for how long, but if it's more than a night or two I could sublet it or something."

"Nah, dude, don't worry about it." Ryan's voice is slow and easy. "The key's on top of the door jam; make yourself at home. But what happened to your place?"

"I… it's a long story, and I'm kinda done with it for today. Is it cool if I explain later?"

"Sure, all right." There's some noise in the background, then Ryan says, "Listen, I've gotta go. But are you sure you're okay?"

Dan wonders just how bad he must sound, and forces some levity into his voice. "Yeah, man, I'm fine. Just tired. Go be a rock star."

"Yeah, okay. Look, I'll call you tomorrow, all right?"

"I'm fine, Ryan."

"Then I'll just call to tell you about how cool everything is with me!"

"All right, then. I'll talk to you later." Dan clicks the phone shut and pulls out onto the road. He's glad he thought to ask Ryan about the apartment. The closest hotel he knows of is another twenty minutes down the road, and he really doesn't have the energy to deal with the drive, and then the check-in… and Ryan's place isn't luxurious, but it's homier than a hotel could ever be.

He's at the apartment a couple minutes later. The key is right where it's supposed to be, and he wonders if everything just goes more smoothly when Ryan's involved. Maybe the band needs a roadie. With a horse.

There are no sheets on the bed, but Dan finds some in the bedroom closet. Everything else of Ryan's is gone, so Dan assumes that the place came furnished complete with linens. Unexpectedly simple... the apartment must still be benefiting from the Ryan Effect. He makes up the bed and falls into it, and it seems like he's asleep immediately.

He's not sure what time it is when he wakes up. He left his watch and his phone in the other room. It's pretty well dark outside, so he's slept for quite a while. He feels better for it. He's still not exactly chipper, but at least now he can think about maybe making a plan. And the first step of the plan almost certainly involves a little Wild Turkey. He goes out to his duffel and pulls the bottle out, then finds a glass in the cupboard by the sink. He pours himself a good-size glass and takes a big sip, then goes over and sits on the couch. He's at loose ends again, and he never does well without something to do.

He thinks again about calling Chris, trying to get some advice on the legal side of things at least, and then remembers the time difference. There's no point in getting the man all riled up in the middle of the night. Jeff's busy with his boyfriend, Ryan's enjoying his new life... Robyn's good at times like these, but she's happy at the Kaminski's, so Dan shouldn't drag her into it all. That makes him wonder what they're going to tell the people at the barn, how his absence is going to be explained.

His stomach rumbles a bit, and Dan tries to think of the last time he ate. He'd missed lunch, so that bowl of cereal in the motel was it for the day. Maybe Tatiana's right to worry about his ability to feed himself. But Dan doesn't want to think about Tat, about her sweet concern for him, or the way that two strangers and a boardroom full of so-called experts have the right to decide that Dan's some sort of a threat to her.

He decides to think about food instead. He remembers that Ryan had said that Zio's made in-town deliveries, so he finds their number and calls them up, orders enough food for dinner and for the next day's breakfast. There are several messages showing on his phone, and he thinks about listening to them, then decides to get another drink instead. He turns off the ringer for good measure. He just sits there on the couch, thinking about his family, and how he'd let them down. He thinks about the lengths Evan goes to trying to protect Tatiana, compared to the total disregard Dan had given his own sister's safety. It's no wonder Jeff gave priority to Evan. Evan cares about other people, so he deserves to have people care about him.

It's surprising how fast he can drink when he's got absolutely nothing else to do, and Dan is definitely well into the bottle by the time he hears the knock on the door. He finds his wallet and heads over, but when he opens the door, he doesn't see what he expected.

"You're not a panini," he says, and Evan stares at him.

"No, I'm not. I'm the guy who's been trying to get hold of you all goddamn afternoon."

Dan peers hopefully around Evan. "Did you *see* a panini?" He knows he's being a little inappropriately flippant, but he's hungry. And drunk. Also, Evan can go fuck himself.

Evan shakes his head impatiently. "No. Can I come in?"

Dan starts to step back, but then swivels around and steps forward, blocking the doorway again. "Wait a second. How did you know I was here? Did your spies tell you?"

"Take it easy, Dan. It's a small town; I drove by and saw your truck—not exactly international intrigue." Dan reluctantly moves aside, and Evan comes in. Dan figures he can kiss the Ryan Effect goodbye now, because Evan's radiating enough energy to destroy all the calm in a Buddhist monastery. Evan crosses over to the coffee table, picks up the bottle of Wild Turkey and looks at the amount missing. He looks back at Dan, evaluating.

"Do you want a glass?" Dan doesn't really want Evan to feel at home, but he also doesn't want to be completely churlish. He'd like to keep at least a little high ground here. Evan just shakes his head.

"Could you... could you maybe just come over and sit down? Or at least... could you at least step away from the door?" Evan shakes his head. "Jeff said that you booked out on him earlier—this would all be a lot easier if you'd stop running away."

Dan raises his eyebrows. "Really? It seems like that might be the easiest thing for everybody. You could get rid of the awkward employee, I could start over somewhere that they actually *let* people start over, without dragging up ancient history all the time."

Evan shakes his head. "Yeah, you're mad, I get it. But do you have to be such a fucking drama queen about it all? And did you have to drag Jeff into it? And getting shitfaced is really productive. I mean, you should have stayed put, let me figure it out, and I'd have taken care of it." He looks a little disgusted. "Would it kill you to have a little fucking faith in me?"

Dan just stares at him. "Stayed put—I'd have loved to have *stayed put*, Evan, but they kicked me out of the house!"

"Yeah, and thanks for calling to let me know! I mean, I could have come down right away and straightened things out, but instead I've spent all fucking day in meetings and chasing your melodramatic ass around!" He sighs as if suddenly exhausted, and sinks down onto the couch. "I changed my mind—I do want a glass."

Dan wants to keep fighting, but he doesn't really have anything to say, so he goes and gets a glass instead. He hands it to Evan and then finds his own and fills them both up. He sits in the armchair and stares at the wall, nursing his drink until Evan speaks.

"Okay. First off… I'm the boss." He sees Dan's lips starting to curl into a sneer, and waves an impatient hand. "Shit, Dan, take it easy. I mean the boss of the whole company, including the security department. If I say you're okay, then you're okay. So stop—" He waves a hand frantically through the air, as if imitating Dan's frenetic actions. He apparently can't find the right word, though, and drops his hand back into his lap. "Just *stop*."

Dan leans back into his chair and takes a drink. He's beginning to feel a bit stupid—alcohol should help with that.

"So, when they called me and said that they had serious concerns and were recommending against keeping you, I figured I had to have a look at what they had a problem with." He looks over at Dan. "I tried to call you to make sure it was okay for me to see whatever it was, but you were busy, I guess." The sarcasm is crystal clear, and Dan takes another drink.

"So then I went into a meeting with the security team and looked over the evidence." Evan looks over at Dan, and for the first time there's a little bit of understanding in his face, a hint of compassion. "I'm sure that was a bit of a shock, man. And, honestly, I can see why they were concerned." He takes a deep breath. "I told them that if I didn't know you, I'd agree with them, and I wouldn't let you anywhere near Tat." Dan recoils a little, and Evan says, "Not because that's right, or because it's fair, but just because... it's Tat. I can't be careless with her safety just to make a point about how people shouldn't be judged by their families or deserve second chances or whatever."

He rubs the back of his neck and looks over to be sure that Dan is still listening. "But I told them that I did know you, and that a character reference from the head of the company should be enough to override their concerns, and that we can discuss other security measures if they want to, but that you stay." Now Evan's looking a little pissed off again. "I don't have a precise timeline, but I'd guess that I was telling them all this at about the same time that you were fucking my boyfriend." Dan freezes. He figures he's lucky that Evan only looks a *little* pissed.

There's another knock on the door, and Dan almost falls over he's so eager to have something to do other than trying to avoid Evan's eyes. This time it *is* the food, and Dan pays the delivery kid and stops by the kitchen area to find a plate. He pauses for a second. He's a little afraid to talk to Evan, but he manages to say, "Do you want a panini?"

"I'm not gonna eat your dinner, Dan."

"No, it's my breakfast. I ordered two."

Evan seems to be thinking about it. "Yeah, okay. You can have breakfast at your house tomorrow."

That doesn't sound quite right, but Dan pulls out another plate anyway and walks over to lay everything on the coffee table. He sorts out the food, only sighing a little when he hands the sandwich over to Evan, and then sits back down in the arm chair. They both eat quietly for a while, but Dan pauses before starting his second half.

"So that's it? We just forget about the whole thing, everything goes back to the way it was?" He's really not sure that's possible for him or for anybody else, but he wants to hear Evan's take on it.

Evan shrugs and finishes his mouthful. "Not quite. The security guys still want to work a few things out—an understanding that you'll notify them if your sister or father gets in touch with you, that sort of thing." Evan looks at Dan. "I know it's a bit insulting, and I understand if it rubs you the wrong way, but... I like that they're paranoid, you know? Tat's... she's casual as hell, totally sloppy about security, and the only reason I've got the luxury of letting her stay that way is because they do all the worrying for her. So, if you object, you need to tell me about it, and we'll figure something out. But it'd be great if you could go along with it."

Dan nods thoughtfully, and Evan shoots him another look. "How drunk are you? 'Cause there's some more stuff I'd like to say, and I'd really like to get it off my chest now, but there's no point if you're not even gonna remember any of this."

Dan thinks about lying. He's getting a pretty strong feeling that he may not have behaved all that well through this, and he'd rather put off being hit over the head with that fact. But there's no point in postponing the inevitable, so he admits, "I'm not memory-loss drunk. And, honestly, even when I'm sober I lose half of the details in these little conversations of ours, so... go ahead."

Evan gives him an odd look, then takes a moment to organize his thoughts. "Okay, first thing, and I think I've already mentioned this once or twice—you have got to talk to me, Dan! I mean, whatever we are, if we're friends or even if I'm just your boss, you've got to let me know what's going on and what you need me to do. You know? I realize that you must have been pretty spun to hear all that shit about your family, and I'm sure it sucked a lot to get grilled about your own... mistakes. So I'm not saying you're not right to be upset. But"—he leans forward intently—"I trusted you before all this came up, and I still trust you. I trust you with my sister's safety. I don't think it's asking too much for you to trust me to try to help you out."

Dan thinks maybe he *is* too drunk for this conversation. He can't really think of anything to say back to that. He just looks at the floor and nods instead.

Evan continues thoughtfully. "Okay, so the next thing is more about the personal side of things. I can't really do this anymore, the way we've been going."

Dan looks up in surprise. He guesses he shouldn't be shocked. He's been totally indecisive about the whole relationship, and then he'd gone mental today. Evan's right to want something a little less dramatic. He nods, and stands up. "Yeah, okay. I get that. I, uh...." He kind of feels like he should leave, but that doesn't make sense. Why isn't Evan the one who's leaving?

Evan just frowns at him. "Jesus Christ, Dan, you're running again. Sit down and listen for a minute, will you?"

Dan sits down obediently, staring at his shoes, but he mutters, "I *was* listening."

Evan voice is almost patient. "But I wasn't done. I'm... God help me, I'm still into trying to figure out a way to make this work. But... okay, yeah, you've got to calm down a little, but also... I think I need you to make a choice." He holds up his hands quickly. "I don't mean tonight. But, sometime pretty soon, okay?"

Dan tries to figure that one out, but he can't quite make it. "Okay, what are my choices again?" He cuts his eyes up to watch Evan's response.

Evan grins a little. "Okay, good job of asking for clarification!" He's being patronizing, but it's light enough that Dan doesn't worry about it. "I think there's three options that would work for me, more or less. I've got a personal favorite, but I really think I can live with any of them as long as I know what's going on and have some time to adjust." He pauses, and Dan takes another drink, bracing himself. "Okay, option one is that we're purely business associates. Not friends, not anything else. And if that's the option you take, then I'm in no place to say anything about you fucking Jeff. That'd be between me and him, because you and me would just work together."

Dan decides to gloss over the difference between working *with* and working *for* someone in favor of clarifying another point. "We didn't fuck."

"What?"

Dan is vaguely pleased to have shaken Evan out of his calm presentation style. "We didn't fuck. I didn't fuck your boyfriend. We messed around some, that's all."

Evan takes a moment to reflect. "Okay, well, that's good to know, actually. He just gave me a sort of general idea—"

"We didn't kiss, either," Dan interjects. "In case you wanted to know."

"You didn't kiss. Okay. Good. But, actually, you should stop telling me things you didn't do, because then whatever you leave off the list, I'm gonna know that's what you *did* do, and I don't need that information in my head." Evan's voice is a little strained.

Dan nods. "Fair enough."

Evan tries to get back to his list. "Okay, that was option one. Uh, option two... option two is that we're just friends. You and me. And I don't mean to be a princess about this, but with this option you can't fuck Jeff." He catches himself. "Or mess around, or whatever. I know that's a bit controlling, but... it works okay, me and Jeff being with other people, but not if I know them, not if.... I can't be wondering all the time, you know? 'Hey, Jeff was busy on Friday, and Dan was busy on Friday... I wonder if they were together?'" He seems to be talking to himself as much as to Dan. "I can't be doing that. So, yeah, that's option two. I'd like to be your friend, but I was wrong, thinking that I could handle it if you and Jeff were together, and I wasn't part of it. Okay? If you and Jeff are together, and I'm not involved, then I really can't know about it."

Dan forces himself to look at Evan. "Sorry about today. I mean... sorry if that bugged you."

Evan laughs a little bitterly. "'Bugged me'? Yeah, it fucking bugged me!"

Dan squirms a little. "We thought you said it was okay...."

"Yeah, I said it was okay. Sometimes I say stupid shit, all right? It's *not* okay!"

"Okay...."

Evan gives him a sharp look as if he's trying to decide if Dan is saying "okay" he understands, or "okay" is what Evan had said and should stand by. Dan raises his hands in surrender. "Okay! It's not all right for me and Jeff to screw around if you and me are friends! I get it!" Then he knows he shouldn't, can't believe he is, but it must be the bourbon talking when he mumbles, "Fucking shame, though. Your boyfriend's smoking hot."

Evan spins his head around to stare at him, and Dan is a little glad that there are no weapons handy. "Too early to joke, Dan," Evan growls. Dan nods meekly and takes another drink. It finishes the glass, and he thinks about getting more, but decides that Evan might not appreciate that. Besides, there's only one more option to go—he can make it.

Evan has regrouped after the inappropriate comment, and is looking doggedly determined to continue. "Okay, so... option three. And, seriously, this is still my personal favorite, even after all this insanity today, so... that's saying something." He smiles sadly at Dan, but Dan thinks he'll wait to hear the option before smiling back. "Option three is all of us together. I still think we could make it work, and I still think it would be fucking awesome. The thing is…. I'm not saying we need to jump into anything, but I need to know that you're into it. I don't mean I want a guarantee, or a time line… although either of those would be great…. I just… I need to know if you want it and are just taking your time getting comfortable with the idea, or if you really don't want it and are just looking for a way to let us down easy." Evan rubs his stubbled jaw line. "Let *me* down easy, I guess."

Dan doesn't really know what to say. Luckily, Evan isn't quite done yet.

"So, yeah, I don't expect an answer on that stuff tonight, I just…." He runs his hands through his hair and makes it stick out at awkward angles. He looks tired, and really young. "I feel like we almost lost it today, you know?" He takes a quick look at Dan. "I don't know, maybe we *did* lose it, or maybe we never had it… I just…." He's sitting forward on the sofa, his elbows on his knees and his hands hanging between them, and his head flops down so he's looking at the floor. Dan wants to reach out to him, smooth his hair back into place and make him feel better.

But he doesn't do it. Evan gave him three options, and Dan absolutely understands why Evan needs to figure out which one Dan wants to choose. The problem is, Dan kind of needs to figure that out too. And until he does, he needs to make sure that he's not making any false promises. He needs to start taking responsibility for his actions again.

"Yeah, it's—" Dan doesn't know where he's going with this, doesn't even know why he started talking. He takes a moment, and then starts over again. "I'm tired, and I'm drunk, and it's been a hell of a day. I… I appreciate you taking the trouble to track me down and lay it out like this." He smiles ruefully. "I get a little worked up sometimes."

Evan snorts. "Yeah. I got that." He scoots forward so that their knees are almost touching, and when he speaks, his voice is lower, and a little husky. "And I've got no problem with it at all. But I want to be the one to work you up, you know?"

And Dan is amazed, because he does know. He looks at Evan and feels the same draw, the same heat that he'd felt with Jeff in Kentucky. He just stares for a second and then nervously licks his lips, and sees Evan's darkened eyes follow the motion. "Yeah, I…," Dan whispers, and then he stands up abruptly and turns away, walking over to the kitchen and running the tap to get some cold water. He wonders if he just has an undiscovered fetish for guys who drink Wild Turkey in dingy apartments.

He fumbles a glass from the cupboard and puts it under the tap, then takes a deep drink. The water is still running, so he doesn't hear it when Evan comes up behind him, but he feels it when two hands come to rest on the points of his hips, holding firmly but not tight, and when Evan's stubbled jaw leans over and rubs over his own. "I can give you some time to decide," Evan murmurs, his lips ghosting over the skin of Dan's cheek. "But I really, really hope you chose option three." One of his hands runs up and tangles in Dan's hair, twisting his head around as Evan shifts their bodies, and then Evan's mouth is on Dan's, firm lips pushing his open, tongue following immediately, confidently. Dan kisses back, but Evan is taking the lead, pulling Dan's body into his, moving his head around to find the best angle, and kissing, so deep, so wet. Dan's hands come up of their own will and grab hold of Evan's shirt, not trying to move or control him, just hanging on, struggling to find some balance in the swirling storm of the kiss.

It's over too soon, Evan pulling away a little and then a little more, until their mouths part, but their bodies are still pressed close together. Evan looks down dazedly, and the hand in Dan's hair loosens its grip and runs forward, smoothing down over Dan's cheek and jaw line as Dan stares into Evan's eyes. "Holy shit," Evan whispers. "That wasn't part of the plan." He releases his hold and takes a step backward, Dan's fingers stretching and then releasing their grip on Evan's shirt. "I gotta go. You.... Please don't run anymore, okay?" And then he's the one running, striding toward the door and yanking it open, and Dan can hear the thud of his feet hitting the bottom stairs before the door even swings shut.

Dan stands in the kitchen, staring at the door. This day has been... confusing. He takes another sip from his glass, then realizes that water isn't going to cut it. He heads into the living room, looking for the bottle of bourbon. He's got some thinking to do.

chapter 37

DAN is hung over when he wakes up the next morning. It's not surprising, considering how much more he'd drunk after Evan left, but it's disappointing. Dan's not usually an optimist, but somehow he's always able to convince himself that he won't feel any serious effects from drinking. His head and stomach welcome him back to harsh reality.

He's not quite sick enough to throw up, but he's sick enough to wish he could. Instead, he staggers into the shower. "Linens" apparently doesn't include towels, so he dries off with a clean T-shirt and then pulls on jeans and a different shirt. The shower helped, but he still feels crappy. He stumbles to the kitchen and looks for coffee, but just as he'd suspected, the Ryan Effect has dissipated and there is none to be found. He finds his keys and heads for the truck. He really needs coffee, and some grease to line his stomach.

He finds them both at the diner out by the highway, and by the time he's done eating he feels almost human. He finds that he has the energy to start thinking about his day.

He tries to remember what specifically Evan had said the night before about Dan going back to work. He'd said he'd make it okay, but… had he said that it was already taken care of? There had been a lot of "stay put"s and "trust me"s, but had there been anything concrete? Dan doesn't want to show up at the barn if he's not cleared to be there, but he really doesn't want to talk to Evan quite yet, either. Evan's options from the night before are still spinning around in his brain, and he really has no idea what he wants to do. Until he does, it'll be pretty damn awkward talking to the guy.

Dan decides to phone Linda. She's up on all of Evan's business, as far as Dan can see, and if she doesn't know, she can find out. He steps out of the diner and lets the cool morning air go to work on his headache as he dials his phone. Linda picks up on the second ring.

"Good morning, Dan."

"Hey, Linda, how are you?"

"I'm lovely, thank you. How about you?" He tries to sense if there's anything more than politeness in the question, wonders whether she has any reason to think that he's not entirely fine. But he can't tell at all—she's quite a professional, and he's really not good at subtleties.

"I'm all right, thanks. Uh… I was doing some stuff with the security people yesterday, and they asked me not to go back to the barn until they'd cleared it." He waits for any sound of surprise from her, but he doesn't get anything. "Evan said he'd clear it up, but I just wanted to double-check before I went back out there."

"Hmm." Linda sounds like Dan just asked her if she knew a good cookie recipe. "I'm not sure, and Evan's not available, but I can give a call over to the security department and check on things. Is it all right if I call you back in a couple minutes?"

"Yeah, thanks, Linda. That'd be great." She hangs up, and Dan wonders if there's anything he could have asked that would frazzle her. He bets not.

He's not sure how long he's going to have to wait, but it's not like he hasn't got a lot to think about. He honestly has no idea how to go about deciding what he wants with Evan. Puppet-Chris suggests a "pros and cons" list, and Dan honestly can't tell if he's joking or serious. It's a little worrisome.

Dan thinks about calling the real Chris, but he wants to keep the line open for Linda. He tries to think it through for himself. The first possibility was just business with Evan, leaving the way open to more with Jeff. But Dan isn't sure that's a real option. He believes that Evan would offer it, but he's not sure that Jeff would. Jeff and Evan might be having problems, but the reaction to the phone call the day before showed that Evan still has a hell of a pull on Jeff. Even with Dan being as tempting as he knew how, Jeff had chosen Evan. Dan wonders how pathetic he's prepared to be. Can he accept that he'll always come second, and still try to have some sort of relationship with Jeff?

Or should he look at the second option, friendship with Evan, nothing with Jeff? Or maybe friendship with Jeff, he supposes, but he's not sure he could maintain that without going crazy. After the kiss last night, Dan's not sure he could maintain just a friendship with Evan, either. After what's been developing between them all, just friendship seems a little pale and unexciting. Dan decides that it's the option of last resort.

So that leaves option three. The one Evan wants him to pick, Dan remembers, shivering a little as he can almost feel Evan's stubbled cheek rubbing against his own. Dan thinks about it hard, tries to imagine how it would work. Not just physically, but emotionally. Are they really saying they'll admit him as an equal partner in their relationship, or would he just be an associate member, an occasional visitor, a novelty toy? He can't imagine them being crazy enough to offer the former, and he's worried that he might be weak enough to accept the latter.

The phone rings, and he picks it up with some relief. Thinking is hard.

"Hey, Linda."

"Hi Dan. I spoke to Bill Albanese in security, and he says that you're cleared to proceed, all the same access as you've had all along."

"Really? That was… fast."

"Were you hoping for a little vacation time?" Linda's voice is warm and teasing.

"Uh, no, not really. Just… great, okay." He checks his watch. The horses will have been turned out by now, but he can check on the competition horses in their pastures, and…

"Oh, Dan, while I've got you…."

"Yeah, what's up?" Dan had almost forgotten that he was still having a phone conversation.

"Evan asked me to get hold of someone he met at the event on the weekend, and I've been having trouble getting through. Evan said the gentleman knew you, though… do you have a number for Sean Dubois?"

Dan's brain stops working for a second, and when it starts up again, it's a little jerky. Evan. Looking for Sean Dubois. Dan can only think of one reason why Evan would be looking for Sean, an underemployed professional eventer. Evan had said that he was okay with keeping things strictly business, but maybe he wasn't. Dan manages to pull himself together enough to say, "Uh, no, sorry, I don't."

Linda sounds as if she's aware that Dan hadn't reacted well to the question. "Well, I'm sure it's not about anything important. I'll just keep trying the original number, I guess. Thanks, Dan."

"Yeah, thank you, Linda," Dan says, but it's like his mouth is moving by force of habit, with no connection to the rest of him. His mind is far away, spinning wildly and inefficiently, trying to process contradictory information. He hangs up the phone and sits down on the fender of the truck.

Is Evan planning to replace Dan if he doesn't go along with his proposition? Or is he going to replace him anyway? Evan had said he wanted the three of them to get together, but he hadn't mentioned how long he thought they should *stay* together. Dan realizes just how much he doesn't know about Evan's plans. Or Jeff's, really—Dan knows that Jeff will put Evan first, but would that extend to supporting Evan if he tried to fire Dan? He wonders just what *they're* putting on the line in all of this, compared to what they're asking of him. Or maybe they're not asking as much as he thinks they are. Maybe they're just looking for a quick fuck, and he should do it and get it over with. Jeff's hot, Evan's hot, who says it has to be all emotional? They'd talked about being "interested," but Evan's also apparently "interested" in Sean fucking Dubois, so what does that mean? But why should Dan give them the satisfaction? If this whole thing has been a lie or a game to them, why should he let them win?

Does Evan honestly have the balls to come to Ryan's apartment and lecture Dan about trust at the same time that he's sneaking around behind Dan's back, trying to hire his replacement? Did Dan actually let himself feel bad for overreacting to the security problems? Sure, Evan trusts him. He trusts him to be a total loser who's too stupid to even know when he's being used, trusts him to move across the country and work his ass off trying to get a bunch of horses in shape just in time for someone else to swoop in and take over. Dan leaves the bumper and sits on the seat of his truck with his feet out the door, and he bends over and puts his head in his hands, pressing in and trying to stop the pandemonium.

He feels the urge to drive again, to climb in and just take off. He's been fooling himself all along, letting himself think that he could do the job without Justin, thinking that he somehow belonged in that nice house, working in that nice barn with all those nice people. He's not nice, and the security guys had seen that in about a second. They must be pissed off now, thinking that he'd gotten away with it all, thinking that Evan trusts him. Evan should tell them that he's hiring somebody new, make them feel better. Hell, maybe he already had, maybe that's why Evan's busy, he's busy laughing his ass off with the security guys, thinking about the poor dumb dropout who thinks he belongs anywhere near the mighty Kaminski. Hell, if Sean wants this shit, let him have it. Dan's had enough.

Dan thinks about Justin and how everything had been simple with him. They'd loved each other, loved their jobs, their horses… their lives. And now Dan has this. This mess of confusion. Dan remembers the funeral, remembers how Chris had talked about Justin's intensity, and his certainty. Dan misses that. He needs that. And then he remembers other things about those days in Kentucky. He remembers riding with Jeff and Chris, going up Justin's hill in the dark, and feeling the night, letting the horse guide him. Why can Dan be so sure when he's on a horse and so totally confused all the rest of the time? He remembers Jeff and Evan at the funeral, too, and Tatiana's gentle hug, and her kind words at the visitation. He thinks of how much Evan loves his sister, and how beautifully she's turning out.

And he picks up his phone and dials. It rings a few times and then a voice mail greeting comes on, followed by a beep. Dan hopes he's doing the right thing.

"Hey, Evan, it's Dan. I think… I kind of need to talk to you…. Just give me a call when you can, okay?" He hangs up. If Evan has been fucking with him, leading him on, he just opened himself up to more lies and confusion. But Dan really wants to trust him. It wouldn't mean everything is going to be easy, or even make that much more sense, but it would give Dan another point to anchor himself to. He's just climbing into the truck when his phone rings. Caller display says Evan—is the guy just screening his calls?

"Hello."

"Hey, Dan, it's me. What's up?"

"Linda said you were unavailable. I thought you'd call back later."

"Uh, no. I was in a meeting, but I saw your name on the phone, so I took a break. Is everything okay?"

Dan's already committed, really. "I was just… I was talking to Linda, and she said that you were trying to get in touch with Sean Dubois. I just, uh… I just wondered why."

There's a second of silence, and then Evan says, "Shit. Did you think I was looking to replace you?" He seems to interpret Dan's silence correctly. "Okay. Thanks for calling and letting me explain."

Dan's still silent, waiting. Hoping.

"Sean did talk to me on Sunday, like you said he would, looking for rides. But he also said he was looking at maybe getting out of riding entirely, and becoming a sales agent. You know, matching up buyers and sellers. I meant to talk to you about it, about maybe hiring him or somebody like him. But then things got a little hectic with the security stuff, and it slipped my mind. But I asked Linda to get in touch with him so I could get some more information. That's all. Seriously, Dan, your job's safe. Regardless of how things turn out, or what you decide or whatever." He waits for a second. "Dan? You good?"

"I'm gonna move out," Dan says abruptly. He surprises himself a little, but as soon as he says it he knows it's a good idea. He believes Evan about Sean, but still… it's a good idea to move out.

"Huh? Out of your house? Why?"

"Because it's not my house, it's your house. I…. It's too close, you know? It's just too much. My whole life is tied up in that place, and… it's too much."

There's a pause, and then Evan quietly says, "Does this mean you're trying to… trying to keep it just business? Trying to avoid me?"

Dan groans a little. "Not really. I'm still… I'm pretty fucked up, Evan. I mean, this thing with Sean… I…." He takes a moment to try to collect himself. "Okay, you said that option three was me being interested in something more, but no guarantees, right?"

"Yeah…."

"Okay, the thing is… yeah, I'm interested. I have been for a while. In both of you, not just Jeff. But… I really don't see it working, Evan. I mean, there's just too much in the way. You know?"

Evan's voice is quiet. "No. I don't know. I mean, yeah, there's stuff we have to work out, but I think we can do it. I think it's worth trying, at least."

"Yeah, okay, but that right there, that attitude—that's why I've got to move out. Because… okay, you can say you won't fire me, and I believe you. Well, I believe you most of the time. But if we *try* this, and it blows up as badly as it could, I really doubt I'm going to want to keep working there. And when the security thing happened—that was like they took everything, you know? Not just my job, but my home. I can't have that much tied up one place."

Evan doesn't say anything for a moment. "Are you sure you want to be deciding this now? I mean, you had a rough day yesterday, and…."

"Yeah. Evan, people move all the time, it's not a life-changing decision. The house was great while I got settled in, and now I'll find somewhere else. No big deal."

"Well, whatever… I mean, we don't really use the place, so if you want to get your own spot, that's great, but the house will always be there."

"Okay, yeah."

"But what about these other things that are in the way?" Evan's starting to sound like he's moving back into his "let's get things done" mode, and Dan isn't sure whether to be amused or terrified. "We should talk about them, right? I mean, talking worked this time—you could have freaked out about Sean, but you didn't. You just called me, and we talked, got it straightened out."

"I freaked out a bit," Dan confesses, and there's another pause.

"Did you go over to Jeff's again?" Evan sounds like he's mostly joking but not entirely.

"No! It was… it was an internal freak out. Didn't last quite as long."

"And you pulled yourself out of it. Seriously, I think this 'talking' thing could really work for us. So here's my plan. We take today to all calm down a little. Regroup. And then tomorrow we meet up for dinner, somewhere quiet, and we figure out the obstacles, hammer out the details."

Dan smirks. "Like, a dating contract?"

"Yeah, exactly!" Dan tries to ignore Puppet-Chris's victory dance, and resolves that he will never tell the actual Chris. Or else he will tell him, while he's explaining the final piece of evidence that convinced Dan that things would never work between him and Evan. "Dan?" Evan interrupts.

"Yeah, uh. The contract idea is insane. But… okay, maybe we should at least talk through stuff, see what you guys are thinking about." A thought occurs to him. "But is Jeff okay with the timing? His show's this Friday, right? Should he be concentrating on getting ready for that?"

"I don't know. Last time we talked about it he was almost ready, but... I guess I could call him and find out." Evan sounds reluctant, almost petulant, and Dan has a sinking feeling.

"Are you guys fighting? Are you mad about him and me?" There's no answer. "Because, seriously... we thought it was okay with you, and I was pretty fucking persistent, man... and when it came down to it...." Dan doesn't know if he really wants to say this part. "When it came down to it, he chose you. I was... well, I was doing my best to distract him, and the phone rang, and he thought it was you, and—"

"Dan! Seriously, this is between me and him."

Dan hears that pretty clearly. "Yeah. So that's the way it's going to be, in your version of the damn contract? You and Jeff can talk about me all you want, but I don't get to say anything about either of you? That's good to know, man. Thanks for clearing that up."

"No, I didn't mean it like that...."

"Really? So how did you mean it?"

"Fuck. I don't know. Okay, yeah, you have a right to talk about us, too, I guess... but... yeah, okay, I heard what you said. I'll give him a call and see if he's free for dinner tomorrow night. Okay?"

"And be nice."

Evan snorts a little. "What?"

"You should be nice when you call him. You love him, remember?" Dan's teasing, but he means it too.

"Yeah, thanks. So I'll call him, nicely... and then I'll call you back and let you know?"

"Okay. But, Evan... I mean, okay, you're right, it's worth talking it out, but... talking doesn't solve everything, you know?" He can barely remember all the things that had jittered through his mind earlier, but he's pretty sure that at least some of them had merit.

Evan sighs. "No, not everything. But, seriously, Dan, if you want this... and I want this... and Jeff wants this... let's make it happen, you know? Let's get it for ourselves."

"Jesus, you sound like a motivational speaker." Dan laughs a little.

"Well, is it working? Are you motivated?"

"I'm motivated to hang up. I'm gonna go to work, and then I'll move my stuff out tonight. I can come back and clean the place… oh, not tomorrow night… the next night?"

"Nah, man, don't worry about cleaning it. We've got people who can do that."

Dan shakes his head. "You have people. I don't. I can clean."

"Whatever. Knock yourself out." Evan mutters something that sounds like "Stubborn bastard," but Dan doesn't ask him to repeat it.

They hang up, and Dan lies back along the bench seat, his feet still sticking out the door. He stays like that for a minute, staring at the ceiling of the truck and wondering what the hell he's doing. In the space of five minutes he's gone from freaking out and hating his life to feeling reasonably content, although still totally uncertain about his future. And still a little hung over. He pulls himself back up to a sitting position and swings his feet inside the truck. He doesn't have to worry about Evan and Jeff until the next night, and in the meantime, he's got horses to train. It may not be a lot, but it's enough. At least for now.

chapter 38

DAN drives to the barn and throws himself into his work with enthusiasm. It's hard for him to believe that he saw the horses only the morning before. It feels like it's been weeks. The staff doesn't seem to have even noticed that he was gone, and Tatiana is there, too, bright and cheerful as ever. He supposes that Evan wouldn't have mentioned any of the previous day's events to her, and she seems unaware of the trauma caused in the name of her security. He has a quick flash of resentment, wondering why she gets to be so blissfully ignorant while he is put through the third degree, but after about two minutes of her gushing about Sunshine and Chaucer and all the other exciting things in her life, he finds that he's forgiven her. He *likes* it that she's unaware and that she can still be a kid even with the dangers in her world. He realizes again that Evan's doing a good job with his little sister.

Dan takes Tat with him when he checks on the horses that had competed on Sunday. They need at least a couple days to rest after their exertions, so he doesn't ride them, but he has Robyn walk and trot them on the leadline so he can watch for lameness, and he runs his hands over their muscles to check for the heat of injury. He explains what he's doing to Tat, and he's impressed as always with her focus and her interest in learning. He sort of hopes that she doesn't become a serious eventer, because he doesn't want to see her take that kind of risk, but he thinks she definitely has a future in the horse world, if she wants it. A future she could earn herself, not one that she buys with her family money.

Ryan calls around lunchtime. He's just waking up, and Dan teases him about the rock and roll lifestyle. Ryan agrees ruefully, and gives a quick summary of what he's been up to. He sounds happy, and more excited than Dan's ever heard him, so Dan's happy on his behalf.

When Ryan asks how Dan's doing, he's not sure how to respond.

"Oh, yeah. Better today, for sure. Sorry about the drama yesterday."

"Dude, there wasn't really any drama…. You just sounded down."

"Yeah, it… I dunno. Some stuff came up, and I didn't deal with it all that well, and… whatever. But, yeah, I think I'm gonna find somewhere else to live. The house is really nice, but it's just not really me, you know? And I think I need a bit of breathing room from the whole Kaminski experience."

"Especially if you're gonna start dating him," Ryan says quietly.

Dan's temporarily speechless. He'd known Ryan was aware of his interest in Jeff, but…. "What? Why would… I mean…."

"Dude, I thought he was gonna punch me that first night in the bar." Ryan laughs a little. "And he eased off, but still… he wasn't exactly subtle. And a guy like him—what he wants, he gets, right?"

"Wait. No…. What do you mean… a guy like him? I thought you thought… Jeff?" Dan is aware that he's not making a lot of sense. Maybe he can treat this as a rehearsal for the conversation the next evening. He obviously needs some practice.

"A guy like him: rich, good-looking, smart, ambitious—the whole package, right? And, honestly, from how I've seen him treat *other* people, he seems like a pretty good guy too."

"Yeah, but… I don't know, man. I mean… I don't know. It's complicated."

"Yeah, no shit. He's been seeing Stevens for years, right?"

"Wait a second—how come you know all this?"

"Dude, he's the biggest piece of gossip around. The whole package. And single. And fucks men and women? And lots of each? Jesus, it's a small town… there's people who could tell you what that guy has for breakfast." Ryan sounds amused by the whole scene, but Dan doesn't think he's able to be that sanguine himself.

"Shit." Dan really hadn't considered that other people might be aware of his… situation. It's one more item that makes him uncomfortable about the whole thing. Puppet-Chris tells him to add it to the 'con' list, but Dan hasn't admitted that he's making one. The less the puppet knows, the better.

Ryan sounds a bit more thoughtful. "So, you're thinking about, what… both of them? The town would love that."

"Jesus. The town cares?"

"Dan, man—you saw those girls grab onto your first day at the restaurant—if the town cares about you, you'd better *believe* they care about Kaminski, and a Kaminski threesome? Hell, yeah, they'd care."

"Oh, God." Dan groans and cradles his head in his hands. "This just gets messier and messier."

Ryan's voice is gentle. "What about you, man? Forget the town, and forget Kaminski... what do *you* want?"

Dan thinks for a minute. "Fuck if I know."

"Okay, put it this way... if you were stuck on a desert island somewhere, just the three of you... would you be getting it on?"

Dan smiles at the thought. "Would there be lube?"

"Coconut oil or something. Be creative."

"Okay, side question—does this not bother you at all? I mean, this conversation is just about killing me, and you seem fine with it." Dan isn't sure if he really wants the answer to that. "Am I just... am I flattering myself to think that maybe it would bug you a little?"

Ryan takes a second before answering. "I went into this thinking we'd be friends. And then I bailed before we got to be much more. I... I've got no right to lay claim to you, man. You know? And, I don't know... I guess I'm pretty good at being content with what I've got, and not bitching about what I haven't."

Dan nods to himself. It goes a long way toward explaining the Ryan Effect. And it bought him a little time on the desert island question.

"Yeah, okay. Uh, desert island—sure, yeah. They're both hot, I like them both... hey, if you were there you could join in too."

"Thanks. So, it's just what other people think that would slow you down? I don't know, man... should that really matter?"

"Well... maybe? Or... I don't know, it's not just what other people think, it's what I think. I mean... Evan's my boss, which is... bad, for me. And on a desert island, we'd all be stuck there together. Nobody's gonna leave, or nobody's gonna see somebody else and want them instead."

"Huh. Yeah, life isn't simple, I guess." Ryan sounds smugly aware that his own life actually is fairly straightforward, but Dan can't really resent him for it.

"Yeah, thanks, that's helpful." Dan smiles. "Okay, I should get back to work, I guess. But do you have your landlord's number, for the apartment? Maybe I'll get in touch, see if I can get a couple months there before I decide what I'm doing longer term."

"Uh… no number, actually. He's a bit of a crazy hippy. He does pottery, and he travels around to all these craft shows… he's hardly ever home. I just leave notes for him in the mailbox of the house, and he leaves notes in the mailbox of the garage—it works out all right. His name's Wendell." Ryan laughs. "He may not even know that I gave notice yet."

"Wendell? Okay. Great, thanks. And, you know… thanks for listening to me babble."

"Anytime, man. I gotta say, though, it's a bit sad when the sex life of some damn horse trainer is that much kinkier than the sex life of a rock star like me."

"Well, you're still new at it… I'm sure the kinkiness will build once you're on the road."

Ryan laughs, and they hang up. Dan goes back to the horses. Having the competitors taking a rest means that Dan has more time for the younger horses, and he really enjoys the chance to work with them and see where they're at. Before he knows it, Robyn and Michelle are calling it a day. Tat looks tired as well, but she seems determined to stay as long as Dan does.

He turns his last horse, an off-the-track Thoroughbred filly, into her pasture, and finds Tat waiting for him at the gate.

"Hey, Dan." She seems a little shy, as if she's building up to a difficult question, and Dan starts to get a bit of a sinking feeling. He really has no idea what Evan has told his sister about… anything, really. Dan, and Jeff, and Dan and Jeff and Evan…. And he doesn't know what she's supposed to know, or even if there's anything to tell her. He looks around frantically for an escape.

"Hey, Tat!" He suspects that his greeting is a little overenthusiastic, considering that he's just spent most of the day with her. He tries to bring the energy level down a notch. "What's up?"

She smiles bashfully. "I just… I wanted to say that… Evan doesn't always tell me all that much. I mean, he tries to protect me from a lot of stuff. But… I could tell something was going on yesterday, and I think I kind of know what it was… and I just wanted to say that I'm sorry. You know… if it was what I think it was."

This is so much better than what Dan thought she wanted to talk about. "Oh, no, Tat... I don't know what you thought it was, but, really... there's nothing for you to be sorry about."

She doesn't look quite convinced. "But if... if they made you feel unwelcome, or as though you were... I don't know, as if you were *dangerous* or something, just because they're being all paranoid about protecting *me*... I should be sorry about that, shouldn't I?" She's looking at the ground as she talks, but then she lifts her eyes up to Dan at the end, and he almost wants to cry.

"No, Tat, you...." He doesn't know how much detail he wants to go into. "You're lucky—you've got a family who cares about you, wants to keep you safe, and helps you know how to do the right things. I wasn't quite so lucky." He smiles ruefully, and wonders if that was enough to make her understand, or just enough to rouse her curiosity. "So... I guess... if you want to be sorry, like, it's too bad that everyone isn't as lucky with their families, okay, you can be sorry like that. But don't be sorry like it's your fault." He shakes his head. "It's not your fault."

He gets another bashful look, and then she nods. "Yeah, okay." They both rest their arms on the fence and look out at Sunshine grazing. Dan gives himself a mental pat on the back. He handled that all right. "Hey, Dan?"

"Yeah?" He almost *hopes* she's got another question, just so he can answer it as smoothly.

She turns her head to look directly at him. "Do you like my brother?" And there goes Dan's confidence. He keeps his eyes resolutely on the field.

"Uh... yes? I mean... I think almost everybody likes your brother, don't they?"

She leans over and gives him a little hip check. "No, you know what I mean. Do you *like* him?" Dan just stares out at the horses, hoping that one of them will do something, anything, to distract this girl from her question. But the horses just keep grazing, and Tat continues. "'Cause he likes you. I mean, he likes Jeff, too, but... you can like two people at once, right?"

"Uh... yes? I think you can like two people at once."

"Yeah. I know it's none of my business or whatever, but... I just wanted to make sure that you know... if you like him, that's cool with me.

I mean, I like Jeff, too, but… you know."

Dan has a brief moment of wanting to shake her. No, he *doesn't* know. Is everything really so clear to everyone but him? Is he just adding extra complications where they don't need to be? Then he remembers that he's talking to a fifteen-year-old girl. Maybe she shouldn't be the arbiter of what's simple or complicated.

He realizes that she's still waiting for a response from him. "Okay, well… thanks for letting me know."

"Are you guys going to, like… date?"

"Sweet Jesus, Tat, I don't know!" Possibly that was an overreaction, but she looks more amused than upset.

"All right, all right…." She gets a mischievous look in her eyes. "Hey, if I promise not to ask any more questions, can I ride Monty tomorrow? Just on the flat, not for jumping!"

Dan shakes his head. She can have his truck if she stops asking questions, but it's probably better she doesn't figure that out. "Uh… that might work. He should just have a light work out tomorrow, if anything… We'll check his legs in the morning, and if he's all right, you can give him a try. Just walk and trot, probably…."

She squeals and gives him a quick hug, and then Evan's Cherokee is pulling into the barn parking area. Tat gives Dan another sly look. "Hmm… Evan said he'd come by and drive me home, but I think I feel like a walk… maybe you should go say hi…."

Dan feels his face flame, and he tries to put a little warning in his voice when he says, "Tat…," but she just laughs and skips away toward her brother.

He hears them exchange greetings but keeps his eyes on the field. He doesn't really want to explain his blush to Evan. The bastard would probably think the whole thing was hilarious.

He hears Tatiana call out a goodbye to him, and he turns to wave to her. Evan is coming across the grass toward him, looking a little hesitant. Dan smiles a greeting and then turns back to look at the horses. Conversations without face to face contact are his favorite.

Evan comes up and stands beside him, leaning his own arms on the fence, just close enough so that their elbows touch. Dan is hyper-aware of the contact, and finds himself wanting to lean into it. If he's honest with himself, he wants to turn Evan toward him and lean into him with a whole lot more than just elbows. Dan may not be a fan of face to face *conversations*, but that doesn't mean he sees no value in the position. It's reassuring, in a way. It's nice to know that Dan isn't going through all this for a guy he doesn't even really want.

Evan watches the horses for a while, then says, "So I talked to Jeff. And I was nice." He cuts his eyes toward Dan, who lets the corners of his mouth curl up a little. "And he said dinner tomorrow is a good idea. He said he's going stir crazy trying not to worry about the show, so he can cook. It'll give him something to do."

Dan hadn't thought about that. He'd assumed they'd go to a restaurant. Evan seems to sense his reaction.

"We could just go out, but if we're going to have a real, honest discussion about all this—some privacy might be good. And Jeff's place is more private than mine, and way more private than a restaurant."

Dan nods. It makes sense. It's just that the last time he'd been at Jeff's, he hadn't exactly been on his best behavior. It'll be a bit awkward to go back, especially with Evan there. But he guesses he just needs to suck it up. He can't avoid the place forever. "Yeah, okay. Uh... what time?"

"I said I'd go there straight from the office... so maybe six or so?"

Dan nods again. "Okay, yeah." Evan shifts a little, so his whole upper arm is against Dan's, and when he speaks, his voice is quieter, but intense.

"I've been thinking about you all day, Dan. Thinking about that kiss, and all the things I want us to do. It's been driving me nuts."

Dan's actually been okay, working with the horses as a way to keep his mind off things, but now that Evan is right here, Dan's having a little trouble forming coherent thoughts. He's not sure what his voice would sound like if he tried to speak, so he just nods.

Evan seems to understand the reason for Dan's silence, and he leans in closer. His lips are right by Dan's ear now, and just like the night before, Dan can feel them on his cheek when Evan speaks. He wonders if this is a favorite technique of Evan's and wonders how he'll be able to stand it if Evan does it much longer. "You've got to give us a chance, Dan. We can figure everything out. I know we can." He turns a little more toward Dan and moves in slightly, and Dan can feel Evan's hardness up against his hip. He lets out a little whimper and turns his head, his eyes shut tight, his mouth finding Evan's by feel. This time it's Dan who leads the way, pushing almost too hard against Evan's lips, licking into his mouth, rolling his hip against Evan's groin. Dan shifts his body so they're facing each other, still squeezed in tight, and their hard lengths are rubbing against each other through their clothes. Evan gasps a little at the contact, and Dan trails his lips away from Evan's mouth, kissing and sucking along his jaw line and down his neck. He's so turned on he can barely breathe. Evan leans his head back, exposing his throat for more attention, and just then Dan hears laughing voices from the direction of the barn, and he rips his mouth and body away from Evan.

Dan turns to look back out at the horses, but Evan stays in the same position as if frozen there. After a moment he groans and lets his head fall forward.

"Dan, there you are!" calls Sara from the barn. Dan turns his head to look at her and Devin. "We're going into town to get some dinner... do you guys want anything?"

Dan glances at Evan but he doesn't seem to be too coherent, so he just decides for both of them. "Nah, we're good, thanks," he calls back, and Evan comes back to himself enough to raise an arm to wave at them before turning around and facing the field.

He waits a while, either to make sure Devin and Sara are gone or to gain a little more control of himself. "Jesus Christ, Dan—" he starts.

"Yeah," Dan replies, and then he grins. "Wasn't today supposed to be a cooling off period, or something?"

Evan laughs a little. "Yeah, something like that." He shakes his head a little. "Okay, I was gonna offer to help you pack up your stuff tonight, but...."

Dan nods. "If I get you anywhere near a bed, you're gonna end up in it. And it'd be better...."

"More fair to Jeff," Evan agrees, "although I don't know if that exactly makes sense. I mean, you and him got together on your own...."

"And you didn't like it," Dan reminds him.

Evan doesn't answer for a minute. "I fucking hated it." Then he grins. "Since when are you Mr. Sensible?"

Dan shakes his head. "I turned over a whole new leaf, man. This is the new me."

"Yeah. Great fucking timing on that, you bastard." Evan keeps looking out at the horses. "Hey, you need to teach me to ride."

Dan can't stop himself from smirking a little. "I thought we agreed that it would be better to wait until tomorrow."

Evan shoots him a look. "Seriously? It's your full-time job, and you still pick up on all the dirty expressions? Wouldn't it sort of wear thin after a while?"

"Dude, I had my tongue down your throat two minutes ago. I'm still fucking hard. Excuse me if I've got sex on my mind."

Evan groans a little. "Jesus, don't remind me. Okay, then, I'm gonna head home, find some dinner. I'd invite you up, but... same problem applies."

"Shit, man, I almost forgot. Your sister... I had a bit of a weird conversation with your sister."

"Well, yeah. Weird's pretty normal with her. What was this one about?"

"Uh... I think she gave us her blessing." Evan looks up in surprise, and Dan shrugs. "I don't know, dude. She... she asked if I liked you, and then she said *you* liked *me*, but that you liked Jeff, too, but that she thinks it's okay to like two people at the same time. It freaked me out a little."

"Jesus. Is that what she was smirking about when she said she'd walk home?"

"I guess so, yeah. She also seemed to know a bit about yesterday. You might want to talk to her about that. I think she believed me when I said it wasn't her fault, but... I'm not really sure."

Evan rolls his eyes dramatically. "This is what she does! She sneaks around and eavesdrops, and then I've got to make her feel better about whatever she overhears. It's... it's not a good system."

"Maybe you should tell her upfront. You know... make sure she's got the facts right, make sure she's not misinterpreting anything."

"That's what Jeff says. Jesus, are you two gonna gang up on me about my sister?"

Dan raises his hands. "Okay, I'm obviously in no position to be giving advice about anything family related. Sorry."

"No, I didn't mean it like that." Evans waits for Dan's shrug, then looks up in the direction of the house. "What did you tell her about us?"

"I, uh… I told her she could ride Monty tomorrow if she stopped asking me questions."

Evan bites his lip a little, then gives up and laughs out loud. "Yeah, okay. Fair enough. Damn, I should remember that one."

"Dude, get your own bribe!"

Evan's eyes are warm, and Dan kind of wants to stay there forever, just basking in the affection from the other man. But he doesn't honestly think it will stay as simple affection for long, and he really does think Jeff would be hurt if they did anything without him. Dan notices that his thinking on the next evening seems to have shifted. Originally it was a meeting to talk, for Dan to explain his serious reservations about their suggested arrangement. But somehow it seems to have morphed, and now he feels like he's going into it expecting to have some sort of sex with at least one of the guys. He's not sure when or why things shifted, and right now he's not too concerned about it. He feels like the tension has ratcheted up to the point where something needs to happen, especially between him and Evan, or they'll both explode. So he can still express his serious reservations about an actual relationship, but that shouldn't mean that he can't get a little action. Or a lot of action, maybe. He's open to suggestions.

But until then, Dan needs to get the hell away from Evan. "Okay, so… oh, you want to learn to ride. You don't mean right now, do you?" His eyes shift down to Evan's crotch, where he still looks at least partly hard. "'Cause take it from me, that's pretty uncomfortable…."

"No, not right now," Evan is quick to say. "Just… someday. Sean was saying that these are good times to buy horses, 'cause of the economy being so bad, so maybe we could be on the lookout for some good eventing prospects, but also for some horses just for riding around on, you know? Like Smokey or maybe a bit bigger, for me."

"Yeah, that'd be great. We could build a run-in shed in the big paddock, and keep the extra horses in there. Smokey'd be happier out all the time, if he had some company. Most horses would, really, but the stalls are convenient when we're riding them every day." Dan's getting enthusiastic about this idea, and he notices that his body is calming right down. Apparently horses are his anti-aphrodisiac—which is just as well, considering his job.

"Excellent, yeah. I've got another... there's another idea I've been working on, but it's not quite put together yet. Hopefully I'll have it figured out for tomorrow." Dan gives him a curious look, but Evan just shrugs and grins. "Okay, then. I'm gonna go.... I'll see you tomorrow, right? Six o'clock at Jeff's."

Dan nods. He kind of wants a kiss goodbye, but he doesn't think it's a good idea. There's no telling where that might end up. Apparently Evan has the same thought, because he's looking a bit regretful as he walks back toward the car.

Dan waits until he hears the Cherokee start up and drive away before he turns and heads up to his own truck. He doesn't really have much stuff to pack up, but he figures he may as well get to it. Maybe he'll even start on the cleaning tonight. Lord knows he could use the distraction from his thoughts. He feels like his head could start spinning again, and he really doesn't think there's any productive decisions to be made right now. He needs to hear what Evan and Jeff have to say and how they respond to his concerns. He's not optimistic, and he's going in with some pretty serious reservations, but he finds that he's really, really starting to hope that they're able to convince him. He doesn't honestly know what he'll do if they can't.

chapter 39

DAN makes it through the next day largely by working his ass off. It occurs to him in the late afternoon that he may have worked a little too hard and that it might have been better to save a little endurance for the evening, but then he thinks of Evan and Jeff looking at him with heat in their eyes, and his dick lets him know that it has access to hidden energy reserves. So he figures he'll be okay.

He heads home about half past four. It's remarkable to him how quickly he's started thinking of the apartment as home, considering that he never did get around to thinking of the guest house that way. It's especially ironic considering that he doesn't even have any legal right to it… when he'd gone to put a note in the landlord's mailbox, he'd found Ryan's thirty-day notice still there, and just added his note to the pile. He has no idea if the landlord will let him stay, but for twenty-six days, at least, it's home. He's not saying that he wants to live in the apartment forever, necessarily, but it's good for now.

He showers and spends a few minutes worrying about clothes. What does one wear to dinner at a friend's that may well turn into a wild threesome? Clean underwear, definitely, but other than that he has no idea. He settles on his usual jeans and a button down shirt. If the guys don't like him in that, they might as well figure it out now, because he doubts it's going to change. He does go to the trouble of shaving—stubble can be sexy, but beard-burn is no fun.

He takes a minute to consider just how disappointed he's going to be if he ends up not getting any action. He'd jerked off in the shower, hoping to take the edge off, but he's getting hard again just thinking about everything. His mind may still harbor some doubts, but his body has pretty clearly decided.

He's ready to go at about half past five, and then takes a few minutes to talk to Justin's picture. Even *it* seems more at home in the apartment. The picture's warm tones hadn't really fit against the cool white walls of the guest house, but the apartment is painted an indeterminate beige-y color that isn't exactly inspiring but does seem to be a better backdrop for the photograph. Dan mentions this in the first couple sentences of his monologue. He figures he should warm Justin up before jumping right into the threesome stuff. But there's really no graceful way to transition from talk of interior decorating to telling your boyfriend that you're going to have sex with two other men, so eventually Dan just goes for it.

"So, yeah. I, uh… neither one of us was exactly a virgin when we got together, right? Maybe I was a bit further away from it than you, but, come on… you got your share. So, uh… I don't know, maybe you did something like this before me. But I think you would have mentioned it. I don't know if it's a good idea or not, man, but it really looks like I'm gonna do it. I mean, they're both good guys, and… yeah, you know, I want both of them. And you're not here." Dan has to get the hell off that train of thought. Showing up with red eyes would definitely not be sexy.

"Jeff's cool—very Zen, very… gentle. He was great in Kentucky, with—" And there's another area that Dan shouldn't really delve into if he wants to maintain his composure. Then again, he's having a conversation with a stolen photograph, so maybe it's not his *composure* that he's lost. But he continues anyway. He doesn't want to feel like he's sneaking around. "You'd like him. Well, he'd probably put you to sleep, a little, but… in a nice way. And you'd like Evan, too, I think. You guys are kind of alike. You're both intense, and you go after what you want. He's gotten stuff a bit easier than you ever did, so, you know, he's a bit more laid back, but… I don't know. Hey, maybe it's like a compliment, right? It takes two of them to add up to one of you?

"So, yeah, that's what I'm doing. It could all end up in a big mess… but at least I tried, right?" He touches the picture gently. There are marks on the glass over Justin's face where his fingers have rested so many times. He'd thought about cleaning them off, but had decided to leave them. "I miss you, baby. But… I'm still here, right? I gotta try to put a life together. So… this is what I'm trying." He pulls his fingers away and raises his eyebrows, trying to get himself into a lighter mood. "God help us all."

And then he's out the door and into his truck, on the way to Jeff's.

It's not a long drive, maybe about ten minutes, but it's long enough for Dan to get ridiculously nervous. He can feel his shirt sticking to his back and wishes he could blame the heat, but the air coming through his open window is cool. He sits forward a bit, trying to get a breeze circulating between himself and the seat. He wishes he'd brought a change of clothes, although he supposes it might be a little awkward to show up for a casual dinner with an overnight bag.

He pulls into the driveway with plans to stand outside for a bit and collect himself, but Jeff is sitting on the porch, Lou at his side, beer in his hand and feet up on the railing. He looks cool as a cucumber, the bastard. Dan wonders again just what those two are risking with all this. He guesses maybe they have nothing to be nervous about. And that means he doesn't, either, he reminds himself. He's not sure if he wants anything, so it's not like he's desperately hoping for a certain outcome. And sex is sex. If he doesn't get it here, he can always get it somewhere else. That helps a little, and he pulls himself out of the truck and walks toward the house.

"Hey, Dan," Jeff says softly, and maybe he is a little nervous, because his eyes don't seem to be quite as still as they usually are.

"Hi. Evan not here yet?" Dan's voice sounds fairly normal. He bends down to greet the dog.

"No, not yet." Jeff nods his head toward a galvanized bucket by the porch steps, full of ice with several bottles of beer sticking out. "Help yourself. Or I could get you something else, if you'd rather."

"No, this is good, thanks." Dan pulls out a bottle and twists off the lid, takes a long pull. It feels perfect, and he takes another swallow which is almost as good. He looks around the porch and takes the seat next to Jeff's, with a little table between them. Jeff looks pretty damn comfortable, so Dan kicks his own feet up on the railing. Physically, everything is lovely. Mentally is a different matter.

They sit quietly for a while. The front yard isn't quite as landscaped as the back. It's mostly driveway and lawn, but there's a huge pine tree near the road, and a pair of squirrels are having some sort of interaction. It's not clear whether it's friendly or hostile. There's certainly a lot of chasing and chattering. In one overly ambitious move, one of the squirrels launches itself from a branch of the pine tree to a branch of a smaller tree on the neighbor's lot, and just barely makes it. The little creature is hanging on by the nails of one paw, and Dan feels Jeff tense and half-rise beside him. Then the squirrel squirms a little, and manages to pull itself up and start scolding again, as if the whole thing was its partner's fault. Jeff sits back down in his seat, and Dan waits for a few breaths. Then he can't resist.

"Do you rescue a lot of squirrels out here?" he asks, his face as straight as possible. Jeff doesn't respond. "'Cause that was a close call. Were you gonna run over there and catch him? Or just give him first aid after he fell?" Jeff's still silent, and Dan looks over at him.

Jeff's fighting to keep his face serious. "I guess I'd have done whatever I could, you know. Whatever it took."

Dan nods. "That's... that's beautiful, man." They're still grinning a little when Evan pulls in behind Dan's truck.

The driveway's not that wide, and Dan feels a little panic when he thinks maybe his vehicle is being blocked in, but calms down when he sees that Evan is parked far enough to the side that Dan could still get by. Still, that reaction maybe wasn't a sign of total comfort with the situation, Dan reflects.

Evan gets out of the SUV and waves, and then takes a moment to take off his jacket and tie, throwing them both on the passenger seat. Dan's not sure how he feels about that. Evan looks hot in a suit, but two pieces of clothing off already makes Evan that much closer to naked, which can only be good.

Evan crosses to the porch a little slowly, almost hesitantly, and Dan gets a bad feeling. Evan had said that he'd been nice to Jeff on the phone, but Dan thinks maybe this is the first time they've seen each other in person since... since Dan's unfortunate display. He pulls his feet down off the railing. They were blocking the way between Evan and Jeff, and Dan thinks maybe he's done enough blocking there already. Jeff stands up and seems a little tentative himself, but when they get close enough they both go in for a hug, and Dan sees that Evan closes his eyes as he buries his face in Jeff's neck. Dan feels terrible. There are more important things happening at this dinner than just deciding whether he's going to get laid.

The hug doesn't last long, but they're both smiling when they pull apart. Evan looks over at Dan. "Hey, man." He looks a little sheepish, but Dan just smiles.

Jeff clears his throat. "Uh, I've got some stuff to do in the kitchen. Do you guys want to move back to the deck, or...?"

"We can hang out with you, man," Evan says, and Dan nods. It occurs to him that the chairs on the porch are the same ones from the deck in the back, and he doesn't really think they were out here the last time he was. He wonders if Jeff had planned to wait on the deck, so that Dan and

Jeff wouldn't be in the house together before Evan got there to chaperone. He wonders if it was for Jeff's peace of mind or for Evan's. Maybe for both.

"But, uh… I just need to talk to Dan for a minute first." Evan waves the papers in his hand at Jeff. "It's just some business stuff. We can stay out here?"

Jeff nods, and Dan is confused. Evan hasn't taken too much interest in the business side of the horses thus far… what's so important that it has to be talked about now? He looks inquiringly at Jeff, who just shrugs and heads into the house. Evan comes over and takes Jeff's seat, setting the papers on the table.

"Sorry for the drama, man… I was hoping to get this settled earlier, but… well, I've already been asking the guys to do it pretty fast, and we wanted to be sure it was right. And I wanted to talk to you about it now, because it might have an influence on what we talk about later. But I wanted to make sure you understood that it's totally separate from any personal stuff. So that left now as a time to talk. Is that cool?"

Dan thinks for a second. "Yeah, I have no idea what you're talking about. But… okay."

"Okay, yeah. I guess that was a little convoluted. But I'll make it more clear. Uh, first off, I wanted to emphasize that this is a business decision. You know how important you are to the barn… I really don't want to be involved in the business without someone I can trust running it. And, annoying security crap aside, I totally trust you. So I know you've been worrying about me maybe firing you, and I can say all I want to that I'm never gonna do that. I understand that you can still worry about it. But… I've been just as worried about you maybe quitting. I mean, that show on Sunday was a big eye-opener… I knew you were good, and I didn't really think you'd have trouble finding another job, but… people were drooling over you, man."

Dan frowns. "I don't really remember anyone drooling over *me*."

"Yeah, not to your face… they were too intimidated! Seriously, man. It was like if Bill Gates showed up to some local entrepreneurs' club."

"Whatever, man." Dan just shakes his head.

"Yeah, okay, you don't have to believe me, but I think you can believe that it would be really bad for the barn if you left."

"I wouldn't leave you in the lurch, though. I mean, I could try to find someone to replace me... not Sean, he's a good rider but not much of a trainer... but I'm not exactly irreplaceable."

"You'd be *hard* to replace. But... here's my solution. I want to make you more attached to the business. Make it so that it's equally hard for either of us to walk away. And then, if stuff doesn't work out on the personal level, we'll still have to find a way to get along, or else we'll have to mutually agree to dissolve things."

Dan looks with some trepidation at the stack of papers. He's heard of non-competition contracts, where people have to agree to not take a job anywhere else in the same industry if they quit working for their original company. Dan can't think of what he'd do if he wasn't working with horses.

Evan reaches over and pulls out a stapled bundle. "So this is what we came up with. It's modeled on a couple other contracts, some in the equestrian business, but really more from restaurants with top chefs, and a few other fields. Anyway, you'll want someone to look at it, but I think it's fair."

He passes the pages to Dan, but Dan doesn't even look at them, just waits for Evan to explain.

"Yeah, so... it's a partnership agreement. Uh, there's lots of details, but the big picture would be that we'd form a business partnership that would own the horses. Uh, obviously I'd be putting up most of the money, so I'd own most of the business, but you'd have the right to buy in... there's a bunch of stuff about valuations and whatever, but you'd buy in at a fair price, whenever you want, up to a maximum of you owning fifty percent of the business. The business would hire you as the head trainer, and your salary and stuff would stay the same, but you'd also get profits... you know, if we ever make any. So even if you quit as the trainer, you'd still be tied to the company, because you'd want to make sure your investment was doing okay."

Dan's not sure if he's hearing this right, and just waits for Evan to continue.

"Yeah, well, that's from my perspective. From your perspective... you'd have less money right now, because you'd be sinking some of it into buying the company, but you'd be building something for the future. And you'd be an owner of the horses, which just makes sense. You put so much into them, it's like they're yours already, really… this would just… reflect that. And honestly, it's not like you seem to need as much money as you're making. I've never seen you buy anything but alcohol and paninis."

Evan pauses for breath, and then looks at Dan a little anxiously. "So… general impressions? I mean… obviously we can go on the way we have been, but… I thought this might be better… you know, especially because then I wouldn't be your boss. Or, I would be a little bit, but you'd be your boss too."

Dan is pretty sure he misunderstood something. He kind of wants to leave the house right now and find the nearest fax machine to send this all off to Chris. Sex is good, but a chance to own the horses, even partly… but he must have misunderstood.

"Okay… let me… okay, let me say what I think I heard, and you can tell me when I go off the rails." He tries to control his voice. He doesn't want to make a fool of himself by acting too excited and then finding out that he'd gotten the wrong idea. "So, what I heard… we'd start a new company, and you and me would be the partners."

Evan nods. "Okay, or… I didn't want to confuse things, but maybe Tat instead of me. It'd be a bit different, because it'd have to be in trust or something, but… you know, the horses are her thing. And, it'd take it even further away from me being your boss, which would be good for both of us, probably. But, yeah, you and a Kaminski would be the partners."

"Okay. And I'd… okay, let's say the company would be worth a million dollars. Just for easy math. So then, say I put in a hundred thousand now. I'd own ten percent of the business?"

"Yeah. Have you got a hundred thousand?"

"Fuck, no. But, you know, for easy math." Evan grins, and Dan continues. "So then, next year, we'd… what, we'd get somebody to say how much the business is worth then? And let's say that… for easy math, let's say that it doubled. I know that's not gonna happen, but…." Evan nods, so Dan continues. "So now the company is worth two million, and if I put in another hundred grand from somewhere, I'd buy another five percent?"

Evan looks a bit apologetic. "Yeah, I know it seems like it's gonna take a long time for you to get up to fifty percent… I mean, if you think the company is going to grow that fast, it would make sense for you to get a loan from somewhere—if the banks won't give you one, I could, if it's cool with you—and then buy your whole fifty percent right at the start. But, honestly, man, I don't think it's going to grow that fast."

"Yeah, no… it's…. Okay, so… what about the barn, and the paddocks and everything?"

"They'd stay part of the Kaminski property, and the business would pay rent. Again, we could get somebody to do a valuation… it's in the contract. And if I get some horses just for fun, then we could just figure out a price for boarding them at the barn. Same with Smokey, if you keep him there. Or… you're using Smokey for barn business, sometimes, so maybe you want to sell him to the business. Whatever makes sense."

Dan sits back a little. He feels like Evan just nonchalantly pulled up a chair and offered Dan his dream come true. He's in a bit of a daze, and Evan seems to be misinterpreting it.

"So, like I said, we don't have to do this. And, yeah, this is totally separate from anything that you and me and Jeff talk about later. I just wanted to say it now, because I thought that one of your objections later was going to be that I'm your boss. So… if we're changing the business relationship, as a totally separate thing… it might affect things later…." Evan trails off and looks at Dan a little anxiously. "So…?"

Dan still doesn't quite trust himself. "Seriously? I mean… are you sure?"

Evan seems relieved. "Yeah, man, like I said—it's good business. Restaurants do it when they've got a hot chef without a lot of money. They want to get him invested in the business so he won't get hired away. Same deal here. So… you're into it?"

"Yeah! I mean… I've got to send it to Chris and everything, but… it sounds really good. It sounds… Jesus, man, it sounds incredible."

"Okay then. Hey, Jeff's got a fax… do you want to send it out now? I mean, there's no big rush, but if you want to get it started…."

"Yeah, okay. Let me just…. I'll call Chris, get his fax number, let him know…." Dan is having a bit of trouble putting his thoughts together. He thinks about Monty, and Sunshine, and even stubborn Winston, and the idea of being an actual owner of those beautiful animals is overwhelming. Evan is looking at him with a bit of concern again, but Dan smiles at him. "Okay, I'm just gonna call Chris. Have you got a pen so I can write down his fax number?"

Evan indicates the pen clipped to some of the papers. "I'll go in and keep Jeff company. Is it okay if I tell him about this?"

"You didn't tell him?"

"No, like I said, this was a business thing. I mean, I think he'll think it's a good idea—he knows you don't like the idea of working for someone you're involved with." Evan stops himself. "Not to get ahead of ourselves. So when you're ready to send the fax, let me know." He smiles happily and heads indoors, and Dan sinks back in his chair and takes a minute to collect his thoughts.

He pulls out his phone and dials Chris, who answers in a more official manner than usual.

"Hey, Chris, are you still at work?"

"Yes, I am."

"And are there important people there who can hear you?"

"Yes."

"Okay, that's cool, though, because I'm calling as a client. Evan just... I don't know, I think he just offered to go into business with me. With the horses. But there's a contract. It's, like, twenty pages maybe.... Can you have a look at it?"

"Sure, I can do that."

"Tonight?"

"If that works for you."

Dan laughs. "I want to have all my conversations with you when you're in the same room as important people. You're much more agreeable."

"Well, I'm not sure about that...."

"Uh-huh. Give me your fax number. And make sure you bill me for this, okay?"

Chris gives Dan the number, and they hang up. Dan heads inside and sees Jeff standing in the kitchen, Evan perched on a stool. They both look up expectantly when Dan comes in, and Jeff gives him a warm smile as if sharing in his good fortune.

"Hey, Jeff. Is it okay if I use your fax?"

Jeff nods, and Evan hops off the stool. "I'll show you where it is."

They go into the office and send the document, Dan anxiously watching each page as it feeds through the machine, Evan fondly watching Dan. As the last sheet rolls through, Dan turns and looks at Evan. "This…. I don't know what to say about this, man. But… thanks."

Evan shakes his head. "No. I don't want you to feel that way… like I said, it's a mutually beneficial arrangement. So, you know, let's have dinner, put this out of our minds, and then whatever else we talk about… it's a whole other thing, okay?"

Dan's not really sure he can do that, but he figures he needs to at least try. "Yeah, okay. Dinner. Right." He follows Evan out of the den and back to the kitchen, where Jeff seems to have everything all ready.

There are several foil packets of various sizes, and a large plate with three seasoned steaks on it. Jeff is just adding some fresh peas to a big green salad, and he looks up from his work when they return. "All ready to go?"

"Yeah, thanks," Dan says, and looks at the food. "Everything looks—" he catches himself. "Well, everything pretty much looks like tinfoil, but something *smells* really good."

Jeff hands him the salad to carry, and gives the steaks to Evan while he himself juggles the various foil packages. They go outside and Jeff carefully selects one bundle. "Potatoes," he explains. "They take a bit longer." He puts them on the grill and closes the lid, then comes over to the table where Dan and Evan are sitting. He pours everyone some wine, and he and Evan chat a little about a favorite musician who's just put out a new album. Dan just sits and listens, feeling perfectly content.

He wonders if he's somehow slipped into someone else's life, with his California-style leisure time and his prospective new business. It feels good, but strange. A part of him wonders how long he can enjoy this before someone finds a way to take it away. Or before he messes it up himself.

chapter 40

CHRIS phones back just as they're finishing dinner, and Dan excuses himself to go answer the call. The Californians have apparently decided to hold off on any serious discussion, so the meal has been casual, with light talk about nothing very important, but between thinking about the horses and thinking about sex, Dan really hasn't contributed much of value. Hopefully talking to Chris will resolve at least one of the outstanding issues.

Dan goes out on the front porch and sits on the steps. He's almost afraid to ask for Chris's opinion of the contract, but he knows he has to.

"So?" he manages.

"So, it looks good, man. It's not really my area, but we've got a lawyer who does a lot of that stuff, and I'll run the details of it by her tomorrow. But, big picture—congratulations, Dan, I think you may be going into business."

"Okay, but…." Dan isn't sure how to phrase this. "Is it *too* good? I mean—is he just giving it to me, or…."

"No, man, it's fair. I mean, he's not giving you anything but an opportunity, right? He's not offering it to you for less than fair market value. He's just agreeing to sell something to you for the right price." Dan can hear Chris shift out of lawyer mode. "Why, is there some reason he might be giving things to you? What have you been up to, Danielle?"

"Nothing!" Dan isn't sure how much Chris needs to know. "Yet. But… I'm over at Jeff's right now. We just finished dinner, and then we're gonna look at our options, you know?"

"Well, what are you doing talking to me, then? Go get 'em, Tiger!"

"Yeah, thanks, that's… really disturbing. But, seriously—the contract is good, but not too good? You'll talk to the woman tomorrow, and if she says it's okay—I can go ahead and do it?"

"Absolutely. I mean, Evan's got the money and the lawyers to be pretty damn tricky, but I really don't see it here—it's detailed, but it all makes sense, and it seems fair." Chris pauses. "And the other... you're okay with that? I mean... you know what you're doing?"

"No, I have no fucking idea what I'm doing. But... it really looks like I'm gonna do it anyway."

"Huh. Is this... should I be worried?"

"Nah, man, it's fine. I mean, worst case scenario is hot, meaningless sex, right? How bad is that?"

"Well, *worst* case scenario is an earthquake and then a volcano and a tsunami. With a forest fire. And Ebola. But there's also the possibility of *crappy*, meaningless sex...."

Dan thinks for a second. "Based on the samples I've had so far, I don't think that's gonna be a problem." Chris groans as if he doesn't want to hear any more. "Okay, I better get back in there before they think I've booked out on them. Thanks, though. You'll call me tomorrow after you talk to the other lawyer?"

"Absolutely."

"Great. I'll be able to give you details of the nasty man-on-man action—" There's a click as Chris hangs up his phone. Dan grins in victory and then heads back out to the deck. Jeff and Evan are talking quietly, and they look almost guilty when Dan appears.

Jeff smiles sheepishly. "We were just discussing our strategy for tonight. Got any suggestions?"

"I don't know... what did you guys come up with?"

Evan looks down at his hands. "Well, so far... alcohol."

Dan smiles at him. "Dude, I've been reading business books—I think alcohol is a tool, not a strategy. The strategy would be, like... enhance honesty and lower inhibitions. No, wait, is that the goal?" Dan frowns for a second. "Okay, actually, that's a good question. What is our goal?"

Evan looks a bit surprised that someone else is trying out the logical, methodical approach. Jeff just looks amused. Neither is talking, though, so Dan gives it a shot. "I mean, are we just trying to get into each other's pants? 'Cause, honestly... I think we can just go for that, without too much strategy needed. But if we're trying to, like, communicate and form a long-range plan... that might take a bit more work."

Evan looks a little dazed. "Go back to the part where we can just get into each other's pants. I liked that part."

Dan looks at him for a second, and then over at Jeff, who looks back at him, waiting. So Dan goes for it. He's a little surprised by his own boldness, but then, once he gets started, he does tend to be hard to stop, and Evan got him started with that kiss in the apartment a couple days ago. He crosses the deck toward the table, and goes around to Evan's side. Evan's sitting with his legs underneath the table, so Dan can't really get the kind of access he'd like, but he does what he can. He drops to his knees next to the chair, and reaches a hand out to wrap around Evan's neck and bring their mouths together. Dan makes the kiss wet and deep, and he's completely aware of the fact that Jeff is watching. It doesn't take long for Evan to get into it, and he brings his own hand up to the back of Dan's head, leaning forward and bending Dan's head back. Dan goes with it, arching his whole body, until Evan is almost out of his chair to follow him.

They're both a little startled when Jeff speaks. "Okay, boys. I'm enjoying the show, but... do we want to just go for it, or do we want to talk things over first?" He sounds pretty calm, but Dan can't be sure. He tries to think how he'd have felt watching someone else making out with Justin, and he pulls away from Evan quickly. He never would have been okay with Justin screwing around with other people, so obviously his comfort level is a bit different than Jeff and Evan's, but still…. Jeff's right, they should figure things out. Evan groans a little, but he lets go of Dan's head without any resistance.

Dan stands up and goes back to his chair. The other two are still looking apprehensive, so Dan decides that he might as well take charge. After all, Jeff and Evan have already discussed this at least somewhat, so Dan's the one who needs the most information. "Okay… how about if I ask you guys some questions?" They both nod, and he tries to think of how to begin. "Okay, let's start big. What *is* your goal here? I don't mean tonight, I mean… ultimately. The last time we talked about all this, you said you were 'interested'. I guess I'm not sure what that means. I'm getting that you're after a bit more than a one-night thing, but… how much more? And how do you see it working?"

Jeff looks over at Evan, and then speaks. "I think that depends a lot on you, Dan."

"Yeah, okay, but… best case scenario. Let's say I'm up for whatever you want. What *do* you want?"

It looks like Jeff's going to field this one, but he needs a bit of time to put his thoughts together. "We didn't plan for this. At all. We went out to Kentucky to buy a horse for Tat, and we came back with a barn full, and you. And, you know, we don't regret it at all, but… it's spun us around a little too. I think… to some extent, I think we just want what we can get. Physically, yeah, obviously. But also… you."

"You make us better," Evan says quietly, and he grins as Dan stares at him in surprise. "You do, man."

"You do." Jeff agrees. "We kind of fell into a pattern, there. And it wasn't a bad pattern, but… we could be more. The casual thing… it was good, and it was right at the time, but then it stopped being right, and we didn't see that, or we…. I don't really know, Dan. Evan and I have talked about it, but we haven't really been able to figure it out. We just… it just feels right to have you with us."

"Okay, that's… that's a little more philosophical than what I was looking for, maybe." Dan tries to figure out what he needs to know. "Okay, typical week. Monday, Evan and I go to work, Jeff… paints something, I don't know. That night I have dinner and go to bed… you guys get together. Tuesday, Evan's busy with Tat, but Jeff and I both have some free time. Can we get together, or am I only part of this if we're all there? Wednesday night, I go to a bar, and a hot guy wants to go home with me—is that allowed? Thursday, Evan has friends over—do they know how I fit in?" Dan laughs, but there's not much humor in it. "What are the chances *they* know, when *I* have no fucking idea?" He blows a big breath out. "I'm not looking for some formal declaration or something, I just…. I can do casual, I'm pretty sure. It's… it's all the rest of it that's confusing, you know?"

They're all silent for a minute, and then Jeff says, "Okay, let's turn it around for a second. If we're agreeable, what do *you* want?"

Dan thinks about it. "Maybe just casual, you know? I mean, you guys are a couple, and sometimes we all just fuck around. Would that work?"

Evan frowns. "Are you saying that because it's what you want, or because it's what you think you can have?"

"I don't know, man. I mean… yeah, maybe for now. I… okay, honestly? *I'd* be happy if we just did the thing where I get to mess around with one of you at a time." He holds his hands up quickly. "I know that didn't work out so well last time, so I'm not really suggesting it, I'm just saying, from my perspective… I honestly don't know about this threesome thing. Do you guys do it a lot?"

They both look a little startled. Jeff shakes his head. "I've never done it, either, Dan… it just seemed like something worth exploring." He turns to Evan, waiting for his input.

"I, uh…." Evan looks a little bashful. "I've done it a few times, but never with all guys. I mean, two guys and a girl, or two girls and a guy, but… no, I've never done three guys, either."

Dan's flabbergasted. "Well, what the fuck? I mean, do you guys even know what you're doing? In terms of the mechanics of things? Do we take turns while one person watches, or…?" He trails off, and just shakes his head at the other two men.

"Well, I've seen porn!" Evan defends, and Dan just looks at him.

"Okay, Captain Pornie, walk me through it," Dan challenges. "I'll be the pizza guy, and Jeff can be the plumber. You can be… hey, why don't you be the high-powered young executive?"

Evan grins at him with a glint in his eye. "Okay, fine." He laces his fingers together and flexes them in front of him as if he's warming up. He sits back in his chair and his eyes focus on the eaves of Jeff's roof, and then he begins.

"The young executive comes home after a hard day and finds that his sink is backed up. He's angry—he's been told that this has been fixed. So he calls the plumber, who comes over and gets to work. But the executive can't help but notice the plumber's tight ass and sexy voice." Evan cuts his eyes teasingly over toward Jeff. "And before you know it, the plumber's still on his back, but now the executive is over top of him, fucking his mouth. Everything's going along great until the doorbell rings. The executive wants his dinner, so he pulls out of the plumber's mouth and tells him to stay put, and then he goes and opens the door for the pizza boy. The executive did up his pants, but he's still obviously hard, and the pizza boy asks if he needs any help with that."

Evan takes a break and looks at Dan. "So, how's it work for you so far?"

"So far the pizza boy isn't getting any action. It's not working for me at all."

"Oh, you want some action, huh? Okay, so the executive says fuck yeah he wants some help. Pizza boy's tip is in the kitchen. So they go in there and pizza boy almost leaves when he sees the plumber, but he's not the kind of guy to freak out and run away. Is he, Dan?" Evan asks pointedly. He's joking, mostly.

"Fuck off and get on with the story, man."

Evan laughs a little huskily. "Yeah, you like the story *now*. Okay, so the executive tells the pizza boy to strip, and the plumber sits up, 'cause this is getting good. And the pizza boy looks like he's not gonna do it, but then the executive grabs him and gives him a really hot kiss, lots of teeth and hands, and then he pushes the pizza boy away and tells him to strip or get out." Evan looks from Jeff to Dan. "Obviously the executive is a bit of an ass, and the finer plot details could be changed in any reenactment."

Jeff shakes his head. "You are enjoying this too much, kid."

Evan grins wickedly before continuing. "So the pizza boy strips down, and the plumber and the executive just stare at him for a minute because he's so beautiful. And then the plumber crawls forward, wanting to get his lips around pizza boy's cock, and the executive stops him, but then says, yeah, okay, do it. 'Cause the plumber's a bit of a bitch, and he won't do a thing unless it's okay with the executive." Evan glances over for a reaction, but Jeff just shakes his head. "And the executive makes the pizza boy sit down on a kitchen chair, and the plumber goes to work on him. And then the executive pulls his dick out again and gives it to the pizza boy to suck on, and he goes to town, slurping around like it's an ice cream cone. Like it's a fucking panini."

Dan's torn between laughing his ass off and getting pretty damn turned on. He shifts in his chair a bit to give himself a little more room, and Evan notices and smiles like he just won the lottery.

Evan shifts in his own chair before continuing. "Okay, so, this is a porno, so continuity isn't exactly crucial. So now they're in the bedroom, and they're all naked, and the pizza boy is leaning up against the headboard, and here's the twist, the *executive* is sucking him off, while the plumber is giving the executive a deep, deep rim job. Everybody's happy, and then the plumber pulls up and starts fucking the executive, really hard and fast, making it hurt a little 'cause he can tell the executive is kinda into that shit."

Dan laughs out loud, and then settles down when Evan gives him a mock dirty look.

"Okay, so, where was I? Oh, yeah, getting fucked. So, they go at it like that for a bit, and then the pizza boy decides that as totally outstanding as the executive is at giving head, he wants something else, so he slides down the bed until he's underneath the executive, and the executive leans down on him so their cocks are together, and the executive is getting fucked so hard that he needs both his hands to hold himself up, but the pizza boy brings *his* hand down and starts jacking them both together, and the pizza boy and the executive are making out this whole time, lots of sloppy kisses and necking and whatever."

Evan looks over at Jeff. "So, it's a porno, so they're gonna want the money shot. But, I don't know... I think maybe the plumber's a bit of a rebel, and he's gonna come in the executive's ass. What do you think, Jeff? Money shot or depth charge?"

"Depth charge? Jesus, kid." Jeff's looking pretty ruffled himself, and Dan's glad to see it. Jeff rubs a hand over his face. "Yeah, he stays in for sure. A little harder, a little deeper...."

"Yeah, and then he goes off. And the executive can feel it, and that sets *him* off too. So that leaves just the pizza boy. The other two take a minute to recover, and then they give the pizza boy the full treatment. One of them blows him while the other one sucks his balls, and then they trade around and one goes up and works on the guy's nipples, and finds all his little sensitive spots and marks them for future reference, 'cause they're all gonna want to do this again. So, finally the pizza boy comes, hard, right down the plumber's throat 'cause the plumber is fucking awesome at that. And then they clean up a bit and all fall asleep together on the executive's huge bed. The End." Evan is pretty clearly proud of himself, and Dan really can't blame him.

After an appreciative silence, Dan says, "Okay, yeah, so maybe there's some merit to the whole threesome thing."

Jeff and Evan both laugh, but no one seems to know just how to proceed. Or at least Evan and Dan don't know. Jeff seems to think that the best thing to do is to sit there and watch them like they're baby pandas, and he wants to see their next adorable trick. Dan's thinking that it's about time to wipe that smugness off his face, but he tries to hold back a little. If they want to talk, he can talk.

"So, are we all good with casual, then? I mean, if we're together,

great, if we're not, we're on our own?" Dan sees them exchange glances
and he looks from one to the other. "Because I'm not really looking to tie
myself down when both of you are free to sleep around—that doesn't
work for me."

Jeff clears his throat. "What if we were interested in changing that?
We could keep things a little loose, but what if we wanted to make it a...
well, not monogamous, I guess... duogamous? Whatever—what if we
wanted it to be an exclusive thing?"

Dan hadn't really expected that, and he has to think for a second.
"No. That's... no. I mean... you guys have each other, right? You love
each other. That's great, but... where does that leave me? I'm fine being
the junior partner if we're just screwing around sometimes, but not if I'm
not allowed to look for something else with someone who might... you
know, someone who might turn into something for me." Dan's proud of
himself for that. He's worth having someone love him. Justin had loved
him, and Justin wasn't stupid. He just needs to keep reminding himself.

Evan leans forward. "Okay, but why couldn't that be us? I mean,
okay, right now—we like you and we want you, a *lot* for both of those, but
okay, you're right, we're not full on in love. But maybe we could be...."

Dan looks at Jeff in some alarm. What is Evan talking about? But
Jeff is looking back levelly at Dan, acting for all the world as if he agrees
with Evan's crazy ideas. "Maybe...." Dan needs to nip this in the bud.
"Maybe anything could happen, I guess. But, really... what are the
chances? Seems a lot more likely that you'll decide that it was a fun little
experiment but it's time to get back to real life. And then I'm left standing
there, all... attached... to two guys who are moving on."

Evan shakes his head stubbornly. "I don't see why it's more likely
that you'll get 'attached' than we will."

"Yeah? Okay, how 'bout if one of you does get attached? But only
one of you?" Dan shakes his head. "It's hard enough with two people.
Throwing a third into the mix is... I don't know, doesn't it seem like we're
asking for trouble?"

"So what are you suggesting?" Jeff asks. "Are you saying it's never
going to happen, or just that we should start slow and proceed with
caution?"

Dan looks at Jeff and then over at Evan. He already feels more than
he should for both of them, and a part of him is screaming that he should

get out now before he starts caring even more. The chances of this ending up well are so slim. But… he wants it. Wants something. He just needs to be smart about it. "No, I can't say it's never going to happen. But, yeah, I think we should start *really* slow. And just… I don't know… I think we've got to stay totally aware of the potential problems."

Evan looks a little impatient. "So, slow with everything? Like, the physical too? Or just the emotional?"

"No, dude, I'm ready to go with the physical! I mean… is that cool with you guys?"

Evan nods enthusiastically, and Dan laughs a bit as they both turn to look at Jeff. He seems a bit more thoughtful. "Are we sure that we can keep the two separate?" He looks at Evan. "He's not wrong about it being risky."

Evan looks subdued for a second, then stares Jeff down. "A couple days ago… that was the closest we've ever come to calling it quits. Right?" Jeff nods reluctantly, and Dan feels bad again. Why had he dragged other people into his issues? But Evan is still talking. "I think we've come too far to back down. We're"—he looks at Dan—"I think we've pretty much committed ourselves to seeing this through. If we don't do this…." He looks back over at Jeff, and smiles sadly. "If we don't do this, we're going to have a hell of a time hanging on, aren't we?"

Jeff looks down at his hands, then over at Dan. "I think he's right. I think… Evan and I are pretty well committed to making some sort of change. A change bigger than just both of us fooling around with the same person. It… we're all off balance, somehow. And I think—we both think—that you could balance us out again. That we could care about you just as much as we care about each other, and… I don't know, that it would take some of the pressure off." He looks over and can clearly tell that Dan isn't convinced. He laughs regretfully. "Yeah, I can't really explain it. You're probably right that we should start slow, but… I just want you to understand. I *can't* keep the physical separate from the emotional. Not with you. So, if you want to protect yourself and keep it casual, okay. But just… be aware, okay? This is important to me. And to Evan. And to the two of us together."

Dan feels overwhelmed, like maybe this is a bit more than he signed up for. It's crazy, for them to think that he's going to somehow save their relationship. He kind of wants to run, to get the hell out of there and find somewhere calm and safe. He could always jerk off thinking about Evan's story, he doesn't need to stay and see how it plays out in reality. He's pretty sure that leaving would be the smart thing to do. He tries to consult Puppet-Chris, but he's just as confused as Dan is. Great.

Dan looks over at Jeff and Evan, both sitting and watching him, and he realizes that it's too late. There's no way he can stand up and walk away from them. Not just because he wants them, but because he cares about them, and if they think that he can help them, then that's what he wants to do. He's nervous again, but he's committed. He stands up, and he can tell that Evan thinks he's leaving. Dan shakes his head gently, and smiles at Evan, then at Jeff. "Okay," he says.

Jeff seems relieved and satisfied, but Evan wants clarification. "Okay? Okay to what?"

Dan shrugs. "Okay. I'm gonna try to keep myself from getting too into this, but, yeah, I understand that it's important to you guys, and I'm not gonna be careless about that. And I do need to start slow with any… emotional commitments or whatever, but… I'll try to be open to at least the idea of more." He tries to look less serious and more sexy. "Is that enough? Or do I have to go pick up a fucking pizza or something? I mean, what's a guy got to do to get some action around here?"

Evan looks at Jeff as if for permission, and when Jeff speaks his voice has that honey-dipped growl that Dan can't resist. "All you got to do is ask, Dan."

Dan tries to make his own voice even half as sexy as Jeff's, and it comes out warm and smoky. "All right, then. I'm asking." He turns and starts toward the house.

Dan isn't sure which of the two moves faster, but he knows that both of them have caught up to him before he gets to the door of the house, and then their mouths are on him, their bodies pressed against his, their hands everywhere. Dan lets his overworked brain turn off as he gives in to the sensations. He's pretty sure that at least this aspect of things is going to work just fine.

chapter 41

SOMEBODY gets the door open, and then they're all stumbling inside. Dan feels himself pressed up against the wall, Evan leaning in against his right side, a rippling, writhing flame, and Jeff on his left, slowly flowing lava. It's no surprise that Dan's skin is burning. He wonders if that's all he is, more fuel for the furnace of their desire, but then their hands lace together over his stomach and work in under his shirt, and he stops caring.

Evan's lips find Dan's sensitive spot just under his ear, and he gasps in response, tilting his head to give better access. He feels Evan's mouth curl up. "Jeff, try here," Evan murmurs, and he uses his hand to guide Jeff's head to the exact spot on Dan's other side, and then they're both kissing and nipping, and Dan doesn't even know what to do, he can't move for one without blocking the other, so he just tilts his head back against the wall and lets the chills run down his spine, one hand wrapped around Jeff's shoulder and clutching, the other... oh, the other is near Evan's waistband. Dan runs his hand down over the outside of his fly, along Evan's hard length, and he feels Evan moan in approval.

Jeff's attention is caught by the sound, and then he's pulling away, and Dan feels cold on that side. He forces his eyes open and looks over to where Jeff is standing, one hand bracing himself against the wall, the other absentmindedly rubbing at his jaw.

"Evan. Kid, hey," Jeff says softly, and Evan lifts his head up a little from Dan's neck, glances over toward Jeff. "Let's slow this down a little, huh? I want this to last."

Dan isn't sure about that idea, and he gives another little rub to Evan's cock through his pants. Do they really need to slow down?

Evan groans and his hips jerk toward Dan, but he keeps his mouth away, and then pulls his whole body back. "Yeah, okay," he says huskily. "Should we... bedroom?"

Jeff nods, and then Evan has one of Dan's hands and is leading him toward the bedroom, while Jeff trails along behind them, holding Dan's other hand. It's a bit like they're going on a field trip in elementary school, with everyone ordered to buddy up, but Dan kind of likes it. He likes that he feels connected.

When they get to the bedroom Evan pauses, and looks over at Jeff as if for instructions. Jeff smiles. "I wasn't lying outside, when I said that I liked the show. And I've got a few years on both of you—I'm thinking that my recovery time might not be where yours is." He gestures toward an arm chair by the wall. "How about if I watch for a while, see how things are going?"

Dan isn't sure about that. He'd been enjoying having two times the usual sensations, and he's not sure he won't get self-conscious if Jeff's watching. And it somehow doesn't feel right for Jeff to be left out. Then he has an idea. "Watch? Or direct?" Dan sees Evan's eyes flare with interest, and they both turn to look at Jeff.

Jeff's voice is gruff when he says, "Jesus, Dan. You're gonna kill me, here." He sits down with one hand on the arm of the chair, the other resting on his straining fly. Dan really wants to go over and release that pressure, remind him what Dan can do with his mouth, but then Jeff sees him looking and shakes his head. "You want me to direct, you need to wait until you're told to do something." Dan gives a little snarl, mostly playful but hopefully enough to make it clear that he's not going to give up on the idea entirely.

Jeff leans back and looks at them. "All right, too many clothes. Dan, why don't you start? Unbutton Evan's shirt. Slowly." Dan's not crazy about the "slow" part, but he obeys. Evan's chest is gorgeous, all ripped muscles and golden brown skin, and Dan's mouth is on it even as his hands are still working the lower buttons. Jeff gives him a moment to enjoy, and then says, "Now slip the shirt right off. Drop it on the floor," and Dan does that without even lifting his mouth from Evan's nipple. Jeff laughs a little. "Determined, isn't he?" he asks, and Dan can feel Evan's stomach moves as he laughs.

"Okay, that's enough of that… Evan, lace your fingers in his hair. Lift his head up." Dan lets it happen, but once he's far enough away to see Evan clearly, it's all he can do to not move back in. He wants to taste every inch of that tanned skin, wants to…. "Okay, Evan, your turn. Let's get his shirt off." Evan doesn't waste any time, and Dan cooperates—he definitely sees the importance of getting naked.

Evan pulls back a little and looks over to Jeff for more instructions, and Dan is really regretting his suggestion that Jeff direct. Jesus, he could have been three-quarters done by now, but instead he's still standing there half-dressed and achingly hard. "Dan, you're looking a little impatient… is there something you'd like to do?" Dan's hands dart toward Evan's fly, but Jeff's voice is a little sharp. "Wait!" Dan freezes and looks over at Jeff, whose eyes are as dark as his voice. "Ask me, Dan. Ask me if you can do it."

Dan's about ready to revolt. "This power thing—are you thinking this is a permanent situation, or is it just for right now?" He knows Jeff can see the rebellion forming….

"It's just for now, babe. Let me enjoy myself while I can." Jeff almost sounds defeated, and Dan really doesn't know what that means, but he doesn't like it.

"Oh, I can help you enjoy yourself," he suggests with a purr, but Jeff shakes his head.

"Evan's waiting for you, Dan. What do you want to do for him?"

Dan looks back at Evan. He'll play the game for a little longer, he supposes. "I want to suck him off." He pauses. "Jeff. May I please give Evan a blowjob?"

Jeff sounds a little out of breath. "Oh, yeah, Dan, you can do that."

Dan's falling to his knees at the same time that he's undoing Evan's fly and pulling his pants down, and so his first view of Evan's cock is up close. And Dan just wants to get closer. It's big, and dark, and beautiful, sticking out totally straight, leaking at the tip. Dan takes a quick lick there, feels Evan's hands flutter at his shoulders in response, and then starts in on the rest of it. Evan's a bit too big for Dan to take all at once, but he's confident that he can work up to it, and he relishes the challenge. He lets his lips go a little loose to start with, just curls them over his teeth and focuses on depth. He takes Evan as deep as he can, feels him hit the back of his throat, changes the angle a little and tries to relax. He keeps Evan mostly in his mouth, just bobbing a little bit, letting the tip of Evan's cock hit his throat, working on the angle… and there it is, and he hears Evan's groan as his cock slides past Dan's gag point and right down his throat. Dan holds still for a second, working his tongue along the bottom and swallowing to keep Evan happy, and then he's ready to move.

He thinks about just staying still and letting Evan start thrusting. Dan loves it when guys do that, but tonight he feels like he's already given away a lot of control, and he'd like to keep what he has left. So he starts moving, tightening his lips and bobbing his head, sucking his cheeks in, and he keeps his tongue working too. He remembers what Evan said about the executive being a bit into pain, and he feels Evan's hips twitch when Dan tries a little brush with his teeth. Evan's groaning now, his hips jerking periodically, and Dan wonders if he's actually going to get this, if Jeff is going to let him make Evan come.

Then Jeff is there beside him, and Dan hadn't even noticed that the man had left his chair. "Jesus, Dan, you are so beautiful like this." Jeff runs a hand up Dan's chest and over his face, resting his fingers on the place where Dan's lips are moving back and forth over Evan's skin. "So beautiful." Dan feels Jeff fumbling for his hand, and he recognizes the familiar shape of a bottle of lube. "I want you to work him open while you're sucking him. Not much, just one finger, but lots of lube. And then when you're done, when he's come down your throat, I want you to put him up on the bed on his knees, with his shoulders against the mattress, and I want you to fuck him hard. Is that good, babe?"

Dan nods enthusiastically, Evan inhaling sharply at the changing pressure on his dick. Dan gets a finger slicked up and brings it around behind, circling Evan's hole teasingly. He thinks about what Jeff had said, about not stretching it too much, and thinking how tight that's going to be around his cock is almost enough to bring him off right there, without even being touched. He brings his free hand down to press on his dick, and Jeff sees it and grins a little wolfishly. Dan doesn't have time to respond to that, but it's not like Jeff isn't straining the limits of his clothing, and he's not even touching anyone.

Dan slides his finger in, silky smooth in the heat and all the lube, and works it around to find the right spot. Evan's fighting to keep still now, his hips jerking like it's only his willpower that's keeping him under any sort of control, and Dan decides to give in. He lifts his free hand to find Evan's and brings it to his head, then sinks back a little to get a better balance. Evan looks down like he's not sure of the message, but Jeff's been here before with Dan, and he gives a little moan. "Do it, Evan, he wants you to." And that's all it takes to get Evan's long, fat cock shoved down Dan's throat. He swallows around it, letting it go deep, but Evan's already pulling out and driving back in. Dan works his finger more as Evan's rhythm get more erratic, and then Evan's hands come off his head entirely. Dan understands the signal, but he sucks Evan down deep anyway, swallows around him, knows he's drooling a little but doesn't worry about it at all. Evan makes a shuddering, hoarse shout when he comes, and Dan chokes a little but loves it. He keeps working until Evan's hand comes to ease him off, and then Evan falls down to his knees in front of Dan, and he brings both hands to the back of Dan's head and holds him still to give him a deep, soft kiss. Which is well enough for Evan, but Dan's still rock hard….

Jeff clears his throat. "Your turn, Dan." He doesn't have to mention it twice. Dan breaks off the kiss and pulls Evan to his feet, kicking Evan's pants the rest of the way off before undoing his own. Evan seems to perk up a little at the thought of getting to see the rest of Dan. Dan tries to take it slow and draw things out a little, but that's just not going to happen. He's *way* too far gone for any sort of subtlety. He'd taken off his shoes and socks earlier, and he's glad of it because he really doesn't think he'd have the patience for laces right now, and fucking someone while wearing running shoes is really not that classy. Although he's been in positions where he'd have appreciated the traction….

But then Jeff is there behind him, and Dan doesn't mind that he's being slowed down because Jeff's hard cock is pressing through the fabric of his jeans and rubbing against Dan's ass. Jeff eases Dan's pants and underwear down, and Dan grinds back a little. It's been a long time since he's been fucked, and he was relieved that Jeff had asked him to top tonight. But all that hesitation is gone when he feels Jeff's cock, *right there*, nestling in like it's going home. He arches his back, grinding back with his ass at the same time as he twists his head around for a kiss, and Jeff's hand is strong where it holds his neck, keeping him still for a deep kiss. Then Jeff's hand is gone, and Dan hears the crinkle of a foil wrapper, and Jeff's warm hands are around him, smoothing the condom on. Dan and Justin had gotten tested for everything under the sun and given up on condoms, so it's been years since Dan used one. He thinks it might not be a bad thing to have a little less sensation tonight, might help keep him from embarrassing himself. Although now Jeff is smoothing lube on, and he seems to be taking a little extra care….

"Shit, man, stop. I'm not gonna last."

Jeff smiles into Dan's neck, rubbing his stubbly cheek along Dan's smooth skin, but at least he stops with his hand. Jeff leans forward a bit so he can reach Evan to give him a little more lube, and the motion pushes Dan forward, too, sends his cock under Evan's ass and between his legs. Evan and Dan moan together, and then Jeff's hand is back on Dan's cock, moving it up and guiding it into place.

"Slow and steady, babe. He likes to feel the stretch, but we don't want to hurt him," Jeff murmurs, but Evan must not have gotten the memo, because as soon as he feels Dan there he's pushing back, and Dan moves back a little but then hits Jeff, who doesn't give. "Okay, apparently *he's* driving." Jeff sounds amused, but Dan doesn't really worry about it because he's pretty much totally concentrated on the sensation of his cock being engulfed by Evan's tight, hot ass. Evan's pushing back steadily, but once the head of Dan's cock is inside, Evan starts rocking a little, pulling away from Dan and then pushing back a little closer each time. Dan's dick absolutely approves, and Dan tilts his head back again, finding Jeff's lips with his. He's not really kissing, more just moaning into Jeff's mouth, and Jeff is there, whispering soothing words and helping Dan to keep still. Finally, Dan is all the way in, one hand behind him grabbing onto the seam of Jeff's jeans, the other resting on Evan's back, right at the top of his ass. Evan stills, and Dan kind of wants to stay there forever, frozen in perfection. At the same time, he very, very much wants to move….

Evan's hand snakes back and grabs Dan's hip, pulling him forward. Dan goes, his dick doesn't give him a choice, but Jeff doesn't come with him, and Dan misses him. That lasts for about two seconds, until Evan braces his arms on the bed and arches his back, and growls, "Go hard, Dan, I want to feel it." Dan wants to feel it, too, so he doesn't argue. He draws back and pistons in, slamming fast and hard, then does it again and again. Evan is pushing back into every thrust, a low keening coming from his throat, and Dan really doesn't think he can last much longer. At least Evan has already come, so Dan doesn't have *that* to worry about, and Jeff has moved around so he can see both their faces and he looks almost as into it as Dan is. Dan can feel the orgasm building in his spine, but he doesn't want to give into it, wants to keep driving into Evan, wants to keep hearing him make that sound.

He manages to hold off a little longer, but it's like stopping a tidal wave with a sheet of paper, and it's not long before Dan loses his rhythm, loses his mind, can hear himself gasping as if he's somewhere far away, somewhere in a land of heat and colors and friction and… he drives deep as he shudders, and Evan stops pumping and just pushes back, bracing himself to hold the extra weight as Dan gives a few more weak, erratic thrusts and then collapses on Evan's back. Evan eases himself down flat, bringing Dan with him, and he just lies there for a while, Dan gasping into his neck. Then Jeff is there, too, smoothing Evan's hair out of his eyes, kissing Dan on the temple. It's lovely, but….

"What the fuck, man? Do you not want to come?" Dan doesn't understand how anyone can be this Zen when his dick is as hard as Jeff's quite obviously is.

Evan laughs a little weakly. "See, man? I told you you're weird." He turns his head a little in Dan's direction. "When he gets turned on he goes all gentle and shit… it's freakish." Judging by the way Evan is nuzzling against Jeff's hand, he doesn't seem to have any real complaints about it.

"Damn." Dan doesn't really understand that, and he thinks it might be time to do something about it. He runs a hand down between his chest and Evan's back, fingers slick in their combined sweat, and then curves down over Evan's ass to hold onto the condom while he eases himself out. Evan gives a sleepy little whimper of complaint, but Dan knows from experience that Evan really does *not* want to leave things like that for too long. He ties the condom off and scoots out of the bed looking for a trash basket. While he's up, he decides to slip into the bathroom to pee. Then he washes his hands and splashes a little cool water on his face. Time to regroup.

When he goes back in the bedroom, Jeff has his shirt off and is stretched on the bed beside Evan, leaning over him and kissing him gently while his hand plays along Evan's ribs. The love between them is almost palpable to Dan, and he feels like an outsider, an intruder. Then Jeff looks up and sees him watching. "Isn't he sweet like this, Dan? All fucked-out and relaxed?"

Dan looks at him a little sadly. "Yeah, he's beautiful." He smiles, but he suddenly feels naked, and he heads over to where his pants are bundled at the end of the bed. "So, uh… obviously I'm happy to help if you actually want to do something with that," and he nods at Jeff's erection. "But if you're just fading into slow-motion cuddle mode, maybe I'll head out. I've got a lot of stuff to do tomorrow, and it's getting late."

Evan half sits up, propping himself up on his elbows. "Nah, man, you should stick around! We'll wake the old man up."

Jeff looks a little worried, but he tries to sound relaxed. "Or put me to sleep… either way, you should stay, Dan. It's a big bed. Lots of room."

"Oh, no, thanks. I've gotten pretty used to sleeping alone. And, like I said, I've got stuff to do tomorrow."

Evan runs his hand down to Jeff's groin. "Stuff that's more important than this?"

"No, like I said, if… you know, it just seemed like you were settling down for the night." Yeah, this is awkward.

"Come here, Dan," Jeff murmurs, and Dan squirms. He's already at the foot of the bed, how much closer does Jeff want him to get? He shuffles forward, holding his jeans in front of him like some sort of unattached loin cloth. He wonders if he looks as stupid as he feels. Jeff looks at him for a long moment, and then he smiles tenderly. "Dan, am I still allowed to direct?"

Dan doesn't think that's a good idea. "You're allowed to suggest…."

Jeff nods slowly. "Okay, then. Here's my suggestion. My request." Dan nods, and Jeff continues. "I'd like it if you'd climb back up on the bed and kiss me while Evan sucks me off. Does that sound like something you might do?"

Dan laughs a little nervously. "Kiss you? Yeah, I think I could handle it." Jeff and Evan just look at him expectantly, so Dan walks around to the other side of the bed. He sets his jeans down carefully, making sure he won't have to fumble around to find them later, and then he climbs onto the bed and stretches out along Jeff's body. Jeff smiles contentedly and gives Dan a sloppy kiss, and then Evan leans over Jeff's chest and joins in. It doesn't really work very well, and it ends up being more like two people kissing while one person randomly licks their faces or something, but… it's a good thought.

Then Evan eases down Jeff's body, trailing kisses along the way, and Dan can feel Jeff lift his hips to let Evan work his pants down. Dan honestly can't believe it took this long to get them all naked. He's lying on his side, with his torso leaning over Jeff, and he brings his top leg over Jeff's thigh, pulling out to bring Jeff's legs apart. Evan murmurs his approval, and then Dan feels Jeff gasp and figures that Evan must have gotten to work. He looks down, and Jeff lifts his head up so he can watch, too, and it really is a beautiful sight. Evan's moving slow and concentrating hard, and he might not be getting Jeff quite as deep as Dan can, but it looks like he's doing some interesting things with his lips, and Dan's almost sorry that he's already come. He wonders how long it'll be before he's ready to go again, and then Jeff stretches up to catch Dan's mouth in another deep kiss, and he feels a stir in his stomach that suggests that it really won't be that long.

For now, though, it's Jeff's turn, and Dan focuses on kissing him back. Jeff has one hand tangled in Evan's hair, and the other slides around behind Dan's neck, his grip tightening as he gets closer and closer to the edge. When Jeff stops kissing him, Dan pulls back enough to be able to see Jeff's face, muscles tightening into a gasp as his eyes stare into Dan, and then through him as Jeff's body arches and spasms. He's still gasping and coming down when Evan slides up toward them, and Dan begins to shift back a little, making room. Evan catches his shoulder, though, and instead of kissing Jeff as Dan had expected, Evan leans over and catches Dan's mouth, and he can taste Jeff's come on Evan's lips, salty and bitter and perfect.

Evan pulls away eventually, leaning down for a quick peck on Jeff's lips, and then he starts squirming and rearranging and manhandling until somehow they end up with Dan in the middle, Jeff stretched out on his left side, Evan on his right. Dan isn't really sure how that happened, and he's not at all confident that it's a good idea.

"I should, uh…." He gestures vaguely toward the door, but Evan doesn't seem to be paying any attention, just snuggles in and smiles.

"Come on, man, stay for a bit. Just a nap, even. It's a comfy bed, right?"

Jeff is making himself comfortable as well. "You could still leave before morning, if you need to."

Evan looks at Jeff assessingly, then back at Dan. "If there's two of us, I bet we could get him to make us waffles for breakfast." He gives a quick kiss to the side of Dan's chin. "His waffles are awesome, man."

This is moving way too fast. The plan had been to keep it casual, to take it slow. But Evan's right: the bed is comfy. And Jeff's right; he can still find his way out later, if he wakes up. And… and he wants this. He wants to stay in this safe, warm cocoon, with these two incredible men, and maybe it won't work, and maybe he'll end up being hurt, but he feels like he's strong enough to take that chance. He doesn't know if his confidence will last forever, isn't even sure that it'll last through the night, but for now, he feels good.

He relaxes his body, slides down a couple inches until his head is more comfortable on the pillow, and he lets his eyes drift shut. For now, at least, he's found the place he's supposed to be.

Coming in August

The sequel to Dark Horse
By Kate Sherwood

Out of the Darkness

"It's hard enough with two people. Throwing a third into the mix is… I don't know, doesn't it seem like we're asking for trouble?"

It hasn't been easy, but horse trainer Dan Wheeler is beginning to build a new life for himself, finding his place in California with his lovers Evan Kaminski and Jeff Stevens. When things are going well, it's spectacular: there's affection, humor, and passion. But things don't seem to go well all that often.

Dan continues to struggle with the loss of his previous lover and sometimes doubts that he even deserves to be happy; Evan is jealous of every rival for Dan's attention—including Jeff; and Jeff worries that he's too old for the younger men and wonders if he should bow out completely. Despite his resolutions, Dan has grown attached to the other two men, but he's not sure that's enough. He knows that it hurts to be together—he needs to decide whether it would hurt even more to be apart.

http://www.dreamspinnerpress.com

KATE SHERWOOD started writing at about the same time that she got back on a horse after a twenty-year break. She'd like to think that she's far too young for it to be a mid-life crisis, but apparently she was ready for a few changes!

Her writing focuses on characters and relationships, people trying to find out how much of themselves they need to keep, and how much they can afford to give away. Kate finds that real-life monogamy is much easier to maintain when she gets to spend time with so many different men in her stories.

Lightning Source UK Ltd.
Milton Keynes UK
UKOW06f1112160615

253583UK00014B/589/P